WINGS OF THE ETERNAL WAR

Part Two of Shadowed Kings
Book Nine in the Pantracia Chronicles

Written by Amanda Muratoff & Kayla Mansur

www.Pantracia.com

For those who serve their country.

The Pantracia Chronicles:

Visit www.Pantracia.com to discover more.

Chapter 1

Summer, 2597 R.T. (recorded time)

A warhorn's cry reverberated through the air, making their drake balk.

Dani stiffened in Liam's arms, turning her cloudy eyes to the rising sun.

The drake lifted its massive head, grey dawn flashing on its pale blue scales. Claws lashed at the soldiers it'd fought alongside only hours before, cutting through steel.

Isalica's horn blew again.

"What is that?" Blood and grime marred Dani's skin, streaking heaviest over her chin and clumping sections of her white hair.

"The order to retreat." Liam's spine straightened as he looked at the military encampment they defended, bodies and debris strewn across the summer grass turned red. "Shit."

The drake thrashed, spinning without command to dig its claws into a Feyorian who'd risen despite his injuries. His scream died beneath another longer blast of the horn.

"We need to move. Cover the troops as they make for the east pass." Liam squeezed Dani's right side, and the Dtrüa turned the drake. "Straight ahead. Go."

"Have you figured out how to control this thing yet?" Dani sent the drake forward, gripping its reins with gloved hands.

The beast ran, its wingless body gracefully speeding over the rugged terrain.

Liam's gut clenched as the sun crested over the horizon. He poked her abdomen. "Don't even think about it."

"Think about what?" Dani peered over her shoulder at him, and he wondered what she could see.

"Oh, don't even pretend." Liam shouted over the wind rushing around them. Even in summer, it bit at his skin, making him shield his face partially behind Dani's shoulder. "You're staying right here on this drake. I already told you I'm not letting you out of my sight."

The drake plowed through Feyorians rushing to catch Isalicans with their backs turned, the beast's tail finishing those who'd dodged. A foolish soldier ran at the animal, but the drake caught him in his wicked jaws and threw him sideways.

Blood sprayed with the release, dappling Dani's once-white leathers with a fresh sheen of red. She closed her eyes, cringing.

Wyverns howled in the sky, daybreak glimmering off one's ember scales as it dove beyond the camp's spiked barricade, landing within.

The Dtrüa looked up. "It will be more effective if we—"

Several trumpets echoed through the air in three sharp blasts, followed by the shouts of soldiers.

Liam planted his feet against the drake's saddle, lifting himself to peer over Dani and the drake's lowered head. He squinted into the sunrise, his heart pounding as light shone on unmarred armor through the whipping Isalican flags.

"Feyor sent no troops to attack from the east." Dani guided the drake at a walk, head turned towards the encampment where a wyvern tore apart the tents.

"Reinforcements." Liam sighed near her ear. "Just in time."

"Little late, if you ask me." Dani huffed, rising in her seat. "I know you don't like it, but we need to split up. Take the drake."

Liam growled, tightening his hold around her waist. "No, you're staying right here with me. Reinforcements or not, I—"

"I love you." Dani pried one of his hands off, her form shifting in his grip. Fur twisted over her body, still covered in ash and blood. Her paws pushed off the drake's back, forcing him to release her, and she leapt to the ground. She glanced in his direction before racing for the suffering encampment.

"Damn it." Liam slid forward in the drake's saddle, and the creature's head swiveled back to him.

Please don't eat me.

The drake chuffed before it delightfully mauled a Feyorian beneath its claws.

Guess it's eager to show its old masters how much it hated them.

Liam dug his left heel into the drake's side, encouraging it away from its current carnage back towards the encampment that Dani sprinted for. Her dark shape blurred among the trampled and burned foliage, darting between the logs forming the outer wall.

Somewhere in the distant east, the deep howl of a drake echoed with another sound of the Isalican battle horn, and Liam's mount lifted its maw to respond. Along the ridgeline beyond the camp, Liam spotted the snowy shape of another drake, two riders on its back.

Please let that be Matthias and my sister.

Katrin had surely gone to find the prince when Dani gave her the other tamed drake. She'd earned its trust by healing it after the Dtrüa's insistence.

"This is insanity," Liam grumbled as he turned to see the Feyorian troops pause in their advance. He jerked his drake to the side, narrowly missing a hurled spear aimed for its throat.

The drake rumbled beneath him in a growl, claws digging into the ground as it hopped over its lifeless victims.

"Let's make sure Isalica knows we're on its side, big guy." Liam patted his mount's neck before he encouraged it forward, back into the fray.

A deeper horn sounded from the west, Feyor's grey banners disappearing between the pines. The army's line broke, and soldiers turned in response to the call to retreat.

The drake lunged after the fleeing soldiers, snapping two within its jaws before Liam redirected him.

Liam circled around, hesitant to advance on the new Isalican troops. He let the drake pace the line like a wildcat, head low to the ground and body still rumbling.

A wyvern launched from inside the camp, and a group of horseback Isalicans emerged from the main gate. They maneuvered towards him, swords drawn.

The drake turned, but Liam pulled on the reins.

"Shek." He remembered Dani using the word multiple times and put every ounce of command he could muster into it. "Shek!"

Pausing, the beast quieted. It lifted its head, exposing its neck to the approaching soldiers as they rode closer.

Liam lifted his hand in greeting to his compatriots, hoping they'd spy the steel insignia still pinned at his left shoulder, even if it was coated in gore.

Please notice that I'm an ally.

As the riders grew closer, they slowed.

"Talansiet?" Micah's voice carried over the breeze as they lowered their swords. "Gods, I thought you were a Yorrie."

"Can't imagine how you'd make that mistake." The humor felt dry as he watched the grim frown on Micah's face. He recognized the men at his side as soldiers from the 134th battalion. They wouldn't know that Micah acted as the prince's stand in.

Best to keep the ruse going, especially with Feyor this close.

Liam lifted his hand to his chest in salute. "Orders, your majesty?"

"Accompany me to the reinforcements. They need to know not to, you know, kill you." Micah sheathed his sword.

Despite the recent horrors of the battlefield, a smile twitched on his lips. "That would be preferable."

Something screeched high in the sky, and everyone looked up.

A scream cut the air as someone fell from the back of a wyvern, landing with a crunch fifty yards to Liam's left.

"Nymaera's breath." Micah glanced at Liam before nudging his horse into a canter towards the approaching forces.

The rising sun behind them glowed off their armor.

Katrin would say the gods sent them.

Liam narrowed his eyes at the corpse that'd fallen from the sky, tracing the path it'd taken.

Two wyverns disappeared into the clouds, but he couldn't tell if either had a rider.

He chewed his lower lip. "Dani... You better not..." he muttered, but already knew better.

Urging the drake after Micah, Liam stayed behind the horses, which kept casting wary glances back. He could sense the draconi beneath him tensing as they grew closer, and he gave it another reassuring pat. "Easy, boy. Friends."

The front line of the reinforcements readied their stances, but Micah lifted his arm.

"Stand down." He rode closer, and weapons lowered.

The ranks of fresh soldiers stretched across the horizon, and Liam counted the flags designating the different battalions. Mouthing the count, a weight lifted off his shoulders. Thousands, at least.

Thank Nymaera.

A commander moved through the ranks on the back of a dappled Percheron stallion. He stopped next to Micah, exchanging quiet words with the stand-in prince.

"Dak." Liam braced himself as the drake shifted, lowering to the ground so he could dismount.

The creature remained lowered, still taller than the horses in front of it.

Liam stepped forward, but the beast shifted. He turned towards its head, larger than his entire body, and held out his hands. "No." He tried to find the words, but couldn't. "Stay," he commanded. "Just... stay."

The drake whined and pushed his nose into Liam's hand with a groan.

"By the gods." The commander gaped as he pulled his horse back from the creature. "How—"

"Apologies, General." Liam recognized the man from Nema's Throne and gave a respectful salute. "But time is of the essence. You need to command your men to leave the draconi on the field alone. Do not attack them. Only the Feyorian soldiers themselves."

"Crown elite." The general narrowed his eyes at Liam. "Explain."

"We have an ally on the field who is altering their loyalty to Isalica, like this one." Liam gestured to the drake behind him, who nudged his back, making him stumble.

Damn it, don't make me look bad in front of a general.

Gritting his jaw, he glowered at the drake. "Shek."

It whined, low and long.

"Do what he says. No attacking the beasts. We can use them and the chaos to our advantage." Micah glanced at Liam.

The general lowered his voice. "But you don't know where your other half is?"

Micah's gaze dropped to the ground. "I do not. I lost track of him in the battle." The man's demeanor darkened even more. "We've taken many losses today."

The general nodded, departing to give his soldiers orders.

Eyeing the drake, Micah gave it a wide berth as he approached Liam. "Last I saw, Matthias and Katrin rode a drake away from here."

Liam nodded, relieved for the confirmation it was the prince and his sister. "I saw them. They're out of danger. But what about the others?" His throat caught with the realization that very few things would keep the other crown elites from riding beside Micah.

The prince's double shook his head, sorrow etching his features. "Barim is dead. Stefan is in one of the medical tents in critical shape, and Riez... is probably dead, too." His jaw flexed, and he whispered, "Matthias jumped six times, but..."

Liam closed his hand on Micah's shoulder, grief rippling through him. He'd known the men a fraction of the time Micah had, but his knees wavered.

Barim and Riez, the two he thought least likely to fall in battle.

His chest ached for them, memories of Barim's laughter and Riez's grin flashing through his mind.

It was an honor to serve with them.

"We'll get our revenge against Feyor by turning their own beasts against them." Liam's hand subconsciously slid up the ridged nose of the drake, who purred like two stones grinding against each other. "This will end with more of theirs dead than ours."

Micah cleared his throat, returning the shoulder clap. "Stay alive, Talansiet."

Chapter 2

Katrin's eyes blurred with tears as she stared down at the valley she'd once called home.

The charred remains of the temple behind the encampment held little interest to the Feyorian troops, but a wyvern had toppled the tent erected over the old library for her.

Bodies lay everywhere.

So much death.

Her fingers brushed the soft scales of the drake beneath her, a memory of what all this was about. Feyor's greed for more power.

Matthias dismounted without waiting for the drake to crouch. He landed with a huff on the uneven ground, stalking away from the view of the valley. Holding a hand to his face, his shoulders tensed and body quivered.

Chewing her lip, Katrin commanded the drake down before dismounting. "The troops from Nema's Throne have arrived." She tried to banish the sorrow from her voice as she looked at Matthias, but the good news would mean little after what they'd already lost.

She'd arrived on the battlefield moments too late. Riez had vanished into the sky in the claws of a wyvern, while Barim's shield failed against another's tail. Stefan had gotten up, but he'd been coated in blood, his movement sluggish and weak. She prayed he'd make it to the medical tents.

Assuming they still stand.

Wincing, she steeled her emotions, reaching to take his hand. "Matthias," she whispered. "I'm so sorry."

His hand hung limp in hers, his eyes staring blankly at the rocky northern slope. After a breath, his fingers flexed. "I need to be down there."

She shook her head, fear rising in her throat. "It's still dangerous. And your Art..."

"Is useless, I know. But I can't hide up here." Matthias turned, looking right through her as he released her hand and approached the drake. "They need me."

She sniffed, swallowing. "They probably need both of us. But Micah told us to head east."

"That was before reinforcements showed up." Matthias looked at her with a stern gaze. "I've rested enough."

Over his shoulder, she saw no sign of a resurgence of Feyorian soldiers. Their banners vanished into the shadows of the forest. She pursed her lips as she surveyed the encampment, the wyvern that'd been there a moment before long gone. "All right." It made her stomach feel hollow. "But, please... can we stay together?"

"I'll stay in the camp with you." Matthias's shoulders slumped with unspoken thoughts.

She nodded, hurrying to the drake and climbing onto its back.

We will need healers now more than ever, and they'll need Matthias to command. No time to be cowards.

The prince climbed onto the drake's saddle behind her, grasping the thick leather edge for balance.

"Ayke."

The drake rose to its feet, turning to the ridge. Its claws bit into the rocks as Katrin encouraged it forward, and they started down the steep descent towards the Isalican reinforcements. Another drake stood near the head of it, though without a rider.

Please let Liam and Dani be safe.

She and Matthias didn't speak as they descended, and she missed the feeling of his arms around her with the distance between them. Glancing back, she tried to meet his eyes, but his gaze remained on the abandoned battlefield.

By the time they reached the camp, the reinforcements had moved in, reconstructing several of the tents while positioning massive ballistas drawn behind horses. The first rank of troops had advanced, pressing into the tree line. The distant clash of metal suggested some Feyorians lingered in the forest.

Katrin steered the drake down the wide walkways, surprised when none of the Isalican soldiers reacted beyond giving them space.

The drake tensed beneath her as she slowed its walk and made her way to the medical tent.

Katrin ran her palm over the drake's neck as it crouched.

The beast shook its head, lowering it. It huffed, sending bits of dirt and ash into the air.

She could sense the weariness within the creature, now exhausted and still recovering from the wound she'd healed. Black blood streaked the scales of its neck, along with the red of soldiers it'd slain.

Matthias slid to the ground, landing with more steadiness than Katrin expected.

A man hurried towards him, and they exchanged a forearm grip and one-armed hug. Micah pulled back and shook his head, smacking Matthias's shoulder. "It's damn good to see you're both all right."

Katrin dismounted, and as she did, the drake curled up on itself, wrapping its long scaled tail around its head. It didn't bother to move out of the walkway before closing its eyes.

"What of the others?" Matthias's gruff voice hid his pain.

"Stefan will make it." Micah cringed through a smile. "But that's the only good news I have for you."

The prince nodded, letting out a long breath. "I'll meet you in the command tent."

Katrin tried to listen as she watched soldier after soldier carried into the medical tent. Blood soaked its dirty entrance flap, turning it to a horrible mud.

Micah paused, watching Matthias go before looking at Katrin. "Your brother is safe."

Relief twisted to more sorrow as she spied the growing lines of bodies along the camp's walkways. "Thank you," she whispered to Micah. "But what happens now?"

"The reinforcements are pushing Feyor back. We'll regain the field. I'm not sure why, but the wyverns all retreated." Micah rolled his shoulders, face as serious as she'd ever seen it. "The drakes have been instrumental. I wish I could thank Dani for what she's done."

"Wasn't she with Liam?"

Micah shook his head. "No. Liam was alone on the drake."

A knot formed in her stomach. Her brother hadn't wanted to let Dani out of his sight after her return from Feyor. Yet, if the wyverns were turning back, it had to be the Dtrüa's doing.

But where is she?

She looked after Matthias, but he'd vanished among the soldiers rushing about the encampment, repairing the destruction the wyvern had wrought.

"Will Matthias be all right?" Katrin didn't look at Micah, hugging her own abdomen.

Micah put a hand on her elbow. "As much as the rest of us, perhaps. I... He tried so hard to save them." He lowered his voice. "He might have, too, if I hadn't gotten hit."

Katrin met Micah's eyes. "He'd never let anything happen to you." She hated the image of Micah's corpse that flooded her mind, promptly followed by the image of Matthias beside him. It made her nauseous to even consider.

"He didn't outright tell me I died, but that's the only reason he would have jumped again."

"The gods put limits on the Art for a reason." Katrin spoke the words to convince herself more than the man beside her. "There must be a reason for all of this."

"Let me know if you figure it out." Micah patted her arm before walking away.

"Micah."

He paused, looking back at her.

"I... should try to help in the medical tent, but Matthias..." She looked past the prince's double towards where the command tent stood. "What do I do?"

"Help in the medical tents. I've got our prince." Micah nodded once and strode after Matthias.

Katrin sniffed, rubbing her face with the inside of her arm. She turned to the tent entrance just as the drake lifted its head, lips curling back in a snarl. Her heart leapt into her throat as a man covered in blood rounded the creature's backside, skidding to a stop with its warning.

His black hair stuck to the sides of his face, caught in the streaks of crimson. The armor he wore and the steel insignia on his left shoulder helped her identify him as friend rather than foe. His eyes brought a wave of relief and comfort, so much like her father's eyes.

"Liam." She sighed, approaching him while scanning him for substantial injuries. "Are you all right?"

"I'm fine. Have you seen Dani?"

"Weren't you going to, you know, not take your eyes off her?"

He gritted his jaw. "You know how she is. She transformed in my arms so I couldn't keep hold." He looked over her shoulder at the medical tent. "You haven't seen her?"

"No. But I haven't been inside the tent, yet." Katrin fought to control the sudden worry surging through her. "Where do you think she went?"

"To get a wyvern."

More panic. "What?"

"Just... will you check for her? All the wyverns are gone, now, so I thought she'd be back. So connect, or whatever it is you do with her."

Katrin frowned. "I need to save my energy for—"

"Katy girl." His eyes bored into her, the fear within the deep brown making her stomach curl.

He's never been like this before.

She tilted her head at him, placing a hand on his arm. "Fine, but don't assume the worst if I can't find her."

Chapter 3

Wind tore through Dani's hair, whipping it back from her face. Tears streaked her temples as she laughed, gasping with each dive of the wyvern through the clouds.

Wings beat beside her, carrying her higher until all she could see was light. Her skin chilled, but she didn't care. "Ryke!"

The wyvern banked to the right, straps on Dani's thighs holding her on its back as it redirected towards the sun. Hardly any scents speckled the air. Tinges of blue from the clouds' moisture and blurs of orange from where the wyvern had flown.

Where I flew.

Years prior, when she'd been most involved in training Feyor's draconi, she'd requested to fly with the wyverns. But Nysir had dismissed her desire before she'd even finished her sentence.

"The *blind* do not *fly*."

The words had stung, but Tallos had assured her that the opportunity could come after she'd worked her way up within the Dtrüa. Perhaps even after they were wed.

I never needed them. They needed me.

The revelation struck her, lifting a weight off her chest.

Dani grinned, gripping the handles on the wyvern's saddle.

The back of her mind tingled, and she relaxed her thoughts.

Katrin is trying to reach me.

She'd felt the sensation many times once she'd been close enough again to Feyor's border, but connecting with her friend had always been a risk. One she often opted not to take.

But I'm safe now.

Closing her eyes and entrusting the wyvern, Dani breathed in deep and followed the connection back to Katrin.

I'm here. She projected her voice into the acolyte's head, waiting for the vision to come.

Her friend opened her eyes, blinking in the bright morning sunlight shining off the icy blue scales of the drake beside her. They shone like a fresh snowbank, veins of deep blue patterned along its back and sides like a wildcat.

Dani's breath caught when Katrin's gaze landed on Liam, hardly recognizable beneath the filth.

"Oh good, you're alive. Liam's worried." Katrin spoke aloud, her voice altered as she heard herself. "He also needs a bath."

Liam frowned, gesturing up and down Katrin's body. "You don't look much better. Is she seeing me right now?"

Katrin nodded, her vision bobbing with the motion.

Liam's dark eyes met hers. "Dani, where are you?"

Dani just gazed at him through Katrin's eyes, ignoring his question as she relished in a clear view of his face. *Gods, I love him.*

"Well, get over here to tell him yourself." Katrin looked away from Liam as if punishing her, redirecting her gaze to the medical tent. In her peripheral vision, Dani could see the lines of bodies along the path, but Katrin seemed to try to spare her the sight.

Huffing, Dani held tighter to the wyvern, her euphoria dimming. *All right. Tell them not to shoot me.*

"Tell the soldiers at the ballista not to shoot." Katrin repeated. "Wait, are you really on a wyvern?"

Liam groaned. "I told you not to even think about it, Dani, but you did, didn't you?"

I'll be right there.

Katrin's sight faded as Dani pulled her consciousness back to herself.

Her vision brightened with the sun, and she took a deep breath. "Dak!"

The wyvern screeched and dove, cutting through the clouds. They misted Dani's face before breaking away.

Plummeting through the sky, she angled the wyvern towards the darkest area, dappled with movement and spots of orange fires. Halfway down, she pulled on the handles. "Fah!"

The wyvern's wings billowed wide, slowing their descent. The leather membrane thrummed against the wind as it eased them down, sending gusts in all directions as it found an opening in the encampment to land. Soldiers darted out from beneath it, cursing and shouting.

The beast met the ground, lurching forward to land on the bend of its wings, and let out a roar.

A drake's low howl answered it from nearby.

"Taka, girl." Dani patted its neck. "Shek, taka." Sitting upright, she unlatched the leather straps over her legs, freeing them to jump to the ground.

"You're crazy, you know that?" Liam's voice came from the same direction as the drake's howl, his scent disguised beneath the muck covering him. "That thing is twice the size of the drakes."

Her head still spun, her cheeks prickling in phantom wind still whipping around her. She shrugged. "It can carry two, if you're jealous."

He chuckled as he stepped closer. His hands wrapped around her waist, pulling her close to him. "I'm just glad you're safe. And the battle is over. For now, at least."

Dani buried her face in his neck, holding him tight. "I'm sorry for leaving, but I had to do something about the wyverns."

"You changed everything," he whispered near her ear. "We need to report in, though. Katrin told me Matthias went to the command tent."

Pulling away from him, Dani touched Liam's face and smiled before letting go of him.

The wyvern snorted, exhaling another gust of wind.

"Will it... uh... be all right staying here?"

Dani outstretched a hand, and the beast touched it with its nose. "Buk'toe." She stroked its snout. *Stay here, you're safe.*

The wyvern purred, pressing harder against her palm. The gentle response of agreement rumbled through the Dtrüa.

Satisfied the wyvern would obey her command, she returned to Liam, finding his hand.

"Buk'toe. That sounds like the command I might have been missing earlier." He entwined his fingers with hers, tugging her away from the wyvern. "Hopefully we don't have to stay long. Katrin wasn't exaggerating about me needing a bath."

They moved through the camp, the scent of blood and death still thick in the air. But the familiar beige of the canvas tents returned as well, growing more prominent the further they walked.

Liam paused beside her. "Here." Canvas rustled as he pulled aside the flap for her, encouraging her inside towards the murmur of voices. Armor clattered as two guards near the entrance straightened to attention, but then relaxed as Liam stepped in behind her.

"What'd we miss?" Liam placed his hand at Dani's lower back to guide her.

Dani breathed deep, finding scents of many soldiers inside, only a couple familiar. The dark shapes stood still, their attention on her.

"Dani." Matthias's deep voice made her smile. "I hope you're prepared for how many medals my father is going to cover you with when we return to Nema's Throne."

She huffed, shaking her head. "I need no medals."

The prince strode closer to her, touching the leather near her shoulder. "I doubt you'll get a choice, but a promotion will have to do for now, assuming you want it."

A promotion?

Furrowing her brow, Dani touched what his hands left, finding the cool metal pin. It felt the same as the one on Liam's shoulder. "Are you making me one of your elites?" Surprise rippled through her, and she swallowed the emotion that rose in her chest.

"I trust you beyond measure. Would you do me the honor?"

Dani hesitated, smelling the apprehension emanating from the far corner of the tent. Despite the nerves gathering in her gut, she nodded.

"What is your surname?" The prince's voice held an undercurrent of grief, but she understood his need to ignore it.

"I..." Dani shuffled her feet. "I haven't one."

The pressure on her lower back from Liam increased, but then relaxed. He leaned in to kiss her temple before stepping away.

"All right. Varadani, under order of the crown, witnessed by General Flennick, I hereby pardon you of all crimes committed against the country of Isalica and its people."

Dani's heart sped, and she steeled herself for what he'd say next.

"You will, from this day on, be considered one of our people and have all the rights that come with being Isalican, should you choose to embrace them. Raise your right hand."

Taking a shaky breath, Dani did as instructed.

Matthias's tone gentled. "State your full rank and name."

"Varadani. I am a Dtrüa."

"Where were you born?"

"Melnek, Feyor."

Is this really happening?

"State your loyalties."

Dani swallowed. "I am loyal to Isalica. To you."

"Repeat after me." Matthias paused. "I swear to guard the throne and its secrets with my life, and my word is my bond."

The Dtrüa repeated the phrase, a smile twitching her lips.

"Welcome to the crown elite." Matthias touched her hand, taking it in a firm grip. "Though I'll need your help to find a suitable material to replace that insignia when possible. I don't want to inhibit your unique strengths."

Dani touched the insignia and nodded. "Bone would be ideal."

The prince squeezed her hand and let go. "It'll be done. Now, the two of you should go get cleaned up. Feyor is on the run, and we have time to recoup."

"Sir?" Liam's tone was difficult to place. "Are you sure we're not needed here?"

"You've both already done enough." Matthias's voice faded as he stepped away, moving back to the other scents in the tent. "I'd rather you get some rest before you're needed again. As long as Dani can assure us the drakes in camp won't go rogue, I fully expect you both to take the rest of the day to yourselves."

"The drakes know they are among allies. They won't hurt anyone." Dani blinked in the hazy darkness of the tent. "Thank you."

Matthias fell silent for a breath before he made some kind of gesture. "It's the least I can do. We'll reconvene tomorrow to discuss our next steps."

"Thank you, sir." Liam's fist thumped against his chest in salute, but then relaxed to take her hand.

They walked together from the tent, Dani's mind spinning.

Pardoned. Promoted. I hardly recognize my life.

Liam stepped sideways into her, wrapping his arm around her waist. "I wasn't expecting that."

Dani scoffed. "Me, neither." She gazed at where his silhouette blocked the sun. "I'm officially no longer your prisoner."

"Guess not." He touched her wrist, lifting her hand to his cheek. "Though, I don't think I could ever consider putting those cuffs back on you."

Dani shuddered, the same hollowness from before twinging in her chest. "I have an idea for cleaning up, as long as you're not afraid of heights."

"Heights?" Liam touched her chin. "Honestly, whatever it will take to clean off this gore so I can kiss you again."

Her stomach twisted.

I hardly believe he still wants to after what he saw.

"I can only imagine how awful it looks." Dani tried to disguise her worry.

"You're the fortunate one, unable to see. Though, I guess you got a peek through Katrin earlier." He took her hand again, starting down the path in the direction they'd come from before.

"I did. And if I look anything like you..." She swallowed.

Except he used a sword... I used my teeth.

"So what's the idea?"

Dani turned him down the path they'd taken from the wyvern. "Just a little trip to the clouds."

The wyvern screeched, banking to the left through the clouds. Its saddle, meant to hold up to three riders, kept them firmly in place.

Dani patted Liam's hand on her waist. "Tell me what it looks like."

Light dominated her vision again, hair whipped from her face as they soared.

He leaned against her, his mouth close to her ear as he spoke. "It's remarkable. Beautiful." Liam tightened his hold, his breath tickling her neck. Hot compared to the chill wind. "The trees look more like sticks, and the river like a drip of water over a moss covered rock. The mountains seem smaller, yet bigger at the same time."

She smiled, leaning against his chest and wishing the grime of battle wasn't covering his scent.

Liam nuzzled her neck, clearly less affected by the filth. "I'm so happy to have you back. And now flying. It all feels—"

"Like a dream?" Dani huffed. "I could pinch you, if you want."

He hummed. "You'd enjoy that too much."

The wyvern descended, pushing its thoughts into Dani's mind. It couldn't speak to her in Common, rather portray its feelings through images and impressions.

She exhaled, wind rushing past her as she gave the beast more rein. *That's perfect, thank you.*

The wyvern chuffed at her response, flapping its powerful wings to slow their momentum as they approached the mountain's base. Pine trees scented the air, a jut of rock crunching as the wyvern's claws found their hold. They lurched to a stop, and Dani took a deep breath, catching the sulfurous scent of the hot spring within the forest.

"Dak." The Dtrüa unlatched the buckles on her legs as the wyvern crouched. *Please stay until we return to you.*

The wyvern purred, shaking its neck in agreement.

Liam completed the task first, and he slid from the saddle. His fingers brushed hers as he helped her down with him.

Her boots slid on the loose gravel, and she clutched his arm, clicking her tongue.

Open space.

The sun shone around her, unobstructed by nothing but the wyvern.

"We've landed somewhere rather precarious, haven't we?"

He chuckled. "I'd say so. If you'd slipped right there, you wouldn't be recovering from the fall." Wrapping his arm around her waist, he turned her towards the smell of pine. "Bit of a slope here."

"You underestimate a cat's ability to land on their feet." Dani smirked, letting him lead her. "Only takes a breath to change. I've done it mid-fall before."

"I'm not sure even your panther would have survived that plummet."

"Noted." Dani tightened her grip. "I'd rather not test it."

"Me, neither, considering I just got you back."

Needles crunched beneath their feet as they reached steadier ground, but the terrain remained uneven, forcing them to keep their slow pace.

He never let go of her hand.

Dani clicked her tongue again, and the sound bounced back to her from the encroaching trees. "There's a hot spring around here."

"I can smell it, but how did you find it? Feyor's maps can't be that good."

"The blind can't read maps, anyway." She tilted her head at him.

Liam sighed. "You always make me sound so insensitive. You know what I meant..."

Dani smiled, but discomfort stirred in her stomach. "The wyvern brought us. She knew of the place, not me."

"The wyvern?" Liam turned back towards the creature as they walked. "Hey, she won't leave us, right? We won't get stranded up here?"

"She'll stay."

"What's it like?"

"What's what like?"

Birds called from the trees, needles rustling as a crow squabbled with a sparrow. A very different battle than the one they'd come from.

"Talking to them. To the drakes and wyverns. Bears." Liam bobbed her hand in his. "Can all Dtrüa do that?"

Dani smiled as Liam properly rolled the sounds of the word. "Yes. I mean, I think so. I thought so..." She thought back to when she'd ridden the wyvern the first time, driving away the other draconi. Turning them against their Feyorian riders.

"But now you're not sure?" His steps slowed as he faced her.

"I... It was easier than I thought it'd be, to sway them to my side. Our side. I encountered another Dtrüa in the sky, but even he couldn't keep control of his mount once I spoke to it."

"Maybe they just trusted you more?" He squeezed her hand. "I know I do."

"Maybe." Dani's doubt echoed in her tone.

He tugged on her hand again, resuming their walk through the trees. "Come on, I think we're getting close."

Liam guided her around a cluster of trees, quieting as the smell of the hot springs grew stronger. His hand tightened from time to time on hers, as if he was considering speaking, but nothing ever came.

What is he thinking about?

She couldn't bring herself to ask, licking her bottom lip as she followed him. The metallic taste of blood touched her tongue, and she cringed.

At least I didn't run this time.

Her mind circled the thought, and she wondered what had been different enough to quell the flight instinct that had taken over before.

A rock turned under her boot, and she stumbled, but Liam caught her.

"Sorry, not an easy path through here." A smile colored his tone.

"My fault. I wasn't paying attention."

He slowed. "Something on your mind?"

They stepped from the forest, the air suddenly humid. The ground beneath her boots solidified, a smooth edge where the spring waters had risen and eroded the bordering stone. A familiar dampness hung in the air, the shadows of a cave to their left.

"Nothing important."

Drips echoed as Liam guided her to the deep scents of the spring's cavern.

"I wish you could see this," he whispered. "The water is so blue, and you can see the stones at the bottom perfectly. Most of the spring seems to flow back into the mountain." He stopped, letting go of her hand.

His swords clanked as he unbuckled their sheaths from his back, followed by the gentle clinks of his light armor. "I'm not sure there's any saving some of my clothes with how filthy they are."

Dani sat and pulled her boots off. "I'll clean my leathers when we get back. I doubt Isalicans have adequate replacements."

Liam scoffed. "I'm sure we'd find something. You're Isalican, now, too, remember?"

Nerves tangled in her chest, but she ignored them, removing the pelt from her shoulders. She fell silent, shedding the rest of her outer layer of clothing.

Liam's boots thunked to the stone, his bare footsteps moving closer to her. His hand brushed under her chin. "What's wrong?"

"I know Isalicans have fine leatherworkers. But we have specialized ones to craft clothing for the Dtrüa." Dani turned her face away from his touch. "And nothing Matthias says will change where I was born."

"Maybe not, but it changes where you're going, doesn't it?" His palm cupped her cheek, encouraging her blurry gaze back to him. "And that's the more important part. We'll find someone to make you new Dtrüa leathers. Isalican Dtrüa."

"There's no such thing." Dani's back straightened, and she pulled his hand from her face. "I needn't get new ones."

"All right, so we won't get you new ones." The linen of Liam's shirt rustled as he loosened the collar. "Let's focus on cleaning up. I don't want to fight."

Dani ground her teeth, pulling off her underclothes and slipping into the warm water. Plunging beneath the surface, she closed her eyes. Her hearing muted, blocked by the sound of water swirling around her. Leaning forward, she found the edge of the pool with her toes and pushed off, swimming through the open water. Her hands found the opposite side, and she surfaced, smoothing her hair back.

How can I expect him to understand when I don't, either?

Light splashes rippled behind her as Liam lowered himself in and cleaned his skin.

Dani touched her chin, finding blood still caked on her, and took a breath. Holding it, she sank again, floating beneath the surface and scrubbing her face. She worked her hands through her hair and over her neck until the slime of mud and blood disappeared. Breaking back to the surface, she sucked in a deep breath of the humid air, trying to still the swirling of her stomach. Water dripped over her face, and she wiped it off, squeezing her hair.

Another deep breath came from Liam a moment later, water cascading over him into the spring. He stilled with the water. "Dani..." His gentle voice echoed along the damp cave roof where they'd drifted in.

Resent bubbled in her throat. "I know you hate that I'm Feyorian, but no matter what anyone says, that will never change."

"But I don't hate that." Water pulsed around her as he moved closer. "Just like I don't hate your clicking. It's all part of you. And I love *you.*"

"You fell in love with the helpless Dtrüa you kept in chains, not..." She dipped her chin, touching her canine with the tip of her tongue. "How can you want to be near me after everything last night?"

"What are you talking about?" Liam's hand drifted below the water, finding hers. "I love you just as much today as I did yesterday, perhaps more."

"More?" Dani furrowed her brow.

"Your strength is part of who you are, Dani. Your resilience, despite all of it. Your willingness to do what is necessary, even if you're afraid or you hate it. You rode drakes and a wyvern. You amaze me." Liam lifted her palm to his cheek, brushing over the thin layer of stubble forming there. He kissed the pulse of her wrist. "You can't scare me away."

"I killed soldiers... with my *teeth*. Does that not bother you?" Dani tilted her head, running her thumb over his chin and down the underside. "I use no blade. I *taste* the death. How can you cope with that so easily, when I still struggle with it?"

Liam shook his head, kissing her wrist again. "We all have struggles when we make war our business. But you do what you must to persevere and survive. If that's fighting with your teeth and claws, I see it no different from what I do with a blade. Either way, we're both instruments of Nymaera, and we both survived. And I'm still able to hold you in my arms and kiss you. Even if there is a little blood, it's worth it."

"And if there's more than a little?" Dani blinked, half her vision darkened by the cave, the other still bright with morning sky.

"Even if that wyvern of yours hadn't found us this hot spring, I would still kiss you." He moved closer to her, lifting her chin. His breath heated her lower lip as he hovered just out of reach. "Blood and all." He closed the gap, moving his mouth against hers and sending a shiver down her spine. His arm enveloped her, stroking the path of the shiver beneath the warm water, their nakedness touching.

Dani's hand slipped into his wet hair, bracing her upper arms on his shoulders to lift herself and wrap her legs around his waist.

Weightless in the water, she kissed him harder, her previous agony of being apart from him heating her eyes.

Each movement, he met with more fire. More passion. Liam made the rest of the world disappear. His hard body slick against hers, he traced her lips with his tongue.

She felt him growing stiff against her as he broke away. He ran his hands through her hair, pushing it back from her face as he kissed the bridge of her nose then forehead. "Never forget how beautiful you are to me." He kissed her again, gentler. "Never. And, as long as you'll have me, you'll be mine, too."

Dani's heart twisted at the idea of belonging to another.

But with Liam, it's different. I have a choice.

She nipped his lower lip. "All yours."

Chapter 4

Flipping the parchment over, Matthias studied the next page of the documents Dani had stolen from Feyor. Staring at the shorthand lettering, he inferred its importance despite being unable to read it.

Just need her to explain what it means, if she can.

Alone, he turned another page, and the sound whispered through the command tent. One piece slipped off the pile and drifted to the canvas-covered floor. When he bent to pick it up, his gaze trailed across the tent to the packs on the far side. Barim's slouched onto Riez's, and Matthias's gut knotted.

He straightened in his seat, scenes from the battle replaying in his mind in a continual torturous loop. Of Riez caught in a wyvern's claws. Barim crushed beneath its tail. A bolt in Micah's chest and leg.

I saved Micah, but why can't I stop seeing his death?

The horrible images repeated regardless, making his chest seize. His breathing sped, and he slapped the piece of parchment onto the table so hard that the inkwell fell over. The blackness seeped out of it, but he made no move to right it. His vision blurred as he watched each drip fall from the side of the table.

"Matthias?" A gentle female voice made his chest clench harder, and he looked up, expecting Katrin. But the woman just inside the command tent's doorway was taller, her shoulder-length blond hair the opposite of Katrin's.

He tried to control the anger in his tone but failed. "What?"

"I... came to check on you. Katrin was remarkably vague about what happened, and I..." Merissa stepped closer, her hands clasped in front of her hips. Splotches of blood showed where her apron hadn't protected all of her clothes. "I was worried about you."

"I'm breathing, which is more than I can say for the others. Save your worry for their families." Matthias stacked the papers, rising from his seat.

Merissa pursed her lips. "With all due respect, their families don't blame themselves for the death. But you clearly do." She approached the table. "This isn't your fault."

"Isn't it?" The prince stepped towards her, and she shifted to face him. "I could have saved them, if I'd not been so careless. If I'd saved my energy, but I ran out."

Rage seared through his chest, scorching his muscles into moving. He gripped the side of the table and heaved it over, sending parchment and chairs scattering through the tent. "I killed them! I should have known they'd need me, but I failed them. I jumped six times. *Six* times. And I still couldn't fix it."

Merissa didn't even flinch, her body stiff against his torment. She watched him, her eyes darkening for a moment before she crossed her arms. "All Art has its limits." Her voice drew quieter as her eyes flickered to the mess.

A pair of guards rushed into the tent, armor clanking. They stared, wide-eyed and ready. "Sir, we—"

The prince glared at them. "Get out!"

Both flinched, while Merissa remained like stone. They snapped to attention before bustling back out of the tent.

As his personal healer, Merissa had seen him angry before, but had always given him the space necessary to calm.

I need space.

"This isn't you, Matthias." Merissa's thin face held concern. "You gave all you could to save them."

"But it wasn't enough." Matthias turned from her, his hands shaking. "They're dead, and it is my job to tell their families why."

"And Feyor is that reason. This war. It is the destroyer. The enemy." Merissa took a short step closer to him. "You must—"

Matthias straightened at her advance. "There will be a caravan leaving for Nema's Throne within the week. You'll go with them." His voice lowered, tone softening. "You are dismissed."

"Matthias, I—"

"You are *dismissed*, Merissa."

She hesitated, a distant grinding of her teeth reaching his ears. "Thank you, your majesty." Frustration laced the formality, and the flap of the tent billowed as she exited.

Taking a deep breath, he let out a slow exhale.

The tent flap opened again, and he spun to face it. "I told you..." Sighing, he shook his head. "Liam. What is it?"

Liam lifted his eyebrow at the flipped table. "What the hells happened in here?" He nudged the fallen table with his formal boot, the rest of his attire matching. He donned the more refined appearance of the crown elite, likely still attempting to clean the mess off the battle armor from the day before.

Snapping at people isn't helping anything.

"Nothing." The prince let the Art flood his chest and tugged at time. He watched the table and its contents flow back to their proper positions before closing his eyes to face the tent entrance.

He blinked at Merissa's hardened face. "With all due respect, their families do not blame themselves for the death. But you clearly do." She approached the table, exactly as she had before. "This isn't your fault."

"I appreciate your concern, but you're wrong. It is my fault. I jumped six times, and I probably could have saved the first two for more dire circumstances." Matthias eyed the table, no longer feeling the urge to topple it. "I ran out of energy, and I failed them."

Merissa's shallow steps scuffed over the canvas floor, but she stopped short of reaching for him. "All Art has its limits."

"A stretch longer than a quarter hour would be much more

useful." Matthias softened his dark tone. "There will be a caravan leaving within the week to take the more severely injured to Nema's Throne. I'd like you to accompany them, as they'll need a competent healer."

"Are you certain that's best?" Merissa's brow furrowed. "Katrin is skilled, certainly, but I am your personal healer. And her training..."

"We will find a solution for her training, but this is best. Please be prepared to depart with them."

Something flashed in Merissa's vision, a glimmer from the lantern on the side table making them appear flecked with gold. It vanished as she sighed and lowered her gaze. "I've never held back when I disagreed with you, but I suppose I can't say no, can I?" She gave a small smile.

Matthias narrowed his eyes. "On the contrary, I don't think you've ever voiced your disagreement."

Her smile grew. "Perhaps that's because I've always agreed with you before."

The flap of the tent whipped open as Liam strolled in, running a hand back through his dark hair. His eyes darted to Merissa. "Oh, hi. Didn't know you were already with someone, Matthias. Need me to..." He gestured to the entrance.

"No. Merissa was just leaving." Matthias studied her, crossing his arms.

"I suppose I was." She sounded almost teasing as she started for the exit. "But I may come check on you again, later, Matthias."

"I'd rather you focus your efforts on the wounded. Last I checked, you take direction from me, no?"

Something is off with her.

She gave a respectful nod to him and Liam before slipping out of the tent.

Liam watched the flap settle back into place and approached. He circled the table, righting the fallen inkwell. He glanced at Matthias, a question in his eyes. "Any word on Feyor's movements?" He turned, lifting a scrap of linen to clean the table before dropping it and moving it around with his foot to soak up the ink from the floor.

"Scouts have yet to see the draconi return, but not all abandoned the army." Matthias exhaled, pushing Merissa from his mind. "Where is Dani? I hope yesterday didn't make anything harder for her. We should have discussed the crown elite position in private, first."

Liam chuckled as he looked at the prince, depositing the soiled linen on the edge of the table. "You caught us by surprise, but she's fine. Just still confused about everything, for which I don't blame her. Turning against those who have been her people..." He returned to the opposite side of the table, leaning against it. "She'll be here soon. She insisted I come ahead of her for the meeting. I think I annoyed her with my... *hovering*."

"One day, hopefully she thinks of us as her people." Matthias moved to his chair. "Stefan isn't able to join us, yet. He needs a few more days to rest before the healers will let him out of their sight. But Micah should be here soon. We need to decide what happens next."

Liam opened his mouth to speak, but the flap moved aside and Dani entered, Micah holding the canvas for her. A stern expression clouded his features, which Matthias recognized.

Guess I'm not the only one who feels responsible for those we lost.

Dani clicked her tongue, eyes centering on the prince. "Stefan sends his regrets for being unable to attend." Her hair shimmered in the lantern light, free of the filth from the previous day. Even her leathers were spotless, the steel insignia still at her shoulder.

"When did you speak with him?" Matthias furrowed his brow.

Of all the people Stefan met, he'd never spoken to any of them as much he spoke to the Dtrüa.

"Just before coming here. He's feeling much better, even if Katrin hardly lets him sit up." Dani clicked her tongue and touched the back of a chair.

Matthias nodded, suppressing the guilt trying to surface. "I appreciate you checking on him."

Liam bobbed his chin at the papers in front of Matthias. "Anything helpful in those documents from Feyor? Worth the risk?"

"Plenty. Sit." The prince pulled a chair from the table and motioned for the others to join him. Once they had, he pushed the documents to Liam. "It definitely details their goal to obtain dragons, and how they plan to use them. However, with the symbols all over the maps, it will take some time to decipher which locations we should target, if any. I'm not convinced we need to find them ourselves, not since Dani has swayed those attacking to retreat, and could likely do the same with the dragons if Feyor succeeded."

"If dragons still exist," Liam muttered, dubiously studying the pages.

"They exist." Dani didn't miss a beat. "I learned more while I was home. While I was in Feyor, I mean. This isn't the first time Feyor has ventured into the Yandarin Mountains, but previous journeys have been to steal eggs."

Micah leaned forward. "Dragon eggs?"

Dani nodded. "They were successful on numerous occasions, but the eggs never hatched."

Matthias exchanged a look with Micah. "They could have been wyvern eggs?"

The Dtrüa's face hardened, her lips twitching in a frown. "Or chicken eggs, I suppose."

Liam snorted. "If they didn't hatch, how *do* they know they were dragon eggs?"

"Size." Dani shrugged. "You've all seen the difference between a quail egg and a chicken egg. Wyverns are less than half the size of dragons. We... *They* know the difference."

Micah whistled. "Wyverns are enough on the battlefield. We can't let Feyor get dragons, too. Even if we are able to persuade them to stop attacking, they'll do plenty of damage in the interim."

"And the wyverns aren't gone." Dani's gaze flickered between them. "I may have convinced a few, who convinced others to retreat, but Feyor is ruthless. They'll be beaten into submission again and *will* return."

"So we need dragons to kill them?" Micah sounded hesitant.

Dani sighed. "No. We need them for their authority. I don't know this for certain, but during training, we target the wyverns first. Because the drakes obey the wyverns. If I apply the same logic to dragons…"

"The dragons may hold dominion over the rest…" Matthias tapped a finger on the table.

"I will admit, the damn things seem far more intelligent than I thought they'd be." Liam tossed the bundle of documents back to the center of the table. "The first drake Dani tamed was the one to persuade the second to join us, too, not her. So the theory of hierarchy among them makes sense."

Micah turned towards Dani. "Were you part of any of the training while you were in Feyor?"

"I was." Dani's jaw flexed. "I was not trained as a rider, for obvious reasons, but I helped *domesticate* the beasts. All Dtrüa do. Dire wolves, too."

"How intelligent are they, exactly?"

Dani paused, focused in his direction. "Drakes… are a little more advanced than the wolves. Like herding dogs. Wyverns are like human children. Impulsive, reward driven, can communicate with each other and the Dtrüa with language. They understand strategy, even if their baser instincts are still strong. I would assume dragons surpass both."

"But dragons haven't been seen in thousands of years, and wild wyverns disappeared during the First Great War." Liam leaned on the table to face Dani, too. "We seriously think they've been hiding up in the Yandarin Mountains all this time?"

"Can hardly blame them, seeing what Feyor has done to their cousins." Dani frowned. "I understand that taking my word for it is difficult, but I have no reason to lie."

"I don't think you're lying, Dani." Matthias shook his head. "Your insight is incredibly valuable. I wish I could properly convey Isalica's gratitude for what you've done for us already."

"Feyor will want to change that." Micah motioned at Dani with his chin. "They must know by now she's working with us."

"Like to see them try and get to her," Liam growled, his hand slipping around Dani beneath the edge of the table, making Micah's eyebrow rise.

Matthias frowned, studying the Dtrüa. "It's likely they will attempt to kill you. I will post extra guards around your tent, but thus far, Feyor hasn't successfully breached our camp with assassins."

Dani huffed. "If they send anyone, it will be another Dtrüa."

"Then we'll need your help to know how best to identify and prepare for them." Micah leaned back in his chair, crossing his arms. "Train our own people how to identify the Dtrüa."

"What about the drakes? Could other Dtrüa get close enough to turn the ones still in the camp against us?" Liam looked to Dani.

She paused, thinking about it. "It's possible. The drakes are smart, and they could be swayed. Chances are, a Dtrüa wouldn't prioritize them, though. Not when I could take more from them..." Her voice trailed off, eyes distant. "I should probably stay with the drakes during the night. Or at least close. They'll protect me, and it will let me keep an eye on them."

Liam frowned and looked about to protest, but then pursed his lips before nodding. "I'll stay with you too, then."

Matthias tilted his head. "That's your call, Dani. If you think it's a good idea."

Dani nodded. "Liam is fine to stay out there with me."

"It'll be good if we can keep those two you tamed fighting for us. Along with that wyvern." Micah's eyes met Matthias's.

"The wyvern won't stay near the camp. She prefers the wild, but I can have the drakes call her back if we need." Dani touched the insignia on her shoulder, and the prince remembered the trinket in his pocket.

Matthias retrieved a replica of the insignia from his coat, this one made of bone. "I had this made, but only if you still want it." He held it out.

The Dtrüa clicked her tongue before reaching. Her fingertips trailed over his palm, finding the piece of carved bone. Her lips twitched in a smile, and she took it. "I am honored. Thank you."

"Matthias." Pain already etching Micah's tone. "We need to discuss sending news to Riez and Barim's families with their belongings..."

The prince's heart weighed heavier, and he swallowed. "I'll write the letters tomorrow."

Chapter 5

Katrin's stomach danced in knots, the activity of the medical tent failing to distract her. Chewing her bottom lip, she glanced up at the doorway again as soldiers walked by.

Dani should be headed back soon. There wasn't enough time this morning.

The Dtrüa had stopped briefly at the medical tent to check on Stefan, and Katrin had caught the glimmer of morning sunlight on the steel insignia on her shoulder. The combination of excitement and dread only made the nausea worse.

Matthias hadn't mentioned his intention to make her one of his private guards. In fact, the prince had said very little to Katrin over the past day. He'd arrived late into their tent, and she only woke long enough to curl up against him. When she'd risen in the morning, he was already gone.

She'd considered seeking him out, but knew if she didn't grant him the distance he needed now, she'd be a hypocrite.

He gave me all the space I needed to mourn the priests and temple.

She idly rubbed her stomach as it flopped again.

Stefan's clammy hand brushed hers, drawing her attention to him. His eyes looked concerned, but not for himself.

"I'm fine." Katrin forced a smile, cupping his hand and lowering it back to his chest. "Don't worry about anything other than healing. I wish there was more I could do for you."

"You do plenty." Stefan swallowed, wincing, his voice gruff.

Katrin reached to the pitcher on the table beside him, filling a glass before helping him lift it to his lips. As he drank, she peeked beneath the blankets at his bare torso, still black and blue with bruises all along his side. Pools of deep red had worked their way towards the surface of his skin as the healers continued to repair the internal damage from the wyvern's tail.

They worked on him whenever they could, expelling as much as they dared without his body rejecting the work. Stefan's lack of connection to the Art slowed the process exponentially, forcing the healers to only work in short sessions so they could retain energy for others.

The crown elite had laid down again, letting out a long exhale.

Looking across the tent, Katrin eyed every full bed. Hundreds of injured. So many more dead. The smoke of the pyres had drifted into the tent, still hovering in the tall peaks.

Gods, I don't know whether to be happy or damn the timing of all of this. I just need someone to talk to about it.

And Matthias was not the answer. But as Katrin looked back across the medical tent, her eyes caught the white of Dani's furs as the Dtrüa passed the tent entrance, Liam at her side.

Katrin reached behind to untie her apron, lifting it over her head as she stood. "I'll be back to check on you soon." She grazed her hand over Stefan's as she placed the soiled apron across her chair and began dodging through the maze of cots. She nearly slipped as she hit the muddy path, slick from the early morning rain storm rolling away.

"Dani!" Katrin pulled her skirts up to avoid getting them dirtier than they already were.

The Dtrüa stopped, facing her. "Katrin. Is something wrong?" She let go of Liam's hand and stepped closer. "Is Stefan all right?"

"Yes, I'm sorry. Everything is fine." Katrin eyed her brother, and he tensed as if he also expected trouble and needed to be ready to defend them. "I just..." Her heart pounded. "I need to talk to you."

Liam narrowed his eyes. "Katy, what's wrong? I know that look."

Katrin scowled. "It's fine. I was just hoping I could talk to my best friend, if that's all right. Alone. Or do we need your permission?"

Liam lifted his hands. "Whoa, you know I didn't mean it like that. Of course you two can have some time." His hand caught Dani's briefly and leaned to kiss her temple. "Give a shout if you need me to come rescue you, since Katrin seems rabid."

Dani smirked, but her expression held something else beneath it. "I'm good at dealing with wild animals. I'll find you after."

The anger seemed foreign as it bubbled up, but Katrin swallowed it. She just glared at Liam's back as he walked away. Taking a deep breath, she rubbed at her uncomfortable stomach again. "Can we walk?"

"Of course. What has you so worked up?" Dani clicked her tongue as they strode forward, stuffing her gloved hands into pockets at the back of her leather breeches.

Katrin shook her head, brushing the straight strands of her hair behind her ear. "It's probably nothing. But with the war, and the battle. The bodies..." She steered them towards the close northern edge of the camp, staring at the snow-capped mountains. "And I'm worried about Matthias..." She huffed a laugh at herself. "What isn't there to be worked up about?"

Dani's brow furrowed. "Matthias is putting on a rather convincing show for the rest of us, but I can smell his anger. It heats the air differently than fear."

"I don't blame him for being angry." Katrin crossed her arms, a chill summer breeze sparking goosebumps over her skin. "I just hope it's not at himself. I suppose that's the hardest thing about having the Art, sometimes. We always feel as if there should have been something more we could do."

"And when you're him..." Dani shrugged. "He already carries the weight of the world on his shoulders."

"I wish he could share that weight sometimes. I worry that I'm just adding to it instead of helping though."

"How could you be adding to it?"

They'd reached the empty training arena the crown elite typically used, and Katrin gripped the smooth top rail of the fence, leaning against it. "By giving him one more person to worry about. Maybe two more..." Her abdomen clenched as she leaned it against the fence.

Dani moved beside her, and they stared ahead together.

Chewing her lip, Katrin's eyes felt heavy. "My moon cycle hasn't come." Speaking it out loud suddenly felt insane, and she shook her head. "It might just be late, but there's this feeling..."

The Dtrüa tilted her head, narrowing her eyes at her friend. "Your scent changed. I noticed it the moment I saw you again, but I thought little about it." A smile spread over her lips. "This is a good thing. A blessing. You needn't fear Matthias's reaction."

"But I'm not even sure... And this timing..."

"I recognize the shift now. You are with child, and the timing could certainly be worse. Everyone needs a little hope right now, and what better provider of hope than a baby?" Dani touched her shoulder. "This is a *good thing*."

"I'm pregnant." Katrin said the words out loud, hoping they might help settle it more permanently in her mind. Looking down at her abdomen, she tried to imagine what the child looked like within her. Matthias's child. They hadn't even talked about children, but it would have been naive of her not to consider the possibility, considering their time together.

I knew I should have spoken to an apothecary for a tonic.

But the unknowing turned to a strange elation at the idea. A lingering excitement so twisted with the nausea that it was hard to place.

A baby.

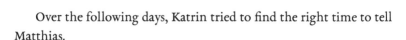

Over the following days, Katrin tried to find the right time to tell Matthias.

The prince kept busy, returning to their tent late at night and starting his meetings early in the morning. His grief followed him everywhere, taking the spark from his gaze.

Losing Barim and Riez weighed like a pit in Katrin's stomach, constantly swaying her from telling the prince about their child. She tried to tell herself it would give Matthias something to look forward to, but a little voice at the back of her head whispered doubt. The happiness could add to his guilt, even if the deaths of his elites weren't his fault.

Katrin stared at the center post of the tent, laying on her back on the cot she shared with him. He hadn't returned yet from his meeting with the general, but she welcomed the time alone to imagine what their future looked like once all the chaos settled.

She flinched, a sharp pain rolling through her from her abdomen that promptly subsided. Touching her belly, she rubbed the sore spot, already familiar with the aches that normally came with her moon cycle. Though this one didn't belong with her pregnancy.

The pain doubled back again, and Katrin couldn't help the small cry that escaped her as she hunched over her stomach. Her eyes heated.

Dani! She called out blindly with her mind as she sought her friend, trying to remember how to breathe. Another reprieve came for only a breath before the hollow ache restarted.

Something's wrong.

Only a few breaths passed before the flaps on her tent moved, a white blur of fur darting inside. Fear of the growing pain overrode any that might linger from seeing the massive cat rush into her tent.

The panther trotted to her, sniffing near her hands. Dani's whiskers tickled her skin, and the cat lifted her front paws onto the cot.

The big cat's face shifted, fur retreating over her until the Dtrüa's human form emerged. "When did the pain start?"

Another shudder echoed through Katrin, and she cringed. A warm, wet sensation touched the inside of her thighs, and she reached down before answering her friend. Her fingers returned thick with red blood.

Dani squeezed Katrin's arm. "I'll get Merissa."

The Dtrüa's words sounded so far away as Katrin gritted her teeth against another crippling wave of pain, refusing to cry out. She nodded frantically, trying to twist her legs to the edge of the bed. Her vision blurred as she watched her friend retake her panther form and race from the tent.

Oh gods, please, no.

The breeze trailed Katrin's hair to the side, strands drifting over her face as she stared at the horizon. Her eyes felt swollen, her throat raw. The pillows Merissa had given her within the medical tent were probably still wet from her tears.

Dani sat next to her, silent.

Katrin clawed at the ribbing of her corset, betrayed by her own body. Everything weighed impossibly heavy. She could still smell and feel the blood that had flowed from her.

"I can't tell him." Her voice sounded foreign as it drifted over the summer wind. Thunderclouds rimmed the sky, but she couldn't tell if they were coming or going.

"He can only be there for you if he knows." Dani touched Katrin's hand. "You need his support."

Katrin shook her head. "No. He's already mourning enough. He doesn't need this, too." Her nails scrapped along her corset, her limbs numbing. "I can't." Her voice caught in her throat, and Dani wrapped her arms around her.

"You'll get through this." The Dtrüa squeezed, resting her head on Katrin's shoulder. "You just need time, I promise."

"It feels silly to be so worked up over this." Katrin rubbed her eyes. "I wasn't even sure I was pregnant until four days ago. But those four days..." She'd imagined so many times what it would be like to hold the child, to see Matthias doing the same. To imagine what their family could be. The happiness they would find.

She pulled her knees to her chest, burying her face between them and rubbing the tears away with her skirt.

"It's not silly." Dani's voice softened. "What can I do?"

Katrin shook her head, the knot in her hair falling loose.

"Nothing." She sniffed, forcing her head up. "I have to find my own way through this." She closed her hand over Dani's, the thoughts she'd had while crying in the medical cot echoing through her soul.

Dani tensed and whispered, "I may have made a mistake."

Katrin narrowed her eyes, nerves vibrating to life as she looked at her friend's milky eyes.

"I asked Matthias to come out here after his meeting this morning. I can hear him coming, but I can ask him to go. I'm sorry, I thought you'd want him with you." Dani rolled her lips together.

Katrin couldn't hold in the whining groan as she closed her eyes. Lifting her face to the sky, she steeled every muscle in her face against letting more tears come. Wiping her cheeks, she shook her head. "It's all right. I can't avoid him forever." She patted Dani's shoulder before scooting away just enough to wrap her arms around her knees again. "I'll be fine," she lied as she smiled at her friend.

Dani's shoulders drooped, and she nodded, rising. "I will be close if you'd like to talk after." She touched Katrin's face before walking away. Matthias spoke to her as she passed him, but the words didn't reach Katrin's ears.

The prince approached her from the side, eyes etched with worry. He circled in front of where she sat on the log, kneeling. "Gods, Katrin. What's wrong?" Touching her cheek, he stroked his thumb under her eye.

Looking at his face, Katrin studied the eyes she'd dared imagine on the face of a baby. And her heart broke within her chest. Shutting her eyes, she tried to hold in the tears, but a warm trail flowed down her cheek, anyway.

Matthias's feather-light stroke brushed it away. "Oh, Kat." He wrapped his arms around her, pulling her into him. "Whatever it is, you can tell me." Kissing the top of her head, he stroked the back of her hair.

She shook in his arms, unable to hold in the sobs that started again as she gripped his tunic. The scent of him, his strength, tried to rebuild her, only to be torn down again by the ache in her empty womb. "I'm sorry." She sniffed. "I'm so sorry."

"You have nothing to be sorry for." Matthias pulled from her, meeting her eyes. "You're scaring me. Please tell me what's going on."

She shook her head, biting hard on her lip to control more sobs. She tasted the copper of her blood, and it sent a shudder through her body as she imagined seeing it on her fingertips again. "I..." She looked down, unable to look in those eyes. "I can't do this. I'm not strong enough."

"Can't do what?" The prince dipped his chin to catch her gaze. "Do you want to leave the camp?"

She nodded, but then shook her head as she looked away again. "I think I need to leave more than just the camp behind, right now." It hurt to say it, but she ground her teeth to stop from crying again. "I'm going to go home. The caravan headed for Nema's Throne will go directly past my family's farm. I... can't be here."

Matthias blinked, and he nodded. "Whatever you need. I can brief Micah and leave him in charge while—"

"No." She breathed hard as she met his eyes. "I can't be with you. Not right now."

The prince stilled, recoiling his hand from her as he sat back on his heels. "You're leaving me?"

Katrin winced, wringing her hands together in her lap. "I need to."

He cleared his throat, looking at the ground between them. "Why? Is it because of the last few days?" Looking at her, he ran a hand through his hair. "I know I've been preoccupied, but..."

"No, of course not." She touched her stomach again, unable to stop herself from the action as the pain tingled. "This isn't because of you. I told you, I'm not strong enough. *I'm* the one who needs to leave." She wanted to stand, to walk away before he could look at her more like he was.

The pain in his eyes only doubled hers. But her knees wouldn't work.

"I'm sorry." Her voice cracked.

Matthias cringed, then steeled his face. "You won't tell me why?"

She shook her head, trying and failing yet again to hold in the tears. "No."

The prince stood, his hand drifting towards her before he stepped back. His mouth opened, but no words came out before he turned and walked away.

Katrin refused to turn after him, staring at the white caps of the mountains before her. She closed her eyes, letting the quiet tears fall, dripping from her chin to the dandelions at her feet.

Silence reigned for only a few breaths before soft footsteps hurried up behind her.

"What just happened?" Dani sat sideways on the log, facing her. "Matthias looked... not happy."

"Why would he be happy?" Katrin swallowed, resisting the temptation to wipe her face again. "I'm leaving."

"What?" Dani gaped at her. "What are you leaving, exactly?"

"All of it." Katrin rocked to stand again, but a flash of pain caused her knees to fail at supporting her. She put her hands behind her on the log to stop from falling backward, her body jelly. "I can't be here right now. I can't look at him."

"That will pass. Don't throw it all away, Kat. You need support right now."

She gritted her teeth. "I won't get it here. Not on the front lines of a war."

Her anger heated her gut. Anger at Feyor. At her body. At the gods. At everything leading her astray. "I need to let my head clear so I can think objectively. I haven't been able to do that since I set eyes on Matthias. Maybe all of this has been a giant mistake."

Dani balked, rising from the log. "All of this?"

"No." Katrin rubbed her forehead, wishing her head didn't feel stuffed with linen. "Yes? I don't know. Maybe that gods' damned vision that convinced me to follow Matthias wasn't a vision at all. It was just a girl's daydream about escaping the life she was meant for." Her eyes roved over the charred black skeleton of the temple, summer buds attempting to grow within the ash. "I shouldn't have ever left."

Flashes of the white panther stalking through the trees of her dream made Katrin's breath catch, but she squeezed her eyes shut.

The Dtrüa took a step towards her. "But look at what you've gained."

She scoffed. "Gained? All I see is loss. The border, the temple. Barim and Riez. No new information from the library on dragons. Then, when I dared to hope, to be happy at the prospect of a child, I fail at that, too." She gripped hard at her stomach, imagining tearing the flesh beneath her corset. She gritted her jaw, heat swelling again with the anger. "I'm going home, Dani. I'm leaving this afternoon with the caravan. I have no place in the temples, and certainly not in a royal palace."

"But—"

"I need to be alone." Katrin glared at Dani. She wouldn't have needed to speak to Matthias if the Dtrüa hadn't summoned him. She could have just vanished. "I need time. Just go away."

Dani's chest rose faster, and her jaw flexed before she sucked in a breath. Dropping to all fours, the Dtrüa took her panther form and bolted away. She ran for the tree line rather than the encampment, disappearing among the foliage.

Katrin breathed, quaking in her roiling fury. Before she realized her own movement, she was back on her feet, pacing through the grass. Finding her quarterstaff where she'd left it against the outside of the battlement, she clutched it. With a mere whisper of thought, her emotions flooded with her Art into the wood, and it crackled beneath her palm.

Black lines, like lightning strikes, radiated down the oak from her grip, shimmering embers beneath them. Swinging the staff in a smooth arc, she cried out as it slammed into the log she had been sitting on.

The wood ruptured in her hands, splinters digging into her skin as she lifted it and slammed again. The staff, weakened by her Art, exploded in a rain of cinder and ash.

Her gut quivered, and she stared at her shaking, bloody palms as her knees gave out. Collapsing against the grass and dandelions, Katrin surrendered to the pain.

Chapter 6

Didn't expect Katrin to accompany us.
The stubborn prince still insists I leave.
Though I doubt he suspects me.
It's too bad Katrin won't come all the way to Nema's Throne.
She might have proved a better vessel.
So close to Matthias.
But now...
She's weak.
Broken.
She bores me.
Matthias must return to the capital eventually.
And when he does, I'll be waiting.

Chapter 7

"What the hells is this?" Liam stormed into Matthias's tent, clutching a scrap of parchment with Katrin's handwriting on it.

Matthias looked up, his eyes sunken. "I don't know, Talansiet, how about you tell me?" He rose from where he sat at the small side table next to his cot.

Liam paused, furrowing his brow. "You didn't send her away?"

"Away? Who?" Matthias pushed his chair beneath the table, his movement sluggish.

The blame he placed on the prince vanished. "Katrin." He lowered his fist. "She went with the caravan this afternoon. I was busy with training exercises in the western field and she didn't even bother telling me in person."

Matthias pushed aside the papers he'd been looking over, not meeting Liam's gaze. "So she left, then." He cleared his throat, letting out a breath. "I hope she finds whatever she's searching for."

Liam eyed the prince, trying to read whatever he could from the man's posture and expression. His face was hardened, eyes dark. "Did you talk to her?"

Matthias nodded, finally making eye contact. "I did. This morning."

"And?"

"She said she was leaving the camp. Leaving me. To go home."

"What the hells happened?" Liam tucked the note into his back pocket as he took a step forward. "Did you have a fight?"

The prince scoffed and threw his hands up into the air. "Nope. She wouldn't tell me why. Nothing happened. One day, we were fine, the next... not fine. I don't know what happened, and I couldn't find Dani after to ask her."

"She included an apology to Dani in her note." Liam pursed his lips, but worry rose. "She just... left?"

Matthias ran his hands over his face, scratching his beard. "Yes, Liam. I don't know what else to tell you." His voice dropped with his gaze, a hollowness echoing in it. "She said she couldn't be with me anymore."

"Nymaera's breath." Liam ran both hands back through his hair. He sighed, his shoulders slackening. "Not like you needed more worries right now. I'm sorry, Matthias. At least we know she'll be safe at home?"

The prince nodded again, jaw flexing. "Safe at home." His deep monotone voice sounded distant. "Definitely safer than being here." He strode past Liam, pushing the tent flap open. "I'll go check on Stefan. Let me know if you find Dani. Last I saw her, she was with Katrin outside the east gate."

Liam stared at the entrance as the canvas fell back into place. The pain of his sister's secret departure lingered, but Matthias suffered far worse. His mind wandered to Dani, paranoia crawling into his chest.

She'll be devastated, too. What is Kat thinking?

Making his way through the camp, Liam took the less popular paths to avoid the monotony of stopping to receive a salute every five steps. Squeezing between tents, he first visited the small tent he and Dani had established at the edge of the paddock the drakes occupied.

Both were present, and Brek gave his customary growl that Liam chose to interpret as a greeting rather than residual anger about the crossbow bolt.

"Seen Dani, boys?" Liam glanced between them as Ousa thrust his head over the high fence for scratches on his scaled nose. The soldier obliged, still marveling at the fact that he could touch the creatures Dani had named.

Guess we're keeping them.

Ousa whined as Liam walked away, leaning in to check the tent and finding it empty. "East gate, it is."

Dark clouds rolled in, and the air warmed with the scent of a coming thunderstorm. Sharp winds whipped through the pines, prompting Liam to walk faster before the rain came to wash away any trail he could follow.

Climbing the slight hill from the gate to the fallen log near the pine forest, he spotted Katrin's broken quarterstaff. The base of it remained almost intact, but the top had shattered into more pieces than he could count. The charred end showed her Art's participation in the destruction, and it only brought more questions.

Scanning the ground, he spotted the giant paw prints of Dani's panther form in the wet dirt. Her trail led into the forest in a straight line, not wavering.

Following it, he continued even as light rain fell from the clouds, dappling his face.

Picking up his pace, he came to where the trees thinned and a cliff disrupted the terrain.

It overlooked a valley, and a pure white panther laid at the edge.

Her front paws draped over the side, ears swiveling with his approach.

Looking at her, he couldn't help but appreciate the beauty. Thick drops of rain fell onto her coat, dripping down her sides without being absorbed. The ridge of pines beyond created a pristine backdrop for such a magnificent creature that should have sent him running for the safety of camp. But the danger of her only made him want her more as he stepped forward, the fear of her being gone, too, fluttering away.

"There you are." He crossed towards her furry head, crouching before sitting to let his feet dangle over the cliff side.

The panther groaned, and she shuffled sideways, laying her head in his lap.

He stroked the fur on top of her head back between her ears. "You had me worried."

Dani huffed, rolling onto her side. She looked up at him, cloudy eyes flickering over his face. Her body shifted. Skin emerged over her face as the fur retreated, forming the pelt around her shoulders. "Worried about what?" Her soft voice relaxed his insides.

His hand ran over her hair instead of her fur, brushing the long strands behind her ear as her head rested on his thigh. "I thought maybe you'd left, too, when I first read Katrin's letter."

A solemn expression took over her features. "Oh." Her eyes darted away before returning. "I would never leave without..."

"Without telling me?"

Dani scoffed. "Without *you*." She gestured in a circle with her hand. "Not very far, at least. I've done that, and I needn't do it again."

He playfully brushed his fingertips over her earlobe. "Then I'm a very lucky man, indeed." His chest panged with guilt that he could still touch the woman he loved, while Matthias was alone. Chewing his lower lip, Liam studied Dani's perfect face. "I don't want to be apart from you again, either. The last three months..."

"Are you planning a trip without me?" A smirk danced over her mouth. "You needn't worry. I'm not going anywhere. The bond is broken, and I need never return to Feyor."

"But you still think of it as home, don't you?" He continued to trace her face. "Do you miss it?"

Dani hesitated, brow twitching. "Old habits, I suppose. I never had much of a home, and I'm learning it has less to do with a place and more to do with who is there. I miss things, sometimes, but I don't want to go back. If anything, my recent time there only reminded me of that."

He hummed in understanding, following her shoulder and arm down to her hand. Entwining his fingers with hers, he lifted her knuckles, kissing them. "More for me to be grateful for, then."

"I won't leave you, Liam." The Dtrüa centered on the fears he couldn't deny. "I know that's what you're thinking, after seeing your sister leave Matthias."

He sighed, nodding against her touch so she might feel it. "I can't help it. She just... left. And I don't understand what happened."

Dani's jaw clenched, her gaze altering to the sky as raindrops still fell. "In time, I'm sure she will explain."

"If she's even thinking at all," he grumbled.

A distant rumble echoed over the mountains, a flash of light preceding another boom of thunder. The raindrops grew heavier, falling faster, and Dani rolled her face to hide it in his stomach.

Liam smiled as he hunched over her to further protect her, enjoying the sensation of the rain dribbling past his collar and down his back. Leaning forward, his lips brushed her cheek. "I love you, Dani. And I'm grateful for every moment."

The Dtrüa peeked at him before sitting up and crawling into his lap. Rain dripped down her face, sticking to her dark lashes. "And I love you." She draped her arms over his shoulders, kissing him.

He sank happily into the movement of her mouth against his, the growing storm unable to quell his desire for her. His hands ran up her hips and over her sides, pulling her closer. The idea of ever losing her made his chest ache and his throat tighten.

How did I fall so fast?

His breath sped as he broke away from her, unwilling to move too far. Water ran through their hair, attempting to break through where their heads touched. Chest thrumming, he felt foolish for the thoughts still coursing through his mind. Crazy. But he was desperate to know.

"Can I ask you something?"

"Anything." Dani grazed her lips over his, her hands at either side of his neck playing with the thin leather strap holding the panther tooth pendant she'd given him months ago.

He kissed her as the words caught on his tongue, untangling them with the affection. "You don't have a surname, and I'm wondering if you'd like to share mine." His thumb brushed over her jaw, and he opened his eyes to watch her face. "If you'd take mine, as my wife?"

Dani pulled back from him, blinking. "You... You want to marry me so I have a surname?"

Liam flinched, sudden guilt wriggling in him. "No, no, that's not the reason. I'm trying..." He sighed and shook his head with a slight laugh. "Dani, I love you. And I want to marry you. To be your husband and love you forever."

Her breath came faster. "You're serious."

"Of course I'm serious." He tried to interpret the look on her face, the tightness of her mouth, but couldn't. "Why wouldn't I be?"

"It's... pretty fast."

"Our lives can be pretty fast." Liam took her hand between them, pressing hers to his chest. "Especially considering the war right now. I don't want to waste any time."

Dani bit her lower lip, her eyebrows upturning in the center. "Is this because Katrin left Matthias? Or that we lost Barim and Riez?"

"Do either of those things matter in this? I'm talking about us right now. And how much I love and want to be with *you*."

Dani touched her forehead to his. "I want to be with you, too. But we've only experienced a small part of each other. Battles. War. Prisons and..." She huffed with a smile. "Interrogations. Liam, how can you be sure? What will we be like outside of a war?"

"None of it will change how I feel about you."

"You don't know that. There are things you don't know."

Liam swallowed. "Are you saying no, then?" His stomach twisted, but he fought to control it.

"I'm saying... I'm saying I need time to think about it." Dani pulled away and touched his face, running her thumb over his brow. "I meant it when I said I'm not going anywhere."

He tilted his head into her touch, savoring the feel of her over his wet skin. The rain had turned to a thick misting as more lightning crashed over the Yandarin Mountains, the low rumble echoing the feeling of his own body. "Not a no, at least." He tried to find comfort in his own words as he brushed his hands up into her hair and pulled her close to kiss her. "I'm not the most patient, but for you, I'll try."

Dani smiled, nipping his bottom lip. "Not a no." She pulled at the hem of his tunic, freeing it from his pants.

He moaned against her lips, caressing down to her backside with his hands. "Something else in mind?" He smiled as he kissed the corner of her mouth, tasting the rain on her skin.

Dragging her nails over his sides, she flicked his belt open. "I don't want to waste any time. And we've never made love during a thunderstorm."

Chapter 8

One month later...

With his usual abundance of patience, Matthias took Dani's hand and traced her finger over a symbol.

She closed her eyes, focusing on the shape.

"Does that one mean anything to you?" Life had returned to his deep voice, especially since Stefan's full recovery, but the prince's demeanor still wasn't the same.

Dani shook her head. "No. I've never encountered it before, either. Where did she draw this one?" It'd become habit to avoid saying Katrin's name.

He knows who I mean.

Matthias sighed. "It's at another of the mountain peaks."

"They could mean nothing." Liam's blade rasped against the whetstone in the tent's corner, his teal scent tinting the air. "She's always doodled in the margins of books."

"No, it means something. They repeat through all her notes, not just in the margins. If I cross reference all the symbols with those from the Feyorian documents, these three are the only ones constantly repeated. They mark the three highest points of the Yandarin Mountains. It's not a coincidence."

Liam huffed. "Would have been nice for her to just write it in Common. Same goes for the Feyorians." His sword returned to its sheath, and a new blade ran along the stone.

Dani felt a flicker of gratitude for Liam's continued attention to no longer using the derogatory title for her people. He hadn't said Yorrie in weeks.

Matthias paused, tension surrounding his dim shape. His voice lowered. "Have you spoken with her?"

The Dtrüa had tried many times to reach her friend that week, her desire to fix their friendship finally outweighing her hurt for how they parted ways. To her disappointment, she'd had no success.

Dani shook her head. "She's closed off. Or she's too far."

The prince inhaled a deep breath, pacing away. "I got word of the caravan's arrival in Nema's Throne yesterday. It confirmed they left her at her family's home."

"I think she's angry with me." Dani dipped her chin, Katrin's last words to her still stinging.

Liam stopped again. "She apologized, though, so I don't think she's mad at you, Dani. Whatever happened, she just needs time."

"I thought this would've been enough time," Dani whispered, turning from the men.

"What do you mean, enough time?" The prince's pacing paused. "You never explained why you think she's angry with you."

Dani clenched her jaw. "I summoned you that day, thinking it would be good for her to talk to you. I knew not..."

Matthias stepped closer, and she cringed. "Why did you think she needed to talk to me?"

Dani hesitated, the information Matthias was missing weighing like a rock in her stomach. It had plagued her for weeks, since the day Katrin left, but the Dtrüa had held her tongue. The information wasn't hers to share, even if she struggled watching the prince suffer in the unknowing.

The crate beneath Liam creaked as he stood, depositing his blades on top of it. "It's just us here, Dani." His voice grew closer. "If you know what made my sister leave, I think Matthias deserves to know."

Dani's eyes burned, and she slowly faced them again. "Two days after Feyor's attack, Katrin learned she was pregnant."

"What?" Matthias's whisper sliced through the tent like a blade, making her flinch. "Are you saying she's out there carrying my child?"

Tears welled in Dani's eyes, and she shook her head. "She lost the baby. The night before she left..."

The air stilled, breaths held in chests.

"Shit..." Liam's whisper broke the silence first.

Matthias turned from her, sucking in shaky gulps of air. "You were in my tent that night."

"I had to change the bedding..." Dani swallowed, her throat tightening. "I'm so sorry. I knew... I knew not what to do."

"That's why she left." Matthias's tone sounded strained.

"Seeing you reminded her of what she'd lost."

"What *we* lost." The prince's voice shook, his breathing coming faster. "I had a child."

Dani bowed her head, hot tears trailing over her cheeks. "She thought you already had enough to deal with."

Liam's touch brushed her shoulder, his lips pressing gently against her tears before he moved away, stepping to Matthias. He paused, the raging silence in the tent growing again.

"Matthias?" Liam whispered.

"I'd like a moment, please." The prince spoke through clenched teeth, and his pain radiated in a haze of maroon over Dani's senses.

"Of course." The Dtrüa turned, clicking her tongue and crossing to the tent's exit.

"Sure," Liam echoed, but his footsteps lingered before he followed her, snatching his weapons along the way. "I'll... check in." He said over his shoulder before they both slipped outside.

Dani clicked her tongue again and walked a few paces away in a rush before facing Liam, holding her palms out. "Please don't be angry."

"I'm not angry." Liam's voice remained far too calm as he stepped to her. His warm, calloused hands took hers, squeezing them. "Dani, I'm just sorry you've been carrying that, too." He pressed his lips to her forehead, a chill autumn breeze rushing around them as they shivered. Wrapping his arm around her waist, he turned them down the hard mud pathway. "Let's get inside, though. Too cold out here."

They walked together, Liam's grip tight around her even as soldiers saluted them before he turned down the familiar route towards the back of their tent. The wind howled through the distant Yandarin Mountains, echoed by the slow rumble of Ousa and Brek's playful growls as they tussled in their paddock nearby.

Dani and Liam's tent had grown to something far more permanent, including an extended wing that partially covered the drakes' pen so they could seek shelter from the harshening weather.

Liam tugged the drawstring of the flap as he nodded to the two guards positioned outside. "You know I rarely ask for favors, Private, but could you fetch us some tea?"

The soldier's armor clanked as he shifted in salute. "Sir."

"Thank you." Liam held the flap aside for her, the welcoming scents of their home filling her nose.

The flap closed behind them, and Dani stepped farther into the space. "I wanted to tell you, but—" Another scent dappled her vision and she froze, the yellow tinge wafting through the tent.

"What the hells…" Liam's sword scraped out of its scabbard faster than she'd ever heard, his arm suddenly around her waist and pulling her behind him.

"Please, I'm not here to harm either of you." The gentle voice drifted through the tent at first, as if Lasseth's shape was still forming as he spoke. His cloak whispered against the canvas floor as he stepped back.

"Liam, stop." Dani pried his arm off her. "I know him." She recognized the tension in Liam's scent, the steady calm he took before a fight. She gripped his forearm, squeezing.

The soldier remained ready. "How the hells did you get in here?"

Someone yelped outside as the drake's side of the tent shifted. The flap that led to the outdoor paddock lifted, Ousa's snout emerging beneath with the bright spot of daylight. The drake huffed.

"Shek, taka." Lasseth's order rang clear, and the beast snorted before abandoning its search.

"You're a Dtrüa." Liam stayed poised, and Dani didn't let go. "But can't say I expected one to shift from shadow instead of an animal form."

"He's not like me. Not really." Dani pulled on Liam. "Lasseth is the one who introduced me to the woman who broke my bond. He's a friend."

"She might also add that I'm the one who stole the documents you and your prince have been pouring over." Lasseth's voice held a smile.

"That, too." Dani finally let go of Liam, approaching the Shade until he closed his arms around her in a hug.

"Glad to see you're safe." Lasseth let go of her, poking the bone insignia at her shoulder. "And getting the credit you deserve."

Liam cleared his throat.

Dani coughed and stepped back. "This is Liam."

"I assumed." Lasseth chuckled. "Chivalrous, isn't he?"

"Uh huh..." Liam sounded unimpressed. "What are you doing sneaking into our tent, Lasseth? As a friend, I'd think you would have knocked."

"Knocking on a tent tends to make little noise." The Shade sighed, and Dani could imagine Liam's eye roll. "I came with a warning, Varadani. Resslin is on her way. For you."

Dani's heart sank, fear ebbing into her stomach. "When did she leave? From where?"

"Yesterday, from Melnek. You're fortunate I have faster traveling methods than she does."

Resslin's mountain lion form would take at least a week to reach their camp.

Dani took a deeper breath. "She's coming to kill me?"

"That she is." Lasseth's cloak rustled as he crossed his arms. "Nysir never returned, and King Lazorus has decided she is personally responsible for the defection of a Dtrüa during a time of war. You are the sole source of her embarrassment and ruined military career."

Liam stepped away, making a wide arc around the edge of the tent as if trying to get behind Lasseth.

The Shade hesitated before striding closer to Dani again, taking her hand and pushing something cool and smooth into her palm. "A gift, from our mutual friend."

Dani studied the leather string necklace, finding a long, smooth piece of carved bone as a pendant. "What is it?"

"A charm. If Resslin is close... it will react with heat and light."

Nodding, Dani pulled it over her head, tucking the pendant under her leathers. "Thank you, both of you. I appreciate the warning."

A voice outside drew her attention.

"Sir, I brought the tea you requested."

Dani faced Lasseth again. "Hurry, you should..."

His scent had already dissipated, disappearing by the time the soldier lifted the tent flap.

"Nymaera's breath," Liam hissed, approaching where Lasseth had been, but Dani knew he was already gone.

The soldier halted next to the doorway, the tea set clinking together on the tray. "Sir?" Confusion tainted his tone as Liam sighed.

The private moved without Liam saying anything, likely waved in by the crown elite.

"Thank you." Liam's tone sounded far too exasperated as he poured water and the private departed.

Dani stood still, pressing the gift from Ailiena against her collarbone, memorizing the way it felt so she'd recognize any change.

Thank you, Rahn'ka.

"Being with you is never boring." Liam poured a second cup, the sound coming from the low table near the corner of their tent, pillows and blankets spread along the floor to sit on. "You never said much about the man who helped you get out of Feyor, though I feel his ability to dissolve into shadows would have been good information to have."

"I'm sorry," Dani murmured.

"So he isn't a Dtrüa? He sure seemed to have Ousa fooled." Liam crossed to her, taking her hand to guide her towards the tea and rest. "Can you tell me?"

"I know little of his past. Just that he is a Shade, whatever that means. He worked with a woman, Ailiena, to free me from the bond to the other Dtrüa."

"Never heard of a Shade. She's one too?"

"No, she is something else entirely. I wish I could explain."

"But she has the Art capable of creating an object that will sense when a particular person is near..." Liam kept hold of her as they sat on the wide pillows on the floor. The wooden tray ground along the table as he pulled it closer, spoon tapping against the rim of the tin cups.

Dani nodded. "If he says that is what it does, I trust him."

He placed a warm cup in her hands. "Then I do, too. Even if his Art is creepy. But this Resslin..."

"She was the first cat Feyor created. I was to be her protégé before Tallos claimed me. My superior in rank and skill. She's got fifteen more years of training than I do. I was to begin my training with her once... once Tallos and I were wed."

I probably should have told him that part sooner.

His breathing stopped, the tent growing still with him. "I..." His cup tapped on to the table. "I didn't realize you two were *that* close. I knew he was possessive, but..."

Dani sipped her tea. "We were betrothed when I turned sixteen."

"When were you supposed to wed?"

"A few months ago."

The fabric of the pillows rubbed together as Liam shifted. "I guess that didn't work out so great..."

"Please remember that I had no choice." Dani reached for him through the darkness of her vision, finding his forearm. "I think it worked out exactly how it was supposed to."

His hand closed over hers, skin rough as he took her hand. "No regrets, then?"

"A few," Dani whispered. "But I can't change what I've done, and

I regret nothing that's happened between us. I'm sorry I haven't answered you, yet, I just—"

His touch slipped away. "Don't worry, I know I surprised you. Surprised myself."

Has he changed his mind?

Liam sipped his tea, letting the quiet between them grow.

Dani's thoughts drifted to the day on the ridge when he asked her to be his wife. The thought of being bound to someone again brought an array of emotions, ones she had difficulty sorting through.

A low rumble of Brek's whine shook through the air as the drake nosed his way back inside to the warmth of the paddock within the tent. Hay crunched beneath him as he settled into his usual spot, snorting.

The ground vibrated as Ousa pursued, his rumbling purr playful, but he received a low warning growl from Brek.

Dani closed her eyes, the growl provoking images of Tallos's bear form. He'd come for her, in Omensea, and nearly killed Liam to get to her.

I can't let him stand between me and another Dtrüa.

Brek growled again, more pronounced.

"Ousa, back off. He clearly doesn't want your attention," Liam grumbled to the pair of drakes, their exchange stopping.

Ousa whined, the sound unusually high pitched for the size of the drake.

"I'll get you a snack to distract you in a minute."

Another whine.

Liam sighed. "All right, all right." He stood, putting his tea aside, before walking to Dani. He touched the back of her head, leaning down to kiss her hair. "They're more demanding than I imagine children would be." His tone had lightened to something more amused, but his words weighed on her heart.

He thinks about children? But what kind of children could I possibly give him?

Dani swallowed, pain prickling her insides for what Katrin and

Matthias suffered. Her breath quickened, and she shut her eyes tighter. The hollowness returned to her chest, and she touched her sternum.

I wish this feeling would go away.

She put her tea on the floor.

Ousa trilled as Liam crossed to the paddock gate inside their tent. The gate creaked when he opened it, making his way outside where they kept the unwanted parts from the camp's butcher.

Dani opened her eyes, gazing at the teal trail left behind after Liam's exit. "How could I ever be enough?" she whispered, knowing her words wouldn't reach his ears. She bowed her head, pressing her palm to her chest. "I'm not even whole."

Ousa thundered out of the tent behind Liam, leaving Brek snoring on his bed of hay, uninterested in food. The drake howled happily from outside, a crunch following that sent a chill up Dani's spine, knowing full well the damage the drake's jaws were capable of.

Liam's scent returned through the loose tent flaps, his boots shuffling on the hay lined floor.

Standing, Dani chewed her lip. "It's all right if you've changed your mind."

"Hmm?" He latched the gate behind him. "Changed my mind about what?"

Footsteps tapped over the ground outside the front of their tent, and Dani tilted her head to listen.

Matthias's gait.

Afternoon light brightened her vision as the tent flap opened, the prince's navy scent tinging her sight. "Good, you're both here."

Dani faced him, exhaling the emotion she harbored about Liam's proposal. "What is it?"

"I need you both to pack up. We're leaving the camp tomorrow morning."

"Leaving?" Liam approached the prince. "Are we retreating from the valley?"

"No. I'm leaving Micah in command with Stefan. We're going to pay your folks a visit, Talansiet." Matthias's voice had recovered since they'd last spoken, but it still held underlying tension.

"Sir?"

The formality surprised Dani with how close Liam and Matthias seemed.

Silence hovered in the tent, and she could imagine the unimpressed look on the prince's face.

Liam sighed. "Are you sure that's a good idea?"

"I know Dani's inability to connect with Katrin doesn't mean anything is wrong, but the bottom line is that we need to understand her notes on the dragons. Once she's explained what they all mean, we can continue our planning."

Dani rolled her shoulders. "Will make it more difficult for Resslin to find me, at least."

"Resslin?"

"Oh, nothing shocking. Just a Dtrüa bent on killing Dani."

The prince grunted. "Fantastic. Hopefully not another bear?"

"Mountain lion." Dani spoke the words through clenched teeth. "I'll explain everything later."

"So are we traveling with the prince, or a crown elite?"

"You're traveling with the prince. I don't need any attempts on Micah's life if I can help it. But it's just us three going, and we're taking the drakes."

"That'll be a fun surprise for my parents. And the cows..." Liam's tone held his smirk.

Dani's stomach twisted at the idea of seeing Katrin again, even if the acolyte had apologized through her brother.

She'll find out I told Matthias the truth.

"You don't have to see her, you know. Dani and I could just go. Be there and back again within a week with Ousa carrying us." Liam had moved back near Dani, picking up his tea without sitting down.

"I'll accompany you in case we need to continue on to Nema's Throne. But I will spend my nights in town, rather than at the farmstead." Matthias took a step back. "We'll leave at first light."

Chapter 9

Matthias glanced at the back field, where Dani worked with the drakes. "You should have mentioned your family ran a *cattle* farm."

The Dtrüa stood with Ousa and Brek, lecturing them in a distant field about the rules of not harming any of the cows.

"I did mention it," Liam grumbled, brushing dirt off his breeches after an excited Ousa had knocked him on his backside. "Ousa thinks we've brought him to a feast."

"Think Dani can sway them?" The prince stared at the woman as she darted in front of Ousa, pointing.

The drake crouched, crawling over the tall grass like a playful dog.

Liam chuckled. "It's pretty ridiculous how cute I think drakes are now. They were just vicious killers before."

"Seems she's changed your mind on a few things, then." Matthias quirked a brow, looking forward. His gaze settled on the farmstead they approached, and a knot tightened in his gut.

Maybe she'll be in town, and I won't have to see her.

Liam clapped a hand on Matthias's shoulder. "I'll get you a horse as quick as I can. But I better check in with my old man first. He'll still beat my backside, crown elite or not, if I take one without asking."

"Of course." The prince nodded, trying to ignore the rising nerves. "It'll be kinder on everyone if I leave this one to you two."

The toasty scent of baking pies drifted from the homestead's front windows, open with rose colored curtains flapping in the autumn breeze. Behind, the rolling hills met the base of the mountains, topped with barren maple trees, mounds of yellowing leaves on the grass. The cattle stood frozen in various positions across the land, their heads turned towards the drakes.

Leaves rustled in the wind as they blew across the path leading to the squat house, the door opening despite the fifty yards they still had to walk. Smoke rose from the man's pipe, his plain boots and breeches stained with mud.

Matthias slowed his steps and came to a stop. "You know, I think while you talk to your folks, I'll see if Dani needs any help."

Liam cast him a sideways glance. "I thought you wanted to check on Kat?"

"No, you can. I don't think I can see her right now."

As if the gods were seeking to punish him, Matthias's eyes flitted to the window beside the porch where Katrin stood within. She didn't look up as she worked, bits of flour speckling her cheeks, black hair framing her face.

Matthias's heart twisted, and he backed up a step.

A dog yipped as it pushed past his master through the doorway, a blur of black and white fur as it dove off the front porch straight for Matthias and Liam. Its tongue lolled out the side of its mouth, tail wagging as it charged at Liam, who crouched.

"Tuks!" Liam fell backward as the herding dog barreled into his chest, barking and licking. "Still alive, old man?" He scratched the animal, only further exciting him.

Matthias chuckled, forgetting himself before he looked up and met Katrin's gaze. His breath hitched, and he swallowed his smile. "Come get me when you have permission for the horse."

"Sure. Stable is the one on the right, around back. I'll meet you there after I talk with Pa." Liam looked up at the man on the deck, who puffed another cloud of smoke from his pipe. The hint of a smile curled his clean-shaven face.

Another woman, very much like Katrin, joined her at the window before the acolyte disappeared.

The prince tore his gaze away and turned, walking towards the stable near where the drakes occupied a field. Lifting his eyes from the road, he watched Dani make her way to him.

They met halfway, concern etching the Dtrüa's face. "Did you see her?"

The prince nodded out of habit. "Only for a second, but she's safe, and that's all I needed to know. How are the drakes?"

Dani huffed. "Persistent. They've got minor negotiating skills, but I think I talked them out of eating *just one*." She rolled her eyes. "They should be all right. Is Liam fetching you a horse?"

"Yes. I'll be fine in town."

"Maybe I should go with you."

Matthias furrowed his brow. "Why? Liam said it wouldn't be a problem having you here."

Dani shifted on her feet. "I know he said that, but... I'm not really, um... I don't do families well. They'll hate me. Can't I come with you?"

The prince huffed. "No, you're going to be the braver one of the two of us. Try to enjoy yourself, they'll love you."

The Dtrüa sighed. "Fine. But if it goes poorly, I'm blaming you."

"Sounds fair." Matthias chuckled as she kept walking towards where Liam greeted his father with a handshake, Tuks running excited circles around their ankles.

Exhaling, the prince turned away and continued to the stable. He slid the barn door open, greeted by the scent of hay and horses. Walking inside, he strode down the center, eyeing the stalls on either side. Half of them were piled with hay and feed. Two draft horses occupied the larger stalls, with three quarter horses in the others.

A chestnut with a blaze on its forehead peeked out at him, snorting.

"Got nothing for you." Matthias spied a small white bucket hanging near the cross ties and scooped a handful of oats from within. "Or maybe I do." He approached the horse, holding out his flat hand to let the animal munch the treats.

Footsteps echoed through the barn, and Matthias breathed a sigh of relief. "That was fast, I thought..." As he turned, his gaze landed on Katrin rather than Liam.

She'd tied up her hair again since he'd seen her in the window, streaking bits of flour through it, in addition to the spots on her cheeks and brow. She still wore her apron, equally coated. Her feet were bare, despite the chill, as if she'd run out of the house so quickly she didn't have time to put anything on them.

Matthias clenched his jaw, anger battling with the hurt, and he looked away.

"I heard Liam asking Pa for a horse..." she whispered, voice barely reaching him. "You're leaving?"

"Yes. I'm staying in town." He stroked the horse's nose, letting the animal nibble his skin.

Hay crunched beneath her foot, but then she froze again, still so far away. "Oh." Rubbing her hands over her apron, she stared at her feet. "I... don't know why I came out here. But I..." She hesitated. "I just need to say I'm sorry."

Emotion heated Matthias's veins, and he faced her again. "For what? Leaving me with no explanation or for not telling me I lost a child, too?"

Her eyes widened, flashing to meet his before averting again. Her chest rose in suddenly rapid breaths as she wrapped her arms around herself, shirking back slightly. "Both." Her eyes closed, thick black lashes stark against her cheeks. "I didn't know how to tell you, but I guess Dani must have done it for me." A tinge of anger touched her tone, but it faded with a slow exhale. "I should have. But you already had enough loss."

"I don't think that's why you kept it from me." Matthias patted the horse and stepped away from it. "Because you knew for days that you were pregnant, and you didn't tell me that, either."

"There was never a good time."

"Never a good time? To tell someone they're getting the greatest gift?"

"No! I hardly saw you those days. You came to bed after I was asleep and left before I woke up. When was I supposed to tell you? I was lucky if I got to even say good morning!" Her hands balled at her sides, and she defiantly met his gaze.

Matthias huffed. "What was that? Four days? What about the four *months* you spent holed up in a library? I was there the whole time."

Katrin's lips pursed. "That's not fair."

"This wasn't just your loss, but you didn't let me share it with you. You left me in the dark, broke my heart, and left me to learn the truth a month later from someone else. I've only known about this for a week. A week ago, I lost the possibility of a child, so don't tell me what's not fair." Matthias strode towards her, wishing for the fresh air outside.

"At least I spared you the excitement! The joy, the dreams, and the hope. Only to have it all torn away. At least you didn't have to see the blood, feel the pain..." She gripped at her abdomen as she stepped aside from him. "At least you didn't feel betrayed by your own body. Just looking at you..." She cringed, closing her eyes.

Matthias passed her, halting at the open barn door and spinning to face her. "Don't you get it? I wanted all of it. *All of it.* With you. I wanted to share the joy and be there when things don't go the way we want them to. You didn't even give me the chance to feel the grief that I deserved as much as you did. You hid this from me, and now... Now I guess at least you don't have to see my face." He walked outside, taking a deep breath of chill autumn air.

"Don't *you* get it?" Katrin shouted as she stormed out the barn doorway after him. "That's the worst part of it. Your face is all I've seen since I left. I haven't been able to stop thinking about you and how you're right... I did take those things from you. And it wasn't right, it wasn't fair... but how do we go back? How can we make it like it was before again? I can't reverse time and take it all back like you."

Sorrow crept through Matthias's chest, and he shrugged as he backed away from her. "We can't, Kat. We can't go back, even if we wanted to. And just like I have to live with my regrets, you must live with yours. I hope you find peace here."

Her voice broke. "I miss you." She sagged against the doorway of the barn, her face flushed with streaks of tears. "I'm just scared. And all I can think about *every night* is how I wish you were here to hold me, kiss my hair, and assure me I'm safe. That everything will be all right, one way or another. I messed up, Matthias."

Matthias's eyes burned, but he shook his head. "And I would have said and done those things, but you left me. I can't just forget that."

Katrin's lower lip wobbled as she nodded, sagging further against the door. "I know," she whispered. "I'm just..." She rubbed at her abdomen. "I'm sorry."

"For what it's worth, I am, too. I wish you hadn't endured all that." Matthias swallowed through the tightness in his throat. "I want to forgive you, but this is so fresh for me."

"Then why are you here?" Katrin's voice hardened as she swallowed. "Why come here?"

Why did I come here?

"Because I still love you, and I wanted to see for myself that you were all right." The honesty spilled from his mouth before he could control it. His anger waned. "Liam will explain the rest."

"Well, I'm not all right." Katrin's red-rimmed eyes met his before she strode towards the back porch of the house. "I thought I was, at least for a little while. But I'm not. I guess you can probably see that for yourself, too." She waved her hand up and down herself without fully looking at him.

His frustration mellowed, and he fought to keep the smirk from his face. "I see a woman covered in flour. Do you get *any* in your baking?" He'd hardly intended to repeat the phrase, but memory coursed through him of the first time he'd said those words to her in the temple kitchen.

Katrin scowled at him, recognition flashing in her eyes. "I recall you liking my baking." She sighed, brushing more flour from her apron. Silence lingered as she stared at her dirty bare feet on the leaf covered path. "Will you stay?" She chewed her lower lip as she looked up. "There's plenty of space here. If you do still love me, please stay."

Matthias hesitated, watching her. "I don't want to make things uncomfortable for you."

She shook her head, strands of her hair falling loose. "It won't."

The prince rolled his shoulders, his heart yearning to be near her despite the damage she'd done. He breathed, the sweet scent of the pie on the windowsill promising comfort. "If I didn't know better, I'd say you baked that pie just to further tempt me."

The barest smile touched her lips, and it almost made his world crack in two.

Katrin stepped onto the porch. "It will be done cooling soon. Come have some." She paused at the door, turning back to face him. "I still love you, too."

The words resounded through him, his resolve weakening. He met her dark eyes, wishing he could wipe away the tears lingering on her lower lid. His chest ached at the thought of turning from her now. "All right. I'll stay."

Chapter 10

Katrin refused to let out the sigh of relief that waited at her lips. "Good." She nodded, steeling her face not to show her emotions.

"Kat! I think your peach pie is ready to come out of the oven!" Lind shouted from inside. Her voice, so much like her little sister's, made Katrin almost think she heard herself.

She snatched up the hem of her apron and wiped away the tears, forcing a broader smile on her face as she opened the back door. "I'm coming!" She slipped inside, leaving the door open for Matthias, hoping he would take the invitation.

Seeing him sent her heart reeling, bringing back all the painful memories of her miscarriage, which she'd struggled to forget. His face made her knees weak and threatened everything.

And here I am, asking him to stay. What's wrong with me?

Hurrying across the main sitting room past Pa and her sister's husband, Katrin spied Liam rubbing his boot against the back of his leg while he spoke to them. Fresh leaves, matching the ones she'd brushed from her bare feet, cascaded to the rug.

She narrowed her eyes at his guilty gaze.

He overheard me and Matthias fighting...

"Ouch!" Lind recoiled from the oven door, shaking her hand.

"I told you I've got it." Katrin bumped her sister out of the way, tossing a damp cloth from the counter at her. "You're too clumsy to get anything out without burning yourself."

Gathering up the edges of her apron, Katrin reached into the oven and withdrew the pie, eyeing the golden crust. She hefted it and its iron pan onto the counter as Lind danced around her to close the oven's iron door.

Matthias strode into the back doorway, hesitating as he took in the room. The tall prince hardly looked like he belonged, clearing his throat as he stepped inside.

Liam patted his father's shoulder as he walked towards him. "Sorry, Pa said it's no problem, so let's get you that horse." He gestured to the door.

"Aren't you going to introduce us first, Li?" Lind held the damp cloth to her burned hand, eyes sparkling in Matthias's direction.

Katrin's cheeks warmed as she busied herself with the neglected dough on the counter, glancing up to find the prince's eyes on her.

"Nah, I like leaving you in suspense." Liam gestured for Matthias again.

"I don't think I need the horse, after all," the prince murmured to Liam before turning to face Lind and offering his hand. "Matthias."

Lind smiled warmly and accepted his hand. "Pleasure to meet you. I'm Maralind, and that swell-looking fella over there is my husband, Storne." Her confidence would have wavered if she knew of Matthias's lineage. Or that they'd lost a child.

Katrin had confided in her sister about the deep-voiced 'crown elite' and the romantic connection they'd shared. And based on the sideways smirk Lind gave her, she'd have even more opinions about the man who'd inadvertently taken Katrin from the temple.

I hope she waits until we're alone.

"Shall I tell Ma to make up another bed, then?" Pa rose from his chair, teeth clicking around his pipe.

"Only if it's not a bother. I don't wish to put you out."

"Of course not." Lind glanced at Katrin with a subtle lift of her eyebrows only a sister would notice. "Better food here than at the inn in town, anyway. Kat bakes some nice sweets."

"I'm familiar with your sister's cooking, she's quite—"

A familiar howl sounded outside, rumbling like the call of a lion and eagle together. Tuks lifted his head from the rug where he lay, barking and howling back.

"Hush, boy." Storne's burly hand brushed over the dog's snout, and the whole room froze, still listening.

Then a child's wail sounded from down the hall, and Lind sighed. "Good job, Tuks. Woke her up again." She tossed her rag to Katrin before bustling away.

Katrin winced and looked at Liam. "I can't believe you brought the drakes."

Liam shrugged and gestured at the prince. "It was his idea."

Matthias frowned. "It seemed like a bad idea to leave them at the camp without their handler. Speaking of, where's Dani?"

"Getting the tour from Ma." Liam sauntered into the kitchen, eyeing Katrin before circling around her to the far counter. "She insisted I stay and fill Pa in while she took care of it."

A lump of regret solidified in Katrin as she thought about how she'd left things with her friend. She'd already forgiven the Dtrüa for telling Matthias the truth, even if she wished she could have done it herself. The thought of Dani finally being close again sent a spiral of excitement through the acolyte.

"I really can manage on my own." The Dtrüa's voice came from the hallway opposite where Lind had gone.

"Nonsense, let me help." Ma's kind tone made Katrin cringe.

"Ma, lay off it. She probably knows the house better than you, now." Liam's voice drew Katrin's attention to where he'd snuck behind her, picking at the pie's crust. Plucking off a piece, he hurriedly put it in his mouth before she could swat him.

Dani and Katrin's mother emerged from the hall.

A patient, uncomfortable look clouded the Dtrüa's face as Ma led her by the elbow. "I should go check on the drakes."

"Liam, will you guide her to the door?"

Liam groaned. "Ma, no, she can handle it on her own. Hands off." He slipped behind Katrin again, grabbing a larger piece of filling and crust. He hummed as it went into his mouth. "Tastes good, Katy girl."

"Get out." Katrin smacked him harder on the chest. "And let the damned thing cool properly."

Dani stiffened before easing her arm out of the older woman's grasp. "I'll be fine, thank you." She clicked her tongue, crossing the room for the door behind Matthias and hurried outside, whispering something to the prince as she passed him.

Matthias chuckled, trying to hide the expression with a cough.

Katrin's heart fluttered at the sound before she focused on the closing door behind the prince. Her gut tightened, her entire body a tumble of emotions she couldn't fully comprehend.

Dani.

"Just let the bread dough rise. Don't touch it." She shook a finger at Liam. "And keep out of the pie."

Izi sniffled, gurgling in discontent from being woken from her nap as Lind re-entered the room, the toddler on her hip. Izi's black hair matched her mother's, but it held her father's curls. She stilled on seeing unfamiliar faces in the room.

Having the child in the house had been both a blessing and a curse.

"Where are you going?" Liam frowned as Katrin shoved her apron into his hands.

"I need to speak to Dani. Let's just hope this conversation goes better than my last one." She glanced at Matthias, who quirked an eyebrow at her.

"I'm still here, aren't I?" The prince's tone was gentle, something else lingering in his gaze.

Katrin winced, putting on her slippers next to the front door. "I guess you are." She smiled, hoping he would see the gratitude in it.

She left the chaos of the front room, Liam already making his way to the niece he'd never met with Tuks inserting himself in the middle. Once on the porch, she took a deep breath of the chill air, catching whiffs of her father's pipe.

I wonder what that's like for Dani.

The Dtrüa jogged towards the drakes, already halfway there

despite remaining in her human form.

She'd nearly forgotten what the two massive beasts looked like, their scales shining icy blue in the sunlight. They snapped at each other, razor teeth encouraging the instinct to turn and run the other way, but Katrin lifted her pale skirt and hurried after her friend.

As she grew closer, the Dtrüa's voice carried over the air. "I said no, Ousa! Brek is right, no eating cows!" She pointed a finger at the smaller of the two. "Shek. No cows."

The drake Katrin had healed huffed in victory, turning from the other and sniffing the air. His eyes found the acolyte, and he lumbered towards her with a rumbling purr.

"I guess that means you remember me." Katrin held out her palm, smiling as the drake nuzzled against it, guiding her hand up his snout. "Brek, is it?" She stepped into his enormous head, running her hands over his smooth, leathery scales. She touched the scar that remained at his throat, where a break in the scales marked his close call with death. Scratching around it, she kissed the side of the drake's nose as he purred. "I missed you, too. But not nearly as much as I missed Dani." She looked at the Dtrüa, who stood still, facing the other way.

Dani turned her head, hesitating before facing Katrin. "You're not angry with me?"

"With you?" Katrin paused, but Brek moved his head to encourage her to continue scratching, and she obeyed. "I was worried you're angry with me... Gods know I deserve it."

Looking down, Dani twisted the toe of her boot in the grass. "But if I hadn't brought Matthias to you, you wouldn't have left him. Plus, you already know I told him the rest about a week ago..."

"I don't blame you," Katrin whispered. "Even if I hadn't seen Matthias in that moment, I still would have left. I needed this time. But I shouldn't have said such awful things to my best friend, first." She patted Brek a final time before stepping away despite his protesting whine. Taking Dani's hand, Katrin smiled. "I know why you told him, and while I'm upset about all of it... I don't blame *you*."

Dani's gaze lifted, and her lips twitched before she pulled her hand free and leapt at Katrin for a hug. Wrapping her arms around the acolyte's shoulders, she squeezed. "I wanted to warn you he was coming here, but I didn't think you'd want to hear from me."

Something in Katrin's chest lifted as she gripped Dani. "It's probably better you surprised me with this. Less time to overthink." She pulled away, keeping her hands on the Dtrüa's shoulders. "But I'll always want to hear from you. Nothing should ever come between us."

The Dtrüa smiled, tension lingering in her face. "Must we return inside?"

"There's no rush." Katrin took both her hands, entwining their fingers. "Ma can be overbearing, but she'll settle after a few hours."

"She thinks I'm an invalid."

"You'll prove her wrong plenty fast, and besides, Liam will talk to her. Assuming he's not too busy stealing all the sweets in the kitchen." She bobbed their hands. "How are things between you two?"

Dani hesitated before nodding with excessive enthusiasm. "Good. They're good."

Katrin paused, studying her. "What's wrong?"

A cringe crossed Dani's face. "You cannot tell anyone."

A flutter of panic entered Katrin's body. "I won't." She steeled her eyes from looking at Dani's abdomen.

"Liam asked me to marry him."

"What?" The potential jealousy subsided, settling into surprise at her brother instead. "Liam asked you to... what?"

Dani nodded. "The day you left."

"Well, that's unexpected...." Katrin glanced at the house. "Liam can be rash, sure, but something like that... He's not the best at committing to any kind of responsibility. Hells, he joined the military to get *away* from having to take over the farm. What did you say?"

"I haven't answered him, yet."

Katrin bit her bottom lip and cringed.

"I cannot see the face you're making, but I can imagine." Dani huffed out a sigh. "I doubt it matters, anyway."

"Of course it matters!" Katrin shook her hands wildly. "Why wouldn't it matter?"

"Well, that's the thing... I think he's changed his mind. And if he didn't a week ago, he will now."

"Why do you think that?"

"He said he surprised himself with it, and he hasn't brought it up since. Being here will only confirm that I'm not the kind of person he wants to spend the rest of his life with."

"Surprise for Liam means nothing. He surprises himself when he wakes up in the morning..." Katrin pursed her lips, tightening her hold on Dani. "Besides, you're wrong. I've seen how he looks at you."

The Dtrüa sighed and tugged Katrin to begin the walk back to the homestead. "I'm a fighter, not a wife. Not a mother. I know nothing about cooking or children."

"Well, then you're the perfect match, because that's Liam, too. He doesn't want this life, Dani. Not really. He ran away from it."

"And is this the life you want, now?"

Katrin fought to control her initial reaction, channeling the calm she'd studied for years. At least until Matthias had distracted her. "We're not talking about me, we're talking about you and Liam. What kind of life do *you* want?"

Dani shrugged. "I've only ever known one kind. I never had a family."

"Then this will be an excellent opportunity to experience it. And my family is far from perfect, so I suspect it to be a very accurate representation." Katrin bumped her hip against Dani's.

"Are you and Matthias together again?" The Dtrüa's question hit her like a brick to the stomach. "He wants a family, I can tell."

"Which is precisely why we can't be." Katrin cleared her throat to hide the emotion creeping up. "I can't give him that."

Dani furrowed her brow. "Just because this happened once, means nothing."

"Except I'm fairly certain it will happen again. And again."

"You cannot know that."

"But I feel it." Katrin touched her abdomen. "The continued bleeding, the pain no matter what part of my cycle I'm in. Something isn't right, and I have to accept it as the will of the gods."

Dani stopped and faced Katrin. "As awful as you feel right now, that's a bunch of horseshit. It hasn't been that long, and you can't write off a family in your future because of it. You don't get to give up. I won't let you."

Katrin closed her eyes, trying to let the breeze bring her the calm she needed. "I... can't go through that all again, Dani." Her voice weakened with the words. "I don't want to risk it ever again. And Matthias deserves far better than me, anyway. I'm just an acolyte." She laughed dryly and shook her head. "Not even that, anymore. I don't know what I am."

"You're lost." Dani's voice softened. "That's all. Be patient with yourself. You of all people know healing takes time."

Katrin sucked in a breath, cursing herself. "How's Stefan?"

A more genuine smile graced Dani's expression. "He's good. Fully recovered and managing the encampment with Micah." She turned towards the homestead and clicked her tongue. "Ready to go inside?"

Her relief abruptly turned to anxiety. "I can't believe I asked Matthias to stay..."

"Hmm." Dani strode towards the steps, slowing until her boot hit the first one. "Wonder why you did that?" Her playful tone matched her smirk.

"Because I'm a masochist." Katrin couldn't help but return the smile. "The baby's awake, and the racket she makes might be a bit distracting, just so you know." She hopped onto the porch, moving past Dani to the door.

The Dtrüa clicked her tongue again. "I'll try not to scare it."

Katrin snorted. "If anything, she might save you the trouble of clicking."

As the door opened, crashing echoed from the sitting room,

wooden blocks toppling over one another as Liam cheered.

"No! The Great Library of Capul has fallen! What have you done, Izi?" Liam scooped the toddler up into his arms as she burst into wild giggles, kicking at the blocks.

"She's got a knack for destruction. A bit like her Uncle Liam," Pa mused from his sitting chair, puffing to relight his pipe.

Dani stood rigid next to Katrin, who tapped the Dtrüa's lower back to encourage her forward.

"Maybe Uncle Liam needs to introduce Dani to the destruction."

"No, no, no." Dani backed up a step, holding her hands out. "The small human will see me."

Liam was already on his feet, taking the toddler with him as he laughed. "Oh, yes, and that would be horrible." He tickled Izi as she looked at Dani, a curious glint in her dark eyes. "It's all right, Dani. She won't bite you. At least, probably not." Before the Dtrüa could protest, Liam plopped Izi directly into Dani's outstretched hands, stepping in to help support.

Dani gasped, gripping the toddler at the middle and keeping her at arm's length. "Oh, Nymaera, it smells funny."

"All right, now bend your elbows..." Liam put a hand around her waist, the other encouraging the movement. "Embrace the smell." He smiled broader than Katrin had seen in a long time, and it made her heart lighten.

Gods, I missed them so much.

The Dtrüa cringed, bringing the child closer, but still held her in the same awkward way. "It won't stop squirming."

Katrin leaned over Dani's shoulder, placing a kiss on Izi's forehead. "That's normal. Just... imagine she's a dire wolf pup. Not much different, I suspect."

Izi reached across the gap between her and Dani, fingers roving curiously over Dani's cheek and jaw. "Hi," she squeaked, before enthusiastically repeating it. "Hi, go! Hi."

Dani froze, wrinkling her nose as the toddler's hand explored her face. "Why is its hand sticky? Dire wolf pups are never sticky."

Liam snorted. "Better not to ask." He kissed Dani's temple. "Want me to take her back? You're doing great."

"Please take it... take her. Take her back."

He laughed louder, plucking Izi back from Dani's hands, and placed her on his hip as he leaned against Dani's shoulder. "How about a little further away, then. Izi, can you say Dani?"

"Da!" Izi declared, tugging on Liam's tunic.

"Good luck," Katrin whispered in Dani's ear as she turned to the kitchen, mentally sorting through what needed to be done for dinner.

I need to finish my bread dough, too.

Where she expected to see Lind stood a tall, handsome man.

What in Nymaera's name...

Matthias donned a clean apron, kneading her ball of dough.

"No, no, what are you doing?" Katrin rushed forward, glowering at the dough in his hands. "That was supposed to be rising."

The prince swatted her hand, scowling. "No, *that* one is rising." He motioned behind him, where a cloth lay draped over her dough.

Katrin gave him a double take, narrowing her eyes at the dough Matthias worked on. "Where did you get that?"

"I made it." Matthias used a kitchen knife to slice it in half before cutting the two pieces each in half again.

"That's not bread dough."

"Nope." The prince retrieved the rolling pin from across the counter, giving her a knowing smile as he dusted the counter with flour. "It's pastry dough."

Katrin froze, watching as he rolled out the dough like he'd done it hundreds of times before. She opened her mouth, but no words came out, prompting her to close it again. Her head tilted, and she eyed the vegetables and rabbit meat on the chopping board. "You... cook?"

His words in the kitchen from the second day she'd known him flitted through her memory. *This might just be my favorite room in this temple.*

"Not as often as I'd like." Matthias lifted the dough off the counter, laying it in a fresh pie skillet. He cracked an egg into a small bowl and whisked it smooth before setting it aside. Rolling out a second lump of pastry dough, he glanced at her. "My mother taught me."

He was telling me the truth that night.

"I see..." Katrin watched his hands as they moved, spotting how perfectly clean his apron still was despite the work he'd accomplished. She frowned as she moved around him to gather up her dough, poking it with her thumb to check its progress. Replacing the linen, she turned to stand beside Matthias, watching his hands again. "Impressive," she conceded as she pulled a cutting board in front of her and took up some carrots. "Is there a particular way you'd like these cut, seeing as you've hijacked my dinner preparations?"

"Diced is fine." Matthias smirked at her. "There's some rosemary and thyme in there that should be removed from the stem before—"

"Seriously?" Katrin lifted an eyebrow. She started to speak again, but shook her head as she brought the kitchen knife down through the carrots. "I'm dreaming. Only explanation right now. More cruel tricks of my mind."

Matthias laid the next round of flattened pastry dough into his second pie skillet. "Cruel? Now, now, Priestess, that's a little insulting. All I wanted to do was make you dinner." He chuckled, sending a shiver down her spine. Refocusing on his task, he brushed egg wash over the bottom crusts before putting them in the wood fire oven. Pulling a pot off a higher shelf, he set it on the stove and checked the heat beneath the iron slab.

Katrin scowled, pushing the carrots aside to start on the onions. She leaned close and whispered, "Forgive me, Prince, for my surprise at your apparent knowledge in cooking. I thought you were joking, that night at the temple." She studied the flash of amusement in his eyes. "Your title is something I refrained from telling my family, by the way."

"When they let me commandeer their kitchen, I assumed as

much." Matthias put a chunk of butter in the pot. "It's not often I get to cook while enjoying some semblance of anonymity. Stefan and... *Stefan* would never let me live this down." His expression hardened, and he pulled a wooden spoon from a drawer.

How does he know where everything is?

Katrin refocused on the cutting. "I'm sorry," she whispered, hoping to blame the onion for the water rising in her eyes as she thought of Barim and Riez. "Dani mentioned Stefan's made a full recovery."

Matthias nodded. "He's with Micah."

"Nothing has changed at the encampment, then?" She lifted the cutting board and wordlessly offered it towards the pot.

The prince scooped the onions and carrots into the pot, and they sizzled in the butter. "Nothing worth noting." He pinched salt from a bowl and added it to the vegetables.

"I'm sorry for that, too." Katrin took the cutting board back and returned to prepare the green beans. "I'll leave the rabbit for you, if that's all right. I've never been good at deboning rabbit without making a proper mess." She eyed him up and down in obvious fashion. "Maybe you'll actually get that apron dirty."

"Doubtful." The prince pulled a second chopping board from next to the stove and laid the skinned rabbit out. He chose a thin knife from the block and focused on the carcass, slicing out each bone with unexpected precision.

Seeing him in a kitchen alone would have been startling, but the nostalgic setting of her family home made the feelings even more confusing. Her insides warmed, a familiar yet unwelcome feeling with Matthias. She studied his defined jaw beneath his beard and slowed as her body followed the usual rhythm of slicing the vegetables.

In a blink, he reached for her, grabbing her knife hand with his clean one. "Watch yourself." He gestured at her hands with his chin. "Your knife is sharp."

Furrowing her brow, she looked down to see the blade of her knife precariously close to her finger. If he hadn't grabbed her, she would have cut right into it.

I probably did, and he just went back.

Heat flushed her cheeks at the realization of her distraction, and she set the knife down. "Better I focus on things with duller instruments, then."

Matthias didn't look at her, returning to the rabbit. "Might be safer."

Moving to her dough, she didn't bother checking it again before rubbing flour between her hands. Picking up the ball and bouncing it between her hands, she moved to the section of counter he'd used for his pie crust.

The sizzling from the pot grew louder as Matthias added the diced rabbit meat, still not a speck of muck on his apron.

Katrin plopped her dough down, sending a puff of flour across the counter onto her own apron before kneading it roughly. In her peripheral vision, she watched him again, trying not to imagine more of these situations in the future.

I can't get used to having him near me again, even if there's so much I don't know.

But there didn't need to be secrets.

"Thank you." She lifted her chin to give him a soft smile. "For catching me before I cut myself."

His ocean-blue eyes met hers. "I'll always do my best to help you keep all your fingers." He used a thick cloth to pull the pie crust bottoms from the oven before adding the herbs to the pot with some pepper. Dividing the contents between the two crusts, he returned to roll out the top layers of dough. "Just because we aren't together, doesn't mean I don't care."

The words hurt more than she expected. She lifted and dropped the dough again, with more violence than she meant, flour spattering up. "I know. I don't expect either of us to stop that. So, perhaps we can figure out a way to be civil. To be friends?" She watched him, hiding all the loathing at herself for the suggestion. But that was all she could be to him. It wasn't fair to ask for more after all that had happened.

Matthias's jaw flexed, and he glanced at her. "Friends." The word sounded strange. "Yes, I suppose we could try that." He covered the pot pies with their tops and pinched the edges, brushing egg over them before returning them to the oven. "If nothing else, it will make our time here easier before we return to the border camp."

Katrin slowed in her kneading as she remembered the question she'd been too distracted to ask before. "Why are you here?"

The prince cleared his throat. "With the help of the Feyorian maps and your notes, we've narrowed down the location of the dragons to three points. But we don't know what your symbols mean, and since Dani couldn't reach you, we came here to ask. Liam has all the documents."

"You mean your ferocious crown elite, who is currently laying on the rug building cities out of wooden blocks?" Katrin gestured with her head to the sitting room.

Matthias looked at Liam, a vague smile brightening his face. "One can be both ferocious and loving, Priestess."

The nickname sent a quake through her soul with his second use of it. She chewed her lip as she scored the dough, taking her time to not cut herself as she separated it into even sections. Each small bun received a sprinkling of more flour and kneading. "I don't think I'll be returning to the temples." She watched the silky edges of the bun as she worked it. "So you won't ever be able to truly call me that."

"Does that mean you'd like me to stop?" Matthias wiped his hands on a damp kitchen cloth, leaning sideways against the counter.

I'd like a lot of things...

Katrin heaved a sigh, avoiding his gaze. "Not necessarily. Just thought you should know. But I'll see what information I can give you about the dragons after dinner."

He scoffed. "Your nickname has never had anything to do with your rank, you know. Or even that you came from the temples."

She wrinkled her brow. "Then what does it have to do with?"

The prince shrugged one shoulder. "Priests and priestesses guide people in their faith. Teach those who must learn. While I may have little faith in any gods, you showed me a different kind of faith. Taught me, you could say. That's why I call you priestess, and none of that will change no matter where you take your life."

A crack formed in her heart, and Katrin turned her gaze back to the dough to hide it from Matthias as she plucked up another ball and started working it. "I... need to hurry and get these done so they have some time to rise again before baking." She didn't know what to say to him, and busied herself to work through each bun.

The prince fell silent, nodding before he pulled off his apron. "Of course. Apologies." He walked from the kitchen, joining the others in the sitting room.

Katrin watched as Liam encouraged some blocks into Dani's hand, pulling her closer to Izi while Pa held up a pipe in offer to Matthias. Storne had vanished with Lind, probably enjoying the break with Izi distracted, and Ma was likely readying the rooms for the night.

Her stomach twisted, trying to piece together the boil of questions still forming.

Matthias accepted her father's offer but gestured his head towards the front door. The two walked together to the front porch, doubling the nerves in her stomach.

Matthias and Pa. Together. Talking.

But he's not with you anymore. It doesn't matter.

She wondered if Pa had ever overheard her conversations with Lind. He was always more aware than he often acted with Ma, catching onto the smallest details his children let slip in his presence. The horror of Pa knowing Matthias's role in her life, especially in her recent decision not to return to the temples, made Katrin nauseous.

She closed her eyes as she leaned into one of her rolls, trying to calm her stomach and even out her breathing.

Friends. Just friends now.

Chapter 11

Liam grinned at Izi's delighted laughter as another masterful construction of toy blocks toppled. "Little tyrant." He tickled her, and she shoved his hands away, scurrying through the mess.

"Da-ee, help!" Izi tumbled into Dani's lap, wriggling around to face Liam again.

The Dtrüa lifted her hands away from the toddler, stiffening again. "Liam, what do I do?"

He laughed, sitting back onto the rug. "You don't have to do anything other than decide whose side you're on in this battle. Mine or hers." He lifted a teasing brow, but glanced over Dani's shoulder at Katrin, who still stood rigid in the kitchen, her eyes closed.

"Well, if she doesn't want to be tickled, stop." Dani scowled at him.

"Tickles!" Izi stomped her feet, eyes bright with mischief.

"Oh, come on, beautiful. Haven't you played before?" Liam pushed some blocks across the rug, and Izi kicked at them from her position in Dani's lap.

"Played?" Dani frowned. "Of course I've played, just not... with one of these." She sniffed Izi's head, poking her in the side.

Izi screeched and rocked forward, landing on her hands before she ran around Liam, forcing him to reach behind for her as she exploded with more giggles.

"She's a child. You were one once, too, you know. Just be yourself, you don't have to do anything special."

Dani lowered her hands, her jaw tense. "This *is* myself."

Izi charged off behind the sitting chairs and Liam leaned back to keep an eye on her as she wove through the furniture, hiding from him.

"It'll get easier, and it'll start to make sense. Don't be too hard on yourself." He put a hand on her knee. "I can only imagine how overwhelming all this is for you."

The Dtrüa recoiled. "If your sister knew anything about me, she wouldn't want me near her child."

"What are you talking about?" Liam heard Izi's feet pound as she ran off again, this time in the kitchen's direction.

Katrin's responsibility now.

Liam rose, reaching down to her and brushing her hand. "Let's get some air. Maybe that'll help?"

Dani nodded, accepting his offer and standing.

"Oh, Izi, no. Don't touch that." Katrin scooped the child up, casting an annoyed glance at Liam, but her eyes flitted to Dani. She gave her brother a silent question with the concern in her eyes, but he waved a hand to dismiss it.

"We'll be back in time for dinner. Ring the bell if we're late?"

Katrin nodded. "You should take Dani to the stream out back. I bet she'd like it."

Izi pulled Katrin's hair, freeing it from the knot at the back of her head as he guided Dani to the back door.

Once the fresh air hit their faces, Dani's shoulders relaxed. She clicked her tongue and walked with Liam to the stairs.

"Two steps down," he warned, but knew it would be the last time he'd need to. Alerting Dani to things she couldn't see had become second nature, and he hardly had to think about it any longer.

She slid her foot out, finding the edge before descending.

They remained quiet, stepping onto the path. Leaves crunched beneath their boots. The cows in the field had returned to their mindless grazing, no longer affected by the drakes who lazed about the distant hill pasture. The familiar scents of the farm made him feel relaxed and safe, regardless of what war loomed far to the west.

The mountains ahead had yet to see snow fall, shorter than the Yandarin mountain range they'd been stationed at for months.

"Ahead are the mountains." He leaned close to her, wanting to describe before she asked. "They're all grey stone and craggy, not a lot of trees up near the top, but I can see some of the pine ridge in front of them through all the maples. Only a few leaves are holding on this late in the season, so all the oranges and reds are gone. The cow pastures are to the left, going back towards the mountains, and to the right are all the barns and the stable. It sure looks like they could use some new paint this coming summer. The white is peeling off."

Dani squeezed his hand. "You seem to like it here."

"It's home." He looked at her, studying the worry still etching her face. "But in a week I'll be so restless I can't stand it anymore. That's how it always goes."

"So this isn't the life you want?" She looked at him, gaze hovering near his face.

He narrowed his eyes, unable to stop the suspicion at her question. "It's a nice thought, and it could have been mine, but I chose a different path." He kissed her knuckles. "One I don't regret."

"You might, one day." Dani tilted her head. "You never want a family?"

He shrugged. "I have a family." He paused, tugging her closer. Touching her jaw, he wrapped an arm around her to pull her body against his. "And you're all I really need. If kids are in my future, then I'll be happy for them. If they're not, I'm happy with that, too. As long as I have you."

Dani swallowed. "I'm terrible at this."

He chuckled, tracing his finger down her jaw. "You're not terrible, you're just not used to it. It'll get better with time, and even if it doesn't, you're still gorgeous to me. If anything, it makes you cuter to be so confused with what to do with Izi."

"I know you said I was a child once, too, but Liam... I wasn't. I was young, yes, but I never had a childhood."

He paused, watching her cloudy eyes. It made sense, considering all he knew about how Feyor created the Dtrüa, and it made his chest ache. "Perhaps it's not too late for you to experience it a little. I have an idea."

"What are you doing?" Dani's tone held an air of suspicion, and she took a tentative step back.

Liam chuckled as he stepped after her, nuzzling his face against her neck. He nipped at her earlobe, breathing to tickle her skin. "Why don't you... count to twenty, then come find me?"

"What? Why?" Dani turned her face into his skin, kissing him.

"It's a game children play. I hide, you find. So play with me." He teasingly brought his lips near hers. "I'll make it worth your while." He trailed his finger up beneath her chin as he stepped away. "Though, maybe you should give me thirty seconds. And no panther form, that's cheating."

Dani frowned and closed her eyes. "I can find you without it." She crossed her arms. "One."

He smirked as he turned and jogged down the path towards the distant barn. He paused at the corner, glancing back to see Dani still standing where he'd left her, a slight smile on her lips. It made him grin wider as he dodged around the corner, running towards the broken-down wagon he couldn't believe was still there. It'd been one of his favorite hiding places when playing with his sisters, but he doubted he'd fit below it anymore. Instead, he turned his attention to the pile of leaves and hurriedly picked them up, rubbing them against his tunic.

Maybe it'll hide my scent at least a bit.

He doubled back to the corner of the barn, pressing himself against the wood as he peeked back at Dani.

The Dtrüa walked straight for the barn, a determined look on her face. She paused at the corner, chest rising with deeper breaths than usual.

He held his breath, willing his heart to beat slower as he watched her, a grin crossing his lips as she walked past him, continuing to the wagon at a slower pace.

Before she could move out of his reach, Liam lunged, grappling her waist as he let out a low, playful roar.

He was prepared for her elbow as she instinctively threw it back at him, turning just enough to catch it on his bicep, but then the world tilted and he hit the ground hard with his back, taking Dani with him. He huffed with a laugh as she hit his chest, her hair tickling his face.

Dani huffed. "That's a good way to die by panther, you know."

"You'd have stopped yourself in time." He encouraged her to turn until she sat up, straddling his hips. He lifted his head, enjoying the view of her in the position and smiled. "I'm all right with this result."

The Dtrüa scowled at him. "Somehow, I don't think this is quite how childhood games end." She rocked her hips, sliding her hands up under the bottom of his shirt.

"Most decidedly not." He bit his lip, controlling the moan that sought to escape at the feel of her. He arched his back, pushing against her. "You better go hide before I lose all control and forget about these games."

Dani leaned forward, hovering her lips over his. "You'll never find me." She grazed his mouth with the tease of a kiss before rising off him. She quirked an eyebrow at him before taking off, disappearing around the barn.

He let his head rest against the hard dirt as he tried to remember how to breathe, urging his body that it'd have to wait before it got what it demanded.

One. Two.

He closed his eyes until he got to twenty, then continued to count as he rose. "Thirty," he whispered as his eyes scanned the ground for disturbances among the leaves, having heard her run north for the trees.

Tuning his senses as best he could, Liam set off into the woods, his desire still aching through him. The anticipation of finding her quickened his heart, eliciting the opposite response he'd been trying to encourage. He focused on her boot tracks, fresh in the soft dirt as he jogged up the hill into the grove of trees, listening for movement amid the birdsong.

He couldn't believe how deep she'd gotten into the trees in the time he'd counted, pausing when her tracks vanished within a circle of barren maples, mushrooms undisturbed and flourishing on the forest floor.

Liam groaned, rubbing the back of his head. "Inconvenient," he whispered to himself, glancing around but finding nothing. Sighing, he chewed his lower lip and looked up, just for good measure, but nothing except birds occupied the branches above.

Have you ever just listened?

The memory of Dani asking him the question so many months ago echoed in him. They'd stood in the freezing snow looking at nothing.

Liam pursed his lips and closed his eyes, sucking in a deep breath.

I probably look stupid.

He flexed his hands, urging them to relax as he inhaled again, the nutty scent of the forest seeping through his senses. He focused on his hearing, trying to pick up everything around him. The wind through the remaining leaves, and the distant trickle of the stream. Cows lowed in the distance. A bird's wings flapped.

Leaves rustled, barely audible, a few paces behind him.

Tilting his head, he focused on that single sound, tracing in his mind the steps back towards it. The noise grew closer, the gentle sound of breath accompanying it.

He smiled to himself as he spun, opening his eyes to find a doe standing behind him. It lifted its head from the forest floor, ears perked at him.

Liam sighed. "You're not Dani..."

The deer's nose twitched before it shook and walked away through the trees.

"But still... beautiful, yes?" The Dtrüa's voice came from behind him.

He faced her. "Where were you?"

"You'll never know." She stepped into him, bringing her mouth to his.

With a hum of approval, he wrapped his arms around her to pull her closer. Her hips pressed against his, where he was still eager for more of her. He ran his hands into her hair, diving deeper into the next kiss as he trailed his tongue along hers. They'd had so little time to be affectionate during the travels with Matthias, both afraid to make his loss of Katrin harder. But he missed the feeling of Dani's skin as he slid his hand down her waist, fingers tickling beneath her waistline.

Her steps moved back as he pushed her towards a tree. Their kiss paused only briefly as her back contacted one of the cool maple trunks, his mouth moving hungrily against hers. His hand trailed to the front of her breeches, loosening the ties.

Dani flinched and broke the kiss with a yelp, leaping sideways with her hand outstretched. "What the hells was that?" She swiped her hand on her breeches, nose scrunched up in a disgusted face.

Liam's stomach swirled, but he couldn't help but laugh. "It's a tree, Dani."

"Thank you, sir, but there's something *on* the tree."

"The moss?"

"No, it's not *moss*. Please look. I touched it." She squealed again, still rubbing her palm on her pants.

Liam quirked an eyebrow as he examined the tree. Glowering at it, he stepped around to where Dani's hand had grazed a grey, slime-covered lump. "It's just a slug." He laughed as he plucked the creature off.

Dani whined. "Gross. Stay away from me with that thing."

Liam laughed again as he tossed the creature into the bush and faced Dani. "But it's kind of cute..."

"It's slimy and my hand is still sticky." She growled, looking at her palm as if it betrayed her.

"Aw, it just wants to say hi." Liam popped his finger into his mouth before tracing his wet skin over the back of her hand.

Dani shrieked, leaping back. "Not funny!"

Liam cackled as he stepped after her, catching her waist. He lifted his finger to her jaw, tracing it while holding her still against him. "Sluggy kisses."

Her hand whipped to his, finding his finger rather than the creature. Eyes widening, she glared at him. "You're torturing me with *this*?" She threw his hand down. "What did you do, lick it?"

He snorted. "You haven't had problems with my saliva all over your skin before..."

Dani's tone darkened. "You're gonna pay for this."

"Oh, I'm sure I will." He leaned in to her neck, nuzzling through her hair to kiss her skin, playing with his tongue beneath her earlobe. "But this is why I love you."

"Because I threaten you?" Dani whimpered, trying and failing to sidestep out of his grip.

"Because you will fight in a war and tear out men's throats, but a little slug sends you running." He nosed her ear, letting a slow breath torment her as he flicked his tongue. "Because you're you, and someday... when you're ready... I will marry you."

Dani stilled, breathing faster as she pulled back to touch his face. "I am. I am ready."

Liam's chest pounded as he gaped at her, turning his cheek in her palm to kiss it. "You are?"

"I mean, we needn't rush, but... I want to marry you, too." Dani chewed her lower lip, running her thumb over his chin. "I want no one else."

He hadn't thought he'd been worried about what her answer would be, but hearing her say it made the rest of the world disappear. With his hands in her hair, he pulled her against him again, kissing her deeply. He breathed her in, enjoying the sweet scent of her with the rich forest around them.

Breaking from her just enough, he breathed on her lips. "I will always be yours."

Chapter 12

Teal surrounded her, tainting the bright sky and musty scent of the forest floor. Dani tugged Liam's arm tighter around her, his bare chest pressed to her back under his heavy cloak. Her body still buzzed with satisfaction, a calm dominating her mind she'd never known.

"Can we stay here awhile longer?" She kept her voice low, listening to his breathing near her ear.

He hummed as he kissed her shoulder, trailing his lips towards her neck. "At least until sunset, then it might get a little too cold." His rough fingertip trailed over her abdomen, teasing beneath the curve of her breasts. "Though I'm sure we could find ways to stay warm." He smiled against her skin as he leaned up to gain better access to her neck.

Dani grinned, tracing circles on the back of his hand that wrapped around beneath her. "I can hardly believe I'll be your wife."

"My beautiful wife," Liam whispered as he nuzzled into her hair. "But I shall start spoiling you now."

"Spoil me?" Dani made a face. "With what?"

"Everything. Anything you possibly want."

"What if I want nothing?"

"Then I'll get inventive." He tightened his grip around her, teasingly rocking his hips against her backside as his hands traced down her body. "And you'll just be surprised all the time. Which I rather like the idea of."

"I can live with that." She rolled onto her stomach, propping herself up on her elbows. The cloak slid off her shoulders to her lower back, letting cool air refresh her skin. "Surprises sound fun."

He shifted, his dim shape moving in the bright daylight as one hand continued down her back. His touch slowed over her spine, near the scars he'd pointed out before.

"Do they look awful?" Dani whispered, resisting the urge to hide them.

Liam remained quiet as his fingers walked along her skin, passing unevenly over the less sensitive skin. "Not awful, but there. And knowing what caused them..." He let out a long breath. Circling around an area near the base of her neck, he made her shiver. "These are the worst. And I wish I could go to Feyor and return the favor to whoever did this to you."

"They had the most success on the spine." Dani closed her eyes, the memory of the injections sending sparks of pain through her. The heat that followed, sending her into fits of fever and chills as her body coped with the foreign substance forced into it. She touched her wrist, almost able to feel the cold chains that once bound her. "I wasn't a person to them. Even after they finished their trials. Even my name..."

He retraced the scars again. "What about your name?"

"I used to assume Varadani was my birth name, but it wasn't. They named me after the poison they used to sedate me." She'd overheard a healer in the medical tent instruct someone to give a dying man a dose of it to ease him into Nymaera's arms.

"Varanithe Danilisca." His realizing breath brushed strands of her hair back from her forehead. "I... hadn't even thought of connecting that to you. I'm used to hearing it called Warrior's Lullaby." He huffed, brushing his lips against her temple. "Seems even more appropriate now, in a way. But you know you can change it, if you want..."

Dani frowned. "They named me *poison*. How is that appropriate?"

"Warrior's Lullaby, not the poison part." He groaned. "I was trying to be cute and I'm clearly awful at it."

She scoffed. "You're not awful at it. I'm just difficult."

"I think you're perfect."

Warmth filled her chest. "Have I mentioned that I love you?"

Liam chuckled, tracing his hand over her back again. "I don't mind hearing it over and over again." He flattened his hand over the gathering of scars, his soft lips pressing against her forehead. "And I'll never let anything like what Feyor did happen to you again."

"I cannot do chains again." Dani shook her head, smirking. "The ones you had me in hardly counted, though. I disliked them, but I had every opportunity to free myself."

"Oh, I'm sure you could have. I'd noticed Katrin watching where I put my key every time, like she was planning to break you out. She's not exactly a skilled thief." His touch moved over the scars again. "But you never accepted her offers. Why?"

"She was the only person who'd ever seen me for me, and if I let her free me, I'd have had to run." Dani tilted her head, her hair falling forward off her shoulders. "You never would have let me stay with you all without being bound. So I stayed bound. Even if my keeper was an ass."

He laughed, and it banished the chill of the air. "I was an ass." He nuzzled close to her ear, nipping it. "But I just didn't see you, yet. And now that I do..." He brushed her hair from her face, tucking it behind her ear. "I can't imagine a day without you."

Dani's chest tightened, and she rolled her lips together. "Neither can I, which is why I must ask something of you that you won't like."

His body tensed. "What is it?"

"Resslin is coming for me. You cannot win a fight against her. When she finds me... And she will, it's only a matter of time... I need you to let me handle it." Dani touched his face, tracing it so it would appear in her mind.

His hand closed over hers, his mouth in a frown and jaw tight. "That's a big ask."

"I know." She swallowed. "But I was sloppy fighting Tallos because I was terrified for you. You cannot get involved."

"I have a feeling I won't have much of a choice." Liam rubbed his thumb over hers. "If I can avoid it, I will. But if it looks like I might lose you, and I genuinely believe I can make a difference... I would never forgive myself if I didn't try. Please don't ask me not to try."

Dani nodded with a humorless laugh. "If things were reversed, there's not a power in Pantracia that would keep me from defending you, so I suppose that's the most I can hope for." She lifted her chin and caught his lips in a kiss, exiling her dire thoughts.

He renewed the kiss with gentle fervor, his hand passing down her bare back to cup and squeeze her backside, sending a jolt through her. She rolled to her side, pressing her chest against his as he bit her lower lip, the heat threatening to rise again between them.

A metal clang in the distance made her jump, gasping as she broke the kiss. "What is that?"

Liam laughed as he sat up, tugging her with him. "The dinner bell. I guess we lost track of time." He pressed her shirt into her hand.

Dani snorted. "I wonder how that happened." She let the cloak fall off her naked body. "I guess that means forest playtime is over."

Liam groaned as she stuck her hands into her sleeves, and he leaned forward to stop her arms before they could lift her shirt. Bringing his chest against her back, he bit her shoulder, tracing the curve with his tongue. "Unfortunately." His hand slid around her abdomen, pulling her against the hardness of his body. "And here I was, ready for more."

The dinner bell rang again, more incessantly.

Dani laughed. "There will always be more, my love." She kissed his neck, biting him. "But aren't you even a little curious if our prince really is a secret chef?"

"Very true." Liam released her, and the leaves rustled as he dressed behind her. Her breeches landed in her arms a moment later. "I look forward to being the judge between him and Katrin. I suspect more bitter baking battles throughout the week."

"Sounds not so bad for us." Dani pulled her leathers on, followed by her boots, after Liam found them for her.

"I'm going to get so fat..." Liam sighed.

"I'll help you work it off."

"Oh, I like that promise." He stepped closer, plucking his cloak from the forest floor along with her pelt. He placed it over her shoulders, kissing her cheek. "I will say I'll be grateful if Matthias turns out to be a good baker. I wasn't looking forward to Lind's cake for Katrin's birthday. She didn't get any of the Talansiet baking skills."

Dani paused. "It's Katrin's birthday? You make cake for that?"

"Day before the winter solstice. Ma was thrilled when we showed up because it'll be the first time the family has been together for a birthday in years. I'd honestly almost forgotten. They're planning to surprise her. I figure we're covered on the surprises, considering we arrived with Matthias today."

"Is a birthday something you often celebrate?" Dani tied her pelt, missing Liam's warmth.

Liam paused, and she imagined him studying her.

She cringed. "Why do I feel like I've asked a silly question?"

"Not really that silly when I consider why you're asking it." Liam took her hands between them. "But yes, birthdays are always celebrated. Another year in Pantracia, and the perfect excuse to be spoiled with ridiculous gifts."

Dani laughed. "Sounds fun."

"Speaking of spoiling... When is your birthday? I will need the proper time to prepare."

"Prepare?" She laughed, tugging his hand to walk towards the incessant dinner bell. "Mine *is* the winter solstice."

Liam laughed. "I should hardly be surprised. You and Katrin truly are like sisters, only a day apart. You're turning nineteen too, right?"

Dani nodded. "Strange, isn't it? But if we were sisters, that would make you my brother, so I'm grateful it isn't true by blood."

"I will happily be the vessel who makes it possible by marriage, then." Liam squeezed her hand. "And I'm telling my family about your birthday. It's time you received a proper celebration for it."

Dani coughed. "No, no. You said you were celebrating Katrin's birthday. Not mine."

"It would thrill Katrin to share the celebration with you. Besides, Dani, you deserve it, too."

She clenched her jaw, taking a deeper breath.

I shouldn't fight him on everything. He just wants to do something nice for me.

"All right. But I'm doing it for you."

Liam kissed her cheek as the surrounding scents changed back to the open fields and peeling paint of the barns. "Then while you're feeling generous, I'd also like to tell my parents about you becoming my wife, even if we don't have an exact plan of when, yet."

Dani couldn't help but smile at his tone. "Of course you can tell them. As long as they will approve of you marrying a Feyorian."

"Are you kidding? Ma will be thrilled I'm getting married at all."

"Katrin said you trouble committing to responsibilities."

"She's not wrong." Liam plucked something from her hair as they neared the porch, the dark homestead's silhouette growing larger. "I typically do. Which is why I was a private for so long. But I guess Matthias forced me to see I was capable of more. And you've done the same, just in different ways." He slowed as they neared the porch, but he didn't warn her about it.

He knows it drives me crazy.

Dani poked her boot forward, the toe hitting the stair, and she climbed. "I hope Katrin and Matthias can be happy for us, too. Though they seemed rather friendly while cooking."

Liam hesitated at the top of the step, lowering his voice. "You didn't overhear the argument out by the stables, though."

"I heard the tones, but not the words. I assumed they recovered since he stayed," Dani whispered.

"I honestly don't know why he agreed, or even why she asked based on what I heard. Then to see them in the kitchen like that... I don't understand any of it."

Dani kissed his chin. "Because we were so easy to understand in the beginning?"

The door in front of them creaked open.

"There you are!" Katrin sounded exasperated. "Pa hasn't stopped complaining about how hungry he is since the pies came out of the oven."

The low chatter of the rest of the household overwhelmed Dani's hearing, but she breathed through it. "Here we are!" She gave a wide, overzealous smile.

"You might want to brush those leaves out of your hair, big brother."

Dani smoothed her own hair, quirking an eyebrow in Liam's direction. "You got them out of mine and forgot yours?"

"I can't see mine." Liam laughed as he let go of her.

"Neither can I." Dani huffed.

"You're letting the draft in!" Katrin's father called from inside, his gruff voice sounding annoyed.

"That's better. Get inside." Linen whipped in Katrin's hands, and Liam sidestepped to avoid her strike.

He put his hand gently against Dani's upper back, encouraging her first through the door before shutting it behind them.

Katrin's soft footsteps took her back into the kitchen.

The bulk of conversation hovered to the immediate left of the doorway, where the dining table was. Sound bounced off the hard wooden surface, allowing her to pinpoint where each person sat, leaving three empty spaces at the close end of the oval table.

Matthias laughed with Liam's father, something about Zionan tobacco, but the meaning was lost to Dani.

The Dtrüa crossed to the table, finding the back of one of the empty chairs.

"Liam, help her with her chair." Katrin's mother lectured.

Dani held up a hand. "I'm fine, really." She pulled the chair out, sitting with the others. "I can function a lot better than—" Something cut through the air, and she gasped, reaching for the projectile that flew from Matthias's direction. She caught the object, gently squeezing it with a sniff. "Did you just throw bread at me?" She chuckled and set the dinner roll on her plate.

"I did not make those to become projectiles," Katrin growled from behind, something sizzling between her hands.

"Sure worked to prove a point, though." Liam pulled his chair out beside Dani, but paused to take the savory pie from Katrin to place at the center of the table.

Silverware and ceramic chimed as another roll flew, but landed in the middle of the table.

"May have taught Izi it's okay to throw food, though." Lind leaned over her plate to recover it, but a smile softened her words.

"She's got a good arm." Matthias's sheepish tone made Dani stifle a laugh. "Apologies."

Pa chuckled. "Seems an acceptable price to have all our children under one roof again. Can I get you some more of that ale, Matthias?" He scooted his chair out before the prince even answered.

"Stay put, Pa. I'll get it." Katrin hadn't even sat down yet and walked around the table to Matthias, lifting his mug off the table. "And don't wait for me. Dig in while it's hot."

"Don't need to tell me twice." Liam's chair ground closer as he slid a metal utensil under the crisp pie crust, lifting a piece to her plate first. "Pass the salad, Ma?"

"*Please*," his mother prompted. "Did the military purge you of all your manners?"

"Please." Liam accentuated the vowels before he placed a bowl on the table between them and dished it onto their plates. "It'll be hard to go back to the camp after getting used to all the fresh food here."

"Katrin's been a great help with maintaining the garden." Storne's strong voice came around a mouthful of food. "I was never much good at it. So you can thank her for the salad."

"Since you can't thank me for the pie." Katrin returned, replacing Matthias's mug before coming around the table. "Anything else before I sit?"

Liam moaned. "Damn, Matthias."

"Language." Ma's fork clanked.

"Darn, Matthias," Liam repeated with a smile. He picked up the bowl of salad again, passing it over Dani to Katrin as she settled beside her. "Katrin's got competition indeed. Who'd have thought... you, of all people."

"What, Talansiet, men can't cook?" Matthias's knowing tone held an air of challenge as the prince's utensils clinked.

Dani touched the crust of the potpie before finding it with her fork. "That's rather outdated thinking, Liam. Maybe you should get him to show you a few things."

"That's not what I..." Liam sighed, filling his mouth with another bite instead of finishing the sentence.

"So when you lot going to explain those fancy insignias on your shoulders?" Pa had taken a large swig of his drink before speaking. "I ain't a military man and don't recognize the significance, but if you're away from the border in a time of war..."

"I told you Liam got a promotion, Pa." Katrin poured a rich smelling sauce over her salad. "Did you want some for your salad, Dani? Liam's a heathen and likes his plain."

"Please." Dani had no idea what she was agreeing to, but it smelled delicious. She took a bite of the potpie and the flavors hit her tongue like nothing she'd eaten at the military camp. "Where did you learn to cook like this?"

"My mother taught me." Matthias sipped something. "Many years ago. She thought everyone should know how to prepare meals." He redirected his speech. "Those insignias mean they are a part of the crown elite."

"Crown elite?" Lind tore a piece off a roll, putting it in front of Izi. "As in... personal guard to the royal family?"

Storne whistled. "That's one hell of a promotion. What's your assignment that makes it so you can come visit us?"

"Something still important to the war and, conveniently, it's here. Katrin was doing some research at the border that might lead the prince to what he's looking for." Liam's fork scraped on his plate, trying to get every bit of pie off it.

"The prince? Prince Alarik or Prince Seiler?" Ma, who sat beside

Matthias, sounded astonished. "Kat, you never said you were doing work like that. Did you actually meet one of the princes?"

Katrin choked on her bite, chewing for an extended time before answering. "Yes, I met Prince Alarik, Ma. But it's really not—"

"Was he handsome like they all say he is?" Lind bubbled with excitement.

Dani clenched her jaw to keep the smile from her face, stuffing another bite of dinner into her mouth.

Poor Katrin.

 Chapter 13

"No, Lind, he's horribly ugly. A disappointment, really." Liam took a large bite of his salad.

What did I do to deserve that?

Matthias gaped at his friend, trying not to laugh. "Don't let him hear you say that, or you might get demoted."

Liam shrugged. "Would be worth it." He glanced at Dani as she tasted some of the dressing Katrin had put onto her salad, the Dtrüa's face twisting in contemplation.

Katrin's cheeks reddened. "The prince is a fine-looking gentleman, but that's irrelevant to what I was working on. I'll give Liam the information tomorrow, and they'll all be on their way back to the border again."

"Nonsense. Liam's already agreed to stay for the week." Ma reached to Matthias, patting his wrist. "You're welcome as well, of course. And Dani."

"We appreciate the hospitality." Matthias closed his hand over hers. "Perhaps you'll let me use that kitchen of yours again."

"Of course!" Ma beamed, her face so much like Katrin's, especially in the smile. Her hair was knotted the same, but streaked with silver. "Do you work with the prince, too? I don't see one of those fancy insignias on your shoulder."

Matthias cleared his throat, unable to find the will to lie to the woman. "Actually—"

"Ma, I think I forgot a batch of rolls in the oven." Katrin broke into the conversation, her mother's gaze turning in surprise.

"So get them..." Lind encouraged Izi's little fork to the pie in front of her.

"I... need Matthias's help." Katrin pushed back her chair, placing her napkin next to her plate. Her eyes met his, silently pleading with him.

Her mother frowned. "Don't be ridicul—"

"You don't mind, do you, *Matthias*?" Katrin's eyes widened in silent insistence, and she bit her lower lip.

The prince scowled, but rose from his seat. "Lead the way."

She dashed to the kitchen. When she reached the oven, she swung the door open. Using their bodies to shield it from the rest of the family, she slid an already baked tray back into it before silently sealing the door.

As she faced him, her gaze drifted over his shoulder to the table. "You can't tell them," she whispered. "Please, don't."

Matthias kept his voice low. "I won't lie to your family."

"Lind knows you and I were together." Katrin stepped closer. "She could tell I was a mess when I first arrived, and I confided in her even if I didn't tell her who you were. She knows that you... Matthias... are the man I love." She broke his gaze, shaking her head. "If she realized you're also the..." She stopped before she said it, taking his hands between them. "Please. You don't have to lie, just... avoid the full truth? They're already crazy enough, considering I *work* with you. If they find out who made them dinner..."

The prince took a deep breath and let it out slowly, trying to hide the hurt her words caused. "You realize you're telling me you're... what? Ashamed of who I am? Embarrassed?"

Her eyes widened, and she opened her mouth.

He pulled his hands from hers and held one up. "Fine, Katrin, I'll steer clear of the truth, even though *you're* the one who asked me to stay." Turning from her, he walked back to the table, forcing a smile as he took his seat. "Wrenin, Liam mentioned you brew this yourself. It's delicious. Do you grow the hops, too?" He sipped the ale, enjoying the bitterness.

"East field. Ferment it in the basement. Yez hates it, says it stinks." Katrin's father beamed in appreciation as he drank his own mug.

"It does stink." Katrin's mother wrinkled her nose in distaste.

The oven door clanked shut again as Katrin pulled her cleverly replaced rolls back onto the counter, a little browner than they'd been before. She didn't move, her hand still in the linen wrap she'd used to pull the tray from the oven as she stared at nothing.

I should have stayed in town.

"Did you take Dani to the stream?" Lind spoke across the table to her brother.

"I don't know if we made it that far." Liam grinned, shifting a little closer to Dani. Her body straightened in the usual way it did when he touched her beneath the table. "Got a little distracted."

"Hope it's not those damn badgers again. I've filled in their den at least a dozen times in the last month." Storne cast a curious glance at Matthias, an interested glint in his green eyes that shifted to Katrin.

She brushed her hands on her skirt and stoically walked back to the table before settling next to Dani again. She didn't look up from her plate as she ate.

"I noticed no badgers." Dani looked at Liam.

"We wanted to tell you all something, though." Liam put his fork down as he watched Dani, the love in his eyes unmistakable. His gaze flickered to Kat, but then back to the rest of the family. "Dani and I have decided to get married."

Yez gasped, her fork clattering to the table as she leapt to her feet and danced around towards them.

Matthias stared at them, the weight in his breeches' pocket heavier as he hid the bitter sweetness that accompanied the news. "Congratulations." He smiled, lifting his mug to his mouth before his emotions tainted the joy. "I mean, I'm shocked she's agreed to this, but I'm happy for you both."

Liam's mother wrapped her arms around her son's neck, pulling him into a rough hug.

"Geez, thanks." He breathed, but met Matthias's eyes.

The prince nodded at him, grateful for the distraction. He slipped his empty hand beneath the table and pushed on the piece of jewelry he'd gotten made for Katrin.

Why did I even put it in my pocket this morning if I didn't plan on seeing her?

Now that he had seen her, he was certain she wouldn't want it.

Dani let out a whoosh of air as Liam's mother gripped her in a solid hug.

Matthias buried his regret with a chuckle, gaze drifting to Katrin. Her eyes met his, and he looked away, determined to keep the smile.

How can we ever just be friends?

Four days later...

Matthias held the banner of colored fabrics over the doorway, looking back at Yez. "Is that level?"

"Little higher." Yez adjusted flowers on the side table beside the front sitting area, a fire already blazing in the hearth. The vibrant orange and blue of the flowers perfectly represented the two they were to celebrate that day. Wrenin had returned from town only a quarter hour earlier with the fragrant additions to their decorations, having bought them from a local greenhouse.

Matthias fixed the banner and glanced at the layered chocolate cake he'd baked, iced with white buttercream frosting. "Yez, did you say there were a few extra flowers?"

"Over there." She gestured with her head to the back door and dining table.

The prince collected the remaining six blooms, three of each color, and brought them to the cake. Breaking the stems a couple inches below the flower, he arranged all six on the top of the dessert.

Ma would be proud of this one.

Thoughts of his mother washed through his mind, memories of her laugh and how they'd cooked together in the last years of her life.

He smiled, turning one of the flowers so it sat just right.

His current life on the Talansiet farm hardly resembled the military days he'd grown used to. Sharing a room with Liam was a small price to pay for the home-cooked meals, family atmosphere, and being able to relax and play with the toddler.

Izi squealed as she ran through the front doorway, her mother close behind. The toddler wore a frilly blue dress, a wide orange ribbon tied at her waist. Locks of curly black hair bounced around her shoulders as she barreled towards Matthias's legs.

"Izi!" Matthias crouched to greet the little girl, and she collided with him. "Is mommy letting you have cake later?"

"Depends on how much dinner she eats." Lind smiled as she admired his work.

"Lind, aren't you supposed to be watching for Katrin and Dani?" Yez had moved on to the bouquet on the dining table.

"Pa's out there. Him and his pipe are less obvious than Izi and me." Lind pinched her daughter's sides, and she pushed harder into Matthias's hands, giggling. "Especially with how cute she is."

"The cutest." Matthias stood, lifting the girl with him.

"Isn't that dress supposed to be for the solstice festival tomorrow?" Yez remained focused on her work while she spoke, much like her youngest daughter often did.

"Yes, but I couldn't wait to see her wear it."

"We will just keep it clean, so you can wear it tomorrow, too." Matthias carried the child to one of the stuffed vases and plucked a small orange flower from the arrangement to give her.

Yez huffed from over his shoulder. "I'd just gotten that one the way I liked it."

The prince gave her a sheepish smile. "Izi gave me no choice. She's very sorry."

The little girl whipped the flower around, pushing it against Matthias's face.

Yez shook her head, the hint of a smile crossing her lips. She shook a finger at Matthias. "You're too charming for your own good.

Whatever woman ends up with you is going to have her hands full."

Lind gave a knowing smile at Matthias before she took the squirming Izi from his arms.

"Lucky for the female population, my life is rather busy, already."

"With baking decadent cakes and pastries." Lind grinned, bouncing Izi and tickling her nose with the flower. "Though, it's a shame. You'd make a wonderful father based on how you are with our little princess."

Matthias chuckled. "I appreciate your vote of confidence. Perhaps one day, things will change." His gaze drifted out the window to where Katrin, Liam, and Dani were walking back from discussing the Yandarin Mountain maps near the drakes. "Wasn't Wrenin going to warn us?"

Lind followed Matthias's gaze and sighed. "He's probably asleep. Ma, they're coming!"

Yez cursed under her breath, something she would have yelled at Liam for, as she fiddled one last time with the flowers. "Go wake your father."

Lind put Izi down and led her towards the door. "Izi, go get Grampy."

The little girl screamed again as she charged across the front porch, tackling Wrenin's leg.

He let out a surprised snore, his pipe nearly falling from his mouth. He grabbed it as he sat up, blinking at Liam, Katrin and Dani as they walked up to the porch steps. "Hey Lind, they're coming!"

"Thanks, Pa..." Lind laughed from the doorway, blocking it with Matthias.

"What's going on?" Katrin frowned, her eyes catching his before she looked away.

Izi charged, and Liam scooped her up with a playful growl.

"Why's Izi wearing her solstice dress?" Katrin narrowed her eyes at her older sister.

Dani hesitated before reaching for the toddler, tickling her near the armpits. "You smell like flowers!"

Matthias smiled at the Dtrüa. Considering how uncomfortable she'd been when first meeting the child, he was amazed at the progress she'd made in only a few days.

"There's cause for some early celebration." Lind leaned against the door frame. "On two counts, according to my brother."

A rosy tinge washed through Dani's cheeks, but the Dtrüa only whispered something to Liam.

Katrin frowned but glanced at Dani and Liam.

"Come on, Katy girl. You didn't really expect Ma to forget your birthday, especially considering how we used to pretend the winter solstice festival in town was for you. But the trick is on you, because it's actually for Dani." Liam poked Katrin's side. "Happy birthday." He leaned into Dani, kissing her jaw. "And happy birthday, tomorrow."

Dani chuckled. "Does that mean I have to wait until tomorrow to have cake? People keep talking about it, but I've never had any. It smells... like chocolate."

"Why didn't you tell me?" Katrin spun to her friend as she jumped onto the porch. She caught Dani's hands and pulled her forward. "I didn't know it was your birthday tomorrow."

"I never knew I was supposed to mention it." Dani shrugged.

Matthias stepped backwards into the house to let the others in. Katrin entered last, and he touched her arm. All the things he wanted to say got stuck in his throat when she looked at him, and his intention faded. "Happy birthday, Katrin."

She held his gaze for the first time in days, a hint of pink rising in her cheeks. "Thank you," she whispered, placing her hand on top of his. "You certainly didn't have to help with all this."

Liam held Dani around the waist, following her as he usually did to whisper things in her ear. They stopped at the first arrangement of flowers, the soldier guiding her hand to examine the petals as he quietly described them.

"I definitely did." The prince dropped his hand, trying to shake the heavy feeling from his heart. "I hope you like chocolate."

"I love it." Katrin leaned out of Izi's way as the toddler spotted Tuks on the front porch, running after the herding dog as he yipped and dodged her.

"Katrin, Dani, come take a seat so we can get to opening your gifts!" Yez called from the sitting area, patting the cushions of the couch. "Storne, we're starting!"

"Coming!" the man bellowed from the back porch and entered with an armful of firewood.

Matthias took a step away from her, swallowing and gesturing to the sitting room. "After you."

She hesitated, eyes dancing down his face as she swallowed and nodded. "All right." She grabbed the edges of her pale blue skirt as she strode around a low table to join the others. "You all didn't have to get me anything. Just being home is gift enough." She settled onto the couch, and Liam guided Dani beside her.

"It's not all about you this year, Kat. Dani gets gifts, too, so you won't feel so alone." Liam stepped around to the dining table, where Yez had arranged the modest collection of packages.

Matthias smirked at the look on the Dtrüa's face.

She definitely doesn't enjoy being the center of attention.

Katrin slid her hand into her friend's, entwining their fingers. "Do you want to see while you open yours?" She whispered the question, and he knew the offer wouldn't make sense to anyone else in the room.

Matthias took a seat across from the women as Dani nodded.

Liam lifted a pair of boxes over their shoulders, depositing them into the women's waiting laps. "These are from Ma and Lind."

Dani's fingers played with the bow of twine, a smile inching across her face. "Look at Liam," she whispered. "I want to see his face."

Katrin gave an exaggerated sigh as she turned over the back of the couch, looking at her brother.

Liam smiled at her before he kissed the top of Dani's hair.

Those two are perfect for each other.

"Oh, come on. Open them." Lind sat in Storne's lap in the chair near the freshly loaded fireplace.

"All right, all right." Dani pulled the bow of her box.

Izi raced over to Matthias, and the prince lifted her to sit in his lap. "Shh. They're opening gifts." He redirected the flower the little girl still held towards her nose and whispered, "Did you sniff it yet?"

"Kat," Dani murmured, and Matthias looked up to find the acolyte's eyes on him. "You mind looking this way?"

Katrin pursed her lips as she looked down, her hands twisting together on her lap. "Sorry."

"I'm sorry we didn't have more time." Yez brushed her hand over Dani's shoulder. "Should fit, though."

Dani shook her head, opening the box.

Inside was a rich chocolate colored leather vest with lighter laces along the sides. White fur lined the inside, framing the neckline.

Liam must have helped with that one.

The Dtrüa bit her lower lip and looked up, Katrin's gaze following hers. "It's beautiful. Did you two make this?"

"Ma's a bit more of a natural with leathers than me." Lind wrapped her arms around her husband's neck, leaning on him. "A joint effort. Do you like it? Liam said you only wear leather..."

"Thank you." Dani ran her hand down the front of the vest, nodding. "He's right, and it's perfect. I love it." She nudged Katrin with her shoulder. "Your turn."

Katrin untied her bundle, revealing a gift of the same style, though hers a full-length dress. It was a deep shade of blue, with blazes of teal and white in the shape of winter lilies on the bodice. "Oh, Ma. You remembered that dress I wanted."

Matthias lowered his gaze, trying not to imagine her wearing it. He pressed a hand to his pocket, feeling the small bulge still there.

I should give this to her later. Might be my only chance.

"Of course I did. Not quite the same as that ridiculously expensive one you spotted in town years ago, but hopefully it does it justice. Lind did the embroidery."

"It's lovely, thank you." Katrin folded it, smiling warmly at her sister.

"Ready for the next?" Liam smirked as he held two much smaller boxes in each hand. "From me, this time."

Dani glanced at Katrin again, and the acolyte nodded. Dani closed her eyes before Katrin turned to look at Liam as he leaned over the couch and placed the small box in her hands.

The Dtrüa pulled on the ribbon, removing the lid. She lifted a small white piece of jewelry from inside, turning it over in her fingers. "Liam, it's beautiful," she whispered.

A ring made of bone. Points for creativity, Talansiet.

Matthias leaned closer, tilting his head as Dani slid the ring onto her thumb.

The thin band widened at the top, spreading into a carved depiction of snowflakes that fit between her joints.

How much do I pay him?

The prince glanced at Liam, trying to remember what the other crown elites earned for their services.

Stefan handled the finances.

Liam kissed her temple. "Not as beautiful as you."

Katrin scoffed, rolling her eyes. "You can't be more original than that?" she teased, but Liam shoved her shoulder.

"Just open yours, Kat."

Pulling on the little orange ribbon, Kat opened her box the same size as Dani's and lifted a ring of similar style, though made of silver. The carved leaves shimmered in the firelight, and Katrin smiled as she slid it onto her hand.

"I figured you two are enough like sisters, I might as well continue the theme." Liam smiled at her before he kissed Katrin's head as well.

"Thank you, Liam." Katrin reached up and patted his cheek before he started towards the table again.

"My gifts are far more practical." Wrenin lifted an eyebrow as he packed a new pipe. "Would you like a pipe, Matthias? It's that weed from Ziona again."

"I'd love one, Wrenin, thank you."

Dani tilted her head. "Are we expecting company?"

Katrin's brow furrowed, and she looked at her mother.

She lifted her hands. "I didn't invite anyone else. I know you hate being the center of attention."

Liam stepped out from behind the couch, his eyes on the windows at the front of the house. "Some riders coming down the drive." He stepped to the corner of the front room behind the door, picking up his sword.

Matthias stood, still holding Izi, but handed the toddler to Lind when the woman reached for her daughter.

Dani followed Matthias to the front door, and he opened it.

"Is the sword really necessary?" Yez frowned as she eyed her son.

"Yes, Ma, it is."

"No, Liam, it's not." Matthias walked outside, gaze trained on the Isalican flag carried by one rider. It bore the royal crest, and he groaned. "Sorry, Kat," he muttered under his breath.

Dani darted outside. "I'll make sure the drakes stay put." She ran around the side of the house, disappearing.

Sunlight glinted off the soldiers' armor as they grew closer, a cloud of dust rising behind them.

"Well, they look awfully official." Liam stepped around Matthias, his shoulders squaring as he assumed his position in front of the prince.

"They certainly do." Matthias crossed his arms as the riders slowed, halting twenty feet from the porch.

"A message for Prince Alarik Rayeht." The front rider made the announcement as she dismounted, crossing towards them before taking a knee. She bowed, then stood and held out a sealed scroll. "From King Geroth Rayeht."

Liam studied the woman. He remained in position, but offered a respectful salute before he glanced at Matthias for direction.

"At ease." Matthias sighed, stepping around his crown elite to accept the scroll. "Is my father expecting a reply?"

"No, my lord." The soldier saluted. "Would you like me to wait in case you'd prefer to send one?"

Matthias huffed. "No, Corporal. You may continue on your way."

"Yes, your majesty." She bowed before returning to her horse and mounting. The two other riders at her side turned with her, a cloud of dirt rising behind them.

Liam chewed his lower lip as he eyed the scroll, his gaze darting to the front door. "So much for anonymity."

Groaning again, the prince turned around.

Everyone else, except Katrin, stood at the front door gaping at him.

Shit.

"My first name might be Alarik..." Matthias cringed, scratching the back of his head.

"I... I don't feel well..." Yez put her hand to her forehead, her husband taking her by the shoulder, his pipe hanging loose in his lips.

Izi squirmed from her mother's arms and barreled into Matthias's legs, tugging on his pants until he picked her up again.

"Ma, don't freak out," Liam pleaded. "He's still the same man."

Yez fanned herself with her hand while Lind just gaped at her child in his arms.

"Come sit down, love." Wrenin tugged on Yez, opening the doorway to show Katrin still sitting on the couch, her face buried in her hands.

Matthias sighed when he saw her. "I tried."

Lind looked from Matthias to Katrin, her cheeks flushing. "Wait, Matthias is really Prince Alarik, and Katrin..."

"Maralind, breathe." Storne's eyes hadn't left Matthias, though, even as he squeezed his wife's shoulder.

"I'm still me. Same person." Matthias glanced around the room, eyes landing on the kitchen counter. "Maybe we should have some cake?"

Katrin sat up, taking a deep breath as she kept her eyes closed, like she was trying to center herself. "It changes nothing, Lind."

"Are you kidding? This is insane!" Lind moved back from the door, crossing to her sister. "The crown prince has been in our house for *days* and you didn't say anything? You were in a *relationship* with the crown prince and didn't say anything?"

Matthias rubbed his forehead. "She wasn't allowed to say anything. It's not her fault."

Katrin's eyes darted to him, widening. "You don't—"

"Everyone was under strict orders from my father not to divulge my location, family or not. I am very sorry if this causes you all discomfort, but I promise I'm still the same person."

"So... cake?" Liam chimed as he closed the door. "This is going to be Dani's first birthday cake, if I might selfishly remind everyone..."

"Where is Dani?" Katrin scanned the room.

The Dtrüa appeared at the back door, letting it close behind her. "The drakes are fine... Did I miss something?"

"Matthias is the crown prince!" Lind gaped.

Dani let out a heavy breath. "Oh good, we all know this now? *Now* can I ask if anyone else finds it shockingly absurd that he can cook?"

"Oh, gods." Yez fanned herself harder. "The crown prince cooked in my kitchen. I've eaten the *crown prince's* cooking."

"Ma, stop," Katrin whined.

"We can return to referring to me as Matthias any time, now."

"Are we doing cake?" Dani walked over to Liam, a strange smile on her face.

"Yes, we are doing cake." Liam wrapped his arm around her waist, leading her to the counter.

Wrenin stepped away from Yez, going to the side table where he'd packed a pipe. "You still want that pipe, Matthias?" He held it out to him.

Katrin sighed, giving a grateful look to her father.

Matthias accepted the pipe and tucked the scroll into his coat. "Let's enjoy it outside, shall we?" He glanced at Katrin. "Save us some cake?"

She nodded, giving him a tight smile. "That will give everyone else in here time to get themselves together."

Wrenin paused at the hearth to light a long starter stick and followed Matthias outside, puffing to start his pipe as he went.

Once outside, Matthias closed the door and accepted the blazing starter. Sheltering the bowl of his pipe from the autumn wind, he inhaled the flame into the tobacco. The sweet smoke hit his tongue, promising comfort as the voices inside took to higher pitches.

Wrenin crossed the porch to his usual chair, but pulled it further down the decking, away from the front room windows. Grinding in protest, the chair tilted sideways before Wrenin plopped into it.

Matthias took the other seat, dragging it with Wrenin's. "You have my gratitude, sir."

Wrenin's eyebrows rose together. "Don't think I quite deserve such a lofty title from you, but you're welcome."

The prince chuckled. "You saved me from that room, so you can have whatever title you want."

Wrenin smiled around the mouthpiece of his pipe, chewing it. "Only a cattle farmer."

So that's where Katrin gets her modesty.

"Pardon my forwardness... *Matthias*, but I have to ask." Wrenin glanced in his direction, a cloud of smoke passing over his weathered face. "You and my Katrin?"

Saw that one coming.

Matthias blew a mouthful of smoke away from Katrin's father. "For a time, yes. I care deeply for your daughter, but it didn't work."

Wrenin hummed, turning to look out over the hills. He didn't speak, taking long draws of his pipe, his eyes squinting as if deep in thought.

After several minutes, Wrenin's teeth clicked on his pipe and he withdrew it, settling it into his lap. "Ain't my business, you understand. But Katrin is a smart girl. Certainly far smarter than me. And when she came home the way she did, I knew something must have gone real wrong." He twisted his pipe in his calloused hands before he lifted it back to his mouth, taking another slow draw. "Father's intuition, maybe, but I knew it had something to do with a man." He cast a sideways glance at Matthias.

The prince nodded, watching his pipe and choosing his words carefully. "When she left me, I thought it must have been something I'd done. Or not done. But I've since learned that while it had everything to do with me, it also had nothing to do with me. I wish I could undo the events that led to her return home, but I also think that being here has been good for her. She's lucky to have the family she does."

A wry smile crossed Wrenin's features. "A very political answer."

Matthias chuckled. "I don't mean it to be, but her reasons aren't mine to share."

He nodded again. "Problem with all the smarts she has, sometimes, is they get in the way. She overthinks things to the point of convincing herself that she can't do anything right, so why even try. Been doing it since she was as little as Izi."

The prince studied the ashes in his pipe before looking at Wrenin. "What did you do about it? To help her see her own potential?"

"Showed her a lot of patience." Wrenin blew out a breath. "Time. She'll usually find her way around. Just letting her know she's loved and safe and supported."

Matthias opened his mouth to speak, but the front door swung open and ricocheted off the exterior wall.

Dani lunged at Matthias, wrapping her arms around his shoulders and squeezing so hard he almost dropped his pipe. "I love you, I love you. This is the best birthday *ever!*"

Liam appeared in the doorway, lifting his hands. "I tried to stop her, but she's like a wild animal."

Matthias sniffed at her face. "You smell like cake."

Dani pressed a kiss to the prince's cheek in an unusual show of affection before letting go. "I won't even hold it against you that it took you so long to bake." She darted back inside, shouting. "Izi, we need more cake!"

Liam laughed, meeting Matthias's eyes. "Just remember, you created this monster. Not me."

Matthias chuckled and shrugged. "I'm not the one sharing a bed with her tonight."

"Gods save Katrin." Liam grinned before he disappeared back inside, closing the door.

Wrenin chuckled, leaning back in his chair. "How long are you going to ignore that message from your father?"

The prince cringed. "It only says one of two things, and either option doesn't sound very fun."

"Can't avoid responsibility forever."

Matthias smiled, pulling the scroll from inside his coat and running his thumb over the seal. "I don't think I've ever avoided it before. Kind of felt good." He smirked at Wrenin before flicking the seal open.

"Any time you miss mucking cattle stalls, you can come right back here, and I'll put you to work." Wrenin crossed his legs. "As long as you make more of those meat pies."

"I'd be happy to." Matthias unrolled the parchment, eyes darting over the familiar handwriting.

> *Matthias,*
>
> *It's time to come home. We've drafted the treaty with Ziona. Your brother will wed the Zionan princess this winter in the Great Temple and you should be here. I've overlapped it with your birthday. You're welcome. I'm looking forward to meeting the woman you've spoken so highly of. Still doesn't explain your presence at the Talansiet cattle farm, but you can fill me in when you get here. Your willingness to connect with our people only further confirms the great king you will be. Don't delay in your return, you know how much time the tailor likes to prepare.*
>
> *Your father.*

The prince took a deep breath. "Weddings all around, it seems." He gave Wrenin a regretful smile. "Looks like mucking stalls will have to wait for next time."

"Pity." Wrenin frowned. "I was looking forward to that story for the boys at the tavern in town."

Matthias laughed. "The stories you've already got will have to do. I'm sorry, it looks like I will have to steal your son before the winter solstice festival tomorrow."

Wrenin shrugged and stood. "Today is the first celebration with all of them under one roof in nearly six years. It's been a gift already. But I think I'm wanting some of that cake you got Dani all worked up over."

Chapter 14

Holding her plate close to her mouth, Katrin took another bite of the decadent cake and nearly fell over from the sheer richness.

How did he get all those flavors in there?

She hummed as she took another bite, the sharp tang of raspberry preserves so perfectly balanced. "How?" She motioned with her fork over the piece as if it'd answer.

"The trick is balancing the tartness of the berries with the sweetness of the buttercream." Matthias's deep voice startled her as he strode into the house, watching her. "Do you approve, Priestess?"

"You need to teach me how you made this." Katrin smiled before she realized what she was doing.

Storne had escorted Yez and Lind out to the back porch with their plates of cake, leaving the others to the peace of the warm living area, Izi and Dani wrestling playfully on the center rug.

"I wish I had time to do that." The prince leaned on the kitchen island as Liam cut him and his father a slice. "But it looks like we'll be departing sooner than expected."

Katrin's stomach dropped. "Oh."

"Where's the king want us to go?" Liam handed a plate and fork to Wrenin, who moved to his favorite chair to watch Izi and Dani, giving the toddler pointers as they played.

"Nema's Throne." Matthias looked at Liam. "We have a wedding to attend."

Liam's jaw stopped working for a heartbeat, and he swallowed. Licking his upper lip, he looked at his cake. "Nema's Throne?"

What the hells is that about?

Katrin studied her brother, trying to pick apart the obvious distaste for the capital city. But something else Matthias had said captured her attention. "Wedding?"

"The treaty with Ziona is drafted and will be signed after the nuptials."

Suddenly, the cake on her plate didn't seem so delectable. "You?"

Matthias straightened. "Me? Oh, the wedding? No. My brother. Seiler is marrying her."

Katrin caught the relieved sigh in her throat.

I have no right to be grateful.

"Well, it's certainly good timing." Liam cleared his throat, piling another bite into his mouth. "Didn't you just say you'd need to do your research in a more extensive library, Kat? Nema's Throne is going to have the best."

The prince's brow furrowed, and he glared at Liam. "Give us a minute, please."

Liam groaned. "Oh, don't give me that. Fate of the kingdom is at stake and all, isn't it? We don't exactly have time to—"

"Can I borrow you?" Matthias met Katrin's gaze. "For a moment, outside?"

Liam pursed his lips.

"Of course." Katrin slid her plate of half eaten cake onto the counter, casting her own glare at her brother as she followed Matthias's gesture to the front porch. She plucked her cloak from the hook beside the door, wrapping it around herself as she stepped outside. The warm fur tickled her neck as she buttoned it in place.

Matthias closed the door behind him, leading her away from the windows at the front of the house. "I have something for you." He faced her, walking backward as she followed him. "I didn't originally intend it to be a birthday gift, but since we're leaving, it's my last opportunity."

Her chest tightened. "Matthias," she breathed his name, missing saying it. "You don't need to give me anything."

"I do, actually." He stopped walking, withdrawing the little drawstring leather pouch from his breeches pocket and offering it to her. "It's not really my style, and I think it would mean more to you."

She hesitated as she looked at the pouch, wondering why a gift from Matthias felt so much more significant than the others. It felt wrong to think that way, but she lifted her hand to accept the little sack into her palm. "Thank you." Loosening the string, she reached into the bag, her fingertips caressing the cool metal as she withdrew the jewelry.

The sun glittered through the fine colored glass, cut into small circles and held within rings of silver. As light shone through the bracelet, creating prisms of brightness on the porch, her breath caught.

"I found part of a stained glass window from the temple. I thought you might like having a piece of it." Matthias's voice quieted, uncertainty lacing his tone.

Heat pooled behind her eyes, and she turned the bracelet over in her palm, touching each tiny pane of glass. Breath grew shallow as she tried and failed to stop a tear falling down her cheek. "Thank you," she whispered. She looked up at his face, meeting his eyes. They made the rest of her melt like ice in summer.

Before she could question the instinct, she reached to his cheek, her palm brushing over his soft beard. "I don't deserve you. Why would you still give me this, after everything?"

Chapter 15

Matthias's heart pounded, seeing her so vulnerable, and he struggled to keep from kissing her. "Because it will always be you, Kat. No matter where you are, or whether we're together, it will always be you."

Katrin's eyes sparkled with tears, darting back and forth between his. "I've been such an idiot."

Before he could overthink it, he circled his arm around her waist and pulled her into him. Meeting her mouth with his, he kissed her hard, sparks flying over his closed eyelids when her lips responded.

She whimpered into him as she wrapped her arms around his neck, pulling herself against him.

Matthias broke away from the kiss. "Marry me." He blurted the words, but had no desire to take them back. "I don't want to live this life without you. Be my wife. Marry me."

"What?" Katrin's body tensed in his arms as she put her hands on his chest. "Matthias, I..."

He searched her face, loosening his grip and letting her go. "You said you still love me. Is that not true?"

"I did, I do." Katrin's chest rose rapidly in her breath as she stared at his chest. "Matthias, I love you, but..." She closed her eyes and shook her head. "We can't. I can't marry you."

Matthias's throat tightened, and he stepped back. "Why?"

How is this happening again?

He sucked in a breath through clenched teeth, steeling his emotions.

I don't need to know.

Art flooded his veins, and he yanked time into reverse.

Chapter 16

Katrin's palm brushed over Matthias's soft beard. The bracelet dangled from her other hand. "I don't deserve you. Why would you still give me this, after everything?"

A pained smile spread over his face, his jaw working. "Because I care about my friends." He touched her hand, pulling it from his face. "May I?" He gestured to the hand holding the bracelet.

I want to kiss him. But I can't.

Katrin focused on what he'd called her. Friend.

The word, even though she had proposed it, sounded impossibly hollow. She swallowed, but gave a quick nod. "Please." She deposited the bracelet into his hand, turning her wrist over for him. She cursed herself for imagining his lips touching her skin.

Matthias unfastened the small silver clasp and refastened it around her wrist. His eyes shone with emotion, but he looked away. "Please excuse me." He walked around her, back towards the house.

Furrowing her brow, Katrin turned to watch him walk away. It broke something within her as she struggled to remember why they couldn't be together.

It won't work. I have to let him go. I can't give him what he needs.

She shivered beneath her cloak as a stray breeze rustled over the hills, and she pulled it tighter as she stared at the front door of her family home. She already knew there was nothing inside for her.

I don't belong here anymore.

She'd grown beyond the home, but returning to the temples didn't seem right, either. The knot in her stomach doubled as she faced the porch steps, gathering her skirt to sit on the middle step. Touching the bracelet on her wrist, she cringed at the phantom pain in her lower abdomen.

The front door creaked open, drawing Katrin's gaze.

Lind stood in the frame, glancing back over her shoulder before descending the porch steps. Her gaze locked on her sister's. "I can't believe you were courted by a prince!"

Katrin groaned, burying her face against her knees, hands over her head. "Not now, Lind."

The woman snatched Katrin's wrist. "What is this?"

Scowling, Katrin pulled her arm away. "A birthday present." She breathed, soothing the frustration. "I know I wasn't entirely open with you, all right? But it doesn't matter all that much. They're all leaving tomorrow, then things here can get back to normal."

Lind pursed her lips, hesitating as she stared at her little sister. "Kat." She sighed as Katrin turned away from her, and she sat on the stairs next to her. "*Impressive* bloodline aside, Matthias seems like a perfect match for you. Why don't you want to be with him? I've seen how he looks at you. He *loves* you."

"That's awfully bold of you to say." Katrin stared at the fine silver work around the glass bracelet. "I don't deserve looks like that. He's angry, and I don't blame him."

"Why? What happened, Kat?" Lind's tone softened. "You've been holding something back, I can tell."

Another sharp pain stabbed into her gut as Katrin thought about the night she'd kept secret from him. Tears welled in her eyes. Bowing her head, she sought to hide it from her sister. "I should have told him, but I didn't."

Lind put a hand on Katrin's shoulder, rubbing her back. "Told him what?"

Grief tore through her, conquering the walls she'd built. It made little sense that it won now, but with the memory of the temple held within the bracelet, and the look in Matthias's eyes before he'd walked away...

"The baby." She sobbed, hugging her knees. "When I lost it. I never told him about it."

"Oh, Kat." Lind leaned her head on her sister's shoulder, wrapping her arms around her and squeezing. "Losing one is hard. I know it all feels so impossible."

Her sister's embrace encouraged Katrin into her, listening to Lind's steady heartbeat. "And now, seeing him here. Seeing him with Izi." Her body shuddered.

Lind stroked her hair. "It must feel like everything in the world is fated to torment you right now, but you need to remember that it's not your fault. It happens. A lot more often than people talk about. When I lost my first..." She rested her chin on Katrin's head. "I damned every pregnant woman I saw, every child. But it will pass, and more chances for a family will come."

Katrin stilled, forcing her breath to even. "When you..." She lifted her head, meeting her sister's dark eyes, twins to her own.

"You were already gone at the temples. It happened a few times before we had Izi." A sorrowful expression clouded Lind's face. "I planted a rhododendron along the back of the house each time, but do you know what helped the most? What helped me survive?" She paused, tilting her head. "Sharing my grief with Storne. He always reminded me I did nothing wrong, and it was just the way of the gods. One day, we would have a child, and we did. But grief isn't something to be selfish over. Keeping it to yourself doesn't save the other person, it only isolates you."

Katrin shook with a rattled inhale as she laid her head on Lind's lap. "I'm so sorry."

Lind rubbed her back. "It's painful at the time, but try to remember there is a reason. Things go the way they are meant to, even if their purpose is only to strengthen us."

"So what do I do now?" Katrin balled some of Lind's skirt in her hand as she swallowed her tears. "Everything just hurts."

"Be patient with yourself. Grieve your loss. And if you want, there are a bunch of tulip bulbs I've been meaning to plant." Lind squeezed her again. "And just like you will heal in time, Matthias will, too."

"Maybe." Katrin sighed, playing with the hem of Lind's skirt. "But planting something sounds nice. And maybe it will help. It'll be easier when Matthias leaves tomorrow, too."

Lind hummed. "Don't take this the wrong way, sis, it's been lovely having you home... but you should go with them."

Katrin stiffened, sitting up enough to look at her sister. "What?"

"Liam told me he invited you. Nema's Throne? Grand adventure and expansive libraries?" Lind huffed. "You don't belong on a farm. Even if you aren't chasing the love of a prince, you need to find your own path."

"And you think that's in Nema's Throne? Which, conveniently, is the same direction as the prince..."

A smile spread over Lind's face. "It's also the same direction as your brother and your closest friend. I don't know where your path will take you, but you'll never find out sitting here making pies."

Katrin scoffed. "You like my pies." She rubbed her eyes, cleaning them of her tears. "But the libraries there are supposedly pretty remarkable."

Lind patted her back. "There's your answer, then. I will miss your pies, but my waistline won't. Come, let's plant those bulbs before you need to pack up."

Katrin nodded, combing her hands through her hair as she stood. Twisting it behind her head, visions of Matthias came back to her mind. "I..." She paused, letting her hair fall around her shoulders and cloak. "I made a mistake by not telling Matthias before. I shouldn't do that again."

An understanding smile crept across her sister's face. "I'll meet you by the garden?"

Katrin nodded and started towards the front door, rubbing her cheeks again. Sucking in a breath, she straightened and opened the door for both of them.

The front room felt oddly vacant as Katrin stepped inside, her father nursing his pipe in his usual chair, an empty plate on the table beside him. Ma had returned to the kitchen, wiping down the counters with more fervor than she had in days.

"Where'd everyone go?" Katrin smiled to hide her sadness from her parents.

"Storne's putting Izi down for her nap, though I doubt he'll be very successful with all that sugar she ate." Ma crossed to retrieve Pa's plate. "Your brother and..." She breathed as her husband lifted his eyebrows in encouragement. "*Matthias*... are in their room packing. I believe Dani slipped out to check on the drakes."

"House is going to be quiet again." Pa chewed his pipe.

Katrin just nodded as she turned down the hallway to Liam's childhood bedroom, which he'd shared with Matthias for the past few days. She paused before she reached the open doorway, able to hear them shuffling around, though not talking.

Something was bothering Matthias outside.

She chewed her lip, swallowing the lingering guilt and pain. She needed to share it. Tapping her knuckles on the open door frame, she paused as Matthias looked up, meeting her gaze. It left her breathless, as always. "May I speak to you?"

Liam straightened, lifting a hand to his chest. "With me, or without me?" He eyed between them, but focused on Matthias rather than Katrin for the answer.

The prince gave him the barest nod, finishing folding the woolen blankets. "You may as well see how Dani is doing with the drakes. Don't even think about cleaning out your parents' pantry. We can get supplies in town."

Liam bundled a shirt, barely bothering to fold it before thrusting it into his pack. "Right." He hoisted it over his shoulder, and Katrin stepped just inside to move out of his way as he went through the door. He gave her a wary glance, pausing briefly to pinch her chin.

She batted his fingers away, but gave him a smile as he walked into the hallway, nudging the door closed with his foot.

Katrin's stomach whirled as silence fell between her and Matthias, and she watched him while he continued to fold. Staring at his pack, she considered what both her siblings had suggested again, and realized the idea of Nema's Throne thrilled her. She wanted to go. And staying here, where she didn't truly fit any longer, just felt like she was punishing herself.

"I'd like to join you in Nema's Throne." Katrin blurted, unsure if there was another way to say it. "If I may?"

Matthias's gaze darted to her, and his hands stilled. "You what?"

"I want to come with you." Katrin stepped from the door, suddenly regretting losing the stability of the wood behind her. "To Nema's Throne. Liam mentioned the libraries, and... I think I can keep helping with finding the dragons."

"Oh." The prince looked away, stacking the last folded blanket onto the pile.

"I... also want to apologize, but I know it's not enough for what I did." Katrin gripped her hands in front of her, squeezing her own knuckles to keep herself focused.

"You can come with us." Matthias's words were pointed, but lacked hostility. "Can you be ready to leave today?"

"Today?" She shook the uncertainty away. "Yes, I can. But I was hoping you'd help me with something here, first."

"We're rather pressed for time if we want to make any progress before we stop for the night."

"It won't take long, but... I think it's important. For both of us."

His brow furrowed, and he looked at her again. "What is it?"

"I learned something just now, that I didn't know about Lind before. And she told me something she did every time she..." Katrin swallowed, desperately holding in the tears as her voice cracked. "Lost a baby. And I..." She breathed slowly. "Want to try it, too."

Matthias straightened and rounded the bed towards her. "If you think it will help, I think it's a good idea."

"Will you do it with me?" Katrin met his eyes. "Maybe it'll help us both. I know this wasn't just my loss. It's yours, too."

He put his hands on her shoulders, eyes glassy as he nodded. "Of course. I'd like to be a part of it. Thank you for letting me."

Chapter 17
Five days later...

Dani couldn't run any faster. Sharp rocks bit through the snow, cutting her paws. She huffed, trying to beat the exhaustion saturating her muscles with lead.

Liam's shouts of agony ripped through her.

Where is he?

Her surroundings blurred with yellow and orange.

She's gaining on me.

A force tackled her from behind. She shifted, her bones and flesh resuming her human form. Twisting beneath Resslin's pounce, she stared at the two bright eyes. Something else shone red, and Dani braced herself.

Searing pain erupted near her collarbone, and the scent of burning flesh overtook her senses.

Dani gasped, startling awake.

Her chest heaved, muscles aching as if she'd actually been running.

Just a dream.

The quiet night settled around her, Liam's arm draped over her middle. His steady breathing touched the back of her neck. His hand twitched, pulling her gently against him. With a groan, he relaxed again into stillness.

Winter blizzards discouraged the longer trek back to the main pass through the mountains, so instead, they'd skirted the eastern edge of the Yandarin Mountains. And they'd only made it halfway to Nema's Throne. Snow banks, cliffs, and unstable ground had forced them to reroute several times, even with the drakes.

The heat that had burned Dani's chest lingered, and she pressed a hand to the spot.

Her heart jumped, and she reached below her neckline.

The bone pendant from Ailiena warmed her skin, sparking her fear. Opening her palm, she gazed at the dim blue glow.

Resslin is close.

Dani rolled out of Liam's embrace, listening for the drakes on the outskirts of their camp.

Ousa and Brek still slept, their snores overwhelming whatever sounds the night held.

The possibility of Resslin seeking the beasts to turn them against her had weighed on her mind, but the enemy Dtrüa must have decided against it.

The drakes might side with me, instead, but I can't risk it, either.

Smoke shrouded Katrin's scent, where she curled even closer to the warm ring of stones opposite of Matthias.

Liam's cries still echoed in her mind from her dream.

I can't let her endanger them, too.

Dani's pulse sped as she crept away from their camp, resisting the urge to click her tongue. After a few steps, she took a deep breath and embraced her cat form. As she left the shelter of the thick pine canopy, her paws hit snow. Her surroundings brightened with colorful scents, the moon offering enough light to guide her.

Picking up her pace, Dani's strides whispered against the snow, images of her dream flashing as sharp stone beneath scraped her paws. Pebbles clacked as they dropped down the slope. And below, she could hear the roar of the river, too fast for ice to cover it. The ravine smelled of the fresh snowfall, coating what hearty plants still fought the frost.

As she neared the edge, a rock ricocheted down the cliff side, bouncing towards the raging rapids, its echo swallowed by the river at the bottom.

Dani continued on the high ledge instead of descending into the ravine, climbing the rock side as the cliff grew taller.

Seeing empty air ahead, she raced over the fresh powder, steering away from the cliff's drop off. The warmth on her sternum hadn't faded, as if the amulet still sought to warn her despite her cat form.

A musty orange scent tinged the air, and Dani paused, sniffing the snow. The trail led further north, so she padded on at a slower pace.

Resslin's scent grew stronger, speeding Dani's pulse.

"Shift!"

The order cut through the air, and Dani's initial instinct to obey nearly won, but she resisted. She stalked closer to where the voice had come from, the mist of smell forming Resslin's human form.

"Disobeying orders. You have changed." Her superior's voice floated calmly over the air. "Shift, Dtrüa. Now." Resslin stepped from where she blurred in with the cliff side, a dim movement in Dani's vision.

Dani growled, lowering her head. Her claws extended, flexing into the frozen ground.

Resslin sighed. "I've come to talk. Shift so we may do so with some civility."

Talk?

Hesitating, Dani quieted, retaking her human form. Her vision dimmed, the scent colors of snow and pine the brightest. "What could we possibly have to speak about?"

The amulet beneath her tunic pulsed with heat, not hot enough to burn, but she ignored the instinct to pull it free of her skin. It needed to stay hidden.

"What happened to Tallos and Nysir?" Resslin stood stoically still. "I know you are involved in their disappearances."

Dani furrowed her brow, eyes trained on the taller Dtrüa. "I never saw Nysir." She swallowed, clenching her jaw. "But I killed Tallos."

Resslin huffed. "Killed one of our own. You're even colder than Tallos made you seem. A liar, though. Nysir went to that temple you told us about."

Dani's memory returned to the night she'd snuck from the room, thinking she heard Tallos, but ended up saving Liam from a wild bear. Nysir's scent hadn't caught her nose, nor Tallos's. "If he was there, I knew not."

"More lies." Resslin moved, circling away from the ravine. Her leathers were silent with each subtle movement, like a puma even in human form. "Tallos, while a shame to lose, was an arrogant idiot. But Nysir... to defeat the Master Dtrüa. I suspect you accomplished it through deception rather than brute strength."

"I never encountered Nysir. As much as I'd like to take credit, I cannot. If he's with Nymaera, someone else claimed that victory." Dani stepped sideways, keeping Resslin across from her.

Why was Nysir at the temple?

Matthias had mentioned a mangled body, sending her to the cave where it was found. Any scent of the killer had long vanished, but the work could have been Nysir's.

But why torture a priest?

"You've grown bolder since becoming a traitor. How does it feel betraying those who raised you?"

"Raised me?" Dani laughed. "I was not *raised*. I was created. Manipulated. Forced into a life of servitude at the whims of the Feyorian monarchy. You care not about me, only that you lost me. Fewer teeth and claws on your side."

"We made you what you are. What would you be without us? Some hapless blind girl, abandoned in the streets of Jaspa. Unwanted. Broken. Weak."

"Jaspa?" Dani stepped backward. "I was born in Melnek."

Resslin chuckled. "*Reborn* as a Dtrüa." She stalked towards the tree line, pine flooding Dani's senses, and Resslin's position became harder to place.

She must have rubbed herself in pine to disguise her scent.

Dani fought to listen as the Dtrüa spoke, using her voice to envision where she stood, but her words reflected over the sharp rocks around Dani.

A smile colored Resslin's tone. "You were nearly dead when they sent you to us. A husk that we resurrected and shaped. And you were meant to be mine. You could have been great, but look at you. Just a lost, blind girl again. And fighting on the wrong side."

Chapter 18

Snow fell inside the top of his boots, but Liam ignored the shiver as he crouched lower into the shadow of the pine. He'd carefully circled around the ravine edge. Downwind of the two Dtrüa.

The break in the trees along the ravine edge allowed the half moon to highlight Resslin's back, her plain dark hair in a single braid along the back of her head. He'd seen the glimmer of blue light in Dani's palm through his barely open eyes when she'd looked at the pendant and knew what it meant.

And she decided to sneak off alone, of course.

He understood why. He'd promised not to get involved if it didn't become necessary, and he intended to keep his promise. But going alone into the winter night was still foolish, Dtrüa or not.

"I fight for the right side this time." Dani's voice held an air of certainty.

Resslin barked a laugh. "Is that so? Then why are you out here all alone? None of your Icehead friends will fight alongside you, even after all you've done. No matter what you do, you'll be the least important person here. You don't matter to them."

Liam controlled the growl, forcing his fingers to remain steady against the crossbow trigger.

"They're not here because you are my battle. My responsibility, not theirs. I never asked for help."

"Because you fear I may hurt them?" Resslin's tone turned mocking. "Or is it truly because you doubt they'd risk themselves for you? The Yorrie."

Dani shook her head. "What do you want from me?"

"Blood." Resslin's voice lowered. "It's the only way to pay for your sins." The enemy Dtrüa advanced, shifting into her cat form. Tawny fur spread over her body, and she charged.

Dani spun, fur cascading over her form into a blur of white. She ducked, dodging the puma's leap.

Liam let out a slow breath as he lifted the crossbow to his shoulder, fighting all instinct to plow ahead and take Dani's place in the battle. It truly wasn't his fight, but watching as Resslin's claws lashed at Dani's face made his heart thunder.

Wildcat yeowls rang through the air, and Resslin lunged at Dani again. They rolled through the snow, tan over white, spraying cold in every direction.

Watching across the sight of the crossbow, Liam followed each movement, his finger hovering beside the trigger with each even breath.

Wait for the right moment. For the perfect shot. Hopefully Dani will forgive me.

Dani struggled to regain her feet, teeth glinting in the moonlight. The cats rolled again, closer to the cliff edge. Breaking free from her enemy's hold, Dani bolted, but Resslin knocked her to the side.

Dani's paws slipped over the side of the cliff, but her claws prevented the fall. She leapt at Resslin, taking her to the ground. The tawny cat wriggled free, slamming her shoulder into Dani's chest. They rolled, and the puma pinned the panther to the stone.

Resslin swatted at Dani's head before aiming her fangs for her throat.

Kicking with her hind legs, Dani's front paws gripped around Resslin's neck. Red seeped from the fur at his lover's throat.

Liam focused on Resslin's head, but her gnashing teeth were too close. "Shit," he whispered as he moved his aim to the less fatal areas of Resslin's body, his finger catching the trigger of the crossbow the moment he passed to her shoulder.

The bolt flew true, its feathers whizzing through the icy air as it struck Resslin, burying deep.

The puma howled, careening back from Dani.

Seizing the opportunity, the white panther tucked her legs under Resslin and pushed her towards the cliff's edge.

Resslin screamed, her claws raking at Dani's hind legs as she toppled over the edge of the cliff, pulling the panther with her. Rocks collapsed, and Dani's claws scraped along the ground before they both disappeared.

"No." Liam leapt to his feet, charging through the snow and ignoring the protest of his frozen muscles. His boot slipped on the stone as he dropped to the ground, abandoning his weapon. Jagged rocks jabbed into his palms, and he crawled to the edge, praying to any god that would listen.

Breath huffed just below as he looked over, finding Dani clinging to the rock face with her front paws. Her back ones kicked at the air, trying to find something to catch on.

Without thought, he reached to her, gripping her front leg tight. He pulled, but the weight of her panther form rivaled his own. He gritted his teeth, glancing over her shoulder at the white rapids of the river fifty feet below. "I've got you. But you need to shift."

Dani's body rippled, the Art twisting her furs and flattening her face. The pelt beneath his touch disappeared, leaving behind leather over her forearm. She gasped, slipping in his grip before he clamped his hold down on her wrist. Her other hand let go of the rock face, closing on him near his elbow.

Liam heaved Dani up the cliff side, the rocks crumbling further beneath her boots as she struggled to find footing. Sweat beaded his brow when her weight finally shifted, and she crested the cliff edge.

Dani rolled onto her back, scooting further from the drop, panting. Blood oozed from puncture wounds at her throat, scratches marring her face and red staining her thigh.

He sucked in a breath, wincing as the cold bit into his lungs. Leaning over her, he lifted her chin to examine the bite. "You're crazy, you know that?" He panted, moving his vision down to examine the rest of her.

"Am I?" She touched her throat, wincing, but the wound was superficial.

Satisfied she wouldn't bleed out, Liam touched her cheek. "Yes. What were you thinking coming out here alone?" Anger flared, but the relief of seeing her cooled it.

"I needn't put all of you at risk, plus... the drakes. They could have chosen her." She tilted her face into his touch, catching her breath. "I'm sorry I scared you."

"I'm just glad I didn't listen and followed you." The freezing stone beneath them soaked through his breeches, sending a chill up his spine.

"Me, too." Dani reached for him, and he took her hand. She sat up, glancing at the edge. "Think she's dead?"

"There's no way she'd survive that fall, big cat or not." Liam steadied himself before forcing his feet beneath to stand. His legs felt shaky, but he sucked in a steadying breath as he hauled Dani to her feet. "She's gone."

"We should check the river. Even if she landed in the water, her body would wash up on shore." Dani leaned into him.

"There's no safe way down here. We'd have to go downstream, back the way we came." He wrapped his arms around her, unwilling to move.

She breathed slowly, tickling his collar. "I need to know, Liam. I need to know without a doubt that she's dead. Can we take the drakes tomorrow?"

He nodded slowly, brushing his cheek against her cold hair. "All right. I'm sure Kat and Matthias will understand."

The morning sun glinted off the packed snow on the surrounding mountains, a chill breeze rushing down the ravine with the river.

Liam shivered as he pulled his cloak tighter, eyeing where Dani crept along over the worn river stones, Matthias on the opposite side of the water doing the same.

Ousa kept swinging his big head towards the water, his snakelike tongue flicking over his maw. He took a lumbering step, but Liam ran his hand up the drake's neck from below, refocusing his attention.

"No fishing right now. We're going to get moving again soon." Liam eyed Brek across the river, where Katrin scratched his neck before she glanced after the prince.

She was too far away for him to ask what plagued her mind, but he could guess.

"I can't believe they think they can just be friends," he muttered to himself, earning Dani's gaze.

The Dtrüa clicked her tongue, maneuvering cautiously over the river stones towards him. "I doubt it's working."

Liam snorted. "Considering everything, I'm surprised Matthias is all right with her tagging along."

"You suggested it."

Liam shrugged. "I was drunk on chocolate cake. And I didn't think they'd both actually go for it."

Dani steadied her footing, balancing on an insecure rock. "It will get worse if one of them meets another." She sighed. "I found no evidence of Resslin. No scent of a trail. No tracks. And no body."

"Her body is probably halfway to the ocean by now."

Dani shook her head. "No. Animals die in rivers all the time. The bodies always get stuck on a rock or fallen log and end up rotting on the riverbank. She's not dead."

Glancing up to the ridgeline above, Liam chewed his lower lip. "Impressive, if she survived. She has a bolt in her shoulder, too. It'll slow her down at the very least."

"We'll get to Nema's Throne before she can catch up." Dani's tone became distant.

He grimaced at the mention of their destination, a dark pit in his stomach writhing. After his promotion to crown elite, he'd grappled with the reality that he'd have to return.

Maybe if I just stay at the palace, nothing will happen.

"I suppose." Dani stepped closer, but another rock shifted under her weight, making her stumble.

Liam caught her by the elbow, hoisting her against him. "Careful."

"I'm trying. This isn't exactly prime walking area, even for those who *can* see."

Ousa snorted and stepped back from Liam, evidently determining that Liam couldn't stop him with his hands full. The drake gracefully dodged around Dani and Liam, jogging towards the water.

"Ousa, gods damn it." Liam sighed as the drake barreled into the river, howling in delight as he plunged neck deep, spraying water over their packs secured there.

"Will you tell me what Nema's Throne is like?" Dani touched his chin, bringing his attention back to her. "You've been there before, yes?"

Her question made Liam stiffen. "I trained in Nema's Throne. At the military academy there. It's..." He paused, mind rushing back to those days. "Busy. Always something to do, or some party raging somewhere in the city."

Dani's cloudy gaze dropped to focus near his chest. "I'm worried about being in a big city. I could hardly handle Omensea..."

"It should be quieter near the palace. The streets aren't as dense there as they are in the military district. We should just keep you away from Hillboar Street."

"What's on Hillboar Street?"

Liam winced at his own foolishness of mentioning it. "Taverns, entertainment, gambling halls. A brothel, here or there. It's very loud." He'd spent far too much time on that street when he'd been training in Nema's Throne. Every spare iron mark spent.

Dani's eyebrows lifted. "You seem quite familiar with this street. Worried about running into old lady friends?"

"Depends on your definition of familiar..." Liam looked across the river at Matthias, seeking any out he could from the conversation. "And I wouldn't really call them friends."

The Dtrüa frowned. "I wasn't serious, but good to know." Her words were pointed, taking him off guard as she pulled from his grip.

"What?" Liam looked back to her. "Hold on, what are we talking about?"

"You know, some women never wanted that life. To sleep—"

"Whoa, hold on." Liam flinched. "I wasn't talking... No, Dani. Brothels aren't my style. No lady friends."

Dani's brow furrowed, but she didn't return to him. "You said you wouldn't call them friends. If you weren't talking about prostitutes, then who?"

Heat rose in his cheeks. "I had a very different vice on Hillboar Street. And I might have made a few enemies there. Ones I'm not keen on finding out that I'm back in town."

Tilting her head, the Dtrüa narrowed her eyes. "What did you do?"

"That's very accusatory." Liam's chest tightened, worry rising. *Would she judge me for it? If Kofka finds out I'm back in the city...* The crime lord would kill him.

"I'm not trying to accuse you of anything." Dani's shoulders relaxed. "I'm trying to understand."

"Let's just say I'll be staying close to the palace most of the time we're in Nema's Throne. I think that's best for both of us. I shouldn't have even mentioned Hillboar Street." Liam reached for her wrist, but Dani dodged his touch.

"I'm going to check farther downstream for signs of Resslin." She sidestepped, taking her cat form before loping away.

Liam exhaled, hating the version of himself from two years ago. The young soldier who'd gotten into all that trouble in Nema's Throne. Who'd racked up exorbitant amounts of debt to the city's baron of crime. His timely transfer to the border might have spared him temporarily, but he'd been a fool to think he'd ever truly escape his mistakes.

I just thought I'd have more time.

"You find anything?" Katrin's voice rose over the roaring water, pulling his gaze across to her.

Matthias stood, calming Ousa, who'd emerged on the other shore and begun badgering Brek to play with him.

Liam cupped his hands over his mouth. "No, but I'd like my drake back! Then we should get moving."

"Where's Dani?" Katrin's knowing gaze told him she already suspected he'd said something wrong.

Liam sighed, gesturing downstream, and muttered to himself, "I'm a coward."

Chapter 19

The horse beneath Matthias felt foreign after traveling on drakes for so long. But riding without Katrin sitting in front of him was a welcome change, giving his heart a break from the torment of having her close.

They'd arrived at the outer military camp the previous day and left the drakes in an outdoor training arena, despite the wary eye of the commander.

Dani spent the night with the animals to make sure they'd fare well after she'd left.

Composing the proper escort into the capital city took time, delaying their approach to the royal palace. Announcements needed to be made, decorations prepared, and enough carriages and formally decorated guards to rival the Lunar Rebirth parade.

Matthias patted his white horse's neck, glancing at the procession behind him.

A carriage with thick curtains carried the women, hiding them from prying eyes.

Liam rode next to him, but the soldier had originally wanted to ride in the carriage.

He deserves his position, even if he seems to doubt it.

A long line of guards marched in front of them on foot, setting the pace for their journey through the city. Colored papers scattered over the streets, crowds cheering to welcome their crown prince home.

A rock weighed in his stomach.

Barim and Riez deserved to make it home, too.

Matthias swallowed the grief, burying it as he usually did. The men wouldn't want him to dwell on their deaths, but being in Nema's Throne reminded him to visit their families. They would have already received his letters, but he needed to speak to them himself.

The sun glittered through icicles dangling from the high rooftops lining both sides of the street. His father's advisor had even gotten pennant banners hung between balconies over the cobblestone road.

His father had sent him and Liam changes of clothing for them to enter the city wearing. The buttons of his coat went halfway up his neck, thin decorative chains draped across his chest. A steel pin on either shoulder held his cape on, which lay over the back of his horse. A barber had trimmed his hair and beard, making his skin itch where tiny hairs lay trapped beneath the formal attire.

They should have provided another bath after the haircuts.

Matthias looked at Liam, who'd also been attacked by the barber, but they had shaved his face clean.

"Enjoying being the center of attention?" Sarcasm laced the prince's tone.

Discomfort radiated from the crown elite. "No." Liam frowned, looking the part of a stoic guard. "Only upside was the first real bath in over a week. But I think I prefer the border camp where no one cares how perfectly I've shaven. I'd like to see that barber do a good job with Ousa bumping him and insisting on attention."

Chuckling, the prince shrugged. "If you want a demotion, let me know."

"You'd give me one?"

"No." Matthias smirked at him. "I only have you and Dani here, and I need you both. But being home at least means I can pay you for the last month."

Liam looked ahead, giving only a minute nod. "Honestly, wasn't that worried about it..." His eyes flitted towards the dark alleys behind the cheering city folk waving vibrant handkerchiefs and bits of cloth.

"Resslin can't get this close without Dani knowing. You don't have to watch the shadows." Matthias narrowed his eyes at the man's paranoid behavior. He'd been acting strange since the encounter with the other Dtrüa, but Matthias doubted that's all it was.

With a guilty glance, Liam rolled his shoulders, causing bits of shredded paper to fall from the formal navy blue officer coat. "I forgot about these outrageous escorts whenever you or your brother returned home." He bobbed his chin towards the rank of soldiers in front. "I used to be one of those poor guys." The decorative guard uniforms were stuffy and heavy, the steel plating laid like scales along each limb.

"We're at war. My father thought a grand entrance would be good for morale." Matthias spotted a group of younger people waving incessantly at him, so he lifted a hand to acknowledge them. "Changes the mood of the city, even if I don't particularly enjoy it."

"Greater good." Liam never gave in to the attempts to get him to smile or wave, remaining stone faced. He turned back to the street, slowing his horse just enough to make it awkward for Matthias to continue talking to him.

The prince resisted the urge to frown, looking again at their destination.

The tops of the palace towers and ballroom glittered like great ceilings of ice, designed to replicate the refractions of the icicles on the streets. A giant stone structure served as the base, the upper tiers growing more intricate and asymmetrical. Their stone faces were too steep to allow snow to gather, but iced rivers ran over their faces towards the shallow ravine at the base of the castle.

They descended a gentle hill towards the grand bridge, which marked the palace entrance. Beyond, a massive set of curved staircases sat guarded by a formation of at least forty guards dominating the open front courtyard. Pillars rose on either side of the tall double doors at the top, rich with winter ivy's white blooms.

The crowd's boisterous cheering faded as they passed the pair of intricate marble dragons that guarded the bridge, their maws open in a howl at the azure sky.

As Matthias's horse started across the bridge, the guards in the courtyard shifted as one, raising their fists to their chest in salute. A ripple cut through their ranks to open the pathway to the palace front. His father stood at the top, flanked by a pair of personal advisors and his own crown elites.

King Geroth Rayeht started down the stairs, his cape dragging over the lush rug adorning the steps. He wore no crown, but a delicate gold wreath laid over his shoulders, coming to a point near his sternum. His dark eyes smiled, even when his lips didn't. Pausing his descent near the bottom, he waited while Matthias dismounted.

The carriage door clicked as the coachman opened it. It rocked on its wheels, and Katrin emerged, lifting her skirts as she stepped onto the stone. She'd donned the dress her mother and sister had made her, a mountain wind catching the hem. She kept her eyes down, her cheeks pink.

He struggled to tear his eyes away from her, but reminded himself she hadn't worn it for him.

This isn't the moment to be distracted.

Dani emerged beside her, and the carriage driver moved away, exposing both women to the view of the city and the palace for the first time.

The prince approached the bottom of the steps, glancing behind to ensure Liam had also dismounted, anticipating the formality that came next. Facing his father, he lifted a fist to his chest, taking a knee.

Like a wave, every person behind him knelt.

Once the entire crowd had settled into their bow, Matthias met his father's eyes.

"Rise, my son. And welcome home." A smirk threatened's Geroth's lips, and the prince fought the inclination to return it.

Matthias stood, listening to those behind him follow suit in the same wave of motion. "It is good to be home, your majesty."

"Come." Geroth turned, ascending the stairs as cheers erupted through the crowds again. "We have much to discuss."

As Matthias climbed the stairs, he looked back at the three who followed.

Liam had turned towards the woman, brushing close to Dani to whisper something in her ear. To the prince's surprise, Katrin moved ahead first, stepping into line behind him, her hands on her skirt. She'd surely had some formal training on manners and behavior while in the temples, and it showed in her confident stature despite her pursed lips.

Dani moved next, leaving Liam to take up the rear, a small collection of five other crown guards behind him. Matthias had been introduced in a flurry before the procession and didn't recall a single name.

Guards opened the tall mahogany doors as Geroth reached the top, stepping back for them to enter. They remained in salute until Liam passed. The crown guards turned, keeping their backs to the doors as they shut.

The grand entry hall stood three stories tall, lush tapestries and banners rimming the pale stone walls above. The arching marble stairway flowed into the upper balcony on the right side, the hallways beyond impossible to see. Chandeliers glowed with golden Art-laden light, illuminating the vibrant room and its perfectly polished marble floor.

"Matthias!" Away from the public eye at last, Geroth pulled his son into a hug, which he happily returned. Pulling away, the king studied him. "You even let the barber take care of you, I'm impressed."

"You didn't send Astar, so I figured you were trying."

The king chuckled. "Couldn't have that shaky-handed drunk cutting my son's face again, now could I?" He looked over the others. "You're being rude. Introduce me to these new faces. Two elites I haven't even met."

Matthias huffed, gesturing to Liam as he stepped forward, advancing beyond the women. "This is Liam."

The crown elite brought his hand to his chest in another salute, bowing his head. "My king." A tension clouded his voice that Matthias hadn't heard before, but Liam managed to look up and at least not seem utterly shocked at the informal introduction.

At least I warned him how Dad can be.

"A pleasure." The king extended his hand to Liam. The action revealed the uncertainty Matthias had expected, and the soldier stared for a moment.

Liam stood rigid, holding his breath as he accepted the king's hand, shaking it. "Pretty sure it's all mine, sir."

"Humility, I like it." Geroth released his hand, gazing next at Dani. "This must be the new Feyorian crown elite."

Dani took a step forward, bowing her head.

Matthias smiled. "Varadani is both Isalican and Feyorian, and she's been—"

"Pivotal in our defense, I've heard." Geroth offered his hand. "I'd be honored to shake the hand of the woman who tamed drakes and a wyvern for Isalica."

Dani reached, and the king took her hand in a solid shake.

She nodded. "Thank you for welcoming me."

"Of course. My son has impeccable taste in crown elites." Geroth let go of Dani's hand, and the Dtrüa stepped back. His eyes shifted to Katrin. "I can't say I've ever known him to keep the company of an acolyte, but from what I've heard about you, Katrin, I understand why he made the exception." Offering his hand once more, the king grinned.

Katrin bowed her head briefly as she accepted the king's hand, the color in her cheeks remaining. "I hope to continue to be of use during my visit here, your majesty. Thank you for your kind words, though I am no longer an acolyte of the temples."

She's really not returning to the temples, then...

Geroth nodded, releasing her hand. "This may be difficult for you..." He gestured to the three of them. "But I'd prefer you all call me Geroth. Our lives have enough formality outside these walls. There is no need for extra within."

AMANDA MURATOFF & KAYLA MANSUR

Liam and Katrin's brows rose in unison like true siblings.

Dani smiled. "I'm sure we will all be happy to try, Geroth. Thank you." Her lover's eyes turned to her, his mouth tight in surprise.

Matthias grinned, pride rising in his chest for the bold Dtrüa.

Geroth's smile widened. "I like your spirit, Varadani. Come, I'll show you where your rooms are."

Dani strode ahead towards the stairs, clicking her tongue, and walked next to the king. "Please, call me Dani."

Matthias chuckled, elbowing Liam. "Relax. He doesn't bite."

"You meet the king of your country for the first time and have him tell you to call him by his first name," Liam grumbled. "Oh wait, he's your dad. Of course it's easier for you, *Prince*."

Katrin frowned and shook her head as she walked past Liam, purposely hitting him with her wide skirt. "Do you always have to be such a smart ass?"

Liam narrowed his eyes at her. "I'm told it's part of my charm." He tugged at the bottom of his coat, itching his neck where stray hairs likely still bothered him, too.

Geroth and Dani's low voices murmured ahead in conversation, making Matthias laugh.

"Your other half seems to be managing just fine." The prince quirked an eyebrow at Liam.

"She didn't grow up with stories about King Geroth Rayeht and the Battle of Undertown, back before we all were born." Liam ran his hand over his cropped hair, gazing up the grand staircase as the two women and king reached the top. "But we're falling behind. After you, *your majesty*."

Matthias pulled his coat off, laying it over the large bed dominating the main room of his chambers. Retrieving a silk cloth, he dipped it into the basin of water on his table, wiping his neck to clean the hairs off.

Someone rapped on the door that led to his private sitting room, followed by his brother's voice. "I'm still going to get you a birthday gift!"

The prince smiled as he crossed to open the door. "You're getting me a birthday gift on *your* wedding day?"

Seiler casually leaned on one of the columns framing the double doorway into Matthias's bed chambers. With his wavy brown hair brushed to one side, he wore a witty smile on his clean shaven face. His gentle features were far more like their mother's, while his eyes held the amusement of their father. "A wedding day I wouldn't be having if it wasn't for my wayward older brother shirking his responsibilities."

Matthias chuckled. "I'm sure you'll enjoy continually reminding me of that. Where *is* your bride?"

Seiler waved his hand around his head. "Off doing something with her hair, I'm sure. We both know I'm not one to be fawning over her all day, regardless of my willingness to follow tradition." He stepped away from the column, moving into his brother. He pulled him into a strong hug, roughly patting his back. "And yes, enjoying, and will never let you live it down."

"I'd expect nothing less." Matthias released his brother, smacking his shoulders. "Let's walk. Now that I've got that coat off, I might survive." He exited his bed chambers and then his sitting room into the hallway, closing the door behind him.

Seiler clicked his tongue. "Shirking the formalities, now, too. Whatever will Loryena say?"

"It's been awhile. She must be used to Dad's casual atmosphere by now, no? I'm not wearing formal regalia the entire time I'm here." Matthias turned them down a hallway, leading them closer to the dining hall, where drinks and food were constantly replenished all day.

"She finally gave up on me." Seiler gestured at his own attire, a plain tucked shirt and breeches. "Though, she's focused on the wedding right now. I pray to continue escaping her attention." His brother gasped as if suddenly remembering something, his eyes glittering as he nudged Matthias with his elbow. "Speaking of *praying*."

Matthias rolled his eyes. "You did that on purpose."

"And Dad was worried about my tutors..."

"What is it you want to know, brother?" They reached the end of the hall, where two sets of stairs curved to the lower floor. He chose the left side.

"The gossip across the palace is that she's here. A gorgeous young acolyte, or ex-acolyte I suppose. But if she's here..."

"She is aiding in research and spending time with her brother. Nothing else." Matthias descended the curved steps, which led to the northern hallway.

They stepped around the corner, and Matthias hid his cringe.

Katrin strode towards them, a collection of books in her hands, and looked up at their footsteps. Her eyes flitted over Matthias first, averting to Seiler. Pausing, she straightened, recognition flashing through her eyes.

"If it isn't the woman herself." Seiler grinned. "I am the younger, stronger, and more handsome brother." He offered his hand to her, palm up.

Katrin looked unimpressed.

Been awhile since I've seen that look.

"Prince Seiler, I presume?" Katrin shuffled the books into one arm and placed her hand in his. "Am I to believe you were just speaking about me, then?"

Seiler bent, kissing the back of her hand before rising and releasing her. "But of course. Much curiosity reins for the woman who made my ever-responsible, boring older brother abandon his duty to chase an acolyte."

Matthias groaned, running a hand over his face. "Do you mind, little heathen? You're going to make her regret coming here."

"Oh, but I'd be remiss if she left. I'd lose the joy of watching you pine after such a—"

"I highly doubt he's pining. We're just friends." Katrin tucked a strand of hair behind her ear before struggling to lift her books again. "It didn't work out."

Seiler tilted his head and narrowed his gaze at Matthias. "Nope. I know that look. He's definitely pining. Love lost is—"

"And Dad was worried about my tutors..."

Matthias sighed, shaking his head as he regained his bearings. "We're just friends, but you're welcome to pry. I know you will, anyway." They reached the end of the hall, where two sets of stairs curved to the lower floor. He chose the right side.

Easier to avoid her.

"But she's the topic of all gossip in the palace. It might have been that interesting Feyorian woman if it wasn't altogether too obvious she's with that new crown elite of yours." Seiler eyed Matthias.

"Dani is also a crown elite." Matthias turned at the bottom of the stairs, venturing into the southern hallway. "Things didn't work out between me and Katrin. I'd appreciate it if you didn't bother her about it."

"Bother? Me?" Seiler lifted a hand to his chest.

Matthias halted and faced his brother, gripping his forearm. "Jokes aside. I mean it. She's been through some things and doesn't need you reminding her of them."

His brother paused, frowning. "All right, all right." He brushed Matthias's arm off of him. "I'll leave it alone. But you should know that I'm not joking about the gossip, either. The staff is abuzz with it. Everyone knows something must have happened for it not to be you marrying Princess Kelsara."

"It will calm down. Once the wedding gets closer, they'll forget it was supposed to be me. Besides, I hear you two hit it off." Matthias resumed his pace, stomach rumbling.

"She's gorgeous, I'm gorgeous... we'll make beautiful babies." Seiler shrugged. "Zionan blood certainly gives her a mind of her own, though. Hardly get two minutes of that woman's time in the mornings, but she seems level-headed enough."

"Good." Matthias smiled. "Will keep you on your toes." He reached the double doors that led to the secondary dining hall, and the guards swung them open. "Just remember that headstrong blood will pass to your children. I wish you many, many offspring."

Seiler laughed. "It's good to have you home."

"It truly is good to be home." Matthias poured himself a glass of wine, picking a rye dinner roll off the platter of breads.

"How did you convince Dad to host the wedding on your birthday?"

"I didn't. He just knows how much I enjoy that celebration." Matthias took a bite of the bread as Seiler picked up a plate.

His brother chose a turkey leg, licking his fingers after putting it on his plate. "In your honor, there shall be two cakes."

Matthias frowned. "Don't be ridiculous. Let the day be about you and Kelsara as it should be."

Seiler chuckled, looking down at his food. "You know, Barim always..." He paused, his brow furrowing. "Gods, Matt, I heard about Barim and Riez. I'm really sorry."

Matthias nodded, clenching his jaw. "Thank you. And I know. Turkey legs were his favorite."

"I shall remember him every time I eat one."

They stood in silence, looking out the window at the garden in the center courtyard. Water dripped from the parapets around, leaving great gouges in the snow banks where it fell.

Matthias chose an apple once finished with his dinner roll, crunching into the fresh fruit he hadn't had access to for weeks.

"Hey, look who's here." Seiler turned from the window, and Matthias's gaze tracked his brother's to Katrin.

Gods damn it.

"I shall remember him every time I eat one."

Matthias plucked an apple from the fruit platter. "Come on. Introduce me to Kelsara."

"Now?" Seiler narrowed his eyes.

"Yes, now. Or something else. Let's just move on from here."

"Why, brother?" Despite the question, he slid his plate, his food untouched, onto the edge of the serving table and turned towards the door.

Matthias groaned. "Because I'm not ready for the whole Seiler-Katrin-Matthias conversation." He motioned with his head. "Let's go."

Seiler huffed, following his brother's lead. "Fine, but you're going to explain that in greater detail."

Matthias reached the doors and they opened. He glanced sideways, briefly meeting Katrin's gaze as she entered the other side of the dining hall.

Seiler lifted a hand and waved, prompting Matthias to smack him in the back of the head. "Ow!"

"Move."

"She saw you, you know. Might have to jump again to avoid all that. We could use the code word from when we were children." Seiler struggled against his brother's push, dragging his feet in feigned protest.

"I'm not using the code word." Matthias scowled at Seiler, but couldn't help the smile that tugged at his mouth as he let go. They walked down the hallway, and he hoped Katrin wouldn't follow. "Gooseberries. You'd think a couple princes could've been more creative."

Seiler pouted. "Gooseberry pies were my favorite that Cook made." He twisted away, shoving up against one of the paneled walls. It gave way, pushing inward before he slid it easily aside to reveal the old servant's passages they'd frequented as children. "Doubt she'll find us in here." He tilted his head with a mischievous smile, ducking beneath a low-hanging cobweb.

Matthias followed him inside, sliding the disguised door closed. "I knew we were brothers for a reason."

"I never thought I'd see the day." Seiler's voice echoed against the stone, orienting Matthias in the darkness while his eyes adjusted. "My big brother, crown prince... avoiding a woman. I'm so proud... and concerned. What did she do to you?"

Crossing his arms, Matthias leaned against the wall. "Do you really want to know?"

Dread flickered in his stomach at the idea of recounting the painful events that led to that moment. The baby. The miscarriage. Her refusal to marry him that she didn't even remember. He'd tell Seiler it all if his brother wanted to know.

We can't be together again. She's made that clear.

Seiler's boots sounded against the dusty stone. He crouched, a fire starter scratching along the floor before he sheltered the flame with his hand and lit the lantern that lay there.

They'd stolen and hidden them at as many of the entrances as they'd found when they were younger. The lantern sputtered, struggling to catch before Seiler lifted it, snapping the hood in place.

"I'm your brother, aren't I?" Shadows flickered over his brother's face as he looked back. "Tell me."

Chapter 20

This vessel continues to be obstinate.
Fortunate she wrote everything down.
The boring acolyte is back.
Perhaps not so boring.
If she reunites with my prince...
I can use her.
Her and her weak body.
This wedding is proving meddlesome.
Must wait for the right moment.
The right risk.
Lasseth continues to disappoint.
Failure.
His death will be slow.
For now, I must bring a loyal servant into the fold.
Not a Shade.
More subtle.
My auer.

Chapter 21

Three weeks later...

Katrin glared at the hallway ahead of her, willing Matthias to round the corner. She stood in the middle of the rug, clasping a single weighty tome to her chest. He'd walked past the library entrance moments before, and she'd run out to loop around the maze of hallways to land perfectly in his path.

If he's vanished again...

Her knuckles whitened as she squeezed the tome, not sure whether to be angry or devastated when Matthias never came. She'd begun suspecting he was purposely avoiding her the first day they'd arrived, when she'd seen him and his younger brother disappear out the backside of the dining hall right as she'd entered. She'd experimented many more times over the weeks. Every time, he turned before he could be forced to interact.

His Art is the only way he can know every time.

And she was only aware of the times he hadn't jumped far enough back for her to miss seeing him at all.

This is ridiculous. I should focus on the dragons.

Huffing, Katrin stomped around the corner, back to the library. The warmth of the fireplace blazing within welcomed her among the savory scents of parchment and leather bindings, but her chest continued to tighten against her will. She threw the tome onto the study desk with a loud thump, not remembering why she hadn't bothered to put it down before trying to cut off Matthias.

The gold-leafed images on the front shimmered in the low candlelight. The dragons on the book roared, their tongues lashing towards the day-old tea setting she'd forgotten about.

Darkness loomed beyond the large multi-paned window, dusk already fallen despite it being before dinner. She tried to gauge the growing shadows on the mountainside while tapping on her chest, urging it to relax.

He has every right to avoid me.

But the hurt remained.

"Miss Talansiet?" An unfamiliar matronly voice came from the library entrance. "Are you in here?"

Katrin gritted her jaw, rubbing her cheek to ensure no tears had fallen. "I'm here." She faced the library entrance, spying the woman as she stepped inside. She recognized her, though struggled to remember her name.

"Oh, splendid." The silver-haired advisor to the king held a notebook and a stick of graphite. "Everything must have been such a blur when you first arrived. I am Madam Kelnik, but you can call me Loryena. I have a few questions for you and some scheduling information."

"Questions?" Katrin urged her tone to remain patient, despite her foul mood.

"You'll be attending Prince Seiler's wedding, yes?" Her umber eyes hardly looked up from her paper, scrawling notes between glances at Katrin.

"I... hadn't thought about it. I didn't want to presume that I was invited."

"You've been invited by the Isalican royal family." Loryena met her gaze, offering a gentle smile. "I will continue under the assumption that you will attend. After all, it would be rude not to, considering you're... here."

Katrin grimaced. "I suppose that's true. Then yes, I will be attending." The wedding was still a week away, plenty of time to prepare herself for the potentially awkward situations.

"Lovely." Loryena jotted more notes. "The royal family would like to provide your attire. The tailor has an opening for a first fitting tomorrow right after lunch. Your second fitting will be three days later at the same time. Does that work for you?"

Katrin's eyes widened in surprise. "That's unnecessary. I'm certain I could find something amenable in the city..."

Loryena raised her eyebrows. "Dear, when the king wants to give you a dress, you take the dress."

"Very well." Katrin clasped her hands in front of her, already knowing she'd lose an argument with this woman. Straightening, she nodded. "Yes, those times should work fine. Do I need to go somewhere specific?"

"The tailor will meet you in your chambers." Loryena kept writing. "I've also been informed that you do not have an escort. Can I arrange a suitor to accompany you to the wedding?"

"A suitor?"

"Would you prefer a man or woman?"

Katrin's tongue swelled in her mouth. "Neither. I don't require an escort." Her stomach rumbled. "Do I?"

The advisor hesitated, studying Katrin. "Well... I suppose you don't, though it's highly unusual for singles to attend alone. We have many suitable options, depending on your preferences."

"It would be unbecoming if I attended alone, then?"

Loryena nodded. "Your suitor provides a dance partner, conversation, and all the nuptial events are held for pairs."

Katrin winced, wishing she could use Liam, but he'd be attending with Dani. "I would be remiss to decline your offer."

"Wonderful. Would you prefer a man or a woman, then?"

Katrin rubbed her eyes. "A man, I suppose."

"Age, appearance, or status preference?"

Katrin looked up in surprise. "I can be that specific?"

"While I can't guarantee a guest will match a person's perfect choice, I will do my best to find you someone suitable." Loryena smirked, jotting down more notes. "I believe we have five single male guests available to you. I can tell you about them, instead, if you prefer?"

"No, that's unnecessary. Any is fine."

"I think I will pair you with Gaimun, then. He's an avid reader and only slightly older than you."

"You gather all of that information from the invited guests?"

"No." Loryena looked up with a smile. "Gaimun is my nephew. Seems a better choice than Mister Felmer. Bald, in his seventies, wife recently passed away..."

Katrin controlled a laugh. "Gaimun sounds lovely."

"Splendid." Loryena closed her notebook. "He will meet you outside your chambers before the ceremony. If you need anything at all, wedding related or not, come find me. I know I seem busy all the time, but I always have a moment for the prince's guests."

I certainly don't feel like his guest with how he's been avoiding me.

Katrin forced a shallow smile. "Thank you."

The toll of a bell reverberated through the castle hallways, marking the dinner hour.

Loryena chirped in surprise. "The day has run away from me. Shall I see you at dinner, dear?"

Katrin chewed her lip. Matthias would be at dinner, and suddenly her inclination to avoid him rose, even if it was only to be spiteful.

Stop being childish.

"Yes, I will join tonight. I've been taking my meals alone too frequently."

"Wonderful. Please excuse me. I have business to attend to before I can join the meal." Loryena gave a slight dip of her head as she turned and bustled out of the library, her brown skirts swishing behind her.

Katrin leaned against the desk, blowing out the candle. She picked up the tome again, tucking it beneath her arm. If anything, she could bury herself in it to avoid conversation if it became too awkward.

She balanced the tea set in her other hand and shuffled from the library towards the kitchens and dining hall.

A staff member outside the hall took the tea set from her, opening the doors wide. The lavish hall could have seated far more than those currently in attendance. Many large banquet tables sat empty on the far side of the high-ceilinged space.

The dignitaries who lived in the castle had arrived with the summons of the bell, including the king, who stood at the end of the table with a glass of wine in his hand. He chatted with a round, balding man she vaguely remembered as the treasury advisor.

Loryena entered the dining hall from the set of doors across from Katrin, a tall blond woman with her. She crossed the space towards the king, but tapped someone else on the shoulder.

Matthias turned to greet her, a charming grin on his face. Their mouths moved in what appeared to be an introduction, and the prince's attention shifted to the woman. She beamed as he kissed the back of her hand.

The woman took a step closer to the prince, her lips moving again in conversation, but none of it could penetrate through the din of the hall.

The prince's eyes wandered, despite the blond woman's continued chatter, and he paused when his gaze found the acolyte.

Katrin lifted her eyebrows, wondering if she could somehow convey her frustration with him through the gesture. Though he might very well believe it to be colored by the jealousy rising in her veins. She averted her eyes to the nearest seat at the table and plopped her book beside it. Refusing to look at him, she lifted her wineglass to a passing attendant.

Without her needing to speak, the tawny haired staff member poured her glass full.

"Thank you," Katrin murmured as she lifted it to her lips, drinking more deeply than she usually would. The fine merlot ran smooth down her throat, encouraging the next swig.

"I pictured you as more of a white drinker." A male voice behind her made her turn. "And perhaps a less... gulpy one."

The tannin stuck to the back of her throat as she took in the younger prince, and she choked as she lowered her glass. Lifting her hand to cover her mouth, she struggled to swallow. She met Seiler's eyes, fortunately different from Matthias's, even if the similarities were easy to see. They made her ache unexpectedly.

Seiler's eyes narrowed, a smirk lingering at his lips. He motioned to a passing attendant. "Water, please."

"You startled me, is all." Katrin frowned as she lowered her hand, certain no wine stained around her mouth. "I'm fine."

A goblet of water appeared in front of Katrin with amazing speed.

She glowered at it for a moment, but then took it as she set her wine aside and sipped to clear her throat.

"Something on your mind?" Seiler leaned against the back of a chair, glancing behind her before meeting her gaze. "I'm a good listener, you know. And we've not spoken nearly enough."

Katrin pursed her lips, hiding it behind the rim of the water goblet. "I apologize, Prince Seiler. I know I have not been the most social since my arrival."

"On the contrary, I believe there may be extra forces at work keeping us apart." He winked. "Call me Seiler."

She lifted her eyebrows. "Extra forces, huh?" She turned over her shoulder to glance at Matthias, who still spoke with the woman Loryena had introduced him to. The blond stood disturbingly close, her fingers dancing playfully over the decorations of Matthias's jacket.

Heat rose in Katrin as she turned back to Seiler, staring at the similar patterns on his clothing.

"Don't approve?" Seiler's tone lacked the taunting she expected, holding a timbre of curiosity.

Katrin traded her water for her wine. "Not my place to pass judgment."

"Oh, don't be shy. You can tell me the truth."

"All due respect, I doubt that. And I'd rather not." Katrin eyed him before she sipped her wine.

Seiler stuck out his bottom lip. "Suit yourself. Would you prefer I spare you of my company, then?"

She wanted to say yes, but manners dictated otherwise. "I do not wish to deny you my company if it is something you've sought.

Besides, thwarting those extra forces sounds damned appealing."

"It is, indeed. And this time, my brother hasn't erased my progress, so I must assume he either approves or is too lazy to intervene." Seiler's eyebrow twitched.

"Or distracted," she added darkly.

The prince huffed. "Distracted trying to make the best of a boring woman. Can't you tell? He's utterly miserable."

Katrin shook her head, refusing to look at him again. "You would know him better than me."

Seiler tilted his head. "Do you want to be here? In this dining hall, right now?"

She sighed, debating just how open she could be. "Not particularly. Loryena caught me in a vulnerable moment, and I suspected it was better to follow through on what I told her."

Chuckling, Seiler motioned to a staff member to refill their wine. "Oh, the madam can be quite persuasive. But we needn't follow the rules. Shall we?" With his filled wine glass, he motioned to the doors. "Matthias would hate it."

A little wave of delight at the idea made Katrin nod. Retrieving her book, she followed Seiler from the dining hall, wondering at his intentions. In her conversations with Matthias, he'd always suggested he and his brother were close. A little ball of dread gathered in her stomach at what Matthias might have told his brother. Might have confided in him.

"Where are we going?" Katrin sped her step to walk beside the younger prince.

"Somewhere fun." Seiler's eyes glittered with mischief as he looked at her. "You look like you need a little fun in your life."

Katrin narrowed her eyes. "Fun?"

"Yes, that elusive thing that makes people smile and laugh. Ever heard of it?" Seiler paused halfway down the hallway, checking that both directions were clear before pressing both palms to the wall. It shifted inward before he slid it to the side to reveal a passage. He motioned for her to enter. "My lady."

Katrin hesitated as she eyed the secret passage, glancing at Seiler. "Are you sure this isn't how the royal family just gets rid of an inconvenient acolyte?"

"You're anything but inconvenient." The prince smiled, finishing his wine and leaving the glass on one of the decorative tables lining the palace walls.

"That somehow doesn't make me feel better." Katrin studied the darkness ahead, contemplating its existence and Seiler's decision to share it with her. She couldn't imagine many knew of the passage, considering the layer of dust with shallow trails through its center and the low hanging cobwebs.

The perfect place for a murder.

He laughed, walking inside the passage. Retrieving a lamp from the floor, he lit it. "My brother has many strengths, but having fun isn't one of them." He put a fist to his chest. "And I swear on my life, no harm shall come to you." Tilting his head, he took on a serious tone. "Matthias would kill me if anything happened to you, and he hits hard."

"I doubt he would care much, right now." Katrin gritted her jaw before lifting her glass and draining the rest of her wine. Stepping towards the shadows, she slid her glass beside his on the little table.

"Ah, precisely where you're wrong. But even if you're right... We don't need him. Now hurry before someone passes by and sees this door." Seiler motioned again.

What have I got to lose at this point?

Katrin hoisted the book further under her arm as she stepped over the threshold into the passageway, brushing past Seiler as he closed the door behind her.

He held up the lantern, motioning with his head. "This way. Watch your step." Guiding her through the narrow hallways, he reached a spiral staircase which took them down. Pausing at the bottom, he offered her a hand over the crumbling last step.

She studied his offer for a moment, but ignored it as she hopped over the broken rock. "You never told me where we're going."

"I can see why my brother likes you." Seiler motioned again, picking the left hall at a fork. "Are you sure you're not Zionan? You and my future wife have similarities."

Then maybe Matthias would have been fine marrying her.

She grimaced, disguising it with interest in the carved walls. "Can we not talk about Matthias?"

Seiler quieted, and no witty remark came like she expected. They wove through more narrow corridors before reaching a dead end. The prince pulled on an iron bar, and the section pulled in before sliding to the side.

Light streamed in from the hallway, no one in sight.

Seiler exited the passageway, waiting for her before sliding the secret entrance shut. "This way."

Katrin looked up the hall, trying to determine what part of the palace they were in. She recounted their steps in her mind, but the sprawling halls were still mostly unknown to her, even after three weeks.

I'd only recognize it if it was the library hall.

Seiler led her through another doorway, which grew cooler than the halls. Bare wooden paneling formed the walls, donning racks of long and short bows. "Ever used one?" He glanced at her, eyes passing over her body as he approached the wall.

"An archery range?" Katrin tried not to feel evaluated by his look. "No. I've only shot a crossbow."

Plucking a short bow and a flat bow from the middle rack, he slung a quiver over his shoulder. "I'll show you." He crossed to the other side of the room, opening another door.

On the other side, the space opened up into a covered range, a wooden divider keeping archers on one side. Targets lined the middle ground and far wall, with rings depicting the arrow's accuracy.

"As much as I wish I had an image of the man we aren't speaking about, I don't. You'll be stuck with your imagination." Seiler offered her the flat bow. "Unless, of course, your imaginary target is blond and female."

Katrin scoffed and put the book down before taking the bow. Her fingers slid along the waxed string. "And this is to be *fun*?"

Seiler grinned. "Shooting arrows? Of course it is." He lifted the short bow, drawing an arrow from the quiver on his back before loosing it at the targets. It sailed right past the closest one, burying into the dirt floor.

Katrin snorted.

He laughed and drew another arrow, handing it to her. "See? fun."

"You're pretending for me, aren't you?" She tested the string of her bow, pulling it back enough to feel the tension.

He shrugged, walking closer with a hand outstretched. "May I?"

She bit her lower lip, looking at his hands. His deep voice asking the innocent question suddenly transported her back to the icy cave within an avalanche, and she shivered. "Princes and their manners," she grumbled, shaking away any hesitation. "Yes, show me."

Seiler took her hand on the bow, sliding it higher, closer to the notch. He guided her other to hold the arrow nocked against the string. "One finger above the arrow, two below, and aim by looking down the shaft..." He lifted her elbow, and her sight down the projectile lined up. "When you're ready, pull back in a smooth motion and release. Relax your shoulders."

Katrin breathed as she drew back the string, focusing on the shaft in front of her like Liam had taught with the crossbow. Her muscles quaked as she reached her jaw with the pullback, hesitating as she tried to remember all the instructions he gave.

She released her fingers, the bow twanging uncomfortably in her hand as its string snapped against her elbow. Flinching, she lowered the bow with a hiss, touching the sore spot.

"You all right?" Seiler walked in front of her, touching her wrist. "String bite you?"

"I'm fine." Katrin transferred the bow temporarily to her other hand as she shook out the left. "Surprised more than hurt."

The prince looked behind him, stepping out of her way. "Damn good first shot."

Katrin looked down the stretch of range, finding the only target with an arrow protruding from it. Her arrow stuck into the blackened wood of the most outer ring. Brow furrowing, she looked down at the bow in her hand again. "Did you sneak a shot off while I was distracted?"

"Only two arrows out there, my friend. One in the ground, and one not. You did it all yourself." Seiler patted her on the shoulder.

A flutter of excitement jumped through her, but she was determined to stamp it back down. "Probably a fluke."

When she looked at Seiler, the prince was already offering her another arrow. "Only one way to find out."

Katrin accepted it, nocking it against the string before she lifted the bow again. Before pulling back, she checked the position of her arm, ensuring all was free of the string's path. With another steady breath, she released. The bow jolted in her arm, but knowing what to expect now, it was far less awkward.

Her arrow cut through the air, thunking into the same target, one ring closer to the center.

Seiler threw his arms in the air with a short whoop as the thrill rushed through her.

She smiled, lowering the flat bow again. "I guess I can shoot." She looked at the prince, tension fading from her body for the first time in weeks. "Can I have another arrow, please?" She held out her hand.

"You can have all the arrows your little heart wants." He handed her another.

"If I get good enough, maybe I can shoot Matthias in the leg before he manages to avoid me again." She lifted the bow in a smooth movement, loosing an arrow into the target again. It thunked into the wood beside her previous hit.

Seiler laughed, clutching his chest. "Oh, you must. You must. Please let me be there."

She beamed as she took another arrow, ignoring the ache of her muscles. "I just don't understand why he's being such an ass about it all. I thought we were doing better." The words poured out of her before she could stop them. She didn't realize how desperately she'd wanted to say them. Dani had been too busy with crown elite duties to give Katrin an opportunity to vent to her. "Using his Art just to *avoid* me?"

The prince leaned on a post supporting the divider fence. "Matthias has a way of seeing how scenarios play out without letting others remember them. Not entirely fair, but I understand sometimes."

"The problem with all of that is he can't take his own memory of it. So he's just torturing himself."

Seiler pointed an arrow at her. "Yup. That *is* the problem. Which means, sometimes, he's making big assumptions on information that may no longer be valid."

"So what in the hells did I *do*?" Katrin snatched the arrow from Seiler, glaring at it. "Or didn't do, apparently, but I did? It's all so insane when you think about it. I've done nothing, but I'm still being punished for something."

Shaking his head, Seiler sighed. "Look, I know my brother is insanely infuriating with his inability to be open, but he usually just needs time. He's told me how much he cares about you, and that's present tense. If you can put up with his nonsense awhile longer, he will come around and talk to you, eventually. I honestly think he's just hurt and confused. And you wanted to be friends, so..."

"Friends was better than enemies. Than being awkward." She narrowed her eyes at Seiler, waving the arrow at him vaguely. "How much did he tell you?"

Seiler watched her, a subtle cringe twitching his face. "Enough."

Katrin scoffed as she nocked the arrow. She lifted the bow, drawing the string. "You are just like your brother." Loosing it, the arrow struck the closest she'd gotten to the center yet.

"Normally, I'd take that as a compliment." Seiler sighed. "I'm really sorry for what you went through, if I may be so bold. For my brother, too, but... I admire women and their strength for enduring the world's cruelties."

"Cruelties." The word felt sour on her tongue. "Evidently, even if my intentions were to protect him, I ended up torturing us both. I had hoped that planting the flower bulbs together at the farm would help, but they only seem to have made it worse for him. I found closure... hope... but he—"

"He did, too." Seiler nodded once. "Not really my place to say, but I said it anyway. He did, he told me."

"Then why is he still afraid to see me, to be near me?" Katrin swallowed the threat of her emotions, hardening herself. "I'd hoped we'd figure this out together, move forward... together. Now that I know my sister suffered the same and still had a child..."

"Because he's an idiot." Seiler chewed his lower lip the same way Matthias did when thinking. "But does he know this? Have you told him?"

"When would I have told him?"

"Well, I understand you two rode the same drake all the way here. Which, by the way, is insane and I want to meet those creatures."

Katrin huffed. "It was awkward enough by then. I didn't want to make it worse. I could tell something had already changed." She looked down at her wrist, eyeing the bracelet peeking out from beneath her sleeve. It reminded her of his eyes that day, the ones that hadn't been able to look at her after giving her the birthday gift.

"That's the beauty of it, I suppose." Seiler stepped from his spot, drawing another arrow. "Things are always changing, and there's nothing stopping them from doing so again. If you want them to." He offered her the projectile. "And until they do, we can come here, and you can shoot things."

Katrin smirked, taking the offer. She nocked it as she spread her stance again, inhaling a steady breath. A dim haze had descended on her from the wine she'd downed, but not enough to hinder her focus on a new target.

Drawing the string, she aimed and released in a single smooth motion. The arrow sailed true, striking the next ring in, third from the bullseye. "Once I get them pointed in the right direction to find the dragons, I won't be needed here. That'll be a change..."

"I'll be sure to have our librarian *misplace* all the tomes on dragons." Seiler stood behind her and eyed her shot. "You're a natural."

"Whose side are you on?" Katrin glowered over her shoulder.

Seiler leaned sideways, whispering near her ear. "Yours."

Chapter 22

Ousa butted up against Liam's back, making him stumble.

"Whoa, big guy." He reached around, scratching beneath the drake's chin, earning a pleased purr. "I missed you, too."

Brek gave Liam a wide berth, focused on Dani and the bucket of cow parts she carried.

"At least they seem to be adapting pretty well out here." Liam repositioned the scarf around his neck, putting both gloved hands against Ousa's head to prevent him from pushing him over again.

The paddock shared the barracks' outer wall, but the large stone structure only acted as two sides of their enclosure. The fences into the rest of the barracks and stables barely reached the drake's chest, and certainly wouldn't hold them in. But Dani's persuasion had worked, much to the relief of those stationed at the barracks, despite the Dtrüa only being able to check in once a week.

The first two weeks, Liam had declined to join her, despite it meaning she'd go alone to the outer barracks and military stables. It was too much of a risk, considering one of Kofka's peons had probably seen him in Matthias's arrival parade.

But I came straight here and will go straight back. He won't get to me.

Dani emptied the bucket into the trough, other soldiers behind her bringing more. She glanced in Liam's direction, but said nothing, patting Brek's neck.

Each soldier who brought a bucket dumped its contents before hurrying away, trying not to rush. Their unease around the drakes was palpable, eyes never leaving the beast's maw full of sharp teeth.

Ousa abandoned Liam with a chuff, trotting towards the trough and forcing a soldier to dive out of the way to avoid being trampled.

Liam sighed and lifted a hand to the wide-eyed young man in silent apology.

"Crown Elite Talansiet?" Someone spoke from behind him, and he faced the private who gave him a respectful salute. "I'm sorry, sir. I'm hoping I can borrow a moment of your time."

Liam glanced behind him at the drakes as they dove into their meal, Dani walking between them, checking the scales along their bulky bodies. He turned back to the soldier. "Problem, Private?"

"All due respect, sir, not here." He bobbed his hooded head towards the stable structure meant to house the drakes from the weather. "In private?"

Liam narrowed his eyes, nodding as he walked beside the man to the stables. They crossed over the hay strewn ground around the first wide doorway. To the left, two massive piles of hay created beds for the drakes in what would normally have been an open space between the empty horse stalls.

They continued through into the stable district of the barracks, and the private led him to a barn at the back with empty paddocks.

"Wasn't the drake's barn quiet enough?" Liam eyed the private, a nervous roil rising within him.

"An overabundance of caution, but if I may, sir, you are an inspiration. And I am sorry." The private eyed Liam as they entered the open front door of an empty stable.

"Sorry?" Liam followed. "What for?"

The private's head turned towards one of the empty horse stalls, prompting Liam to do the same. Something moved within the shadows, and the stall door slid open to reveal the person within.

He was a monster of a man, broad shouldered and taller than most Liam had ever seen. He'd have made a fine addition to the Isalican military if the Isalican crime lord hadn't scooped him up first.

Liam's heart jumped into his throat. "Mekkin. Fuck."

Mekkin grunted with a wicked smile as he bobbed his chin behind Liam.

The private had vanished out the front door of the barn, which was now being secured by a wiry man with straw-like hair.

"Liam Denethir Talansiet." A smooth voice cooled Liam's blood to ice. "I'm insulted. In Nema's Throne nearly a month... and not a peep from you? No hello for an old friend."

Liam grimaced, wishing he could avoid the piercing blue eyes as he met them. His shoulders slumped, his entire body relinquishing to old habits.

I'm better than this.

Rolling his shoulders, he fought to straighten against the man. "Kofka." He tried to sound confident, his eyes betraying him as they flitted to the silver-capped cane Kofka tapped against the edge of his boot. Perfect streaks of silver framed the sides of the man's black hair, his goatee finely trimmed.

"Did you really think you could enter my city and I wouldn't know?"

"I fully expected you to know." Liam gritted his jaw. "Though a little surprised it took you this long to corner me."

Kofka's brow twitched and pain erupted as Mekkin's fist collided with Liam's side, forcing him to stagger and clutch his ribs.

He whirled towards Mekkin as he bit back his cry of surprise, but the brute of a man snatched his right arm before it could go for his sword, twisting it up against his lower back.

"I'm a patient man, Talansiet." Kofka strode in a circular path around Liam. "But it's time you pay your debts. Without the lip."

"I can get you half of it right now." Liam gasped, grimacing against the sharp twinge of pain as Mekkin twisted harder. "Six gold crowns. And I can have the rest soon."

"That's a good start. But, you see, interest accrued while you were gone. Not to mention your..." Kofka approached, poking the steel insignia at Liam's shoulder with the tip of his cane. "Promotion. Your debt has risen to fifteen gold crowns."

"What?" Liam gaped, forgoing his struggle against Mekkin. "I could buy your gambling hall for that price."

"I have *faith* in your ability to get it for me. Given your new housing situation." Kofka paced away, tapping his cane on the wooden walls. "And don't get any idea about involving your new friends. With what I know, you'd be demoted back to private." He paused, looking at Liam. "Or maybe you'd be put in prison. I have friends in there who would be happy to see you."

Liam pulled, but Mekkin's grip tightened, shoving his wrist higher to the point it might snap. Unable to hold in the grunt of pain, he gasped for air. "All right, all right. I get it. I won't say anything."

Mekkin relaxed, but wrapped a burly arm around Liam's throat.

Liam choked, forcing his hands to remain at his sides. "I haven't yet, have I?" He fought every instinct to reach for the hidden knife in his cloak. He might get lucky with Mekkin... But Frel, the wiry man who still hovered near the door, could hit him with a throwing knife from fifty feet away.

"You have a week." Kofka leaned forward on his cane. "Before I get impatient. I'd hate to spill blood."

"You haven't had a problem spilling my blood in the past." Liam met his icy eyes.

"Who said anything about yours?" A smile pulled at Kofka's lips. "Is there anything a brother wouldn't do to protect his little sister? Not to mention the crown elite you accompanied here. What was her name again? Varani? Verni? Something... Va..."

Liam bucked against Mekkin before he could question the inclination, stomping his boot on the brute's foot. The loosening of his grip on Liam's throat allowed him to throw his elbow back. His fingers grazed the hilt of his dagger before Frel dashed forward, his closed fist contacting Liam's gut with such force it brought the soldier to his knees.

He coughed, gripping handfuls of hay. "Don't you dare touch Dani. Or Kat."

"Dani! Is that her name? That's right. Varadani. Feyorian traitor with no surname. No family." Kofka laughed. "You choose the strangest company."

Liam growled, pushing up, but a kick from Mekkin put him on his back as his vision flashed white. He groaned as his body curled against itself, his dagger thunking on the barn floor beside him where Frel tossed it.

"One week, Talansiet. Then I want my money." Kofka leaned over his cane. "Do we understand what will occur if you don't provide?"

A snarl echoed through the hayloft, drawing all gazes upward. Cloudy, bright eyes appeared over them, the white panther balancing on wooden beams.

"What the fuck?" Mekkin's deep voice came for the first time as he backed away from Liam.

Shit.

Liam cringed as he grabbed his screaming ribs, trying to roll into a crouched position. He didn't want Dani to see this, to know.

Dani leapt from the loft, her body shifting as she descended until her boots struck the floor instead of paws. She slowly stood, breathing in deep, even draws. "Should I call the drakes?" Her voice took a low tone, hands ready at her sides.

"Interesting." Kofka hummed as he stood his ground, Frel taking a small step in front of him. "But no, Miss Varadani. I believe our business here is complete. I look forward to seeing you soon, Talansiet."

Liam groaned, wobbling his head in a defeated nod as Kofka exited the barn, unconcerned with showing his back to the Dtrüa.

Mekkin didn't move, watching them both until the barn's lock clicked and Kofka and Frel slipped through. Then, without another word, the crime lord's bodyguard exited as well.

"I could kill them, you know." The undertone of a growl tainted Dani's words.

"It'd do no good. He's got entire lines of criminal under lords just waiting to take his spot. Wouldn't change anything." Copper tainted the back of Liam's tongue, and he made a face, spitting. Touching his ribs, he hissed as he struggled to sit up.

Dani faced him, scowling. "Would make me feel better." She knelt next to him, grabbing his arm to help him. "It's time you fill me in on what's going on."

"I guess you won't believe me if I try to say it's nothing." Liam sighed, closing his eyes as he considered losing Dani's trust and respect. He already hated himself enough for it. "I..." He chewed the side of his tongue. "Ran into a bit of trouble when I was training here. I mentioned Hillboar Street, and my familiarity with it. I... got in over my head at one of the gambling halls owned by Kofka."

Dani stood, pulling Liam to his feet. "How much do you owe him?"

Liam winced, both in genuine pain and embarrassment. "Twelve gold crowns, but apparently he sees fit to make it fifteen. I skipped town with my transfer to the border, though, to get out of it."

Her jaw worked. "And how much do you have?"

"Six-ish." Liam mentally tried to count the silver florins one crown had been exchanged for already. "It's everything I've made since becoming a crown elite."

"I have two." Dani sighed.

"I'm not taking your money."

The Dtrüa scowled at him. "If you want to wed me, then there is no mine and yours. That's the deal."

"But this is *my* problem. And you're not my wife, yet. It's not too late to back out of that, and hells, I'd hardly blame you."

"Fuck you." Dani spun, stalking away from him.

He blinked, looking after her. "What? What do you want me to say? I fucked up here, Dani. I shouldn't have come back to Nema's Throne. And now I'm putting everyone I love in danger with me."

She turned and glared at him from twenty feet away. "You're a hypocrite. We're not married so your problems are your own? Where was that logic with Resslin?"

He gritted his jaw. "That's fair." Liam's voice lowered as he shuffled towards one of the stable doors, pulling his tunic from where it was tucked. The cold air bit at his skin, but brought some relief to the blooming bruises on his side.

"Damn right it's fair. If you want to be my husband, that means we're partners. It goes both ways. If you take my two gold crowns, we only need to come up with seven more." Dani chewed her lower lip.

"Which is almost equal to what we have. Seven gold crowns is a lot of money."

"We should just ask Matthias. You know he'd—"

Liam's head snapped up. "No. No, absolutely not. This is my shame. I will not involve him."

Dani groaned. "Then *I* will ask him. He won't care. It's nothing to the crown."

"No." Liam pushed all he could into the word. "We can't. Besides my pride, if Kofka gets wind that we even hinted at this to Matthias, it's as good as not paying the debt at all. Only way men like him still exist is by staying out of sight of men like Matthias."

"Can you hear yourself? That's my point. Matthias can take care of him, and then we won't have a problem."

Liam shook his head more fiercely. "It doesn't work like that, Dani. Kofka has men below him, beside him, all around him that will continue his legacy. Continue what he's running here. Cutting off the head of the snake does nothing because it has another head on the other end. Then their threats will still be followed through on. They'll go after you and Kat... and expose every stupid thing I did."

Dani stared in his direction, pausing before tilting her head. "What did you do?"

Liam averted his gaze, even if she couldn't see him. He hesitated, the hole he'd worked to mend in his chest over the years away from Nema's Throne reopening. "Stupid, selfish things." He looked at his gloved hands, imagining how his knuckles had looked those years ago. "Twelve crowns might actually be possible for me to earn now, but before... as a new trainee, barely even a private... I was only making two florins a month. And those vanished into the gambling halls faster than those cow hearts you give the drakes. I... had to find other ways to pay Kofka sometimes."

Striding towards him, Dani softened her tone. "So you did favors for him."

"He made them perfectly enticing. Do this little thing here, and I'll forgive all your debt for the week. This little thing there, and I'll loan you another two florins." Liam ran his hands up through his hair, his voice weakening. "I had a problem, Dani."

"What did you do for him, Liam?" She stopped in front of him.

"Nothing too far. He seemed to know what my limit would be. But I roughed up some others who owed him money. Helped Mekkin when more muscle was needed in collecting a debt."

Dani swallowed, taking a deep breath. "There's no shutting me out of this one. If we're going to fix it, we do it together."

Liam looked into her eyes, trying to read the thoughts rushing through her head. "Fix this together? How do you not hate me?" His chest felt heavy, his entire body sagging against the stable door. "I should have told you."

"You should have." Dani nodded. "But if anyone knows what it's like to make mistakes while under someone else's influence, it's me. I'm on your side. We'll figure this out."

Relief mixed with his guilt. "But just us, all right? No one else can know."

The Dtrüa shook her head. "I cannot promise that." She touched his face. "I can only promise that I will keep everyone else out of it unless it's absolutely necessary."

Damn woman is quoting me.

He sighed, nodding against her hand. "At least promise me you won't sneak off at night and kill Kofka on your own?"

"I won't. We do this together." Dani's touch trailed down his neck to his side, where her fingers gently prodded. "I don't think your ribs are broken, at least."

"Hurt plenty, though." He took her hand, lifting it back to his face, kissing her wrist beneath the edge of her glove. "I don't deserve you."

Dani huffed. "I could say the same thing, my heroic future husband. Give yourself more credit."

He snorted, but his ribs panged in protest, and it turned into a groan. "Oh, I will. For getting us into this mess." He touched her hair, tucking a strand behind her ear. Memory of their morning in bed together, discussing the coming day flashed into him. "Don't you have a dress fitting this afternoon?"

Her nose wrinkled. "That's tomorrow."

"No, that's today." He tapped the side of her nose. "You told me this morning. Gambling debts aren't going to stop this wedding that we're both expected to attend *as guests*. If I have to get dressed up, so do you."

Dani whined. "But I can't shift in a dress."

"Why in Nymaera's name would you need to shift at the wedding?"

She frowned. "Or on a routine trip to check the drakes, right? But there I was, scaling a barn like a feral cat because I could hear you getting punched and the door was locked. I like to be prepared."

"I'll try not to get punched at the wedding, how about that?" Liam took her hand, easing himself away from the stable door. They walked towards the exit, and he took a deep breath through the ache.

"I won't look good in a dress." Dani squeezed his hand.

"You'll be beautiful. Like you always are."

"Fine. I'll go to the fitting. But you're staying in the room so I can keep an eye on you."

"For you to keep an eye on me, I'll have to be no more than five feet from you at any given time."

Dani poked him in the ribs, and he yelped with a laugh. "If you want to be specific, I will keep a nose on you. But it doesn't have the same ring. And I *can* see you, just not what you're doing, what you look like, or if you're even awake. You're a..." She motioned up and down his body. "Dark blob."

He snored playfully. "What? I'm sorry. I'd fallen asleep as we walked." His chest felt lighter, his shame already almost forgotten in Dani's presence.

She laughed, leaning her head on his shoulder. "You sleepwalk remarkably well."

Chapter 23

Four days later...

"Tell me what it looks like." Dani tried not to fidget as the tailor worked around her, adjusting the dress for the second time that week.

The padded chair beside the roaring fireplace shifted as Liam sat. They'd returned to the living space the crown elites closest to Matthias shared, though Dani and Liam had it to themselves with Micah and Stefan still at the border.

"Uh," Liam scratched his chin. "Why do I assume just saying gorgeous won't cut it?"

Dani frowned. "Gendren, maybe you can explain better than my betrothed?"

The tailor chuckled. "I have you in a floor length A-line gown with a white underskirt and a parted navy overskirt with ruching near the hip."

Liam's chair scraped over the ground as he stood and walked towards her. "That's the white bottom dress, and it looks to be a very fine fabric that I'd *love* to see you in without that navy outer bit." His hands roved over her hips from behind. "Here it is... a little folded over on itself at your hips making it... flow over that lovely backside of yours."

Dani rolled her eyes. "Thank you for the translation, Liam."

"I aim to please." A smile had returned to his tone.

After the tense situation at the outer barracks days earlier, he'd been stiff and difficult to read.

Gendren tutted his tongue. "Your bodice is a corset style—"

"Tight. Accentuating all the right places..." Liam supplied, his hands grazed up her sides, difficult to feel through the clothing he described.

Gendren's voice grew tighter. "With a dipped neckline and ruched shoulders. The sleeves are long, opening at the elbow for a cascade of fabric at your sides. It's very tasteful, even if your partner has found a way to make it sound *crude*."

"I did no such thing." Liam traced his hands down her arms. "Besides, I'm merely appreciating your work, Gendren." He nuzzled against the side of Dani's head, his nose brushing her earlobe. "You look stunning."

Dani's cheeks heated. "It feels so restricting. How am I supposed to get out of this thing tonight?"

"Not to worry, we have handmaids to help you after the wedding this evening."

Her stomach lurched, forgetting for a second that it wasn't her own wedding.

"Or I'll happily be here to get you out of it." Liam's hands trailed back down her body.

"Liam..."

He chuckled near her ear, palms roving to her hips, one playfully venturing towards the backside he'd mentioned earlier. Flinching, Liam jerked away from her. "Ow." He whined as he popped his finger into his mouth. "Found a pin, Gendren."

"Serves you right." Dani smirked.

The tailor cleared his throat. "Apologies, and thank you."

Liam stepped around Dani, something metallic jangling on his formal coat. "You going to survive in that until the ceremony? It's about two hours away." Liam took her hand, guiding Dani off the tailor's pedestal.

Dani straightened the necklace Lasseth had given her. "I'll be fine." She smoothed her hands over the skirt, marveling at how soft the material was. "What is this fabric?"

"Silk, miss."

"I've never worn silk before." She touched her waist, where

boning inside the corset held her back straight. "I miss taking deeper breaths."

"Shall I loosen the bodice for you?"

"Please." Dani's body tugged back and forth as the tailor pulled at her laces, giving her more room to breathe. "Thank you."

"Of course. Will that be all for you two? I need to stop at Miss Talansiet's chambers to make sure she is getting along all right."

Dani pursed her lips and motioned with her head for Gendren to lean closer. She kept her voice too low for Liam to hear. "How do I walk in these?"

The heeled shoes required her constant attention to balance in, lacking the comfort of her boots.

Gendren chuckled, whispering back, "Imagine your toe hitting the ground first. Give a little kick with each step, and it will prevent you from stepping on your skirt."

The Dtrüa offered him a sheepish smile. "Thank you."

He patted her upper arm. "Enjoy the celebration, miss." His sewing kits tapped together as he collected them, lifting his pedestal with a brief exhalation.

Liam's hand wrapped around her from behind, his nose grazing lower on her cheek than she was used to because of the height of her shoes. "You do look absolutely wonderful. Fit for a royal wedding."

Dani smiled, facing him. "So you approve of this getup?"

"It's a nice, every-once-in-a-while treat. Though I'll be missing the leathers by the end of the night."

She laughed. "I'm sure I will, too. I shall never understand how women wear these all the time. How do they fight?"

"Katrin shoves her skirts into her belt. Though, I would say most women wearing this getup wouldn't be fighting. I doubt I'd be very effective in my wedding attire." He leaned close, whispering even though they were alone now. "I still stashed a knife in my boot, though."

Dani touched his face. "I'll remember that when I'm undressing you later."

"If I don't use it to cut you out of that corset. And no teasing, or we won't even make it to the ceremony." He ran his hand over her jaw, moving as if he would tuck her hair, even though it was secured at the back of her head with far too many pins.

She shrugged, enjoying the feel of his fingertips. "Would they miss us?"

"Matthias would notice." Liam sounded disappointed. "He's probably already noticed us being a little distant. We've missed dinner the past few days, and for what? We still haven't figured out a plan."

"Time isn't up, yet." Dani kissed him. "Let's try not to think about it and enjoy today. Even if all I'll be able to focus on is walking. Let me hold your arm on the way to the ceremony so I can practice."

The array of smells and sounds of the ceremony left Dani dizzy, and the rest of the evening whirled by in a blur. She struggled to stay centered, blocking out the hundreds of voices and scents bombarding her.

Why must everyone wear perfume?

The procession from the temple back to the palace had provided her the only opportunity for fresh air that day.

Her feet throbbed. "I need to take these off." She whispered the words to Liam, who stood next to her, holding her waist.

"Now?" Liam took her wineglass as she thrust it towards his chest. "We're in the middle of the ballroom. People will see."

"I don't care." Bracing one hand against his shoulder, Dani lifted one foot at a time to unbuckle the straps. "No one can see my feet under this dress, anyway."

He supported her, shifting to help hold her skirt back so she could free herself.

When her bare feet touched the cold floor, she sighed. "That's better." She dropped the shoes, using her foot to tuck them under a table skirt.

Chuckling, Liam nuzzled against the side of her head. "And

you're the correct height again. You holding up all right with all the noise?"

A small orchestra of musicians filled the entire ballroom with the ballads of Isalica, dancers' heels tapping on the marble dance floor. Vapid women's giggles. Boisterous men cheering at each other. Glasses clinking.

Dani cringed. "I'm getting used to it. Just remember that however loud it is for you... it's at least twice that for me."

"Which is why I'm worried." Liam squeezed her waist. "We can step out to the balcony, but now your feet might freeze. They haven't cleared the snow from it yet."

"It's giving me a headache, but I can manage." Dani quieted as the room hushed to the tink of silver against glass.

Voices whispered, murmuring at first before falling silent.

"Thank you all for helping us celebrate such a joyous occasion!" The king's voice rang through the hall, and everyone cheered. "My eldest son has convinced me he should make the toast to the wedded couple this evening, but I can't let him have all the fun. My son, Seiler, and my lovely new daughter, Kelsara, you make a wonderful pair that will lead us all into a time of prosperity. May the gods bless your union and that of our countries. To the prince and princess!"

Dani imagined Geroth lifting his wineglass, and she smiled, retrieving hers from the table to lift it as Liam did the same.

The crowd echoed the king's final proclamation, and she sipped the red wine.

As the crowd settled, Matthias's voice came next. "Thank you, my king. My father has such an eloquent way of wording things, doesn't he?" He paused, a smile in his tone. "See, one perk of being the older brother is I remember our shenanigans in greater detail than my younger sibling. I've never told him this story, but when Seiler was six or seven years old, our mother caught him stealing food from the kitchen. When she asked why, my brother claimed he was hungry. *But you just ate*, she said. But she let it go. At least, Seiler thought she did. The queen watched her son the next day and, instead of confronting him when Seiler once again snuck into the kitchens and pilfered a tray of sandwiches, she followed him. What could a boy his age need an entire tray of sandwiches for?" Matthias paused. "Do you remember?"

"Does he?" Dani whispered to Liam.

Liam leaned close to her ear. "He shook his head."

Matthias continued, "Our mother followed him all the way through the palace to a remote service entrance that she didn't even know about. Outside were at least a dozen children dressed in dirty rags. His age, younger, older. Seiler gave the street orphans the platter of sandwiches and played with them, promising to return the next day. My mother told me this story months later, when I asked why the kitchen now made so many meals to give away. I asked her if Seiler got in trouble... because, I mean, that's what counts, right? But she told me she never admonished him for lying. She never even told him she knew what he was doing. She just left extra platters within his reach and gave him extra clothing when he said he'd lost his shoes. He lied because he wanted to protect others. My selfless little brother fed those children for months before our family could put a new foundation in place to do it for him. I've never met another person with the capacity for compassion like Seiler has. While political marriages start as a bond of countries, they continue as a bond of people. And I can tell you, Princess Kelsara, in no light manner, that my brother will always have your back. Even if our laws all say you are now a Rayeht, Seiler is also a Pendaverin. I wish you both the happiest of marriages and the brightest future for this alliance."

Dani grinned as cheers and shouting rose again, people clapping and demanding the couple's first dance.

The orchestra burst into action, music filling the hall, and the crowd shuffled.

"What's happening?" Dani nudged Liam.

"The married couple is having their first dance... but... It looks like Seiler is forcing Matthias to go with them. The four of them are taking spots on the dance floor."

Dani cringed.

Katrin always wanted to dance with Matthias.

"Where is Katrin?"

Liam paused, leaning away from her. "She was by the center pillar while Matthias was giving his toast, but I don't see her now." He lifted his wineglass, sipping. "Why? You thinking of dancing with her instead of me?"

"No. I'm thinking seeing Matthias dance with someone else might not be fun for her. I should go find her." Dani finished her wine and set the glass on the table.

"Well, I guess that's a no to the dancing, then."

Dani smiled. "I'll come back, and then we can dance. I expect the celebration will last some time." She kissed him on the cheek.

"Want me to come with you?"

"No. Maybe just remind me how many paces the door is away from us." Light sparkled in her vision, but the crowd created a constantly fluctuating blur that kept her from gaining her bearings.

Liam hummed, taking her hand to guide her to the wall. "I'd guess about one hundred or so to the corner. There's a doorway for the staff sooner, though, so don't fall through that. Then another thirty to the left for the main doorway. You think Kat left?"

"Maybe. Probably. I will try to connect with her once I'm out of this chaos." Dani motioned to the table. "Is there an open bottle of wine?"

Liam chuckled as he placed a bottle in her hand. "Good luck."

"Back soon." Dani walked along the wall, counting her paces and skipping the staff doorway as Liam instructed. She rounded the corner to the left, and doors clicked open at her approach.

"Crown Elite Varadani," the guard acknowledged.

She nodded, exiting the room and taking a deeper breath as the noise quieted. Her bare feet hit lush carpet, warming her toes and ceasing the vibrations of the active ballroom. Clicking her tongue, she continued down the hall, closing her eyes. *Kat, you there?*

The sounds of the ballroom grew louder once again as Dani's

vision brightened. She studied the elaborate banister a few feet away, but Katrin's eyes shifted to her pointed shoes. She wiggled them back and forth, rippling the silken hem of red satin skirts. There was a whirl of movement just over the edge of the balcony.

The dancers.

Katrin was somewhere above the ballroom.

Dani hadn't even realized there was a second level, considering it wasn't in use for the wedding celebration.

The acolyte looked at the glass in her hand as she set it on a golden table beside the couch she sprawled on. She picked up a squared decanter full of something amber, and a pungent scent caught her nose. "I'm here." She spoke aloud, allowing Dani to hear her through her own ears. She poured her glass full before lifting it to her lips. "Something wrong?"

Dani slowed her steps, trying to determine where the stairs to the balcony were. *No. But I see the wine I'm bringing may not be necessary.* She breathed deeper, pulling her awareness back to herself. Clicking her tongue, she found a stairwell and ascended to the balcony. Again, someone opened the door at the top for her, and she caught Katrin's scent.

Walking across the carpet, Dani sat with a grunt on the couch Katrin occupied. "I cannot wait to take this corset off."

"Eh, the clothes aren't bothering me." Katrin's feet brushed against Dani's leg. "You look nice. Bet Liam can't take his eyes off you."

Dani took a deep breath, calming her nerves at the renewed noise. "Thank you. I wouldn't know." She smiled, shrugging. "He keeps telling me, though, so I'll assume you're right. Why are you up here? And what are you drinking?"

"I couldn't be down there anymore." The liquid sloshed in Katrin's cup as she tilted it back. She gave a slight hiss as she swallowed. "And I'm not entirely sure, but I'm hoping it helps me forget all this." The glass clinked as she poured more. "Thank you for the wine. I'll need that soon."

The Dtrüa made a face. "It's for me, too."

Katrin chuckled. "All right, you can have some, too. Since you brought your own glass."

Dani touched the tip of the wine bottle and poured for three seconds into her glass before setting the bottle down. "Hiding from the dancers?" She sipped, sitting sideways to put her legs alongside Katrin's.

"Just particular dancers. You get worried or something? I've hardly seen you in the last few weeks."

"Maybe. And I'm sorry about that. I should have set aside more time to spend with you. "

Katrin made a sound with her mouth Dani hadn't heard before. "It's fine. I know you're busy. Crown elite and all. And Liam." She paused. "Maybe you should dance with him."

"I'll dance with him later. I'm sure this will go all night... And you know Matthias is just playing the good host, right?" Dani nudged her with her foot.

Katrin quieted, her nails clicking on the edge of her glass.

Dani tried again. "Have you even talked to him lately?"

Katrin gave a dry laugh. "You mean beyond the basic pleasantries and expected hellos? Or do those count? Is it strange I've talked to Seiler more?"

"Seiler?" Dani tilted her head. "You've spent time with Matthias's brother?"

"He taught me how to shoot a bow." Katrin's glass clinked against the golden table. "And evidently cares far more than Matthias does."

"You mustn't say that." Dani touched Katrin's foot. "Matthias loves you."

"Is that why he's been using his Art to avoid me for a month?" Katrin's voice strained.

"Maybe there's a reason we don't know?" She drank more wine, guilt growing unexpectedly for defending the prince. "Not that it's acceptable, either way. But if it bothers you, tell him."

"How? How do I tell him if I can't even get within three feet of him? I don't even understand why he allowed me to come with you all to Nema's Throne if this is how he's going to be."

Dani fell silent, shoulders slumping. She rubbed her thumb over her wineglass, feeling the etchings.

Katrin sighed. "I'm sorry. I shouldn't be yelling at you. It's not your fault." She picked up her drink again, pausing for another long gulp. "Go dance with Liam or something. I'm going to head back to my chambers and sleep. It sounds far more thrilling than being here right now."

Dani said nothing as Katrin's skirts rustled with her departure. She set down her empty glass a breath later and stood, picking up the bottle.

Maybe dancing will take my mind off everything.

Chapter 24

Matthias sipped his whisky, his mind wandering as Niva talked about something.

Shit. I should be listening.

"Then it curled, and I needed to heat it up to make it lay flat again!" Her tone rose in pitch in her frustration.

Is she talking about parchment?

"But then it didn't match the rest of my outfit, and I had to start all over!"

Her clothing. She's talking about her dress.

"So I went with the purple dress instead, because no matter what I did after that, my hair wouldn't curl again. Too curly, too straight, and then stubborn! Crazy, right?" Niva gestured at him as if he was supposed to contribute now, and he blinked.

"Incredible. Just... ludicrous." Matthias struggled to find words to satisfy her.

At least she couldn't talk while dancing.

"Did you want to join me for another dance?" Matthias offered a hand out to her, but she waved it off.

"Oh, I'm much too tired. I'd rather talk and get to know you better, Prince Alarik."

Nymaera, save me.

He tried not to cringe at the use of his given name. He'd tried and failed to convince her to call him Matthias.

"All right. Have you traveled anywhere interesting lately?" The prince forced the smile back onto his face, hoping for something more stimulating than stories about her hair.

"Traveled? Gods, no. I find the lack of proper accommodations along the road less than acceptable. Far better to stay right here in Nema's Throne, where I can enjoy consistency. I'm sure you missed it horribly while you were at the border." Niva frowned. "I can't even imagine how dreadful that must have been for you."

A vision of the wyvern's claws tearing Riez into the sky, then Barim and Stefan falling beneath another's tail, flashed in a blink. "Difficult is hardly an accurate word."

"What did you even sleep on? In those tents..." She gasped as a thought coalesced in her mind. "And bathing..."

Clenching his jaw, Matthias resisted the urge to tell her how those were the least of his worries. How he'd lost men and people he cared for. How he still had nightmares about the wyverns. The blood.

But being with Katrin made my time at the border so much more bearable.

The prince took a steadying breath. "I apologize. I promised my father I would check on the wedding arrangements from time to time, and I must ensure the cake will be presented soon. Please excuse me." He ducked away before she could offer to join him, weaving through the crowds. Rubbing his temple, he reached the main doors, and the guards opened them with a salute.

"Enjoying the festivities, your majesty?"

"Of course. A joyous day." Matthias forced a smile and exited, letting his shoulders relax as he strode down a hallway. Near the corner where the stairs to the ballroom balcony began, he paused and set down his glass of whisky.

When he looked up, someone walked straight into him.

She gasped, stumbling, and he caught her by the elbows.

"Katrin." Matthias met her eyes and let go, stepping back. He instinctively reached for his Art, willing it into his veins so he could take a different path.

"Stop." Katrin pointed at him. "Don't you dare jump. I know you've been doing it every other time, but please." Her voice weakened before she hardened her face with a frown. "Don't do it now."

Matthias held his hands up, nodding once and letting go of his power. "All right. Not jumping."

Most of his previous jumps had reasons beyond his discomfort at seeing her. Either his brother accompanied him, or he'd been in a foul mood. While he had no excuse this time, the habit had lingered.

"Promise me you won't. Or I'm going to make you walk around these halls with me for fifteen minutes to ensure you can't avoid me this time." Katrin's cheeks were rosy, the vague scent of whisky on her breath.

Clearly I haven't been as subtle as I thought.

He ground his teeth, but nodded again. "I promise, I won't." He studied her, admiring the intricate braids in her onyx hair and the way her red dress hugged her figure. Swallowing, he met her gaze again. "Are you angry with me?"

"Angry?" Katrin glanced over his shoulder at the hallway.

Two guards stood stoically outside the ballroom doors, and Katrin lowered her voice.

"Matthias, I'm furious. But now that I'm finally talking to you, all I feel is relief." She ran a hand up to touch her hair before lowering it with a sigh. Her features hardened again. "Are you enjoying the celebration? That woman you're escorting... she's... *lovely.*"

He resisted the temptation to admire the acolyte and the lithe shape of her small frame. The deep red corset complemented her, the low wavy collar exposing the softness of her chest. More revealing than anything he'd seen her in before.

"I'm happy for Seiler. I think he and the princess make a fine couple." Matthias narrowed his eyes at her, trying to understand why she would mention Niva.

Katrin's eyebrow rose a little, as if acknowledging his avoidance. "A perfect wedding indeed. The ceremony at the temple was..." She closed her eyes briefly, taking in a deep breath. "Inspiring. It makes me miss it."

Something tightened in his chest. "Are you returning to the temples?"

"I... might." Katrin played with the seam on the side of her dress. "I've been thinking about it. The truth of the matter is I don't have anywhere else to go."

Matthias's heart sank. He wanted to tell her she'd always have somewhere to go, but she'd made it clear at her family's home that she didn't see a future with him.

"That story you told about Seiler." Katrin balled her hands together in front of her as if unsure what to do with them. "That was a nice story. He's a good man, and your mother was clearly a noble woman. I still wish I could have met her."

Warmth echoed through Matthias's body. "She loved weddings, always the life of the party. I know my brother comes off as a jester sometimes, but he cares a lot more than he lets on."

"I've noticed." Katrin's lips twitched in a smile, but she chewed her lip for a moment as she met his eyes. She hesitated. "Thank you... for not jumping." She stepped forward, reaching for his arm, but recoiled. Nodding to herself, she gathered her hands in front of her again. "I hope you have a wonderful evening, Matthias." She moved, stepping around him, but he caught her upper arm.

"Wait." Matthias let go, studying her face. "It hasn't been fifteen minutes, yet."

Katrin smiled, and it lit up her face for the first time in a month. "But I still remember, so that's a good sign for at least a little while longer. Perhaps I should start counting those minutes now, instead, so I know I haven't forgotten anything." Her gaze moved down, and her hand grazed his fingers. "Walk with me?"

Matthias glanced at the large doors to the ballroom and took her hand. "Somewhere in mind, Priestess?"

She closed her eyes again for a moment, swallowing as she shook her head. "You know this place better than me. But maybe somewhere with snow?"

He smiled, remembering how he'd asked for snow the day they'd met. Motioning with his head, he led her the way he'd been going, through a few turns before coming to the inner courtyard.

A closet next to the doors held thick winter cloaks for anyone who needed to go outside.

Matthias released Katrin's hand and opened the closet. Selecting a lush grey cloak, he draped it over her shoulders. He buckled the front for her before retrieving one for himself.

Katrin smiled when he faced her again, and she backed towards the door, her hand blindly finding the handle behind her. "Oddly familiar, don't you think?" She opened the door, a chill creeping in with the perfect silence of snowfall.

A frozen fountain stood at the center of the courtyard, barren maples shaped around the inner circle of tiled pathways. They'd been cleared some time earlier in the evening, but now had a thin layer of the fresh snow on top.

Katrin stepped outside, thick flakes landing on her dark hair. She looked up at the sky, white specs catching on her lashes as she closed her eyes and breathed.

Gods, she's gorgeous.

Matthias clenched his jaw as he stepped outside, feeling the agony of her refusal yet again.

I can't do this.

He hardened his emotions. "I told Niva I'd be right back. I—"

"What?" Katrin's eyes blazed as they opened and met his. "Niva? We only just got here? What happened to fifteen minutes?"

The prince looked behind him, his veins heating with potential. "I shouldn't be here, this isn't..."

"So you want to go back to Niva? So why even lead me on just now? Give me hope and then strip it away. For Niva?" The same fire from their first encounter lit her eyes. Katrin tugged her cloak tighter around her. "Of all the women you could possibly escort... you chose her?"

"What is that supposed to mean?" Matthias's mind whirled to keep up.

Why would she seek hope when she just wants to be friends?

"Oh, come on. I spoke with her for two minutes a few weeks ago, and I could look in one ear and see the open sky on the other side. She's completely vapid and lacks any actual personality."

Matthias huffed. "Exactly. That's exactly why I chose her."

"Do you know how insulting that is?" Katrin's voice grew louder.

"Insulting?" The prince paused. "How is it insulting?"

Katrin rolled her eyes, lifting her hood over her head. "How is it not insulting? Is that really what attracts you, then? Women like that?"

"Her? No. What?" Matthias shook his head, raising his voice unintentionally as he closed the door to the hallway behind him. The silence of the snow encapsulated everything for a moment while he stared at her. "Katrin, I chose her because I couldn't choose the person I *wanted* to go with. Being with her is perfect, because nothing she does can *ever* remind me of you."

Katrin paused, her chest rising with rapid breaths. "Why couldn't you choose me?"

Matthias threw his hands up into the air. "Because you said no!" He lowered his hands, bowing his head as the unwritten marriage proposal and kiss flooded through him again. "I couldn't choose you because you said no."

"I said no?" Katrin's brow furrowed. "What did I say no to? I agreed to come to Nema's Throne with you. I–"

"You only wanted to come to Nema's Throne because you didn't remember our conversation," Matthias murmured, staring at the tiled rocks forming the courtyard path before looking at her.

Katrin straightened, her eyes widening. She pursed her lips as the anger in her eyes grew. Her voice became quiet, like the falling snow. "What conversation?"

"When I gave you the bracelet. It went differently the first time." The admission sparked anxiety in Matthias's gut, but he didn't dare jump back.

This needs to happen. She deserves to know.

"You can't just do that, Matthias." Katrin's disappointment oozed in her words. "You can't have a conversation and then take it back with your Art. That's not fair. You gave me no opportunity to even try to make things right again because I didn't even know what I did wrong! You end up suffering alone, and do you know how hypocritical that is with how angry you got with me?"

"I know." The prince let out a breath. "But I was hurt and angry, and I felt like if you could keep me in the dark, then I could, too. But I couldn't..." His throat tightened, and he looked away, running a hand over his face.

Katrin paused for several breaths, her tone softening. "What did I say no to?"

Matthias faced her, gesturing with his hand. "To being my wife. You said no to marrying me."

Chapter 25

Katrin's entire body numbed. She struggled to remember how to breathe as she stared at Matthias, the snow sticking to his deep brown hair. Stared at the hurt in his eyes. The pain.

"Matthias." She sucked in a frozen breath. "You..." Looking down, she tried to compose her thoughts before she lifted her hand and sternly met his gaze. "Don't you dare jump. Just give me a moment."

Matthias shook his head in a slow, defeated motion. "I won't jump. You deserve to know."

Katrin refrained from lashing at him, the liquor still humming in her veins calmed by the chill winter air. She stared at the decorative tiles at her feet, her footprints exposing the fine paint job on each one. Thumbing the bracelet on her wrist beneath her cloak, she tried to remember the exact order of conversations from a month ago. Trying to place what was going through her mind at the time.

That was before I spoke with Lind.

The conversation with her sister had been a turning point. Knowing she was not necessarily destined to be barren. To never give a future king children. To doom a kingdom with no successors. She'd learned so much more just by being in the palace. By talking to Seiler, and reading more of Isalica's proud history.

Steadying herself, Katrin met Matthias's eyes, losing herself in the swells of sea within them. In imagining his lips against hers again.

She lifted her chin. "Ask me again."

Matthias's jaw flexed. "Pardon?"

"Ask me again." She took a step forward but controlled the inclination to reach for him. "To be your wife. Ask me again." Her heart pounded.

The prince approached her, eyes darting between hers. "I never stopped loving you. Through any of it."

Katrin's lips twitched, and her hands moved from beneath her cloak, touching the fine buttons of his coat. "Me, neither."

Matthias touched her chin. "It's always been you, and it will always be you. I don't want to celebrate the joys of this life nor suffer the losses with anyone else. I know you have reservations about who I am, but I promise you. Beneath everything else, I am simply yours." His touch left her face, trailing down her arm as he knelt in the snow. "Marry me?"

Katrin's breath suspended in her lungs as she saw the prince kneel before her. She stepped into him, running her hand over the side of his head. "Yes," she breathed the word as she squeezed his hand. "Yes, Matthias. I'll marry you. *Without* reservation." She lifted his chin as she leaned into him, taking his mouth against hers. The feel of his lips warmed her, banishing the snow's chill on their faces.

The prince stood with the kiss, wrapping his arms around her, and pulled her tight against him.

His hold made the rest of the world blur.

She renewed the kiss as she pushed against him, slipping her arms beneath his cloak to wrap around his neck, lifting herself to her tiptoes.

Matthias broke the kiss just enough to speak. "I love you, Priestess."

Katrin laughed against his mouth, their cold noses touching. "And I love you, Prince." She kissed him again, tasting his lower lip.

"Will you come inside and dance with me?" He trailed the tip of his nose down her cheek, kissing her jaw.

Her stomach flipped. "In front of everyone?"

"In front of everyone."

Katrin grinned at her own wickedness. "Won't Niva be jealous?"

"I'll happily talk to Niva... for the last time." He nipped her neck, squeezing her waist and making her jump. "Please?"

"How can I say no when you ask so nicely?" Katrin tilted her head for him as her heart thundered at the thought. "I'd love to dance with you. Though we should go now before I get other ideas."

Matthias pulled back from her, his eyes bright as he took her hand. "Come." He tugged her to the door, opening it. "Your other ideas can wait."

The feel of his hand in hers made her whole body tingle, the smile on her face uncontainable. Hardly able to take her eyes from him, she unfastened her cloak, abandoning it next to his on the floor of the closet. He seemed just as unwilling to let go of her to bother hanging them again.

I was such a fool.

Laughter rang through the hall, drawing the prince's gaze. His younger brother rounded the corner, his joyous bride in tow. The princess of Ziona's bronze complexion made her emerald eyes sparkle in the vibrant lights of the hall. Her coppery hair hung in relaxed curls over her shoulders and the hem of her royal blue wedding gown.

Katrin bowed her head, but met Seiler's curious eyes as they roved down to Matthias's hand in hers.

His grin widened. "What is this? A happy reconciliation, perhaps in part due to a meddling brother?"

"Not too much meddling." Katrin touched Matthias on his bicep.

"Definitely too much meddling." Matthias squeezed her hand, but his expression didn't falter. "Why aren't you dancing?"

"Took a break to get... some air." Seiler wiggled his eyebrows, backing down the hall towards the ballroom.

"We're just returning. Are you joining us?" Princess Kelsara resisted her husband's pull, looking at Katrin. "You must be Katrin. And I'd love to speak with you more."

Katrin's stomach jumped, unsure how to interpret the princess not only knowing her name, but to suggest even speaking. She bowed her head again. "I am. I'm sorry we haven't met yet, Princess. Though you've been rather busy the past few weeks, understandably."

Seiler huffed, giving up on dragging the woman to whisper to his brother.

"I'm Kelsara." The Zionan princess held her hand out to Katrin, smiling. "Having you at these family events will be wonderful! Sometimes we desperately need more intellectual conversation."

Katrin accepted Kelsara's hand, returning the princess's firm shake. "Don't tease me with such promises. Intellectual conversation? I assume we are leaving the men out of it, then." She cast a playful glance to the princes.

Matthias snorted. "I don't think we're exactly who she's referring to, but I appreciate your inference."

"Loryena could have chosen you a better escort." Seiler made a face.

"It's hardly her fault." Matthias motioned with his head. "Come with me while I let her down gently. Give the women a moment to gossip about us." He gave Katrin a look before letting go of her hand to continue to the ballroom with his brother.

Her hand flexed on its own accord, missing the pressure of his.

Kelsara watched them go before meeting Katrin's gaze again, her big eyes glittering. "Oh, I'm so happy you two are something again. You're all Matthias talks about. And Seiler mentioned you were quite the natural with a bow."

Katrin's face heated. "Seiler was kind enough to teach me, but forgive me... Matthias spoke to you about me?"

The princess nodded. "How instrumental you've been with whatever you're working on. He said he couldn't believe you'd come to Nema's Throne, but he always sounded so sad underneath it. I don't know why, but it seems perhaps you've worked it out?"

She chewed her lip, quickly reminding herself it would be unbecoming of the woman she had to be now. Both as one speaking to Princess Kelsara and as the one on Matthias's arm. Her stomach roiled again at the thought. All those people in the ballroom who would see her and whisper about her.

I came to terms with this before, I can do it again. It will be worth it... to be with him.

"I was reading Frolisian's paper on family bonds, and while I haven't got my sisters with me here in Isalica, I'd love to have another." Kelsara gave her a tentative smile, tilting her head. "Unless I'm reading too much into your relationship with the prince?"

Katrin's heart jumped into her throat. "I'm familiar with the text. I found it to be very enlightening to much of my own upbringing, and heartily agree. It's nice that even in times of war, our families can continue to grow." She thought of Matthias on his knee in front of her in the snowy courtyard, her soul alight. "And I would very much enjoy having you as a sister, Kelsara." It felt odd to leave off the formal title, but she'd have to get used to it. "You are obviously just as observant as your new husband."

The princess smirked, lowering her voice. "There were still some specks of snow on his knee."

"I'm just relieved he finally stopped avoiding me." Katrin looked at the doorway to the ballroom, contemplating all those eyes. "Do you ever get used to it? All the attention?" Her stomach coiled again. "Oh gods, do you think the king will support a union like ours?"

Kelsara offered Katrin her arm to walk together to the ballroom. "King Rayeht is a reasonable man. I can't see why not. And you get used to the attention, but you don't have to endure it all the time. There are perks to being a princess, like demanding solitude when all you want to do is read or train."

Katrin laced her arm through the princess's. "Solitude is an absolute necessity, and I suppose you're right with that. Though, ordering will take some getting used to, as well." As her arm touched Kelsara's, she noted the firmness of the princess's muscle beneath the sleeve of her dress, encouraging Katrin to focus on the other implication. "Do you train often, then?"

"A few times a week." Kelsara smiled. "I am Zionan. My ancestors would never forgive me if I didn't maintain my battle readiness."

Katrin felt foolish for forgetting the details of Zionan tradition, including the position of women among their military. Men took on the traditional homemaking roles rather than their female counterparts, and Katrin imagined what the country was really like. "Would you teach me? Some of the Zionan battle stances? Matthias and my brother, Liam, have tried to train me how to fight, but I find their techniques... counterintuitive for me."

"Of course!" Kelsara beamed. "Most of the women I've encountered here seem to have little interest, but I'd be honored."

"Isalica must be very different from your homeland, and I can only imagine what it is like for you to be here, now."

Guards opened the ballroom doors for the women to enter.

"I will adapt." Kelsara touched Katrin's forearm. "And so will you. It was a pleasure speaking with you. I must return to the wedding events, but let's talk again soon."

Katrin nodded. "Of course." She slipped her hand from Kelsara, giving her a bright smile as she walked into the ballroom.

Dancers still swirled just beyond, and Katrin surveyed the room to find anyone else to gravitate towards. Running her hands over the tight bodice of her dress to straighten it, she glimpsed her assigned escort, his dirty blond hair falling loose from where it'd been slicked back. He sat on the edge of an embroidered couch, his round face twisted in excitement as he conversed with a woman beside him.

Niva.

The blond woman gave poor Gaimun a bored smile. Her gaze drifted from him as he continued to talk, roving over the crowd before landing on Katrin. Niva straightened, jaw clenching as she glared.

Guess Matthias already told her.

Katrin averted her gaze, looking to the opposite side by the banquet tables, still spread near the far wall with various desserts and snacks. She caught the glimmer of chandelier light on Dani's white hair behind the tables, where she moved with Liam in the open floor space.

Liam had one arm wrapped around Dani's waist, encouraging her to take the steps of the traditional waltz the orchestra played, a broad smile on his face. Dani's lips were pursed in concentration, but a smile lingered in her cloudy eyes.

I suppose Isalican dances are not standard education for the Dtrüa of Feyor.

Katrin wove through the crowds, apologizing each time she had to squeeze through. Emerging near the banquet table, she admired the perfect smile on her brother's face, trying to recall the few times she'd seen it.

With a steady breath, Katrin savored the sweet scent of pastries as she drew her power into her veins, projecting a thought towards Dani.

You should see how ridiculous his grin is right now.

Liam hadn't noticed her, even as she stepped to the end of the tables, only ten feet away.

Would you like to?

Dani closed her eyes. "Yes."

"What?" Liam slowed a little. "Yes?"

"Nothing, just keep dancing with me," Dani whispered, touching his cheek.

Katrin's brother didn't argue, returning to the movement, carefully guiding her back and forth before moving her into a gentle spin beneath his arm and then closer to his body.

Accepting Dani as a temporary visitor, Katrin drew on her friend's power, inviting it in. It tingled at the back of her eyes as she blinked, sensing the moment the Dtrüa joined her. She looked at her brother again, happy to allow her friend to see the warm smile still on his lips that reached his dark eyes.

Dani beamed, her thumb trailing over his jaw.

"He loves you so much," Katrin whispered, knowing Dani would hear. "Who'd have thought with how this all started."

The Dtrüa's voice echoed in her mind. *He's all I ever want.* She paused. *You sound like you're in a better mood.*

"Will you just look at your betrothed's face?" Katrin teased. "Don't worry about me. But yes, I'm better."

Oh, I'm looking. I love seeing his face. But I know you saw Matthias. His scent and yours led away from the ballroom together.

Liam stepped closer to Dani, oblivious to the silent conversation as he nuzzled against the side of her head, brushing his cheek against her temple. His eyes closed, hands grazing over her body.

"It can wait." Katrin forced herself to keep looking, even if a slight heat rose in her cheeks at feeling she was invading their privacy. The lingering smile on Liam's face continued as he whispered something in Dani's ear that Katrin couldn't hear.

Dani kissed Liam, disconnecting from Katrin as she whispered back to him. A breath later, her eyes found Katrin. Lacing her arms further over Liam's shoulders, she tilted her head at her friend. "Tell me."

Liam pulled back from her slightly. "I did just tell you." He looked over his shoulder to see Katrin, his eyes widening a little. "Oh, hey Katy girl, how long you been... standing there?" He looked suspicious, glancing at Dani as if realizing what must have been happening. Smirking, he nuzzled against the side of her head again, whispering something else in his lover's ear.

Katrin smiled at him as she approached, rolling her eyes vaguely at Dani. "In my defense, brother, I tried to tell her we could talk about it later."

"Talk about what?" Liam glanced up and down her. "I almost didn't recognize you at the ceremony and procession, all dressed up like that. You look beautiful, Kat."

"And you clean up quite well, yourself." She flicked his collar playfully, running a hand down to straighten the medals adorning the right side of his chest. "I'm sorry I've been rather... distracted tonight."

"She talked to Matthias." Dani leaned into Liam. "Alone."

"About damn time." Liam sighed, but his eyes looked worried as he met hers. "How'd it go?"

Katrin sucked in breath, trying to think of where to start. "Fine. Better than fine." She glanced around to ensure they were far from other potentially listening guests. "I think we both finally figured out just how silly we were being."

"And?" Dani smacked Liam's shoulder, even if her question was directed at Katrin. "What happened? Are you two together again?"

Katrin's heart pounded. "He asked me to marry him."

Dani squealed. "Tell me you said yes!"

Katrin couldn't help but grin as her brother's mouth opened in surprise. "I said yes."

Leaping from Liam's arms, the Dtrüa all but tackled Katrin, wrapping her arms around her. "Finally!"

Katrin caught her friend's hug, happily returning it as she watched her brother's face. "You're going to catch a fly, brother."

Liam snapped his mouth shut, shaking his head as he smiled. "Unexpected, but..." He stepped in, wrapping his arms around both of them as he kissed the top of Katrin's head. "My little sister, officially the future queen of Isalica."

Katrin's chest tightened, everything suddenly whirling around her. "Let's not talk about that, yet."

"Kat." Matthias's voice came from behind her, and Dani let go. "I..." He looked over the other two, narrowing his eyes at them before focusing on the acolyte. "I'm sorry. I tried to talk him out of it."

Katrin met Matthias's eyes, trying to read the worried expression on his face. "Talk who out of what?"

Metal clinked against glass, quieting the crowd and orchestra.

Her eyes widened as a sinking feeling filled her. She peered through the tiers of food decorating the table between them and the main floor of the ballroom, trying to spy who had stopped the celebration.

Seiler stood with Kelsara at the raised platform where Matthias had given his speech. "I apologize for the interruption." He grinned through each word. "It will be brief, I promise."

"Oh, gods." Katrin breathed, trying to stop the room from spinning more than it already was. She stepped into Matthias, grabbing his arm before she could question who might see, and leaned against him. "You told Seiler, didn't you?"

"He was rather persistent." Matthias tugged her hand. "You want to make a run for it? I wouldn't blame you." His eyes danced over hers, telling her that although he made the offer in jest, he'd go if she wanted to.

Katrin breathed and shook her head. "I want to dance." She squeezed him harder, hoping he understood she needed it to stay standing upright. "I think we need to move somewhere more visible, though, if this is really happening."

"Thinking like a queen already." Matthias smiled, pulling her hand to maneuver slowly through the crowd towards the dance floor as her stomach did another flip.

Queen.

"I have an announcement to make, as this day has a reason for more celebration. And no, I'm not speaking of the birthday we've all ignored." Seiler's gaze tracked them through the crowd.

People parted, making space for the crown prince and Katrin.

"Birthday?" Katrin breathed, encouraging her eyes to Matthias instead of the crowd already gaping at them.

"Tomorrow. Mine. Not important," Matthias whispered.

She pinched him. "Not important?" She tried to frown, but the nerves in her stomach prohibited her from anything but a straight face, trained into her through years of service in the temples. Emotion had to be disguised while healing, and she desperately hoped all of that would help now, too.

Seiler cleared his throat. "I'd like to be the first to offer a hearty congratulations to my brother, Crown Prince Matthias Rayeht, on his engagement to Katrin Talansiet."

The room burst into sudden applause. All attention turned to them, like a crashing wave on the beach, and Katrin would have stumbled if it weren't for Matthias's steady grip.

"At least he didn't call me Alarik," Matthias muttered.

The wedding guests parted for the couple as they made their way towards the empty center of the room.

"Are you fully abandoning the name Alarik, then?" She focused on his face, allowing all others to blur at the edges of her vision.

"As much as I can. I've always preferred my middle name." Matthias guided her in front of him as they came to a stop on the dance floor, and Katrin's entire body felt like it was on fire.

"Now is probably a bad time to say I don't remember many of my dance lessons from the temple," Katrin whispered as they faced each other. Their hands parted, and she suddenly felt too exposed with her back to cheering nobles and guests.

"Don't worry, just follow my lead."

"The Lover's Waltz, please, Maestro. For my love struck brother." Seiler stepped away from the podium, disappearing among the sea of people.

Katrin lifted her eyebrows to Matthias, a smile twitching the edges of her lips as she heard the twang of the orchestra begin. She curtsied, lifting the silky fabric of her skirts.

Several dancers joined them, including Seiler and Kelsara.

"I hope you weren't planning on backing out." Matthias smirked. "Because now it's too late. Unless you'd like me to jump, of course."

"Don't you dare." Katrin's eyes blazed as he bowed with the inclination of the music, making her heart leap. "But you better make sure I don't fall. If I do, you have my permission to jump and fix it."

"You won't fall." Matthias straightened and lifted his hand to press their palms together as the rhythm of the dance started.

Sparks flew between their skin, and she forced a steadying breath.

Don't look at the crowd.

She let herself fall into Matthias's sea-blue eyes, relieved that the Lover's Waltz didn't require any switching of partners. And Matthias did exactly as promised, gently guiding each step of her feet that felt entirely natural with him. Each slow and steady movement left her throat tight and body thrumming for the next. The pressure of the surrounding guests remained, somehow making each moment more powerful as they watched, as they saw them move together in harmony.

Halfway through the song, a different deep voice came behind her. "May I cut in?"

"Of course." Matthias spun Katrin and let go of her hand.

King Rayeht caught it. "I hope you don't mind that I steal half a dance with my future daughter." Matthias's father continued the steps of the dance, leading her just as confidently as his son.

"Your majesty." Katrin forgot to breathe as she met the king's eyes, bowing her head and nearly missing a step before the king smoothly guided her through it. "Of... of course not."

Please don't faint, please don't faint.

"Breathe, child." Geroth's hand kept a firm grip on hers. "Relax. You've already won the room."

At his encouragement, Katrin brought in a breath through her nose, allowing the moment she stood extended from the king's arm to steady herself. Her brow furrowed before her training relaxed it a second later. "I what?"

"You don't have to look. Crowds are easy, and you're a natural. They love my son, and that love has already passed to you."

The inclination to glance at the crowd passed through her, stomach churning as she remembered how many would be watching. As her head turned, she only glimpsed Matthias standing at the edge of the dance floor, watching her and his father. She focused on the serenity of his face, the happiness of his smile as someone she didn't recognize held a hand of congratulations out to him.

This is really happening.

Katrin turned back to the king, quickly reorienting on their movements together. "Thank you," she whispered to him. "I'm terribly sorry for the surprise announcement."

Geroth laughed, so similar to his son. "You have nothing to be sorry for. Both of my sons are happy. What more does a father wish for?" He spun her once before bringing her back. "You are a fine addition to the family."

"I had worried I'd ruin the potential of another political alliance. I don't wish to, especially now."

"Nonsense. Nothing makes a better ruler than love." The king nodded at her. "And Matthias has impeccable taste."

Katrin smiled, remembering when the king had said the same about Matthias's choice of Dani and Liam for crown elites.

"Do I get her back now?" Matthias appeared next to them, and his father chuckled.

"I suppose I can't take all her time." Geroth released Katrin and touched her shoulder. "Congratulations to you both."

Katrin bowed her head again in subtle thank you as her sight returned to Matthias.

"You all right?" The prince kept his voice low, taking her hands to finish the dance with her.

"Yes." She beamed, knowing she meant it. "But I'll be even better when I wake tomorrow and find none of this to have been a dream."

The morning light cascaded through the window in the bathing chambers, warming Katrin's exposed back.

The Art laden pipes gurgled beneath the bath's surface, the refreshing rose oils dancing along the wisps of steam.

The crown prince's chambers boasted a far more luxurious bathing area than her own, the crescent-shaped tub inset into the floor with painted tiles. Peeking at the ajar doorway to the prince's bedroom, she smirked at the mangled bed. The sheets lay half stripped to the ground, the pillows strewn at both ends. It'd turned into a morning of thorough spoiling for both of them.

Flashes of the heat between them prickled her skin.

Her breathing quickened.

His mouth had been warm on her skin, and her cries of pleasure still echoed about the room in toe-curling memory.

She'd tried to exit the bed and fetch them food when Matthias had tugged her back by her waist for more sweet kisses. Before she could recover, he slipped away to find breakfast for them. And further spoiled her by starting the bath water before he went.

Katrin slid through the water to the bench seat beneath the surface, pressing her naked body against the edge to unravel the leather binding of her book. It scraped along the ceramic tiles, and she swiped her fingers on a loose towel before thumbing open the gold-leafed pages.

A door clicked open from the sitting room beyond the bedchamber as someone entered, shutting it behind them.

Matthias balanced a tray in one hand as he entered and relocked the bedroom door. He smiled as he eyed her, carrying the tray of pastries and fruit into the bathing area. "A little light reading in the bath?"

"Knowledge doesn't wait for me to be clean." She gazed at the food, her stomach growling again before she abandoned the book. Humming, she moved to the shallow steps of the tub and wiggled a finger of invitation at him. "Join me? But bring that tray closer, first."

Matthias set down the food at the tub's edge. "What are you reading?" He strode away, pulling his tunic over his head as he walked. The muscles in his back flexed as he unfastened his belt, looking at her as he draped his breeches over a chair by a nearby mirror.

Watching him, Katrin didn't hide her wandering gaze, her body heating beneath the water despite the already active morning. Her tongue flicked over her lower lip as she tried to remember what he'd asked. "Hm?"

The prince chuckled, shamelessly striding to her and stepping into the water. "The book, Priestess. What are you *reading?*"

"Oh." Her neck felt impossibly hot as she reached back and lifted her hair, twisting the knot tighter. "Licanthry's Compendium. It has some interesting references to Isalican geography and ecology. I thought it might..." She paused, looking back at the massive volume and turning her back to the ever-distracting man. "Hold some clues to where the dragons might be."

Matthias's rough hands touched her shoulders, thumbs gently massaging. "Such an impressive work ethic," he murmured near her ear, his deep voice sending a shiver down her spine.

Moaning softly, she leaned back into his touch. Her fingers brushed his hip beneath the water. "You're not exactly inspiring me to continue to be studious." Her head tilted as his mouth caressed her neck, and her entire being thrummed. "You're only further proving how distracting you can be. First, you lure me away from the temple..."

"Lure you..." Matthias growled into her skin. "Not exactly how I remember it."

The steam roiled between them, slicking his skin as he pressed against her back.

"Then you seduce me in Undertown. In a setting similar to this, though, I admit... this bath is *far* nicer. There are certainly perks to being with a prince."

"You don't yet know the half of it." He nipped her skin before looking over her shoulder at the book's pages. "Have you enjoyed the library here?"

The familiar rush of excitement she'd felt when first entering the palace's private library mingled with her lust. "It's amazing. More than I imagined. I'm glad Liam suggested I join you all here." She ran her wet hand up into his hair, encouraging his lips closer to her skin. "And I'm grateful for other things, too."

She'd expected the wedding to be bearable, aided by the whisky she'd smuggled from the drink table. But it'd taken a sharp turn the moment Matthias finally stopped avoiding her. Her heart sped with the vision of him kneeling before her in the snow, and she tangled her fingers with his against her bare abdomen.

"Last night still feels like a dream," she whispered, nuzzling against his steam dampened beard. "This morning, too."

"I'm sorry it took me so long to find my way back to you." The prince pressed another kiss to her neck, but it held a heaviness of emotions rather than just his desire. "I was an idiot for jumping so much."

She touched the thick locks of his hair, turning slowly in his grasp. Looking up at his stormy eyes, she ran her fingers over his temples. "I was the idiot first." The hollow that lingered in her gut swelled before the sight of him banished it. Grasping the sides of his face, she placed a soft kiss on his lips. "Thank you for forgiving me. I hardly feel I deserve it and everything else you've offered me."

"No second thoughts?" A hint of worry plagued his tone, even as he tried to hide it with a smirk.

She smiled and shook her head. "Plenty, but none of them have to do with saying yes to you."

His smirk broadened. "You regret meeting my brother, don't you? I knew I should have kept you two apart longer."

Laughing, she pinched his shoulder. "No, I'm annoyed you kept him from me for so long, and I'm grateful Seiler is clearly persistent. He helped me a great deal, more than I'm sure he even realizes."

Matthias hummed and kissed her. "Perhaps I should have gotten him a better wedding gift, then."

She smiled as she kissed him again, teeth grazing his lower lip. "What'd you get him?"

"A winter estate just outside of Silanus." He grinned.

Katrin gaped.

Silanus, the southernmost city in Isalica, served as a popular destination among the country's northern residents. Sought after for its vineyards and tepid winters, the ocean view port town was a place she'd always wished to visit.

"I'm almost afraid to ask what you'd consider *better*."

A fiendish expression overtook the prince's face as he shrugged. "A bigger estate."

Katrin shook her head and chuckled, strands of hair falling loose from her knot. Trailing her fingers along Matthias's collarbone, she realized she actually might visit such a place, now.

As a princess, once we're wed.

Matthias tilted his head, eyes flickering between hers. "Something troubling you?"

"Not... troubling." Katrin looked up at him again, savoring just touching him. "It's just still strange to consider where things are. It feels like only yesterday I learned you were a prince. *The* prince."

"And you're just now remembering all the names you called me when you thought I was a guard?" He smiled. "What words did you use... over compensating?"

"Oh, hush." Katrin shoved playfully at his chest. "You deserved it, clearly, considering how you'd fooled me. Made me fall in love with you before the truth could scare me away."

Matthias laughed. "I did something right, then, it seems." He gripped her waist and pushed her closer to the side of the tub, sloshing water over the rim. "Shit, your book."

Gasping, Katrin spun, plucking the book off the soaked tiles. She grasped the towel, throwing the delicate leather spine onto it. "Oh, no," she breathed as she watched specks of water soak into the open pages. Leaning down, she blew across the parchment, hoping to help dry the liquid before it jeopardized the writing.

The pages rippled with her breath, furling and turning with each renewed gust. She caught several words as they passed through her vision, along with the pictographs of Isalican beasts. One sentence caught her eye.

> ...*the great temperature fluctuations at this location...*

Katrin straightened, her heart pounding as she slammed her hand down to stop the flickering pages. Pulling the towel and book closer, she lifted herself from the water as she hastily turned the pages back to the passage.

> ...*at this location provided an ideal climate for hatchlings. The drakes, while resilient to less perfect conditions, often favored this volcanic geography. Like spawning salmon, they came back year after year until their numbers decreased. Theories of the exact location cloud the academies, assuming lava pools exist near the top of the mountains. See fig. 376 for map reference. Scholar confirmation has never been acquired, but even without the drakes*

> *still using the location, evidence of their breeding*
> *should remain for some time.*

Her pulse pounded in her fingertips as she turned the page, scouring for the map.

"What is it?" Matthias leaned over the edge of the tub, trying to catch her gaze.

Her mouth felt dry as kernels of her research from various texts bubbled into her memory.

> *The dragon's numbers dwindled due to less ideal*
> *breeding ground.*
> *Eggs, with their rocky membrane, require intense*
> *heat.*
> *Spiritual guidance is required to locate the dragon's*
> *lost temple of magma.*
> *The last known dragon remains were in the ice*
> *fields near the tallest peak. It was believed to be*
> *protecting its young.*

Katrin's finger trailed over the detailed map of the Yandarin Mountains, pausing at the second highest peak where a symbol dictated the referenced text passage she'd just read.

"Katrin?" Matthias pressed again, touching her chin. "Tell me."

She was certain the ice fields were near the marker on the map. Near the lava pools, which created the only known environment that'd ever supported what the dragons needed.

"I know where they are." Katrin's breath caught. She turned to Matthias, splashing water over the edge of the tub, but she ignored it as it sank into the pages again. She touched the prince's chest, meeting his confused gaze. "I know where the dragons are."

Chapter 26

Liam's foot tapped a steady rhythm on the tile floor beneath the breakfast table, and he rubbed his knee to make it stop. The jam on his toast wouldn't spread properly, and he grumbled as he added more, his foot starting up again.

He sensed Dani's attention on him. They'd taken their usual spot towards the end of the table, leaving space between them and the various royal advisors, also taking their morning meal.

Matthias was nowhere to be seen, which was unusual for him. Liam had grown accustomed to the prince beating everyone else into the dining hall, already sipping his coffee.

Probably won't be seeing him here in the mornings anymore. Good.

Abandoning his toast, Liam poured more coffee, lifting the rich aroma to his face. He glanced at Dani from the corner of his eye, frowning at the look on her face.

"What?" He tried to disguise the irritation in his voice, but flinched when some made it through.

The muscle at the corner of Dani's jaw flexed. "Nothing. I need some tea." Pushing her chair back, she stood.

He watched her as she strode across the dining hall towards the banquet table at the far end, piled high with pastries and steaming breakfast meats.

"Damn it." Liam ran his hand back through his hair. His fingers caught on the knots he'd neglected to comb out that morning.

I'm a gods' damned mess.

Kofka had haunted Liam in his sleep, only further reminding

him of the deadline fast approaching. The wedding had occupied so much of his and Dani's time, prohibiting either of them from finding a solution to the crime lord's demands.

Dani returned a few minutes later with a mug of tea and a plate with a plain pancake on it. She sat, setting the plate down and sipping the drink. "I'm on your side, you know."

"I know." Liam lowered his coffee, eyeing her plate. "You don't want any fruit with that?"

Leaning back in her chair, she picked up the pancake and took a bite. "Nope."

He snorted, shaking his head. "Suit yourself." He attempted his toast again, lifting it before dropping it back to the plate without a bite. "I can't even eat."

"You needn't panic. We still have time." Dani dipped the pancake in her tea, sniffed it, and then took another nibble with a thoughtful look on her face.

Liam chewed his lip to force himself not to comment on her eating habits. "Not enough time." He groaned, rubbing his forehead. "Maybe Katrin will be safer now, though. More guards, at least."

"Nothing will happen to Katrin." Dani ripped off a piece of the pancake, clicked her tongue, and dipped it in Liam's coffee. "Especially if you let me go visit Kofka myself." She tasted the pancake again and made a face. "This really doesn't work well for dipping."

He frowned at the pancake crumbs floating in his mug. "That's why you put things *on top of* the pancake, then eat it with a fork." He dipped his finger into the hot liquid, pushing the white bits to the ceramic rim to fish them out. "And there's no way in hells you're going to visit Kofka, alone or otherwise."

Dani frowned. "You should tell Matthias."

"Absolutely not. No way." Liam's spine straightened at the horror of involving the prince in his gambling debt.

Her gaze drifted away from him, her head tilting. "He's coming. And his steps are way faster than normal."

"Is Katrin with him?"

"No. He's alone."

"Shit. You think he found out what we're up to?" Liam resisted the inclination to look behind him as the door across the hall clicked open.

"I hope so," Dani grumbled, sliding her plate over to him and pulling his toast closer to her tea.

Matthias strode over to them, and Liam met his gaze. The prince opened his mouth to speak, but paused when he saw the plate next to Liam's mug. "Did you dip your pancake into your *coffee?*"

Liam looked down at Dani's soggy pancake and scowled. He jutted his head towards Dani, but said nothing out loud.

"He just blamed me, didn't he?" Dani took a bite of Liam's toast.

"Well, it *was* you." Liam lifted his coffee, hiding his remaining frown as he met Matthias's eyes.

The prince sighed. "I need to speak to you both in private. There's more food in the meeting room if you didn't get your fill."

Liam's chest thundered. "Everything all right?" He hoped the guilt didn't show in his eyes as he pushed his chair back.

"Not here." Matthias motioned with his head and started back for the door.

Dani stood, still holding Liam's toast, and followed him while looking in Liam's direction. "The sticky stuff on your crispy bread is tasty."

"Jam... fruit. You know, the stuff I suggested putting on your pancake?" Liam topped off his coffee before he followed the prince, his heart in his throat.

He knows. Somehow.

Liam started trying to come up with the excuses he'd feed to Kofka. What he could offer to make up for the prince getting involved. But as they passed a pair of saluting guards stationed in the palace hallway, shame washed through him. He was a crown elite and personal friend of the prince, yet he was considering bowing and begging at Kofka's feet.

A guard opened the door to the meeting room as they approached, Matthias entering first.

Katrin already stood at the table, her hair knotted in a messy bun on top of her head. Her pale yellow dress made her look out of place in front of the military maps and figurines on the table. She leaned over it, a quill in her hand and face set in concentration. She only glanced at them before returning to the map in front of her.

The guard shut the door behind them, leaving the four of them alone.

Matthias's gaze passed over Dani and landed on him. "Katrin figured it out."

Liam's throat seized. "She did?"

How? There's no way she ever knew about my gambling habits...

The prince's mouth twitched in the hint of a smile. "She figured out where the dragons are."

Liam's chest tightened. "Oh, dragons."

Why do I feel disappointed?

He stepped forward, setting his coffee on the edge of the table to peer at the maps Katrin poured over. They were of the mountains, rather than Nema's Throne like he'd assumed.

They don't know about Kofka.

Dread swelled larger, crashing into a wave of anxiety he wanted to share with his ally. He wanted to rely on his friend to help him solve the situation he'd gotten himself into. To help him with Kofka.

Katrin eyed Liam's coffee. "Don't you dare spill that on these." Her quill scratched as she compared between the map and the open book beside her. Its pages were wrinkled and binding splotched with dark wet spots.

"Looks like you already spilled something else." Liam gestured with his chin and Katrin glared.

"Are the dragons somewhere we can get to?" Dani approached the table but circled it to stand by the bright window.

"Only with the drakes." Matthias's eyes lingered on Katrin before he looked at Liam. "We'll need to make some preparations before we go, including getting everyone warmer gear." He paused, eyeing Dani. "For most of us, anyway."

"The mountains, then?" Liam pulled his coffee further from the maps with Katrin's lingering glances.

"According to what I've deduced, they're near Dyndroli's Peak. It will be... dangerous, to say the least." Katrin let out a long exhale.

"Dyndroli's? You mean... the second highest peak that only a handful of people have ever survived scaling?" Liam lifted his eyebrows at Matthias. "That should be easy. Like walking to the baker's."

Katrin scowled. "Your sarcasm isn't appreciated."

"It so rarely is." Liam sighed. He looked at Matthias. "So we leave tomorrow?" An ember of hope suddenly erupted.

I'd love to see Kofka follow me into the mountains. And I'll have made enough just through my pay by the time we return.

"Tomorrow?" Matthias barked a laugh. "Not a chance. We're thinking in three months."

A torrential downpour drowned the ember. "Three months? I thought this was important. We want to get to the dragons before Feyor, don't we?"

Matthias's eyes narrowed. "Liam, it's winter. The few people who have successfully scaled the peak did it in summer and still nearly froze to death. We're already taking a chance by leaving in the third month of spring."

"Feyor only did egg retrieval missions in the summer." Dani shook her head at Liam, sending him the extra confirmation that this wouldn't be a way to dodge Kofka. "A few tried in winter, but they never returned."

Liam pursed his lips, turning his focus to the maps and swallowing the rising anxiety.

"Is something wrong?" Matthias focused on him. "You've seemed off the last week."

Leaning on his elbows against the table, Liam rubbed the back of his neck. "Just didn't sleep well." His voice was tight, despite every attempt to relax his muscles. The nightmares about Kofka made the statement true. "And not used to being in one place for so long anymore."

Katrin narrowed her eyes.

She knows I'm lying.

Liam chewed the edge of his tongue as he met Matthias's skeptical look. The desire to confide in him as a friend conquered the roiling guilt. "Can I..." Nerves bubbled, but he cleared his throat. "Speak with you alone for a moment, Matthias?"

The prince straightened. "Of course. Let's take a walk."

Katrin exchanged a glance with the prince, giving him a brief nod in response to their silent conversation as she flipped a page in her book, running her finger over the handwritten text. "I have some questions for Dani, anyway, about Feyor's missions into the mountains."

Dani's hand brushed Liam's, and he laced their fingers together for a quick squeeze. "Let's hope I survive the next few minutes," he whispered as he kissed her cheek. "If not, I'm blaming you and my conscience."

The Dtrüa nodded. "You're doing the right thing."

Liam stepped out the door with Matthias, the prince closing it behind them. His throat clenched again as he imagined Kofka leaning on his sinister cane. His teeth flashing like a wolf's beneath his dark goatee as he warned an eighteen-year-old recruit. A naive farm boy already too deep in debt.

Pausing just outside the door, Liam stared at his boots as he considered how to make his tongue form the confession. The long hallway ahead suddenly seemed daunting.

"One of these empty?" Matthias motioned with his chin to the guard, and the woman opened the door across the hall for them.

"You won't be disturbed, your majesty."

"Thank you." The prince entered the large study, furnished with several couches and a massive oak desk near the open window. Outside, snow fell in chunky flakes, a line of shining icicles framing the top of the window where they hung from a shallow overhang. A chill hung in the room, the fireplace unlit and empty.

The guard shut the door behind Liam.

Matthias faced him with an even, patient expression. "What's going on?"

Liam examined the room, moving from the door and possible listening ears. He looked at the tapestries on the wood-paneled walls, wondering if there were hidden passageways beyond where Kofka's spies might hide. He'd already come to suspect the castle had some, considering the unexplained walls and gaps in the architecture. It suddenly made him second guess saying anything at all.

"Liam." Matthias drew his attention.

The soldier averted his gaze to the embroidered rug. "I'm... in a bit of trouble. I made a mistake..."

The prince didn't react. "What kind of trouble?"

"The serious kind. The kind that they threatened me not to say anything to you about." Liam heaved a sigh, shoulders rising with the action. He explained from the beginning and told Matthias all of it. How he'd gotten invited to the gambling halls by one of his fellow recruits. How he'd fallen in with a dangerous crowd and then into debt. How the debt kept growing because he couldn't stop. The favors he'd done for Kofka. He couldn't believe how quickly it came spilling out.

Matthias hardly moved while Liam explained, a stoic expression on his face.

"I... don't have any way to get the money I owe him. And he's threatened to do something to Katrin if I don't make the deadline in two days. I don't expect you to bail me out of this with no consequences... but if I could borrow what I still need, then Kofka will have to back off. And I won't ever go anywhere near Hillboar Street again." Liam met Matthias's eyes for only a moment, unable to maintain it as he buried his hands into his pockets. "I'm sorry."

Sucking in a deep breath, the prince slowly exhaled. "I'm glad you told me, even if a little late."

"In my defense, there was a wedding..." Liam tried to smile, but winced when the prince didn't return it. "I know. I just... I was embarrassed and stupid."

"We all make stupid mistakes." Matthias strode to the window, shaking his head. "But giving you the money to pay back Kofka won't fix this. He will add more interest. Hold your crimes over your head... even if he doesn't realize they no longer hold power over you." He met Liam's gaze. "The crown isn't ignorant of Kofka's actions. He's been a pain in our ass for a long time. He always has an agenda, and if he thinks he has a crown elite under that cane of his, he won't let you go just by letting you pay off your debt."

It was all true. Liam knew it as Matthias said it. "I'm sorry I've put you in this position. I never intended it and hoped I could send what I owed before ever coming back to this city... but war and... other things got in the way." He stared at the back of Matthias's head, wishing there was some way to fix his mistakes. "I couldn't face Katrin finding out at the same time as you. She's going to kill me..."

"Give yourself a break, Talansiet." Matthias faced him. "She might beat your ass, but *kill* is a little dramatic." He smirked, lightening the weight on Liam's shoulders. "We *will* need to involve her, though. And I'm sure Dani already knows. There will be a way to use this to our advantage, but I'm not sure how, yet."

"Advantage?" Liam examined the prince, trying to determine how he'd been so fortunate to have him as a friend.

"If we can trick Kofka into showing us what he wants, then we can be two steps ahead of him."

Chapter 27

Dani stared out the window, admiring the brightness of the snow-covered city while the acolyte scribbled on something. "I can hardly believe you and Matthias are getting married." She smiled. "Are you excited?"

Katrin chuckled, her quill scratching on the maps again. "I don't know if it's fully sank in yet, honestly. Even though the entire country probably knows by now." Her dress rustled as she straightened. "Oh, gods, my parents. Ma is going to lose her mind."

"You should send them a letter." Dani faced her friend. "An owl would get it there before the gossip, I bet."

"I'll need to. Lind wouldn't let me live it down, either, if they heard from the village before me or Liam." Her voice brightened. "I really missed him, and I'm still waiting to wake up and for all of this to be a dream."

The book thumped as she closed it.

"Do you know where the Feyorians entered the Yandarin mountains when they went after the dragon eggs?"

Dani sighed. "I've probably seen all the detailed maps, but..." She waved a hand in front of her own face. "They always spoke of passageways into the mountains, and how they often faced rockslides and cave-ins, but I don't know how they climbed so high."

"Cave-ins?" Some papers rustled, Katrin flipping through more documents.

"Maybe they took a tunnel along the way?"

"Maybe." Katrin tapped the quill against something. "There are not a lot of details about the route they took in the documents you brought back across the border. Most of it refers to what happened with the eggs once they were in Feyor. That they couldn't get them to hatch and suspect it was something special about the Yandarin Mountains. Originally, I thought maybe hot springs, but there aren't any near Dyndroli's Peak. I read about lava pools this morning."

Dani's shoulders slumped, and she faced the window again, wishing she could relay what the maps must have shown.

Katrin remained quiet for a moment, a distant tapping against the table. It paused as her skirts brushed along the floor. "Don't worry, Dani. We'll figure it out. And we'll make it to them before any other Dtrüa control them." Her feet shuffled across the floor and ceramic clinked, liquid flowing from a teapot.

Dani tilted her head, not recognizing the scent. "What kind of tea is that?"

"Jasmine. Would you like a cup?" Another cup clinked as she turned it over from its place setting.

Furrowing her brow, Dani clicked her tongue and walked towards Katrin. "No, thank you. Did you add something to it?"

"A little honey?" Katrin set aside the teapot, picking her cup up and inhaling the steam with a deep breath. She started back to the table, the tea sloshing as she blew across its surface.

Dani focused on the scent, tinting her muddy vision with tans and yellows. As more of it clouded her face with Katrin's blow, the bitter smell of ivy berries brightened. "Stop!" The Dtrüa lunged, slapping the mug out of the acolyte's hand.

It smashed into the wall near the door, ceramic clattering to the floor.

The door flung open, the guard's voice following it. "Is everything all right?"

Matthias and Liam's boots echoed in the hallway, their scents joining the room.

"Dani...?" Confusion colored Katrin's tone.

"What happened?" The prince approached them, his voice

changing direction to address the guard. "Close the door. Keep your post."

The door shut.

Ceramic skittered across the floor as someone kicked a piece, then Liam's hand closed around Dani's.

"There are ivy berries in the tea." Dani squeezed Liam's hand.

"Ivy berries?" Katrin remained still, Matthias's gait moving towards her.

"Check the pot for dark, oval seeds." The Dtrüa motioned to the teapot. "I smelled it. Did you drink any?"

"No, it was too hot." Katrin was the first to the teapot, the lid clinking as she set it aside.

"Maybe the cooks thought the flavor would go well?" Liam sounded unconvinced.

"They're poisonous." Dani shook her head. "Not deadly poisonous, but they would have made her sick."

"Let's just say I wouldn't be leaving my bathing chamber for a few days if I had drank it." Katrin put the teapot back on the serving tray. "Who the hells would put ivy berries in my tea?"

"I can guess." Matthias's deep voice quieted the room, and Dani held her breath.

Kofka.

"Shit." Liam groaned and let go of Dani's hand, a chair grinding along the floor as he pulled it out. "He's sending messages already. That he can get into the palace."

"Who?" Katrin's voice grew trite, and Dani imagined her crossing her arms while glaring at her brother.

Liam sighed. "Just promise you won't kill me?"

Chapter 28

Katrin's shoulders tightened with each word out of Liam's mouth. Forcing herself to adhere to the promise she made not to murder her only brother, she fought to keep her anger in check.

He never made me promise not to smack him, though.

"You're an idiot," Katrin growled, glancing at the inconspicuous tea set that'd almost put her stomach in fits for days.

Liam lowered his eyes to the table. "I know."

Katrin eyed Matthias as she shook her head and stomped across the room to the door, tearing it open. Her eyes met those of the startled guard standing beside it. "Find out who prepared this tea, please." While she put the formal word at the end, she wondered at her own firmness.

The guard, wide-eyed, nodded. "Ma'am." She spun, hurrying down the hall and leaving only one guard at the door, who peered in at the shattered teacup on the floor.

Katrin snapped the door shut before he could get a better look.

Matthias raised his brow at her. "That was technically *my* job."

"If there's a criminal leader operating inside this castle, it's in our best interest to trace *who else* he has under his thumb. And I'm perfectly capable." She frowned to hide the tug of a smile on her lips.

"We're already aware of a few who we suspect have ties to Kofka."

"And they're still employed here?" Katrin noted the flinch in Liam's shoulders at her implication.

"They are. Because it's easier to keep tabs on the ones we know about than get rid of them and not know who he'll send in to replace them. This way, we can limit their responsibilities and control what information leaves the palace." The prince stalked to the table, a frown spreading over his face. "Though none that we know of would have had access to preparing food or drink."

"Well, it seems you might have missed one, then." Katrin crossed her arms, heaving a sigh as she turned back to the table and her brother as if preparing to scold a child.

Liam had shrunk somehow, making himself small in the chair he'd pulled up to the table. "I'm sorry, Kat. I never intended any of this."

"I've always looked up to you... Admired you. You knew it was shameful because you've continued hiding it all these years. Gambling? Debts? Really, Liam? What would Ma say?" A fire raged in her veins, making her skin flush.

Dani stepped in front of her, blocking her view of her brother. "That's enough." Her soft voice held an air of finality. "He messed up. He knows it. We need to think of solutions, not make him feel worse."

Katrin glared at Dani. "Solutions? You mean give him the money so he can pay it back then just fall into the same hole again later?"

"I haven't set foot in a gambling hall in two years." Liam's voice only made Katrin's anger rise.

"It doesn't matter! You put yourself in this situation and just helping you get out of it won't teach you anything. You obviously didn't learn from having to do *favors* for that monster. Have you put ivy berries in someone else's tea before, Liam? Those kinds of favors?"

"People fuck up!" Dani stepped closer to Katrin, her jaw set. "People do things they can't even imagine because they are in situations they never saw coming. Your accusations are far from fair, and I suggest you take a *walk*."

Matthias put a hand on Katrin's shoulder. "Maybe that's a good idea."

Katrin tensed under his touch, but it encouraged a breath as she glowered at the Dtrüa protecting her brother. She ground her jaw as she leaned around Dani to glare at Liam, who held his head in his hands, unable to even meet her gaze.

Breathe.

Forcing in a deep inhale, she lifted her hand to her shoulder, touching Matthias's. "No, we need to figure this out." She forced her voice to calm, rolling her shoulders. "Just give me a moment." She patted him before she stepped away from him and Dani, moving to the large window at the far side of the meeting hall. Staring at the falling snow, she counted snowflakes as they fell by the center pane, watching them disappear into the thick drift gathering against the bottom of the window.

A moment later, Matthias appeared next to her. "We've never had a chance to get inside Kofka's organization. This might be a good opportunity."

Katrin glanced at him, his face instantly cooling her frustration. She sighed. "I don't know much about this Kofka, but I assume he's been plaguing the city for a while?"

Matthias nodded, glancing back at the other two.

Dani knelt in front of Liam, touching his face.

Even if he's wrong, she's still devoted to him.

A pang of her own hypocrisy lowered her shoulders.

Matthias has proved he's still devoted to me, despite my mistakes.

The prince gave her a reassuring smile. "Ten, fifteen years now. He runs a group of thugs and contract killers out of his gambling halls on Hillboar Street. He keeps his own hands clean, using extortion, blackmail... gambling debts, to make others do his dirty work." Matthias looked out the window. "It's easy to find and arrest his goons, but not him. As it stands, the communities view him as a philanthropist because he gives back a good portion of his illegal gold to the poor. It's smart. Makes him untouchable without solid proof."

Katrin wrapped her arms around her middle, considering. "Then you have to get proof. Or take care of him in his own way. Use his own people against him."

Matthias hummed. "Right now, one of those people is Liam. I

don't want to put your brother in jeopardy, but..."

Katrin paused, her mind whirling as she considered. "He's put himself in enough trouble, and it's the best option. If Kofka operates in favors, you put Liam in a position to ask for one... then we'll know what he's after."

The prince looked at Katrin, nodding slowly. "Which means we don't want Liam to pay the debt back."

"No, we want him to accrue more." A knot formed in her stomach at the thought.

Matthias looked at Liam, who hesitantly lifted his gaze. "Talansiet. You remember how to lose at cards?"

 Chapter 29

Liam lifted the edge of his cards, peeking at the numbers written in their corners. While his eyes roved to the players across the worn table, the familiar thrill of the growing pile of coins between them all rose in his gut.

Stay focused. I have a purpose here.

Liam had stayed ahead of his meager beginnings, building his confidence that he remembered how to play the game. Though the men and women across from him appeared to have deeper pockets.

Despite it being two years since he'd been inside Hillboar Hall, the smell and the look of the place hadn't changed. They kept the room dim, with a single lantern dangling above each gambling table. The dark wood paneling of the walls and ceiling reflected only sound rather than light.

Smoke hung thick in the air, vapid giggles emanating from the side rooms Liam had never desired to visit.

Dani must hate it in here.

He looked over at where she stood, leaned against a wall. Her simple burgundy dress hid the layer of leather beneath, but the bone amulet from Lasseth hung exposed against her sternum.

A man stood in front of her, talking to her while puffing on a cigar.

"Hey, fella. Are you going to call or fold?" The dealer tapped the table with his deck of cards.

Liam blinked, examining the pot in the middle of the table that'd grown by several silver florins.

Shit, that's getting too rich for my pair of threes.

He considered his instinct to fold as he glanced again at his hand.

"Call." He tossed two silver coins on top of the pile at the center, watching the eyebrows of a matronly woman across the table rise over the rim of her glasses. He steeled the grimace from his face, knowing her hand was better than his.

She proved it when she revealed a flush.

Liam threw his cards into the center, hissing as if physically hurt. But the excitement of the next hand already bloomed as the dealer gathered the cards and shuffled them, prompting for the early buy in of a pair of iron marks.

Folding the straight he drew in the next hand was worse after he'd already called another player's florin.

Careful to only win small pots, Liam steadily tortured himself with each fold and call throughout the evening. When he put the rest of his money in on a lousy high card he justified people would think he was bluffing over, he found himself in a dangerously familiar situation.

Out of money and out of luck.

Liam feigned his frustration as he stood up loudly from the table, flinging his chair back.

"Oh, come now, boy. You've got to have a few more marks on you. Big strapping soldier like yourself," the balding man next to him mused.

Liam had recognized him the moment he came to join the game. One of Kofka's players, hired specifically to cheat gamblers like himself out of their coin.

Liam shoved his sleeves, forcing them back to his elbows. "Give me a minute." He eyed Dani, who smacked the cigar man's hand away from her face.

Her gaze trailed to Liam, and she sauntered over to him. "Did you win?" She kept her voice low, as per their ruse, and touched his chest. "That was the last of our coin."

An inclination flitted through him to keep playing with the

money they genuinely still had, despite already accomplishing what Matthias had sent them to do. He winced, grateful Dani couldn't see it. "No. You have nothing else on you I can use? You sure?"

"Boy!" The bald goon of Kofka's waved Liam down. "Come on back, game's not as good without you. I'll loan you a few to get you back on your feet."

The scenario was all too familiar.

Liam touched Dani's hand, brushing his fingers over the bone ring he'd given her. "Come be my lucky charm?"

"You shouldn't take the loan." She pulled on his hand, whispering, "You owe enough."

Even if he knew she was pretending, the words still stung. But he hid it behind a charming smile. "I've got this. Just a bad streak. I'll play smarter." He tugged her towards the table, giving a nod to the man offering the loan.

He slid a stack of silver florins in front of Liam's seat and tossed two iron marks into the middle for his buy in. "Good lad."

Liam swallowed the bile in his throat as he settled back into the chair, Dani's hand moving to his shoulder. He kissed her fingertips as he watched the dealer flop cards onto the table.

Stack after stack of coin arrived in front of Liam, promptly leaving with each failed hand. He ignored Dani's feigned protests, borrowing and losing at an impressive rate, even for him. The meager wins in between hopefully served the purpose of not making his attempts too obvious. For a period, he even tried to gamble well, but lost more effectively than when he was trying to lose.

This is why I don't do this anymore.

"All in." Liam shoved the rest of his coin into the table, hoping for a moment that his three of a kind would save him, but the bald man chuckled as he laid his cards down to show his straight.

"Sorry, lad."

Liam grimaced, rubbing his face. "Shit."

The sound of boots approaching from behind him sent a shudder down his spine.

Too fucking familiar.

"Talansiet." Mekkin's burly voice rumbled. "Let's not make this harder than it's got to be."

Liam groaned, not needing to fake the wave of fear that went through him. This was the part of Matthias and Katrin's plan he'd hated the most. He chewed his lip as he stood, forcing calm into his quavering leg muscles. He looked at Dani first, who'd moved into a defensive position between his back and Mekkin.

His hand brushed hers. "I'll be back soon."

"Nope. Boss wants her to come, too." Mekkin crossed his arms, the muscles bulging beneath his sleeves.

Liam froze, his grip tightening on Dani's shoulder with the sudden complication they hadn't expected. He was supposed to face Kofka alone. "She's got nothing to do with it."

"Boss says she comes. She comes." Mekkin frowned beneath his scruffy blond beard.

Dani stood straighter, touching Liam's hand. "It's fine. I'll come with you."

The tension in him doubled, and he wondered if he could take Mekkin. He didn't have his sword, required to hand it over to enter the gambling hall. He still had the knife he stashed in his boot, and he was certain almost everyone in the hall had a similarly hidden blade. Mekkin's, on the other hand, was proudly displayed on his hip, a wickedly large hunting knife with an antler handle.

The Dtrüa poked Liam in the side. "We don't need any trouble."

Mekkin lifted a single eyebrow, as if daring Liam to try.

"Fine," Liam growled, gesturing with his hand behind Mekkin. "His office still in the same place?"

Mekkin grinned, knuckles popping. "After you."

Liam hated how well he remembered exactly what doorway and turns to take to get to Kofka's private study at the back of Hillboar Hall. The smoke faded as they crossed through each narrow hallway, slipping past other gamblers and patrons hanging in doorways and against the walls.

His grip on Dani's hand tightened, guiding her while also trying to seek his own comfort with each remembered step over the worn wood floor.

Mekkin filled the entire hall behind them, forced to turn sideways when they encountered others.

Dani clicked her tongue with each corner, fidgeting with the dress she'd complained about wearing.

The door to Kofka's study stood open with Frel leaned against the outside wall, picking dirt from beneath his nails with one of his throwing blades. He looked up, baring his yellow teeth in a grin as they grew closer. His eyes flickered to Dani, moving up and down and lingering in places that made Liam's blood heat.

"Isn't this just a breath of fresh nostalgia." Kofka stood from his desk inside the room ahead, a smug look on his face. "Like the good old days."

Mekkin and Frel stepped inside after them, shutting the door.

The room reeked of memories Liam wished he could forget. The same decorative sofa. The same wide mahogany desk. The same sword mounted to the wall behind Kofka.

"Look, he can pay it back. He just needs more time to make his wage." Dani squeezed Liam's hand.

Kofka chuckled. "I've been more than patient in waiting for Mister Talansiet to make good on his debts. I've already extended far too much goodwill by granting him this extra week, considering he attempted to escape his debts when he transferred to the border." The crime lord settled into his chair, gesturing to the pair of chairs in front of him. "So let us talk business."

Liam glared at the chair. "I'm not roughing anyone else up for you. Not after what you tried to do to my sister."

Kofka grinned, making him more sinister. "I had a feeling your... *friend* here might notice something was off and fully expected your poor sister never to drink any of that tea. But I'd say that you perfectly understood my intention behind the action." He clasped his hands on top of his desk. "But my my, how things have evolved since last we spoke. Another royal wedding coming, and one you are even closer to than before."

"You know I won't do anything to put my sister in danger, so I wouldn't waste your breath asking." Liam's stomach twisted, wondering if Kofka's sights would really go as high as Matthias and his future wife.

He's not that stupid.

Kofka frowned, tutting his tongue. "I wouldn't ask such a thing. I have others who might assist in that, if necessary." He looked away, turning to a glass decanter. Pouring red wine into a short glass beside him, Kofka licked his lips. "Though, my favor does pertain to another acquaintance of yours."

At least he's getting to the point.

Liam ground his jaw. "So that's where we're going back to. Favors in exchange for debt forgiveness?"

Mekkin shifted, drawing his gaze. Beyond the brute stood the side door to Kofka's study, more rickety than the rest of the room. On the other side waited a room, dark with stains and full of wicked memories the soldier longed to forget.

"I think you'll find the task easier than you're expecting..." Kofka sipped the wine. "A man of mine is in the capital prison. Bring him to me, and all your debt goes..." He motioned with his hand. "Poof."

Liam's eyes widened. "All of it?" His gut clenched.

He'd expected a portion, but all...

"That's right. Down to the last iron mark." Kofka smirked.

"Who?" Liam searched his memories, trying to think who he knew that Kofka might find so valuable. He'd worked with a few different soldiers while performing other favors, but couldn't recall anyone infamous being arrested. Certainly not one of Kofka's men who'd be worth that many gold crowns.

"They're calling him a traitor. You should remember him. After all, he remembers you. Your friend Xavis."

The name echoed in his mind, not one he'd ever planned to forget. Following the battle of the border intended to assassinate the prince, he hadn't seen Xavis. They'd left in a rush, making it impossible for Liam to even write a note for the soldier he'd been so close to.

Liam's breath caught as he put the pieces together. "Why would they arrest Xavis?"

"That doesn't matter and isn't relevant to your job. But I want him out before the crown makes an example of him."

Brow furrowing, Liam shook his head again. "I don't understand, though. How do you even know Xavis?"

He and Xavis had met at the border, and the man's jovial personality had drawn Liam to him. If he'd known the man had connections to Kofka...

I didn't even know he was from Nema's Throne.

"Also none of your concern. What matters is that he stays alive. And you're going to ensure it by freeing him and bringing him here." Kofka tapped his cane. "By tomorrow."

"I don't have that kind of power, are you kidding?" Liam gaped. "I might be a crown elite, but I can't pardon someone."

His friend's questions came flooding back. How curious he'd been about the prince's arrival. Where the prince slept, how long he'd stay.

It can't be true. Matthias suspected a traitor, but how many were there?

The archer the prince had killed had been one of them, working for Feyor. What if they weren't working for Feyor at all, but for Kofka?

Unless Kofka is working for Feyor.

Liam gritted his teeth, pushing the conspiracy paranoia aside. It was impossible. Quill, the archer, and Xavis never even spoke to each other. There had to be a different reason the crime lord wanted Xavis.

"What did Xavis do?"

Kofka scoffed. "Nothing. He failed." The man pursed his lips into a thin line, turning them white. "Enough questions."

Failed. If this has to do with the attack on the border, did Xavis fail to kill the prince?

Liam's gut twisted. "I still can't just free him."

"The limits of your power aren't my problem. I suspect your motivation will prove enough to make it happen." Kofka glanced at the men behind them, a silent command Liam didn't understand.

"A few gold crowns of debt is hardly enough motivation for me to become a traitor myself." He relaxed, forcing his body to prepare for the pain from Mekkin's fists.

It didn't come.

The dreaded side door squeaked open.

"You won't be leaving here without providing collateral. A standard you should remember from before. I can't risk you betraying me." Kofka pointed to the side door with his cane, still sitting. "I've even made proper arrangements for our guest."

Liam took a step to peer inside, expecting to find someone there, already half tortured to death. Instead, the chair that he'd remembered at the center of the hay strewn room had been replaced with exposed iron bars. The cage stood just shorter than he was, barely enough space between the vertical metal bars for his own fist. And it was empty.

His heart dropped into his stomach, a wave of nausea threatening all composure.

"What is it?" Dani must have smelled his fear.

Liam growled, turning back to Kofka. "You've got to be fucking joking. There's no way. You're going to have to kill me instead."

"Now, now." Kofka grinned. "I promise I won't hurt her."

"Won't hurt who?" Dani's voice rose, and she gripped his hand tighter.

"You." Liam checked the room quickly, encouraging Dani behind him so he might block her from Mekkin, but Frel circled behind. "It's a cage."

Dani nearly crushed his hand, her breathing quickening. "I can't."

"I won't let them put you in there." Liam took a step back, encouraging Dani towards the now unguarded front door.

"I cannot see where you have a choice in the matter." Kofka's eyes glittered with delight. "She remains while you fetch Xavis for me. It's perfectly reasonable."

Dani pressed her forehead to the back of Liam's shoulder and whispered, "If I kill them..."

Liam's mind finished her sentence for her.

This will all be for nothing, and we'll lose the chance to take this whole place down.

He shook his head, his hand squeezing hers.

Mekkin advanced at a minute gesture from Kofka, his enormous hand clamping down on Dani's upper arm. "Let's go."

Something in Liam snapped as Mekkin touched her. His entire body went taut as he stepped into the man, jabbing his open hand at the tender flesh just beneath Mekkin's right ribs. The big man winced in surprise, giving Liam the opportunity to slam his foot into the brute's knee, making him stumble.

Frel appeared behind Liam, touching a knife to the soldier's neck.

His hand flashed up, ignoring the pinch of pain as the steel cut his throat. He seized it near the hilt, cutting his palm as he lifted his left boot, fingers closing on his own knife.

A second blade poked near his ribs at his back. "Do it, and she dies."

Liam looked up, finding Mekkin holding Dani, the wicked hunting blade at her throat.

The world froze, broken by the clatter of Liam's dagger hitting the wood floor.

His face felt hot, eyes burning as he looked at Dani. Forced to straighten his spine in Frel's grip, Liam squeezed his fist, warm blood dripping to the floor.

"I'll get in the cage," the Dtrüa whispered, holding tight to the brute's forearm. "I won't even shift, all right? No need for more blood." Her voice trembled, but her body kept stoically stiff.

"Dani." He choked on her name, failing to hide the emotion he'd never wanted Kofka to see. "I'm sorry. I'm so sorry."

Her eyes shimmered with tears as Mekkin hauled her into the side room, the cage door open and waiting. She jerked in his grip, and he let her go. He guided her hand to the open barred door with a strange display of gentleness, and she closed her eyes as she walked inside.

"To prove how reasonable I can be..." Kofka swirled the wine in his glass, setting his cane aside with a click. "I'll even allow you to bid your farewell and make your promises of return."

The cage door snapped shut, making Dani and Liam jerk in unison.

Frel's dagger disappeared, and Liam stumbled forward as the assassin pushed him away. The distance to the cage passed in a blur before he reached through the bars for Dani, only able to fit his arm in to just below his elbow.

"I'll be back as fast as I can," he whispered, voice unsteady. He ignored the pain in his palm as he grabbed both of her hands, smearing blood onto her skin.

Dani sniffed, still breathing fast. "I don't like this."

He pulled her hand through the bars, kissing her knuckles as tears fell onto them. "We'll figure this out."

"Just get Xavis." Dani rubbed her thumb over his jaw.

"I will." He kissed her skin again. "I'm so sorry, my love."

Closing her eyes, she gripped a bar. "Do what you must. Go."

Chapter 30

Katrin leaned over the table, a steaming cup of tea in her hand that Matthias had gotten from the kitchen himself. He hadn't seen her put it down yet, as if taking extra precaution to not even let it out of her grip.

"At least we know who prepared the last tea," Matthias muttered, pushing down the anger in his chest. "Just wish I could do something about it."

Play the long game.

"Better not to draw any extra attention right now." Katrin's eyes remained on the map as she traced a path up into the Yandarin Mountains with her finger. Standing back, she lifted her tea to her mouth, sipping. She'd continued to pour over the maps after Dani and Liam left for Kofka's Hillboar Hall.

Matthias glanced out the window, the moon bright in the star-dappled sky. "It's been hours. Maybe something went wrong."

"Hopefully Liam is being smart not to just lose constantly. That'd be too obvious." Katrin met Matthias's eyes as she walked towards him. She leaned with her hip against the table beside him, her eyes darkening. "Or he got distracted just being back in there."

The prince narrowed his eyes at her. "You're too hard on him. I know he's your older brother, but he's still human. I wondered sometimes why he didn't play cards with the guys, but he never did. The biggest concern he had when he was telling me this morning was how you'd react. My mother always said it's difficult to encourage truth when the truth is met with hostility."

She pressed her teacup to her pursed lips. After her sip, she shook her head and nestled her tea in both hands. "Your mother was a smart woman, and I know you're right. I'm just..." She sighed, sliding her cup onto the table beside her for the first time. "It hurts when you find out that your heroes are just people, too."

Matthias touched her chin, lifting it to meet her gaze. "I can relate to Liam. I've let down Seiler more than once. It's difficult to live up to the expectations."

"Hard to believe with how Seiler still looks up to you." She stepped into him, wrapping her arms around his neck.

A smirk touched his lips. "Well. I mean, I didn't gamble myself into debt with a crime lord, but I shot him in the arm with a bow, once." He chuckled, holding her waist. "Then there was the time with the throwing knives, but it's not important."

Katrin laughed, and it shone in her eyes. "I suppose I should be grateful my brother only disappointed me in a way not physically harmful to me." She traced her thumb along his jaw. "And it sounds like perhaps you need some bow lessons *from me*."

Tilting his head, he stared at her. "Have I mentioned today how much I missed you?"

Another glimmer passed through her eyes as they darted quickly to his mouth. "Not nearly enough." Her thumb grazed over his lower lip. "I missed you, too." She lifted herself onto her toes, giving him a gentle kiss.

Matthias returned the affection before breaking it and pulling her into an embrace. He buried his nose near her hair and slid one hand up her back. "My brother and I had a code word for whenever I jumped. Did he tell you that?"

She'd told him about Seiler's archery lessons, but he'd known they were spending time together before her admission. It had surprised him, but in hindsight, he understood his brother's motivation.

He wanted her to feel like a part of the family when I didn't have the guts.

"Code word?" Katrin's lips brushed his neck. "No, he didn't

mention. He did mention the string of secret tunnels only the two of you know about, but refused to show me any of them beyond the one by the dining hall to the archery range."

Matthias grunted. "If he'd told you about all of them, it would've made it more difficult for me to avoid you." He kissed her head. "Whenever I jumped, I'd say gooseberries, then he'd know I'd come back to change something."

"Gooseberries?" Katrin laughed as she pulled back enough to see his face. "I bet the two of you could get into plenty of trouble when you were boys with that kind of Art available."

"Oh, we definitely did." The prince grinned.

She plucked at one of his beard hairs playfully. "I best hope that special ability isn't genetic, otherwise we'll have our hands full some day with a pair of children able to do the same thing."

Matthias laughed. "None of my ancestors had the ability, so I doubt it's genetic." He studied her face. "You want two, then?"

She bit the side of her lower lip with a shallow nod. "I think so. Two sounds like a good number, maybe more. Depending..." Her face spoke the words without her needing to say them.

He nodded. "Anything between none and ten sounds perfect. As long as I have you."

A smile twitched on her face as she nodded, taking a deep inhale to bury the glassiness in her eyes. "At least one," she whispered. "After seeing you with Izi, you deserve to be a father at least once."

"You will be an incredible mother." Matthias smiled, but movement caught the corner of his eye, and he looked out the window. "Is that Liam?" The prince's heart jumped into his throat at how fast his crown elite ran across the snow-covered courtyard in front of the palace.

He's alone.

Katrin followed his gaze, squinting into the darkness of the late evening. "Where's Dani?"

"Something's wrong. Come on." Matthias moved to the door, jerking it open.

They were halfway down the elegant staircase in the castle's foyer when the doors opened and Liam darted in. He slid to a stop on the marble floor as the guards behind him closed the door. Snow fell from Liam's cloak in chunks, melting into pools of water as his red-rimmed eyes met Matthias's.

"What happened?" Matthias jogged down the final steps.

Liam moved before he could react, and the soldier's fist slammed into the prince's jaw. "This is *your* fault!"

Matthias's head whipped to the side as he stumbled backward.

The guards at the door lunged, grappling the crown elite and tugging him back. The soles of Liam's boots squeaked across the floor, stuttering on the tiles.

"What the hells, Liam!" Katrin's grip closed around Matthias's bicep, and she stepped between the two men. "Calm down."

Liam bucked against the guards only once before his glare bored back into Matthias. "She's in a cage right now because of you."

Kofka has ears everywhere. We can't talk here.

The taste of blood still marred his mouth as Matthias jogged down the last steps. He met Liam's gaze, prepared for the coming swing.

Dodging beneath the punch, Matthias grabbed Liam by the elbow and twisted his arm behind his back. He spun the soldier, hauling him to the floor

The two guards surged forward a step in surprise, but hesitated when they saw Matthias pressing his knee into Liam's lower back.

"Matthias!" Katrin gasped, hurrying down the steps. She stopped when she met his gaze, eyes flickering to his split lip.

"Hold!" The prince's command kept the guards at bay, and he lowered his face closer to Liam. "I know you're pissed, and you landed the punch the first time, but this isn't the place to talk," he whispered, his heart pounding.

Liam's body heaved with rapid breaths. "You're a fucking asshole." He bucked against Matthias's grip before the tension in his shoulders relaxed, signaling his surrender. "Let me go."

Growling, the prince released him and stood. He wiped the blood off his lip with his sleeve and looked at Katrin.

She stepped into him, ignoring Liam as he started to his feet. Her hand cupped the prince's cheek as her thumb grazed over his injured lip. A quick flick of power sparked from the pad of her thumb into him, a brief stinging pain.

Running his tongue out over it, he found the split gone.

Her eyes darted behind the prince to glare at her brother, the anger in her eyes confirming she'd put together what Matthias had jumped to undo.

Liam growled as he shoved past Matthias and started towards one of the side halls.

"Watch it, Talansiet," Matthias hissed, following. "You're out of line."

"Forgive me if I don't really give a fuck right now." Liam stormed into the narrow hall that led towards the royal stables.

Stomping closer to his crown elite, Matthias grabbed Liam's cloak to halt him. They'd stopped in the middle of the long corridor, and the prince pushed his shoulder against the wall. The section pressed inward, and he slid it aside. "In," he ordered, glaring at the soldier.

Liam scowled, but stepped boldly into the shadows, muttering something about the secret passage.

Katrin's touch brushed Matthias's wrist as she followed, not giving him an opportunity to protest. Her steps took her to stand between Matthias and Liam, stooping to pick up the old lantern. The snap of her fingers echoed against the old stone walls as the flame inside leapt to life with her Art.

The hidden door sealed.

Liam's knuckles were white in the lantern light as he faced his sister. Though he seemed less inclined to take a swing at her.

"You can't storm into the fucking palace and punch me. You

think Kofka wouldn't hear about that?" Matthias clenched his jaw, anger heating his veins. "What do you mean, she's in a cage?"

"What?" Katrin gaped, looking from Matthias to Liam.

"Kofka caged Dani. Kept her as *collateral* until I finish his gods' damned favor."

"And you blame me for this?"

"It was your idea to go down there and start losing. You put her in this position with your stupid plan." Liam's voice rumbled in a low growl.

Matthias stepped around Katrin, but she sidestepped to keep herself between them.

The prince glared over her at his crown elite. "Did I introduce you to Kofka, years ago? Did I put the cards in your hands? Don't you dare blame this on me. I'm trying to help you."

Liam took a step forward, but Katrin's hand shot out, pressing against his chest.

"Stop it, the both of you," she hissed. "How is this going to help Dani right now?" She gave Liam a hard shove, and the man relinquished a step back.

The prince took a deeper breath. "Is Dani hurt?"

Liam met the prince's gaze, his eyes deep set and swollen. "Not when I left." He lifted his hand, stretching his fingers as if they ached from the punch he'd never landed, but dried blood marred his palm. "This is mine, not hers."

Matthias backed up, still staring at Liam. "What does Kofka want you to do?"

Liam's jaw tightened. "He wants a traitor out of prison."

"Who?" The prince still scowled.

"Xavis Poltesk."

"The traitor from the border attack." Matthias straightened. "He's on trial for aiding Feyor in the assassination attempt on my life. My father's council will decide his fate next week. Likely execution."

Liam paled, his jaw twitching. "Why didn't you tell me Xavis was involved?"

"Do you know him?"

"Yes!" Liam's shout echoed, but then he sucked in a breath quickly and his voice calmed. "We were close."

Matthias lifted his hands, palms up. "How am I supposed to know that?"

"Liam." Katrin's tone softened as she looked at her brother. "I've never heard you say his name, either."

Wincing, Liam turned from them, his boots scuffling through the dust of the passageway as he rubbed his face. "Probably because I'm an asshole and didn't even think about him that much after leaving the encampment."

Matthias let out a breath. "Why would Kofka want Xavis released?"

"He said Xavis had failed. But I don't know in what way."

"Wait. Xavis failed Kofka? Are you saying that Kofka is responsible for Feyor breaching the walls?" The prince swallowed.

"Good to know I'm not the only one who jumped to that crazy conspiracy concept." Liam shrugged, pursing his lips. "But we don't have a choice. We need to get him out to get Dani back."

"I can't just release Xavis. It's not that simple." The prince ran a hand through his hair.

Katrin took back the lantern, lifting it between them. She looked at Matthias. "In Xavis's crimes, is it certain that he is guilty?"

"It is. He—"

"Xavis wouldn't—"

"Liam, he confessed." Matthias stared at his elite. "He admitted to giving information to Feyor to aid them in killing me. He fed them the border wall's shift schedules and told them where I... where Micah would sit during dinner that night."

"Fuck."

"And if Kofka is now wanting Xavis free, that directly ties Kofka to Feyor as well." Katrin's dark eyes widened as they met Matthias's. "This is..."

She didn't have to say the implications out loud.

"Sounds like we need to have a chat with your buddy, Xavis." Matthias crossed his arms.

Liam grunted. "I sure as hell would like some answers."

"We can't just go to the jail and chat with him. Kofka might have eyes there, too." Katrin chewed her lip. "We need to make it look like a jailbreak, then go from there."

"No. I'm not releasing him without talking to him first." Matthias shook his head. "He could be an assassin, for all we know."

"Then I'll order an interrogation. I have the authority to do that, right?" Liam glanced between them.

Matthias nodded. "You do. You don't need my permission. In the hall with the interrogation rooms, take him to the end. I can already be inside waiting."

"Kofka won't get suspicious if you go to interrogate him instead of just breaking him out?"

Liam shrugged. "I'll just say it was part of my cover to break him out. Which... is probably how I'd do it, anyway."

"Exactly. Then we can stage a struggle, and no one will ever know you two weren't alone in that room." Matthias huffed, relaxing his arms. "Assuming Xavis is no longer a threat."

"That he confessed gives me hope he may cooperate." Katrin lifted the lantern again towards the dark passageway ahead of them. "But we should get moving."

"You're not coming." Liam frowned.

"Yes, I am." Katrin cast a warning glare at Matthias, suggesting he shouldn't try to say otherwise, either.

Stubborn woman.

"Fine, but you're staying with me at all times." The prince motioned to Liam's cloak. "Put your insignia back on. I'll see you in there."

Matthias leaned against the wall next to Katrin, positioned behind where the door would open.

Xavis wouldn't see either of them until fully in the small, empty room.

"Can you try checking on Dani again?"

Despite defending himself against Liam's accusations, guilt plagued him for the Dtrüa's predicament. The woman detested chains, for good reason, and the plan had landed her in a cage.

Like an animal.

Katrin closed her eyes but shook her head. "Dani's too wound up. I can't even break through. I can sense that she's there, but I think her anxiety is making the connection impossible."

Katrin, in her pale yellow dress, stood out among the dirty stone of the room, windowless and lit by two wall sconces on the far side.

Matthias nodded, sighing. "Hopefully she won't have to wait much longer."

The interrogation room door swung open, two pairs of footsteps shuffling inside. As Liam guided Xavis past the threshold, the prince kicked the door shut.

The traitor's head whipped to see who'd done it, his greasy, shaggy hair loose around his shoulders. The torn clothing did little to offer warmth, but they did not offer comfort to those on death's row for treason. His dirty face passed from Matthias to Katrin, thick brows furrowing. "What's going on, Liam? Why's your sister here?"

Liam jerked Xavis's shirt from behind him, throwing the man towards one of the barren walls. "You're not in any position to be asking questions after what you've done."

Xavis dropped back against the wall, lifting his hands up in front of him and lowering his scrawny body, lacking any of the muscle he'd had as a soldier. "I tried to tell them when they arrested me. I'm sorry. I didn't know what Feyor intended. I was just doing as I was told." His eyes shifted to Liam's shoulder, lifting his chin in slight defiance. "Congratulations on the promotion."

Matthias crossed his arms, keeping his spot at the wall. "Who told you to feed information to Feyor?"

Xavis's eyes darted to Matthias. "I don't need extra trouble. I've already been plenty good at getting into it myself. You might be a crown elite, too, but I know better than to blab."

Liam jerked Xavis against the wall, making the man wince as his head collided with it. "Answer his question."

Xavis grabbed at Liam's wrist, but for support rather than to wrestle free. "I can't. And they're going to execute me, so if you'll just take me back to my cell... I don't have much longer to wait."

Katrin stepped forward. "You want to die?" Her voice was kind rather than harsh, as if looking to offer Xavis the comfort he didn't deserve. But the tension in her spine told Matthias otherwise.

"Seems the best option available to me." Xavis glanced from Liam to Matthias again.

"So you wouldn't like it, then, if we passed you over to Kofka and told him you ratted him out?" Matthias smirked, tilting his head.

Xavis's eyes went wide, the lantern light flickering against his horror. "No, gods, no. Don't... don't do that. I didn't tell you anything."

Liam jerked again, but released Xavis as he pushed him against the wall, and the man crumpled to the floor.

"Look, I'll make it easy on you. We already know Kofka told you to hand information to Feyor. Tell me why. Why did you try to aid the assassination of the prince and spark a war?" Matthias narrowed his eyes, rising from his spot against the wall.

"War's good for business..." Xavis muttered, his tone dry as if he'd heard the phrase a million times. "But I didn't know they were going to assassinate the prince. Is that what you two are here for, then? A personal vendetta and need to squeeze it in before they cut my head off?"

Katrin crossed the room, waving off Liam as he stepped to stop her. Kneeling a short distance from Xavis, she watched the man shirk back, pressing himself against the wall as if she'd hurt him. "Kofka wants you back, and he's willing to pay a steep price. Why is that?"

Xavis studied her, eyes flicking down her as if looking for a hidden knife she might use on him.

She held out her open palms. "We're not going to hurt you."

The traitor flinched as he looked over Katrin's shoulder at Liam and Matthias, jerking his chin. "Better tell them that."

Matthias frowned. "I'm not making you any promises unless you start talking."

Katrin cast a glare over her shoulder before refocusing on Xavis. "Kofka has something very important to us. But I have a feeling you don't want to go back to Kofka, even if we say nothing about you ratting him out."

Xavis shifted, pulling his knees to his chest. He eyed Liam. "I could tell when we met you were running from something. Broker told me about your gambling debts back home. That's why I liked you, we were both running away." His grip tightened around his knees. "Difference is, I didn't owe Kofka money. But I'm sure he left me in here until now thinking I'd learn some kind of lesson." He sniffed, rubbing his dirty sleeve over his face. "He's always been like that."

Liam straightened. "You told me you joined up to get away from family. You never said anything about Kofka."

Matthias hid his approval at Liam's focus on the task.

Xavis just shrugged, scratching at the stone floor beside him.

"Unless Kofka is your family." Matthias glanced at Liam. "Kofka wants his what...? Son, back?"

"Nephew." Xavis glanced up at Matthias, meeting his eyes as if apologizing for his lineage. "Mom's brother. But he took a shining to me when I was pretty young, and I thought it was neat that I got to hang out in Hillboar Hall when I was only seven after my mom died."

Matthias motioned to Liam for him to come closer, and he turned his back to the room, lowering his voice. "Katrin said we should use his men against him. Even if we kill Kofka, another would take his place, right? What if that man is one of ours?"

Liam's brow furrowed. "Xavis? You want to trust him? He's a traitor."

"He seems no more fond of his uncle than you are. It would give us eyes and ears inside Kofka's organization, and if Xavis ever betrays us, we still have grounds to arrest him. What do you think? You knew him before. Is he capable of something like this?"

The crown elite glanced over his shoulder at Katrin and Xavis. They paused as Katrin whispered something indistinguishable to the prisoner.

She took his dirty hand in hers, and the prisoner stared at the touch as if perplexed.

"This is your call, Liam." Matthias bumped his shoulder. "If you'd rather throw him back in a cell and bring the military down on Hillboar Hall, I can do that instead."

Liam ground his jaw. "Fight like that... Too many people would get hurt. Including civilians. Better to trust him. If I wasn't hearing him admit it out of his own mouth, I never would have believed Xavis would betray Isalica. He was a good soldier."

The prince nodded, facing Xavis again. "We can make you an offer." He strode closer, glancing sideways at Liam, and crouched next to Katrin. "Liam will take you to Kofka. We won't tell him any of this conversation. You'll work for us while working for your uncle, and we will provide you protection."

Xavis straightened, more so than he'd been capable of before, and Matthias realized Katrin must have healed some injuries hidden beneath his dirty clothes.

If I can count on her for anything, it's having empathy for strangers.

"What kind of protection can you possibly offer me? Based on what mutual friends told me back at the border, Liam's pretty deep in Kofka's pockets. How much you owe him, Talansiet?"

Liam growled from behind Matthias but remained still. "I'll owe him nothing once I give him you."

"Do you want the deal or not?" The prince stood.

Xavis licked his dry lips. "Hells of a deal. Keep my head on my shoulders, and my uncle doesn't learn I sold him out, too? And you got the authority for such a thing as a crown elite?"

"No." Matthias huffed, twisting the signet ring on his finger. "But I do as crown prince. That good enough for you?"

Xavis's eyes widened as he averted his gaze, prompting Katrin to smile and roll her eyes at him. The traitor moved with the old muscle memory of a salute, despite still sitting on the ground.

"So, what do you say, Xavis?" Liam crossed his arms as he exchanged a glance with Matthias. "You willing to work for the crown again?"

 Chapter 31

Eyes shut, Dani focused on her breathing. She gripped the cage bars with both hands, keeping the memory of Liam's face at the royal wedding at the forefront of her mind.

Please hurry.

The room stank of blood, old urine, and her own fear.

What horrors the room had seen... Dani didn't want to imagine. Beneath the stench, scents of dirt and steel lingered, mingling with that of the man watching her.

The persistent flick of Frel's knife beneath his fingernails continued for a time, before the grind of a whetstone replaced it. Each movement slow, interspersed with the sucking of his teeth.

Dani's back touched the bars behind her for the hundredth time, and she flinched. She leaned towards the center again, wishing they'd put the cage against a wall instead of leaving her exposed on all sides.

Communicating with Katrin proved impossible. Whenever she stopped focusing on her breathing, she suffocated. Her fear flooded her veins, drowning her each time. Her heart raced, panic threatening to overtake her before she reined it in with a steady inhale.

The night wore on, hours passing without event.

Pretend you're in the cell in Undertown.

Dani swallowed, but no matter how she tried, she couldn't place herself there. She'd had Katrin, and even with Liam's hostility, she never believed he'd harm her.

These henchmen, deep in Hillboar Hall, wouldn't bat an eye at killing her.

I'm in this cage because I let them see me shift.

Cursing her own stupidity, she returned to thinking about her breathing.

Everything felt hot. The dress she'd put over her leathers was too dense, even against the chill that seeped into the room from somewhere behind her.

Dani squirmed, uncomfortable in the linen, and she loosened the ties at the front. She shuffled in the small space, slipping out of the dress to be only in her leathers, but it didn't help with the heat.

Fear prickled her insides as she brushed her fingers over the bone pendant. It scorched, and her pulse quickened as she hid the trinket in her palm.

No. Not now.

The door to Kofka's study gave a low squeal, one she doubted they could even hear. Mekkin's large boots scuffled into the room, kicking bits of hay as he circled the cage. Crossing towards the origin of the seeping cold, he gave Dani a wide berth.

It was too early for Frel and the brute to switch duties, having done so only twice and on a steady schedule before.

Frel's whetstone quieted briefly before resuming, confirming he wasn't about to depart.

"You're in danger." Dani felt around the bars, looking for the lock as her amulet got hotter. She jerked it off her neck, adding the broken leather string into her closed hand to hide the glow.

Frel made a quick hissing sound between his teeth, as if scolding a dog, and ran his blade along the stone slower than before.

Mekkin chuckled, deep and rasping.

"Please." Dani shook the bars at the top of cage with her empty hand. "Resslin is here. She will kill you all to get to me. You have to let me out."

"Forgive me if I doubt you truly worry about our safety." Kofka's voice came from his study, his cane clicking against the floor as he stepped into the doorway.

"*You* should worry about your safety." Dani gritted her teeth, shaking the cage bars harder. "She'll kill you, too, before she kills me. I can stop her if you let me out."

"As thrilling as a wild cat fight would be, it'd be a waste without a pit, a crowd and a wager." Kofka tapped his cane on the door's threshold, as if hesitating in entering the room he used for his more despicable actions.

Dani stilled, her heart thumping against her ribcage.

He can't know who she is.

The amulet pulsed, flaring to nearly burn.

Wood clunked as Mekkin lifted a bar from the worn door that couldn't keep the winter wind out. Its iron hinges creaked.

"You see, Varadani, Xavis is only the icing. You, my Feyorian Dtrüa, are the cake." Kofka's voice sent a chill through her body.

Dani shook her head, dread twisting in her stomach. "You promised Liam you wouldn't hurt me."

The steady beat of Kofka's footsteps moved into the room as a gust of frozen wind rushed in, bringing droplets of ice and snow with it.

And Resslin's scent.

Like crushed cherry blossoms.

Terror screamed through her. Memories of their fight at the ravine's edge and the woman's deadly words.

She'll kill me.

"And I won't." A wicked grin shone in Kofka's voice. "I have no intention of harming you while our deal transpires. What happens to you after you're out of my care..." He sighed dramatically. "Is beyond my control."

Slamming herself against the bars, Dani cried out. The metal rang, echoing through her head as the cage held despite another ram of her shoulder.

"I'll give Liam your regrets for missing him," Kofka crooned.

Dani crouched, feeling around the base of the cage for any openings. She found none, but stashed the pendant under the dress before standing. Straining against the bars, she felt no give within the metal. "He will kill you," she growled, taking a deep breath and spinning when Resslin's scent grew heavier in the air.

The hay of the room crunched under a new set of leather-soled boots, the usual cadence disrupted by a slight limp.

"I knew you weren't dead," Dani whispered, pressing her back against the bars.

The other Dtrüa's scent tinged with yellow-green, the unfinished healing of the shoulder wound inflicted by Liam's crossbow.

Resslin growled, cat-like despite her human shape.

Metal jangled. Coins clicking inside a leather pouch.

"You're *buying* me?" Dani's eyes widened in disbelief, and she contemplated shifting, but the cage wasn't big enough. Her pulse raced, and she tried in vain to connect to Katrin again, but her senses couldn't focus.

Mekkin approached Resslin, and the pouch clinked into his palm before he grunted.

I'm being sold. Like a circus animal.

"Pleasure doing business with you." Kofka's nails tapped on his metal-topped cane.

"The other part of our agreement?" Resslin's voice sounded tense, as if speaking through gritted teeth.

Sharp pain sparked from Dani's neck below her ear, and she gasped. Jerking away from the bars, she damned herself for missing Frel's advance behind her. "What..." She held her neck, tingling and numbness spreading from the spot.

The familiar scent of the Varanithe Danilisca.

The sharp tang of her blood overtook the scent, but only a prick.

Blinking rapidly, she shook her head. "What have..."

The room darkened, light and scents disappearing as she lost consciousness.

Chapter 32

The smoke of the gambling hall stung Liam's nostrils as he followed close behind Xavis. Forced to give up his sword at the entrance again, he felt naked, despite the heavy winter cloak wrapped around his shoulders.

Xavis kept his head low, but a flicker of recognition still shone on the doorman's face.

Liam tightened his grip on Xavis's shoulder as they wove through the tables to the back hall. They drew eyes with each step, especially when Xavis finally pushed back his hood and slowed to walk slightly behind Liam in the narrow hall.

His face remained grim. "I hoped I'd never see this place again," Xavis whispered, casting a wary eye at a pair of men loitering in a doorway. "Hasn't changed a bit."

"Just don't forget why you're here." Liam pushed his shoulder forward. "This is the chance for both of us to make it right."

His stomach roiled, each step threatening to make it worse as he thought of Dani in that cage.

Frel stood outside the door to Kofka's study, slicing a chunk of apple with his knife. His eyes flickered up, and he huffed, kicking the bottom of the door twice.

The latch clicked and Mekkin opened it from inside, a smile spreading over his face as he looked at Xavis.

Liam narrowed his eyes as they passed between the two men, wondering why neither was guarding Dani.

A clap of Kofka's hands brought his attention back to the crime lord, where he sat on his throne behind his desk.

"Well done." Kofka stood, rounding his desk without his cane.

The door behind Liam clicked shut again as his eyes drifted to the closed door between him and Dani's cage.

His blood raced at her being so close, and he wished he could shout his return to her or burst through the door without waiting.

At least she can probably hear me.

Lifting a hand, he pressed his palm against the feline tooth pendant he still wore, comforted only slightly by feeling it dig into his skin.

Xavis straightened as his uncle stood in front of his desk, looking his nephew up and down.

Kofka's grin turned into a frown. "You look a right mess."

"Treason will do that to you." Xavis stripped the cloak from his shoulders, revealing the far cleaner clothes Liam had found before they took him out the back door of the prison.

I'm done waiting.

Liam turned towards the side door, but Mekkin stepped in the way. He glared at the brute's chest. "Out of my way."

Mekkin's burly hand shoved Liam's shoulder, pushing him back from the door. "Not yet."

Xavis had moved away from his uncle, stepping behind the decorative sofa near the center of the room and running his hands along the embroidered fabric unlike anything he'd experienced in a long while. His eyes flickered to Liam with unreadable emotion as he circled to the front and plopped onto it as if he perfectly belonged there. "I missed this." Xavis propped a boot just off the edge of the couch. "I shouldn't have left."

"Good." Kofka scowled, but turned back to his desk to pour wine into a pair of glasses. "Perhaps you're not a complete waste, then."

Liam cleared his throat. "My debt is paid."

A grin rippled across Kofka's face. "Indeed, it is. And then some." He picked up a pouch from his desk and tossed it to Liam. "Your share of the excess."

The coins clicked as Liam caught the thin leather on pure reflex. He peeked inside the pouch, not a single iron mark tainting the gold coins. His heart sped. "What is this?"

"Your payment for returning Xavis to me. We have absolved your debt through a different source."

Xavis stilled as he met Liam's eyes, his arm resting along the back of the couch. His eyes held a warning as the crown elite's blood ran cold.

He spun back towards the side door, and Mekkin stepped aside. Tearing it open, Liam numbed as his eyes landed on the cage.

The empty cage.

He whirled. "Where's Dani?"

Kofka smirked, shrugging. "That cat of yours was worth as much as I hoped."

The room around Liam blurred as the terror flooded into rage. "You sold her?" His voice rose well beyond his control.

The crime lord chuckled. "Business is business, Talansiet. And Feyorian crowns spend just as well as Isalican. Look at the bright side, you've got enough coin to do what you want, now."

His body shook. "Who?" The sound of his own voice was more sinister than he'd heard before.

Kofka waved a hand in a dismissive gesture. "Varadani mentioned her name... I don't remember it. Snarly woman, though."

Resslin.

Panic seared through him. Images of Dani suffering.

The humor faded from Kofka's face. "Don't test my patience. I shared the gold with you. Now, go, while I still feel generous."

Mekkin huffed, shoving the soldier from behind.

Liam's body lurched into action as everything in him turned to ice. Spinning, he grasped Mekkin's wrist, jerking it past his body as his knee struck the man hard in the stomach.

With a great exhalation of surprise, Mekkin stumbled forward, but Liam was already on him. He wrapped his arm around the brute's neck, bracing his wrist with the other hand as he squeezed, hardly able to feel the elbow pounding into his side.

Frel lunged, drawing two knives from his coat.

"Kill him!" Kofka's order accompanied the tap of his cane. "I gave you many chances, young man. You're out of lives, like your cat."

Liam ignored it all, focused on pulling his arm tighter on Mekkin's throat. Wrapping his legs around the big man's middle, he didn't relinquish, even as the brute's blows grew sluggish.

Light glinted off Frel's knives, warning Liam of his proximity. The soldier kicked the back of Mekkin's knee, sending him sprawling towards his partner.

Frel jumped, avoiding the gasping Mekkin as he lashed at Liam's side, but the crown elite dodged the blow. He caught Frel's wrist only briefly before the assassin twisted free and whirled again.

Pain sliced through Liam's arm as he dared a moment to bend for his own hidden knife, turning the crouch into a roll towards the center of the room.

Kofka had returned to behind his desk, while Xavis sat in exactly the same position, a bored expression on his face.

Mekkin stumbled to his feet, beady eyes glaring at Liam, who adjusted the grip on his dagger. The big man barreled forward, ignoring the threat of the blade as he tackled Liam straight into one of the high-backed chairs. They toppled over together. The satisfying sensation of Liam's blade breaking flesh made the pain bearable.

"We have a different room for this!" Kofka's annoyance permeated his tone.

Mekkin pinned him, lifting his fist to strike the soldier's face.

Liam jerked himself awkwardly to the side, burying his dagger deeper into the brute's gut, angling it up towards the delicate organs. But Mekkin's strength continued, pushing all the air out of Liam's lungs. He desperately wrapped his legs around Mekkin, trying to improve his angle.

Xavis's head popped up over the edge of the couch. "You all right down there?"

Liam gasped, the heel of his left hand catching Mekkin in the chin. Latching his legs, Liam flung his weight against Mekkin, forcing him to the side.

Frel circled around Liam's head, knife ready.

"Not here!" Kofka huffed. "I don't want to replace the carpet again."

Blade flashing, Frel lunged for Liam's throat, forcing him to abandon his knife in Mekkin's gut to catch the attack with his already injured palm. Using the momentum of the assassin against him, Liam rolled, taking Frel with him. He kicked him into one of the side tables, shattering it against the wall.

"I don't think they're listening to you." Xavis settled back onto the couch again, putting his hands behind his head.

Liam twisted Frel's knife from his hand, whirling it back down at him before Frel's boots caught him in the gut.

"Useless. Don't just sit there," Kofka snarled at his nephew.

Liam and Frel rolled as Mekkin grunted in pain, his blood splattering as he tore the dagger from his side.

Xavis sighed. "Very well."

Frel's blade pushed to Liam's throat, hot blood trickling down his skin as the soldier's muscles shook to hold the man off. The blade jerked, breaking deeper on one side as Frel fell sideways, Xavis's boot connecting with his temple.

Liam coughed as he rolled towards the couch, Xavis lifting him by the elbow.

Kofka's eyes blazed at his nephew. "You're dead, too."

Liam caught his breath as Xavis moved between him and Frel. The assassin shook his head, spitting a mouthful of blood as he stood.

Mekkin had risen to his feet, a drape from the back of the couch stuffed into the tear in his tunic to staunch the bleeding. His blood dripped from Liam's dagger, now in Mekkin's grip.

"Just like the training arena back at the border." Xavis glanced over his shoulder. "Though, perhaps a little less armed."

"You always leave me the bigger guy," Liam grumbled, squaring himself at Mekkin, the couch still between them. His ribs ached, and he quickly scanned the room for a weapon.

Mekkin didn't give him the opportunity. He shoved at the back of the couch, its legs catching on the edge of the rug as it toppled towards Liam, forcing him to jump out of the way.

Lunging over it, Liam braced his foot on the wooden frame and dove at Mekkin's feet. He wrapped himself around like a snake, grappling the man's legs and tearing him back to the floor.

Mekkin grunted as he smacked his head against the paneled wall, and Liam rolled out from beneath him. Before Mekkin could react, the soldier had his dagger again, and sliced at the inside of his thigh, aiming for the life-giving artery. The leather tore with his skin, the brute crying out as blood sprayed across the fine carpet.

Liam reared back, ramming his knee against the brute's gut wound before lurching back onto his feet.

Mekkin didn't move after him, his eyes glazing as blood pooled.

Back exposed, Frel pinned Xavis, and Liam didn't have the time to consider how. Tossing his dagger into the air, he caught it by the blade, still slick with blood. His body sang with pain as he threw his arm forward.

The dagger soared through the air in a perfect line. It sank into the base of Frel's neck with a throaty squelch.

Kofka backed from his desk, snatching the mounted sword off the wall.

Liam moved, his vision still laced with red at the edges. Prowling around the desk, he met Kofka's eyes.

Dani's face flashed in his mind, the terror she'd shown when locked in that cage. And now Resslin.

Liam didn't think as he sidestepped Kofka's lunge, catching the crime lord's wrist in a vice grip. He turned it, snapping the bone. Kofka screamed, still holding the hilt of his own sword as Liam buried it into his chest.

The rage in Kofka's blue eyes faded into shock. Then nothing.

Liam waited, glaring at the face that'd haunted him for so many years, then let go.

The man's body collapsed to the floor like a pile of discarded meat.

"Shit." Xavis panted for breath, eyes wide. "What do we do now? Frel and Mekkin aren't his only goons."

Liam breathed, wiping his hands on his cloak as he looked at the empty cage in the next room. "Do whatever you want. This hole is yours, now." He stomped across the threshold to the cage. He stepped within the iron door, crouching to the bundle of Dani's dress. He ran his finger over the fabric, taking it against him, if even for a slight glimmer of hope that she would be all right. The white bone shone against the dirty floor beneath, and his fingers found the snapped leather strip holding the amulet.

"You need to get out of here." Xavis watched him. "Take the back door. I'll come up with something to tell them all."

"Blame me if you want. Maybe it'd be good for these criminals to have someone to fear." Liam stood, the bone biting into his palm as he squeezed it. "I need to find her."

Chapter 33

Katrin trembled as she peeked at Liam.

He stared at the bone pendant Dani had been wearing. Looking completely out of place in the clean royal chambers, Liam sat in an overstuffed chair, still coated in blood. His face smeared and clothing stained beyond repair. Refusing to let her touch him, he'd hardly spoken a word since seeking them out in Matthias's chambers. Nothing beyond revealing what Kofka had done.

Meeting Matthias's worried eyes, Katrin shook her head. "I can't get through to her at all." She stepped into him, lowering her voice as her heart pounded. "I can't even tell if she's..." She couldn't say it, but the void between her and Dani remained.

The prince wrapped an arm around her. "She might be unconscious. Maybe Resslin knocked her out."

Katrin glanced at her brother, his shoulders bunched as if he sensed her attention. "I hope that's all it is. Did Liam say anything else?"

Matthias shook his head. "If Resslin wanted to kill her, Liam would have found a body in that cage." He patted Katrin's shoulder before letting go of her and approaching the soldier. "You won't be any good to Dani if you don't let Katrin heal you and rest up. We can start looking at first light."

"I'm fine," Liam growled. "Flesh wounds. And I can't sleep."

I have a few solutions for that if he'd just let me touch him.

The prince crouched in front of him, his voice gentle. "We'll get her back, Liam. Let Kat help you rest. As soon as I know you're all right, I'll send some crown guards out to look for any evidence of where Resslin took her."

Liam grimaced, thumbing the bone pendant again with his bleeding hand. He looked up at Katrin, his face stoic as he stood. "I need a bath, first. Then Katrin can do whatever she wants." He waved his hand dismissively as he moved to the door.

"I'll come check on you soon, then." Katrin pursed her lips at his shallow nod, watching him until he closed the front door of Matthias's chambers behind him.

"One of us should go with him." The prince faced her. "And something tells me he'd rather not have me watch him bathe."

Katrin almost smiled, but shook her head. "Not much better as his sister. But I'll go. You need to go talk to the guards." She touched the prince's arm, trying to hide her worry from her face.

Please let Dani be all right.

"I'll send them out immediately." Matthias kissed Katrin's head. "We'll find her."

The acolyte visited the kitchens before returning to her brother, the sweet scent of tea on the tray tempting her. But she knew better than to sample the concoction she'd put together to help Liam sleep, regardless of what he wanted.

She healed him while he snored on the couch of the crown elites' living quarters.

The guards' search throughout the night proved fruitless, and each passing hour left Katrin more nauseous.

Matthias saved her the trouble of needing to drug her brother the next day by ordering him to stay put in the palace. Begrudgingly, Liam had obeyed, disappearing into the training arena in the palace's basement.

As Katrin entered Matthias's chambers, she steadied her hands to not spill her tray of tea when Lusken dipped his head and walked out of the prince's rooms.

The General.

"What did he say?" Katrin didn't even let Matthias open his

mouth before she spoke again. "Did they find any sign of Dani or Resslin?"

The prince's expression told her everything she needed to know, but he said it, anyway. "No. Not a sign. They searched the entire southern neighborhood, including Hillboar Street, and found nothing."

Sighing, Katrin slid the set onto the low table beside the sitting room fireplace, pouring herself a cup. Without speaking, she walked to the window, nestling her cup of tea in her hands.

Streamers billowed in the mountain winds where they hung above the palace gardens. Several staff escorted their children onto the grounds, clasping spherical paper lanterns painted like moons, planning to release them at midnight. The colorful sunset reflected off the translucent paper as the children ran in circles, gazing up at their creations.

Matthias moved beside her. "With the celebration tonight, I must be cautious, but I ordered him to continue their search with discretion."

"I know she's still here in the city somewhere." Katrin had hoped to celebrate the coming end of the season and year in the streets with her prince at her side, but now everyone else's excitement dampened her mood further.

"Did you connect with her again?" He faced her, the colors outside glimmering off his eyes.

She shook her head. "It was just a blur of scents and sounds for those brief seconds. But us being able to connect at all means she can't be too far. It only ever works at a certain distance." Her frown deepened. She and Dani had discussed testing the bond's range, but hadn't had the opportunity.

"Mmm. I remember. You couldn't connect with her until she'd gotten close enough to Feyor's border again. That's still an expansive distance."

The door behind them burst open without a knock, and Matthias whirled to face the intruder, a hand on the hilt of his sword.

Liam's black hair stuck to his temples with sweat, his cream shirt mirroring his exertion.

"Gods, Talansiet, you have a death wish?" Matthias frowned as two guards entered his doorway, but he waved them off. "What's the rush?"

Liam heaved a breath, having clearly run. "You'd have jumped if you stabbed me." He gestured at the door behind him. "I saw General Lusken's escort in the courtyard. They find her?" His eyes searched the prince before moving to his sister.

Katrin's face must have been the answer he needed.

"Shit." Liam pushed his damp sleeves up to his elbows and stalked towards the couches beside the fireplace.

"They will continue to search through the night." Matthias's tone softened, and he glanced at Katrin. "But you should know that she's likely within city limits."

Liam's head jerked up, the sides of his hair mussed where he'd grabbed at it. "How?"

"I connected with her." Katrin set her teacup on the low table between her and her brother. "Briefly. And I couldn't tell where she was, but—"

"But she's alive, then. What did she say?"

"We didn't talk. I..." Katrin closed her eyes, trying to find the words to explain them to Liam.

"What do you mean you *didn't talk*?"

"It sounds like she's drugged." Matthias crossed his arms, saying the words Katrin didn't have the stomach to tell her brother. "Dani couldn't speak, and her senses couldn't focus on anything. She may not have even been aware of Katrin being there."

Liam growled as he grabbed at his hair again. "Let me go out there and look. With the street parties and parades... the noise... Dani..."

"Nothing has changed, Liam. Kofka's goons will be looking for you. With the celebration, we have extra cover, but we still have no way of narrowing down where she is."

"We can't just sit here and watch the floating lanterns!" Liam rose, but Katrin put a hand on his chest. The sticky damp of his shirt made her cringe as she pushed him back down.

"I'll make you more tea."

"No." Liam's glare could have melted the ice on Dyndroli's Peak.

She pursed her lips and put her hands on her hips, much like their mother would.

"No one is saying we should just sit here." Matthias's tone held forced patience. "We're still looking, but it's like they vanished. Nema's Throne isn't exactly a small city, they could be anywhere. We've tried carrying the pendant with us, but it doesn't react. Maybe it only works for Dani?"

Katrin settled onto the couch across from her brother, turning over two more cups beside the tea setting she'd brought, and poured them each full.

Liam looked at the prince. "I'm tired of this. We need a new plan. It's the Snowdrop Festival, and Dani—"

"Is probably too out of it to notice the noise." Katrin slid his cup across the polished wood and leaned until Liam took it.

He glared at the pale liquid only a moment before he took a slow, distrusting sip. "That doesn't make me feel any better. Did you try the tracking hounds?"

"We did, but they lost her scent quickly with all the activity in the city today." Matthias rubbed his forehead. "And it will only get worse after the chaos tonight."

"She was so worried about it, too. Planned on spending the night with the..." Liam straightened, his eyes shooting up to meet his sister's. "The drakes."

Katrin furrowed her brow. "Do you think they're going to get anxious with the celebration?"

"No, no." Liam shook his head, scooting to the edge of the couch as his eyes darted to the prince. "Yes, but that's not what I just thought of. We should *use* the drakes. Their sense of smell is a hundred times better than the hounds'."

Katrin's eyes widened as she set down her teacup. "They could find her without any trouble at all, Snowdrop Festival or not." She cast a wary glance at Matthias. "Assuming they don't go rampaging about the city."

Liam looked at the prince, hope banishing the weariness in his eyes. "Tonight is perfect. The festival will have everyone distracted, and they won't even realize there's a pair of real drakes moving through the streets with all the massive dragon puppets in the parade."

Matthias looked from Katrin to Liam, pausing before nodding. "Let's brief General Lusken and head to the outer barracks. You're right. If anyone can find Dani, it's those two."

Ousa howled with excitement as Liam secured his saddle, unable to calm the drake despite every attempt.

The roar of the crowds entering the streets as the Snowdrop Festival began made Brek shift away from Katrin, who stood beneath his head.

Trumpets and drums echoed through the barracks, even on the outskirts of the city. The air smelled of the snowdrop flowers strewn across the streets, and the fresh baked sausage rolls traditional with the celebration.

Katrin had always dreamt of being in Nema's Throne for such a celebration, though hadn't imagined riding a drake through it. She tightened her hold on Brek's reins as the drake side stepped from Matthias, chuffing in response to Katrin's pat. "He knows something is going on." She scratched along the side of the beast's face as he leaned down to her. "Shek. Dak."

Brek crouched obediently, despite the anxious shake of his head.

Running her hand along his neck, Katrin mounted, scooting forward in the saddle to let Matthias join her.

Ousa obeyed Liam's command, but his crouch bounced in excitement as the soldier mounted.

"This will work." Liam looked back at his sister, and she didn't know who he was trying to convince. The crown elite whistled to the guard standing near the paddock gate, and the man hurried to open one side.

Katrin leaned forward, pressing both hands to either side of Brek's neck. "All right, boy. We need to find Dani."

The drake huffed at the name, letting out a low whine.

Katrin tried to push images and thoughts of Dani through her touch, urging the drake to understand. "Dani. Find her."

Brek stood without the command, forcing Katrin to dig her nails against the scales of his neck. With a guttural growl aimed at Ousa, the alpha drake padded forward. His body shook with short, breathy chirps to his brethren, tail lashing at the ground behind him.

Ousa snorted back, snapping his jaws in annoyance, but followed.

The guard watched with wide eyes as the pair of drakes bounded into a fast jog from the barracks, turning sharply enough around the outer wall that Katrin had to grip the front of the saddle and lean to keep from being thrown off, Matthias's grip tightening around her. They tore through the grass meadow at the edge of the city, ignoring the winding road that would have led them towards the backend of the celebration parade.

The palace glittered like a jewel in the night, its spires visible above the multistory buildings of the city. Light shone up from the streets, illuminated by hundreds of paper lanterns already drifting on the winter air. Colored paper floated with it, like that thrown in celebration of Matthias's return to the city.

Brek veered right as they neared the edge of the city, skirting the low wall that marked the entrance into the more central part of town. He squeezed so close to overhangs that Katrin's hair brushed the underside of balconies.

Please don't destroy any of these houses.

Brek slowed as he hopped a low fence, turning his head in a low growl at the dog that barked in protest to the shortcut they'd taken around his home. To the dog's credit, he didn't back down, even as

Ousa circled him, nose low and nostrils flaring.

The drake beneath Katrin heaved, his sides swelling with each steady breath as he lifted his head above the wall between them and the crafting district of the city.

She held in a squeak of surprise as Brek hopped, placing his front feet on top of the wall and forcing his riders to lean almost parallel with his back. Stone scraped beneath his claws as Brek climbed over the masonry, leaving gouges in the stone.

Ousa scrambled up behind them, several stones breaking from the top of the wall to crash to the ground with them.

"I think these two will be very necessary for our coming trip to the mountains." Katrin looked at Matthias over her shoulder.

The prince huffed, gripping the sides of the saddle. "Might need to make alterations to their gear so we don't fall off."

Brek slunk through the shadows of the artisan district, moving closer to the chaos of the festival, and Katrin's heart sped.

"You better not be after sausage buns," she muttered to the drake as she leaned against his neck. "Dani."

Brek ignored her as he continued on, the music growing more distinct with the cheers of people. Turning down another road, Katrin glanced to her left, catching glimpses between buildings of the busy street beyond.

People lined the parade route, and bright orbs of light shimmered like massive lightning bugs twisting in the air. Vibrant red cloth undulated against the wooden frames fashioned like a rib cage, fabric wings beating to the rhythm of the drums. A puppeteer commanded the pole of wood controlling the dragon's head, twisting it towards the crowd to roar at children squirming on their parents' shoulders.

Brek wove suddenly into one of the alleys towards the crowded street, and Katrin's heart leapt into her throat. Somehow, the drake had chosen the right road, slowing before they might have been spotted, and dug his claws into a raised portion of the street. He hoisted them over the rim, turning towards the bridge spanning the parade route.

Civilians gathered at the edges, throwing colored paper onto the performers below.

Without hesitation, Brek plowed forward, keeping his body straight until he reached the other side of the parade route. He'd moved so quickly the people watching the parade below hardly moved, though gasps erupted when Ousa followed.

Katrin turned to spy the younger drake slow, despite Liam's determined face. The curious beast sniffed the backs of heads, finding a child on her father's shoulders.

The girl squeaked in delight, reaching for him with a wand of spun sugar.

Ousa's tongue flicked out, engulfing the offering, and the wooden rod snapped in his teeth before he finally obeyed Liam's kicks.

The child blinked in his wake before tugging on her father's collar.

Brek banked again before Katrin could see more.

The streets grew darker, and she no longer recognized the part of the city they entered. Old warehouses with dark windows and empty streets. The alleys were piled high with barrels and crates, the dense stone buildings blocking out the distant celebration.

Katrin could imagine the thoroughfares packed with workers and tradespeople during the day, but during the Snowdrop Festival, everyone had closed their businesses early. "Did the hounds go down these streets?"

"They did, but they didn't even pick up the scent in this district."

Brek slowed, his nostrils flaring as he lifted his head, tilting it in each direction. He turned down another row of warehouses, then another, until Katrin didn't know where she was at all.

A low whistle drew Katrin's attention behind her, spying the bone amulet in her brother's hand. It glowed with a low blue light, getting brighter with each next movement and turn of Brek's.

They found her.

In the shadow of two warehouses, Brek stopped at a low slung building with black-stained bricks. He whined, low enough that

Katrin could barely hear, and she looked back to see Liam clutching the brightly glowing amulet.

Matthias pushed out of the saddle, landing on the ground moments after Liam.

On the ground, Katrin patted Brek again.

Good boy.

Brek focused on the large wooden doors, lowering his head with a low growl, setting Katrin's spine straight.

He lurched forward, but Katrin caught his reins. They grew taut, and her feet slid along the street before he obeyed her tugs.

Ousa moved to go past them, having been abandoned by Liam as he approached the building. But Brek's low growl made the younger drake pause.

"She's going to make a run for it," Matthias whispered, gaze locked on Liam as he spoke to her.

"You might have to jump. Gooseberries, right? So you don't have to explain." Katrin's heart pounded. She wanted nothing more than to burst through the doors and demand her friend's freedom, but it couldn't be so simple. Dani could be used as leverage if they weren't careful, and letting Resslin get away wasn't an option.

"Gooseberries," Matthias muttered, creeping towards Liam. "She will try to run. There's an open window on the south side of the building that she'll leap through."

Liam slowed as he approached the large barn-like doors, his eyes cast down towards the ground where light flickered in a thin line beneath the weathered wood.

"Wait, are you saying gooseberries because you already jumped, or..." Katrin's eyes met Matthias's, and she read the answer, also realizing there was no other way he'd know that much about the building.

Katrin tugged on Liam's shirt, and he swatted her hand before he looked at the prince. An unspoken conversation passed between the two men, and Liam begrudgingly moved south along the outer wall in the direction Matthias jutted his chin.

The prince kept his voice low. "Dani is on the north side. She's alive but chained and drugged, like you thought. Go to her, and I'll cover your back with Resslin."

She nodded, casting a glance back at the drakes.

Brek had turned, blocking Ousa from advancing. The alpha drake's jaws snapped with a rumbling warning.

Ousa whined, and Katrin winced.

Damn drakes are going to...

The movement inside the warehouse stilled, the shadows under the large doors unmoving.

Matthias stared at it, holding a hand towards Katrin to tell her not to move.

After a few breaths, the shadow shifted again. It broadened as the person inside strode silently towards the doors, and Katrin's palms sweated.

Aedonai, please protect us all.

A scuff and a halt.

The drakes stayed mercifully silent.

Matthias surged forward, slamming his shoulder into the left door.

The hinges broke, and the thick pine door crashed inwards, eliciting a grunt from Resslin. The Dtrüa stumbled back, eyes dark as she bared her teeth.

Matthias stepped over the threshold, shielding Katrin as she slid in and to the right. He held his drawn sword at an outward angle, denying Resslin any hope of getting through the front doors.

Katrin forced herself to look away, scanning to the right, to where Dani hung by chains on her wrists.

Resslin snarled, but instead of lunging at Matthias as Katrin feared, the woman pivoted. Her human form melted in the same way Dani's did, fur erupting from her skin. The puma darted for a table near the back of the space, snatching a small leather satchel in her teeth before racing for the open window at the south side.

As Matthias pursued, storming across the warehouse, Katrin wove around the brick support columns on the right.

Dani hung limp, her boots touching the ground but providing no support. Blood dripped from her elbows, only some from where her wrists were cuffed above, shoulder-width apart. Old trails crusted over her pale skin, but most of the crimson flowed from cuts in her forearms. Deep ones.

It made no sense.

Why bleed her out slowly?

A wild cat screamed in tandem with a thunderous crash, and the entire warehouse shook.

Katrin slid to a stop beside Dani, reaching for her gouged arms and gripping the torn flesh with her bare hands to slow the bleeding. She spared only a glance in Resslin's direction as she summoned her power.

Chapter 34

The puma backed away, ears pinned against her head and teeth bared in a hiss. The satchel hit the ground, glass clinking within. Resslin's eyes shone like dark pools, mirroring the mounds of coal near the outer walls.

Liam stepped over the low windowsill, ignoring the splinters in his hand from where the wood had cracked and buckled when Resslin slammed into it after he'd shut it without warning.

The wildcat looked behind her at the prince, who stood with his sword ready.

The Dtrüa shifted, and Liam's throat tightened in surprise. Fur receded and leathers emerged, along with her wide human eyes. "Please," she rasped, holding up empty hands. "I'm unarmed. I surrender."

Low voices came from the other side of the warehouse, stealing Liam's attention. His stomach twisted at the vision of Dani in chains, her hair dirty with pieces sticking to the blood on her forehead. She murmured again to Katrin, impossible to hear. Everything in him yearned to abandon his fight with Resslin to go to her.

"Liam!" Matthias lunged, a glimmer of steel in Resslin's hand.

Raw instinct fueled Liam as he stepped to the side, the edge of Resslin's weapon tearing through the front of his tunic. The cold slice stung across his abdomen, but he caught her wrist and spun her away from the window.

She dropped low to the ground, as if still in her animal form, and Liam pressed his empty hand to the shallow wound.

Matthias's sword cut air as the enemy Dtrüa shifted the moment before his blade struck her. "Shit."

Her claws scraped the floor as she rushed for the unguarded exit behind the prince. She leapt over the fallen door, but skidded to a stop when a drake's snarl vibrated the ground.

Dani cried out as one of the chains holding her slackened in Katrin's grip, and they both staggered as the acolyte struggled to support the Dtrüa.

With a glance past Matthias to the doorway, where he could see Resslin back in her human form and facing the drakes, Liam didn't care if she got away. He dashed across the room, scooping Dani into his arms to lift her and ease the pressure of the chains.

She whimpered against him as Katrin unlatched the second cuff, and Liam pushed her hair from her face. "It's me, Dani." The growl of the drakes seemed a thousand miles away.

"Teal," Dani whispered, her eyes glazed over and directionless.

Matthias stood near the doorway but started backing up.

"Shek, taka!" Resslin's voice weighed with authority, but was tinged with fear.

Brek's growl grew louder, merging with Ousa's as Resslin crossed back into the warehouse, her hands outstretched in front of her.

The prince cast a sidelong look through the warehouse at Katrin, and he shook his head, still backing from the drakes.

The thick pine of the remaining barn door cracked, the frame splintering with the surrounding brick wall. Red clay dust fell from Brek's pearlescent scales as he pushed through, the grisly scar on his throat shining in the lantern light. His jowls pulled back, razor teeth wet with saliva.

"My... drakes," Dani wheezed, her voice hoarse.

Ousa slid past Brek, curling around the larger drake towards the south window, his head low to the ground like a stalking cat. His eyes flickered to Matthias as he took a position between the prince and Dtrüa. Stone screeched beneath his claws as they flexed with anticipation.

"Call them off, Varadani," Resslin's voice wavered. "There's more you should know."

Dani struggled to take a deeper breath, her full weight still in Liam's arms. "Brek."

The alpha drake huffed his acknowledgement of her word, body tight and poised to attack.

Dani shut her eyes, taking her time to breathe before murmuring, "Kill her."

Brek struck, moving faster than Liam had ever seen. He swung in low, his jaws snapping at Resslin's legs before she had any chance to dodge. Flesh squelched, and she cried out, but only briefly before Ousa lunged from the other side, his teeth crunching on Resslin's upper body.

Liam had seen the drakes' destruction on the battlefield, but the sound of Resslin's spine cracking and the splatter of her blood made his stomach turn. He closed his eyes, but the tearing sounds spurred his imagination to depict the carnage, anyway.

The enemy Dtrüa was already dead when the drakes pulled apart from each other, each taking a portion of their kill.

He swallowed the bile rising in his throat, spying Katrin rapidly turn away. The sound of her retching came a moment later.

Matthias circled behind the drakes, giving them a wide berth while carrying the leather satchel Resslin had tried to run off with.

Liam swallowed again, clearing his throat as he looked at the prince. "Don't think she'll be walking away from that one." He touched Dani's cheek, looking down at her. While her eyes were open, they looked more distant than they usually did.

"Not this time." Matthias eyed Katrin, then Liam. "Need help carrying her?"

Liam shook his head, despite the ache suddenly overtaking his body as the adrenaline subsided. Tightening his grip, he shifted Dani against his chest. "Let's move outside."

The prince nodded, swinging the satchel over his shoulder before approaching Katrin and speaking in hushed tones.

The fresh night air greeted Liam like a wave of strength, aiding his muscles in taking her further from the wretched warehouse.

"Where..." Dani tried speaking again, but she coughed and turned her face into his chest. "Teal."

"You're safe, now," Liam whispered, brushing a kiss against her forehead. "I've got you."

———————————————————————

Dani sat on the edge of their bed, only the fireplace illuminating the room in the thick night.

People still celebrated the Snowdrop Festival in the streets, their voices barely audible from within the palace.

"I don't want to sleep." Dani ran a hand over her forearm, cringing.

Katrin had healed the blood-draining wounds, but the Dtrüa had made her stop there. Little cuts and scrapes still marred her skin, the worst at her wrists.

"You don't have to." Liam poured another cup of tea, carefully replacing the pot on the table beside their bed. The tiny grains of sugar hit the tea's surface like pattering rain before he stirred it. He touched her chilly hands and placed the cup in her palms.

They'd sat in silence for the past hour, Liam leaving her side only to tend to the fire and request more tea from the staff stationed outside their chambers. Dani's clarity had returned as the sedatives wore off. The same sedative they had named her after.

Katrin and Matthias had retired to their own chambers at Dani's insistence, though his sister had given Liam a steady, concerned look before reluctantly agreeing. Her obvious worry only made the coils in Liam's stomach worse.

Before he'd left, Matthias had let Liam look inside the satchel when Dani was busy with Katrin. It'd been filled with glass vials. Some small, some thin, wide, round, and even some jars. All filled with blood. Dani's blood. It'd been sloppy, with fingerprints and smudges all over the outer walls of the containers.

The sight turned his stomach, and he'd almost sobbed.

Liam poured tea for himself, folding his legs beneath him as he settled onto the bed beside her.

Dani held the tea with both hands near her chin, breathing the steam. Her glassy eyes were distant, but her inhales steady. "Every time I started to get a clearer head, she dosed me again. How long has it been?"

Liam flinched. "A day and a half, more or less." Regret laced his tone, and he did nothing to hide it. "I'm so sorry."

Her jaw flexed. "It felt like so much longer." She leaned sideways, resting her head on his shoulder. "I never thought Kofka would work with her."

"Xavis proved quite useful in providing a lot of information about Kofka. But it doesn't matter anymore because he's dead."

Dani paused before slowly sipping the tea. "Did you kill him?"

Rubbing his fingertips together, he imagined Kofka's blood between them and nodded. "I was so angry when I returned and you weren't there. I completely lost control."

The Dtrüa turned her face into his shoulder, closing her eyes. "I warned him you would. I'm glad he's dead. And Resslin's dead. You needn't blame yourself for what happened."

"But I do." Liam turned to her as he slid his untouched tea onto the bedside table. He touched Dani's cheeks, lifting her face towards his. He didn't know what he'd do if he'd lost her. "I was so scared Resslin was taking you back to Feyor. That my mistakes had led to it."

Dani shook her head half-heartedly in his touch. "I thought she would, too." Her chin quivered before she swallowed. "Might have been better."

He brushed his fingers along the pale lines still marring the inside of her arm. "Why did she do this?"

Dani hesitated, brow twitching. "She wanted my blood."

His fingers flexed. "Why?"

Dani had explained Feyor's experiments to create the Dtrüa. The intricate spells woven in with blood. They'd used the blood of grygurr and animals to shape Dani's Art for a specific task and certainly had done the same to Resslin once.

But to take the blood of another Dtrüa? To what end?

"I always thought my ability to communicate with beasts came from my power as a Dtrüa." Her soft voice came quieter. "But that isn't true. It makes so much more sense, now. The battle at the border, the drakes." Dani's grip on her tea cup tightened. "I'm different from the other Dtrüa, but I never knew. I think I was supposed to be Feyor's key to domesticating the dragons."

"Resslin said all this to you?" Liam already knew the answer. If Resslin truly believed Dani wouldn't survive long, she'd have no reason not to share everything. The truth of it made his eyebrows rise. "You're the only Dtrüa who can talk to the drakes?"

Dani nodded. "It would seem so, and Resslin thought if she used my blood on herself, she could develop the ability."

Taking the tea from Dani's hands, he slid it onto the table beside his own. He breathed, his mind whirling through the implications. "If you're the only one who genuinely can communicate with dragons, that changes everything. Feyor still has their trainers, but if what you did with the drakes is any indication, those ties aren't nearly strong enough." He took her hands in his, lifting them into his lap. "I already knew you were unique, but you seem determined to keep proving it."

Pulling her hands from his, she wrapped her arms around his neck and crawled into his lap. Resting her head on his shoulder, she pressed her chest to his. "I knew you'd find me."

"I'll always find you." Wrapping his arms around her, Liam relished in the feel of her body against his.

How did I ever exist without her?

He kissed the top of her hair, leaning to rest his cheek against it despite the dampness from the bath she'd taken. She smelled like the lavender oils Katrin had insisted would calm them both. "If you're amenable to the idea, I don't think I'm eager for either of us to leave this room for a while. At least a few days. Duties be damned."

Dani took a deep breath, air wisping past his neck. "I need that. I need you."

Goosebumps formed as he smiled, lifting her chin. "I am yours." His mouth met hers in a gentle movement, parting her lips so he could savor them. The realities outside the palace faded in the sensation of her, encouraging his hand around her waist. He broke the kiss, tracing a featherlight touch down her neck. "Can I get you anything else before this self-imposed isolation?"

Touching his face, she ran her thumbs over his cheeks to his jaw. "Something chocolate." A smile pulled at the corner of her mouth, and she rolled her lips together. "And maybe other food. I feel like I haven't eaten in..." She frowned, shaking her head. "I'm hungry."

Liam chuckled, slipping from beneath her to stand beside the bed. He kissed her forehead, then the tip of her nose, and lifted her mouth back to his again for a long kiss. "Then I will get you something to eat."

"Ask the guards to get it?" Dani's voice held uncertainty. "I want you to stay."

"I will. I'll be right back." He brushed his hand along her jaw as he kissed her deeper. It grew, and he had to force himself to pull away before he lost all sense of himself. "Chocolate and something more filling. I'll be certain to tell the staff to get something decadent."

Dani fell silent as he opened the door and relayed the instructions to the staff member stationed there by Matthias.

When Liam closed the door and looked at Dani, she still stared in his direction, a thoughtful expression on her face.

"I want to marry you." Dani crossed her legs on the bed, tilting her head. "Before we leave for the mountains."

Liam's stomach flipped in a pleasant sensation. "Before?" He started back towards her.

The Dtrüa nodded. "I kept thinking I could die before becoming your wife, and I... I just want to marry you. No big celebration. Something small. Just the four of us."

His smile grew, body warming at the thought. "You don't want something extravagant? All the people marveling at how beautiful you are?" He stepped closer, and she unlaced her legs, wrapping them around his hips. "And at how lucky I am."

Dani finally smiled, shaking her head. "No. But *you* can marvel."

"I do. Every day." He ran his hands up over her thighs and hips. He leaned to catch her mouth again, her hum vibrating against his lips and sending a shock through his body. Pulling her closer to the edge of the bed, he lavished in the warmth of where their bodies met. "I will marry you. Next week. Tomorrow. Today, if you want. I don't care who's there or who isn't, as long as I get to hear you call me husband."

Chapter 35

Two months later...
Spring, 2598 R.T.

Another grating cough shook Geroth, and the king held his chest, waving off his son.

Matthias stood anyway, crossing the study adjoining the king's chambers to retrieve a glass of water for his father. "That cough sounds worse than yesterday."

Geroth cleared his throat, sipping the offered water. "Nonsense. It's not that bad." He coughed again, shaking his head. "It will pass."

I don't remember the last time he was sick.

"Have the healers checked in on you today?" The prince piled the parchment on the desk, having been going over the maps and plans with his father a final time before their departure.

That's enough work.

"Yesterday. They can't find anything wrong." Geroth didn't sound the least bit worried. "Relax, Matty, it's not the plague. I'll be fine."

Matthias groaned. "Why name me Matthias if you're just going to shorten it?"

His father chuckled, and it turned into another cough. He drank again as he cleared his throat. "I named you Alarik, even if you insist on Matthias publicly, now. I could call you Ally?"

The prince scowled. "Matty is fine. But, you know, Matt is better. Just don't use it in front of anyone."

Geroth grinned. "Worried your future bride will start calling you Matty?"

"Obviously." Matthias motioned with his chin to one of the high-backed chairs near the window overlooking the city. "Sit your old ass down. You need to rest."

The king huffed but took the chair, his son sitting in the other. "Are you ready to leave tomorrow?"

Matthias nodded. "I think so. The drakes' saddles have been altered. We have plenty of rations and water. The warmest clothing Isalica has to offer..." His eyes narrowed at another coughing fit. "I don't know if I should leave you, though. What if this gets worse?"

"You get your worries from your mother." Geroth smirked. "I'm a grown man with a palace full of healers. You have nothing to worry about. I even have a new Aueric healer on my roster."

"Aueric? This far north?" Matthias leaned back in the seat. "Who?"

"I don't remember her name... but Merissa recommended her."

The prince exhaled. "Good. At least you're in capable hands, then."

Geroth sipped his drink again, examining his son even though it appeared he looked out the window.

I know that look.

"You be careful in those mountains. As much as you have half a mind to stay because you're worried about me, I have half a mind to keep you here because I'm worried about you." Geroth huffed, shaking his head. "Dragons. It still sounds insane to think they've been hiding in those mountains all this time."

Matthias ran a hand through his hair. "That it does. But I thought I got my worries from Mom? My crew is skilled and prepared. Plus, we'll have the drakes. We'll be all right."

"And you're still determined to take your future queen with you?" Geroth gave him a knowing smile.

The prince barked a laugh. "You say it like I have any say in the matter. Even if I tried to order her, which I would never dare, she would *still* find a way to join us. Better to embrace her company and prepare for it than fight about it."

Geroth laughed, but sucked in a breath to halt the cough. "She's adjusting well to the life of a royal, then. Already has you in your place." He smirked. "Rehtaeh did the same to me."

Matthias snorted. "And I'll be a better man for it, I'm sure." His eyes lingered on his father. He could count each time the king had spoken his late wife's name, and it always made the man's eyes glitter like a frosted window at sunset.

"Women will always make us better." Geroth settled back into his chair. "I'm sorry you can't have a small wedding like your friends did. You know that Loryena is already planning the ceremony."

Groaning, the prince slumped. "Already? We haven't even set a date."

"Details like that rarely slow that woman down. Best to set the date before she does it for you."

"As soon as we get back, we'll choose one." Matthias sighed. "You think I can talk her out of doing a procession through the city?"

"Doubtful. Might as well prepare yourself for the public attention. At least you aren't dealing with all the moping ladies who hoped to win your heart. But Katrin... she's already done well to earn our people's trust and gratitude with her generosity within the city."

Matthias knew she didn't do it to gain favor, but his betrothed had used the past few months to reconnect with the temples and assist the communities. From simple healings to organizing shelter for the less fortunate, she worked long hours serving the people of Nema's Throne.

And she's not even queen yet.

The prince hadn't let her do any of it without an escort of crown guards, even with her protests. The possibility of trouble hadn't deterred her, and Matthias wished he could be there to witness her efforts each day.

"Now that she has the resources to make change, it's like she's taken it all on herself to accomplish. Some fresh mountain air might do us all some good."

In her effort to work beyond herself, Matthias had noted a

growing weariness in her. She needed an escape as much as he did.

Geroth nodded, drinking. "Even though Merissa is on personal leave, are you sure you don't want to take an additional healer? Things can happen, even with your ability to reverse time."

"I know. But the drakes are fitted for four people, along with all our supplies. We'll stick to the plan." Matthias rolled his shoulders, sitting up straighter. "When will Micah arrive?"

They'd called his closest friend and crown elite home to serve as a potential body double in passing. It would keep Feyor from realizing he'd left the capital.

"Next week, give or take. The border encampment has done well, I hear. Partly due to the wyvern they still have. It's a shame you can't fly it to the top of the mountains."

"I wish we could, but its wings would freeze long before reaching the top, according to Dani. But the drakes are better than nothing." Matthias glanced out the window, enjoying seeing the green through the melting snow.

They grew quiet, both satisfied to remain in each other's company without words.

Geroth set his drink aside, the glass thunking against the wood table. "I'll miss having you here, Matty. It's always a wonder to watch your mind work in those strategy meetings. Micah will prove a poor substitute in that regard."

Pride warmed Matthias's chest. "It will be short term." He smiled, looking at his father. "It has been good... being home. I needed it more than I knew."

Geroth chuckled, a cough reemerging. "Glad to know you miss it here. Sometimes I worry I am forcing you to take the crown."

"That's still some time off, Dad. But no, you're not forcing me. If you wanted Seiler to have it, I'd... *probably* support that choice, but the bottom line is that when the time comes, it will be an honor to continue your legacy."

Geroth reached across the gap between their chairs, patting Matthias's hand. "Then be sure to come back so you can."

Matthias nodded, taking his father's hand and squeezing it. "I promise. We'll be back."

"And send that beautiful future daughter of mine here to say goodbye as well." Geroth pulled away, looking at the window as his shoulders shook with a cough, and he grunted in frustration.

"We'll stop by together in the morning again before we leave." Matthias studied his father. "You should rest. I'll handle the remaining meetings tonight."

Chapter 36

All according to plan.
I can always count on Alana.
But Lasseth...
I will find him.
Then Nymaera will greet him and his Rahn'ka lover.

Chapter 37

"So much for spring weather." Liam tugged his scarf over his nose before burying it against the furs on Dani's shoulders.

The winds whipped over the Yandarin mountain peaks, picking up bits of snow and ice that stung any skin he neglected to cover. While the sky remained clear and vibrant blue, the cold bit through all layers of clothing, and he yearned for the fireplace in their private room in the palace.

We're all crazy leaving that kind of luxury for this.

Dani's legs, like his, were latched to the saddle with straps similar to the wyvern's. She wrapped the reins around her palms as Ousa reached up with a front leg, grasping a nearly vertical rock face and hauling them up. "Imagine being here in winter!" His wife glanced back at him, only her eyes visible above the white suede shielding her face.

Tightening his grip around her waist, he craved the shared heat buried beneath the layers. He squinted through the sunlight above them to guess the distance to the top.

Beside them, Brek's claws scraped at the stone, sending a cascade of broken rock below.

The leather hide of an old map flapped in Katrin's grip on the saddle. Head bowed, she appeared to be studying it even as they scaled, unaffected by the heights that made Liam queasy.

Riding the drakes up sheer cliff sides wasn't the same as riding a wyvern.

Wyverns have wings and are more equipped to stop a minor slip.

He tried not to think of the several close calls they'd already encountered. Even the drakes weren't immune to missteps on the treacherous slopes, proven by spontaneous shouts from Matthias not to make a certain maneuver.

We've probably already died and just don't remember.

Ousa slid back on the steep slope as his footing broke away a chunk of rock, but his claws dug in and he curled right.

"Stop!" Matthias shouted over the wind, and both drakes froze. The prince panted, pointing at the ground in front of them.

A shimmering vein of ice ran through the rock, surrounding a stone peak.

"It won't hold. Take the drakes around the sides. We need to find a place to rest." The prince spoke quietly to Katrin, and Dani touched Liam's hand on her waist.

"Guide me. Left?" Her calm voice helped steady Liam's nerves.

He squeezed the left side of her waist, just as he had on the battlefield when they first rode Ousa together. "Yes, maybe ten drake paces or so. That will get us clear of the bit that might collapse. Or did... I suppose."

Dani urged Ousa to the side, and the drake huffed as they took the less direct path. They slid down another few feet before Ousa hoisted himself up a sheer ten-foot cliff, belly scratching along the stone as he crested the top.

The others did the same on the opposite side.

Ahead, the mountain scape flattened into a snowy valley, peppered with pine trees at the edges. The deep green of their needles was hardly visible beneath the thick blanket of snow.

"I'd go straight ahead for at least fifty yards, just to be safe," Liam whispered to Dani as he tried to make eye contact with Matthias, but his own thick layers covered his face.

Katrin shook out the map as she pressed it against Brek's scaly neck, her gloved fingers running over the surface. She paused as she glanced back over her shoulder, exchanging words that Liam couldn't hear.

Brek veered towards them, parting the thick snow that rose to his chest without a problem, as if a snake weaving through sand. He halted at a command from Katrin.

"Wait!" Matthias looked at Liam, and Ousa paused, too. "I don't think I can jump again. Not far, at least. We should be careful here. There's too much snow to see if the ground is stable enough to handle the drakes' weight."

Dani unbuckled the strap at her thigh. "I'll check!" She freed her leg before working on the next one, lowering her voice to speak to Liam. "Just like before."

"Be careful." Liam hated that it'd become necessary for her to tunnel through the snow as a cat to check the rocks for breaks.

Almost better to stay right here until Matthias can jump again.

Taking hold of her wrist, Liam supported Dani as she dropped from the saddle. Her body sank until the snow reached her waist. She wobbled briefly, proving she couldn't touch the solid rock beneath.

Dani fell forward, white fur spreading over her body until her tail lashed behind her. She dove under the snow, disappearing.

Ousa shifted, tail lashing and spraying bits of frost into the air. A spectrum of colors flashed in the water vapors, which would have been beautiful without all the danger involved.

Liam patted his neck. "Easy. She'll be right back."

Ousa lowered his head, letting out a gulping whine. Burrowing his nose into the snow, his sides heaved with deep, snuffing breaths.

A white blur burst from the snow, thirty yards away, and Dani's panther form landed on a jut of rock protruding from the powder. She climbed to the top before returning to her human form, balanced on the tip. "We cannot stop here!" Her voice barely carried so far over the howling wind. "There's something wrong! Go back!"

Well, that's ominous.

Liam tugged his scarf down off his mouth. "How are you going to get back to us?"

"I'll find another way!"

Liam nodded as he patted Ousa's neck. "Veet." It took him a

moment to remember the old Dtrüa command for 'go back,' but the drake didn't obey.

Ousa whined, lifting his head towards Dani.

"She's fine, you big softie. She'll catch up to us. Veet." Liam pulled on the reins, but Ousa shook his head, forcing Liam's grip to slack.

Brek's growl rumbled across the snow, the older, larger drake already cautiously backpedaling.

Ousa snapped his jaws in irritation and took a forward step instead, closer to Dani.

"Ousa, no!" Dani held out a hand, but a tremor shook through the ground beneath them all.

Thunder shuddered beneath the snow.

"Shit."

The younger drake balked, retreating, but the surrounding snow dropped with the ground. It settled for only a breath before collapsing.

Dani shrieked, her human voice morphing into a cat's yeowl as her stony peak ruptured with the rest of the mountain floor.

Liam pushed himself forward against Ousa, bracing his hands behind his neck and praying the drake would find his footing and not land on his back. There was no way he'd be able to free himself from the harnesses in time. The world around him brightened to white, a cacophony of cracking accompanying his plummet through open air.

Ousa howled as his feet beat on nothingness, Brek's deeper bellow answering as he scrambled to grip onto collapsing ice.

Katrin yelped as Brek tumbled. "Matthias!"

Liam tried to find his sister and the prince in his spinning surroundings, but couldn't. He couldn't find Dani, either, as rocks and snow fell with them. Stone, barely visible in encroaching darkness, rushed up, and Liam already knew they'd been falling too long to survive, drakes or not.

Why hasn't Matthias jumped?

The world jolted as Ousa smashed through a thin layer of rock, claws scraping to gain a hold on something but failing.

The attempt propelled them into a spiral and, somewhere above, Katrin screamed. "Matthias, wake up!" Her voice echoed through the expansive space, and Liam's heart seized.

Fuck.

Another jolt rocked through him, Ousa grunting as his claws scraped invisible walls in the dark, but then a fiery burst of air choked Liam's lungs.

Red and orange swirled around him as they fell, and he caught glimpses of the bottom, at least a hundred feet away.

Molten magma bubbled in bright pools, consuming the whole lower portion of the mountain.

Death approached without the flashes of regrets and victories Liam expected. He tore his eyes away to search the glowing cavern.

"Liam!" Dani's voice came from behind him, and he twisted to see her holding onto the spines on Ousa's rump. Her white hair whipped around her face, cloudy eyes directed at him.

Liam unbuckled his legs as he looked at the ground, fast approaching, and realized he'd never reach her in time.

In time for what?

The magma sputtered, heating his skin to burning temperatures as he, Ousa, and Dani met the surface and the world flashed in a kaleidoscope of color.

The heat disappeared, and the sky brightened.

Sky?

Liam blinked, no longer on Ousa's back, but kept falling. A loud splash overtook his senses before it faded in the foggy ebb of water. The cold sent his body tingling as he tried to comprehend how he was still alive within the lava, but the navy blue depths and glittering surface above him left him dizzy.

The crystalline water broke as the drake collided with it.

He swam out of the way as Ousa surged deeper, furiously kicking and sending currents that forced Liam further away.

Dani struck the water twenty feet from him, but her motionless body only sank.

Liam's lungs burned as he crested the water, sucking in a rapid breath before he dove again. Stripping away his cloak as he swam after Dani, he hurried to remove the bulky coat slowing him.

Above him, water crashed again as Brek and his riders landed.

Liam caught hold of Dani's arm, drifting limply as the depths pulled her down. He kicked desperately, pulling his wife closer. With all his strength, he rushed towards the light, Ousa and Brek's dark shapes blotting out the sun.

Sweet air filled his lungs as he gasped, flinging his arm out towards Ousa's saddle. The drake paddled, nearly pulling Dani and him beneath the surface again with the strength of the current he created.

Ousa's mouth hung open in a pant as he turned towards his riders, slowing his feet to allow Liam to hoist Dani up over his back.

"Are you all right?" Katrin's voice sent a ripple of surprise through Liam, encouraging him to face his sister. She still sat on Brek, whose head whipped back and forth to examine their surroundings with narrowed eyes.

Matthias freed his legs, diving into the water.

Liam grunted as he pulled himself onto Ousa, the prince helping haul Dani up with him. He checked the pulse at her throat and held his hand against her chest that swelled with sudden breath.

She coughed, water spewing from her lips as she buckled over in front of him, grasping at Ousa's scales with a rattling breath and more coughing.

Liam sighed, pressing his hand gently to Dani's back. He turned to Katrin, and his eyes widened. Beyond the coast of the lake, massive jungle trees rose against a vibrant morning sky. The ridges and mountains behind them held more green, vines and foliage dominating every inch of the terrain.

Is this the Afterlife?

The magma had burned them alive faster than they could recognize the pain.

Matthias, treading water, stared in the opposite direction. "I tried to jump once we hit the water, but it didn't work past... whatever just happened." He glanced at Katrin before focusing again on the distance. "Where are we?"

Katrin stared at the sky, where a wisp of something like a fine spider web rippled. "I have no idea," she whispered. "But the power I felt when we fell..." She narrowed her eyes, spine straightening with a gasp.

Liam looked up to follow her gaze, but his eyes locked on a pair of distant shapes rather than the power hovering above them.

Two creatures soared along a distant vine-covered cliff side, their enormous wings catching a warm draft from the jungle floor and propelling them over the ridge.

Liam's heart stopped.

Dragons.

Dani caught her breath, holding onto Liam. "Someone tell me what we're all looking at."

Ousa chuffed, veering away from Matthias and moving without direction towards the root-choked shore. Water churned around him as he reached a root, and Liam seized the front of the saddle to hold him and Dani in place as the drake crawled into the wild undergrowth.

"I don't think we're in the mountains anymore." Liam looked back as Brek and his two riders joined them, both drakes dripping onto the bright blossoms and ferns. "I've never seen a place like this. But I think we might have found what we were looking for."

Ousa huffed, turning frantically to Brek and stomping forward. The two drakes exchanged grunts, and Liam could feel Ousa growing tenser beneath them.

Katrin frowned, patting Brek on the neck before glancing at Matthias behind her. They also had an unspoken conversation.

Liam grumbled. "Anyone going to say anything? We should be dead."

"But we aren't..." Katrin wrung the end of her cloak out as she stripped its soaking leather from her shoulders.

"Some of us cannot see!" Dani squeezed Liam's arm. "What is this place, and why are we still alive?"

"I don't know." Liam took her hand. "I don't know how to describe it to you. But there were a pair of dragons out by the ridge. Real dragons. Not wyverns."

"I couldn't tell how big they were. I don't know how far that ridge actually is from us. But whatever we fell through..." Katrin glanced back at the lake, stripping off her outer coat. "Give me a moment to get a little oriented, Dani, and I'll show you."

Dani slid off Ousa but stilled. "What's that sound?"

"What sound?" Liam followed her, struggling to navigate the jungle's brush, taller than him.

"Wings." The Dtrüa looked up. "I think someone noticed our arrival."

Ousa whirled, circling Dani and Liam like a protective parent. His tail pulled them against his wet flank, a growl rumbling from deep in his chest as he lifted his head towards the canopy.

Leaves and branches creaked as everything above them shifted. The sky, lost beyond the trees, flickered back into existence over them as the trunks and vines leaned outward, pushed apart like blades of grass. They reshaped themselves, creating a clearing as the low-lying foliage grew over to reform the land. A new hill rippled into existence beside them, the beating of wings growing louder.

"There's no way we can run in this mess of a jungle," Liam whispered to Dani as he pulled her close and realized her eyes were already closed in concentration. "You're going to have to act fast to get it to trust us."

Ousa's growl grew more ferocious, and Brek moved in beside him, Katrin and Matthias slipping from their saddle.

"It won't work." Dani shook her head. "The way I speak to Ousa or other animals requires a path that isn't there. I cannot talk to it." She pressed her back to Liam, breathing faster.

Katrin slipped in beside, wrapping her arm through Dani's as her brow furrowed.

"Shit." Liam looked at Matthias, and he could see the prince also calculating the chances of their survival against a creature neither had ever seen.

Great wings lowered the dragon, its crimson spiked head angled at them. Its maw hovered open, rows of jagged teeth dripping with saliva. It huffed, whipping their hair back with one breath and silencing the drakes.

As it dominated the air in front of them, its tail lashed behind, a sharp spade at its tip. Each flap of its wings rustled the jungle greenery. Finally, it landed, four legs contacting the ground and sending a shudder beneath their feet.

The dragon stood at least five times as tall as a human, each tooth the size of Liam's arm. It chuffed again, and Ousa shirked a step back, pulling Liam and Dani with him.

"What's happening?" The prince glanced sideways at Liam, but Dani responded.

"I think it's communicating with Brek and Ousa."

"Why can it talk to them, but not you?" Katrin whispered.

"I don't know, it's not—"

"Silence!"

The dragon's bellow stole Liam's breath, vibrating the ground beneath his soaked boots. "Did it just..."

Ousa tossed his head to Liam, giving him a low warning growl that made the hairs on his neck stand on end. The drake turned back to the dragon with an apologetic whimper.

The magnificent beast snorted, crouching lower to the new jungle floor. Its tongue lashed, more sounds like words pouring from it, but Liam couldn't understand the language.

Ousa took another step back, moving in tandem with Brek to tighten their protective circle around the four humans.

The dragon's cat-like eyes narrowed, giving a look that conveyed annoyance around the scales and spiny features.

Katrin whispered it as Liam realized the truth. "They have language. They're intelligent."

The dragon snorted again, lowering its head to be even with the drakes. To their credit, neither of them balked, despite the dragon's jaws being large enough to snap them in half.

"You are not welcome here, humans." The dragon's deep voice rumbled through Liam's chest, like an echoing thunderstorm. "You're fortunate to have our kind protecting you, or you'd be charred cinders already."

Liam met his sister's eyes, astonished to see not fear, but wonder in them as she peered beneath Brek's neck.

"We mean you no harm." Katrin kept her voice steady. "Rather, we've come to warn you."

"Warn?" The dragon sounded amused as it lifted its head again, peering down at them. "Come to warn us before stealing more of our eggs, human?"

Gods, it's smart enough to be sarcastic.

"No! We're not from Feyor. We don't want your eggs."

"Just us, then. And Draxix." The dragon's tail lashed behind it, colliding with a tree at the edge of the clearing, shattering the trunk. "You will not leave here alive."

"Is Draxix the name of this place?" Matthias spoke up. "We have no desire to harm your lands."

Dani stepped from Liam. "I'm sorry about the eggs. I mean, I never stole them, but I know who did."

The dragon growled, jaws snapping in a vicious clash of teeth, which made Liam wince.

Dani held out her hand. "Please. We're not your enemy."

"How did you find the portal?" The dragon took a step forward, and Ousa pulled Dani in closer with his tail again.

"An accident." Liam pushed against the tightening tail. "There was a cave in, and rock collapsed, and we fell..."

"We were looking for you, for your kind, but we didn't know what we'd find." Katrin scratched Brek's neck just long enough to distract him so she could slip beneath his neck, stepping out in front of the drakes.

"Kat!" Matthias followed her, grasping her wrist.

She turned only slightly, pushing Matthias's chest as she stepped forward again, but he didn't let go.

The dragon looked down, a claw crunching into wood beneath its feet as it lowered its head again. "But you admit to looking for us. To seeking a way to Draxix."

"We thought you were in the mountains. We want to protect you from Feyor."

"Feyor." The dragon's tongue curled over its scaled lips as its head lowered closer to Matthias and Katrin. Its nostrils flared as it took in a deep breath. "You are not like the ones sent before. I smell the Art on you both."

Dani patted Ousa's head, and the drake purred. "Feyor wants more than eggs, now. They think they can control you like they control your brethren."

"Like *you* control them?" The dragon turned its attention toward Dani, nostrils flaring again. "You smell more of those who came for our hatchlings."

Liam wrapped an arm around Dani's waist, pulling her behind him.

Even though that thing could swallow us both at the same time.

"I am a Dtrüa." Dani lifted her hands, side stepping Liam's cover. "But I do not control Ousa or Brek. They chose me in a war, and they chose Katrin, because she healed Brek. We are allies."

"War." The word sounded tainted from the dragon's mouth. "Another failure of human society. Though you did not have proper shepherds to teach you peace before the world broke apart."

"The burden of war isn't ours alone to bear. Feyor uses drakes and wyverns, claiming their lives as readily as their soldiers'." Dani stepped forward.

"And you have prepared these two to offer the same for you. They would die for you." The dragon turned back to Matthias and Katrin as Brek gave a low warning growl.

Liam could have sworn the dragon's mouth curled in a smile.

"That is earned through mutual trust." Katrin glanced at the drake before looking back up. "Trust that perhaps we can build as well? We want to protect you and your brethren."

The dragon paused, its massive wings flexing on its back before they settled into a folded position. Slowly, it lowered further to the ground, its legs curling beneath it. "I will listen. Out of respect for the power I sense in you three." The dragon cast a glance at Liam with a shake of its head. "He is of little consequence."

Gee, thanks, dragon.

Chapter 38

"What is your name?" Dani patted Ousa again, urging him aside so she could join Katrin and Matthias.

If Feyor ever found this place...

Liam grabbed her upper arm. "Are you sure? You can't see the teeth that thing has."

Dani lowered her voice. "I must try." She squeezed his arm before facing the dragon. "I am Varadani, and this is Liam. The man with Katrin is Matthias."

The dragon's wings rustled. "My name is not meant for this language. But you may call me Zaelinstra Zamos Ziyarian."

Dani cleared her throat. "Maybe we can call you Zaelinstra?"

The dragon snorted. "Very well. But you best pray to whatever gods your kind still worships that it remains only my élanvital and I who noticed your entrance into Draxix."

Katrin used that word for us.

The Dtrüa redirected her blurry gaze to the acolyte, but Katrin said nothing.

"Perhaps we can reach an agreement that suits us all." Matthias's tone took on a political nature, and she wondered if that would help or hinder the discussion. "My country is at war with Feyor because my land... *Isalica's* land encompasses the mountains that house your portal. We seek to protect it, but our efforts fall in vain when Feyor uses draconi to push us back. If we win this war, we can keep your secret, your lands, and your eggs safe. But we won't win if Feyor continues to use your brethren against us."

"You seem to have this all figured out, human." An amused tone filled the dragon's deep voice. "But there is a far simpler way to keep our secret, one many of my *brethren* would agree with."

"You could kill us." Dani swallowed, playing with the bone ring around her thumb. "It would be easy. But it wouldn't solve your problem."

Warm breath pushed Dani's hair back from her face as the dragon lumbered closer, blocking out the light.

Liam's hand slipped into hers, tightening.

"Perhaps not, but it would make me feel better." Zaelinstra's tongue rolled over its lip with a wet smacking sound.

Dani cringed. "I doubt we taste very good. If we can find this place, so can Feyor. Especially if we lose this war."

"And who are you to come seeking the aid of the dragons for war?" The voice moved further away, and the dragon's head swiveled towards the prince.

"We're the ones who truly want to keep you and your hatchlings safe." Katrin's boot snapped a twig as she stepped forward again. "I found books about your roosts here in the mountains, about the markers that used to lead to Thrallenax. At least that's what the stories called it. The dragon homelands?"

"Draxix is our home now. Thrallenax is gone."

"But you need it for your eggs, don't you? There weren't details about the hatching process, but our ancient scholars predicted it was the extreme temperatures available in the Yandarin Mountains that helped hatch the dragons there. The ice and the lava in the mountain..." Katrin sucked in a breath, as if she'd forgotten to do so while she spoke. "We can help protect the nesting grounds."

Zaelinstra huffed. "*We*? You continue to insist on such things... but *who* are you? Names mean nothing to me."

"I am Isalica's crown prince, and Katrin is to be my wife."

Zaelinstra hesitated, and the pause between them seemed to stretch for an eternity. "You are the future king of the country surrounding Thrallenax?"

Dani imagined Matthias nodding.

"I am. And until the day I am crowned, my father will protect your mountain with equal ferocity."

The dragon's wings shifted, a great puff of wind threatening Dani's balance as Zaelinstra rose. "And how may I trust your word when you have sworn by nothing?"

"What is it you wish me to swear on? I can offer you all I have, as my word is my bond."

The dragon inhaled, its massive snout in front of Matthias and Katrin. "Swear by your future wife. And your seed she carries within her."

Silence descended for a breath before Matthias spoke again. "My what?"

The dragon huffed again.

"I don't know what she's talking about." Katrin's voice raised in pitch. "But I've..."

Dani narrowed her eyes, focusing on Katrin's scent for the first time in weeks. Orange again tinted the acolyte's yellow aura, but the change must have been gradual.

How did I miss that?

"I'm pregnant?" Katrin whispered the question.

Dani wanted to hug her friend, but resisted, even as emotion burned her eyes.

A low rumble echoed from Zaelinstra, a rolling chuckle. "Yes, future queen. And hatchlings are our most sacred possession. It seems appropriate for the future king to swear upon his own to protect ours."

Chapter 39

Katrin ran her hands over her abdomen, already imagining the tiny life within. Nausea grew in her gut, the same feeling she'd been ignoring while they traveled. She'd believed the stress of the journey to be the cause, as well as the culprit for her missed cycle.

Will I lose this one, too?

Matthias squeezed her shoulder before pulling her into an embrace. "I can't believe you climbed a mountain... pregnant." He kissed her head.

"I didn't know." Dread crept in as she realized how taxing the journey had been on her body, and what it would take to return to Nema's Throne.

The prince pulled away and met her gaze. "I see those thoughts spiraling in your head. Relax. We'll find a way." He brushed her cheek with his thumb, smiling, before looking at the dragon. "I swear, by wife and my child, that I will do everything in my power to protect the Yandarin Mountains and the secrets they keep."

Like a statue, the dragon stared at Matthias for several moments before huffing. "Then what is it you ask of my brethren?"

Katrin's knees wobbled, but Brek leaned closer to offer her support as if he knew. She pressed her hand to his flank, his scales supple and warm against her palm.

Matthias's face held his usual stoicism as he turned from her to Zaelinstra. "We need your help with the drakes and wyverns under Feyor's control. I am sorry I have to ask it. I realize your kind would much rather remain secret."

"The myth our kind intended to become has clearly been thwarted by human greed." She surveyed the rest of them. "And curiosity. But I am not one of our most trusted and cannot guarantee such alliances. However, you have offered little more than to keep secret what you already should."

"Well, is there anything you need?" Liam cast Matthias a wary glance before he looked back at the dragon. "Something we can provide?"

Zaelinstra turned slowly to him, her cat eyes narrowing. "Perhaps."

"Protection of the mountains would encompass keeping your eggs safe, too." Matthias motioned to the dragon. "We can build encampments at every pass entering the Yandarin Mountains. There aren't that many. No one would steal another egg."

Tilting her head, the dragon seemed to consider. "Then I will take your offer to the Primeval. But I cannot make any promises myself. It is not my place."

"Prime evil? Sounds ominous," Liam whispered.

Dani elbowed him. "It means ancient."

"That's all we ask." Matthias ignored his crown elites and glanced at Katrin, his eyes still bright. "Much better than being roasted."

She smiled as she reached for his hand again. Seeing the joy made her want to keep whatever hope she could. Her hand warmed in his. "Should we remain while you speak to this Primeval?"

The dragon huffed and shook her massive head. "No. Visitors are not welcome in Draxix. You're fortunate I was willing to listen to your drakes."

Ousa whined, pushing against Dani's back.

"I will show you a way to return to Thrallenax. Your Yandarin Mountains. A way the drakes can travel." The dragon rocked back, standing to her impressive height and forcing all of them to look up.

Katrin squinted as sunlight shimmered off the dragon's crimson scales. "Thank you for your trust in us."

"Do not return. Do not send others here. When we are ready to speak with you, you will know. To betray our trust will have unfathomable consequences." Zaelinstra growled. "Do you understand?"

Chapter 40

Matthias is home again.
Say goodbye.
Only death will follow him.
Until he is mine.
And he will be mine.

One month later...

"You need to come with me." Micah motioned with his head, not giving Matthias a chance to properly greet him before striding away.

"Can't we settle in, first?" The prince glanced back at the rest of their mountain-scaling group. "I haven't seen you or Stefan since the battle. How is his recovery going?"

Katrin stripped her cloak from her shoulders, handing it to the trailing staff member as they moved further from the foyer. She kept up close behind, exchanging a look with Dani.

The hallways were dark, the windows shuttered in a way Matthias hadn't seen in years.

Not since Mom died.

"Stefan is fine, but your father isn't." Micah met Matthias's gaze, worry clouding his expression. "You need to see him."

Matthias's stomach twisted. "My father only had a cough when we left. What do you mean he's not fine?"

"I'm sorry, Matt. It's not just a cough anymore."

The prince swallowed, his heart speeding. "How bad?"

Micah didn't answer, turning into the hallway and ascending the stairs leading to the king's chambers. The rest of his friends' footsteps echoed gently behind him.

"Micah." Matthias caught his friend by the forearm, halting them all. "How bad?"

His stand-in shook his head. "We're going straight there to give you a chance to say goodbye."

Matthias clenched his jaw, heat springing at the back of his eyes. He nodded, unable to form more words.

Katrin kept a firm hold of his hand as they continued, her grip tightening in a silent attempt at impossible comfort. "Are there healers with him?"

"Yes. Merissa is back, too, but they've all failed to combat whatever he has." Micah's tone remained stoic, staying strong for Matthias.

"We should give you space." Dani's soft voice came behind him, holding the empathy he didn't want.

Not again. I'm not ready.

"I'd rather you stay, if that's all right." Matthias glanced at them, unable to hold their concerned gazes.

"Of course." Liam bit his lower lip as he nodded. "Whatever you need." His voice carried the same tones as Dani's, tightening the knot of finality in Matthias's chest.

This is too familiar.

They slowed once they reached the closed door to Geroth's private bedroom. Healers and advisors lingered in the sitting room, falling silent with the prince's approach.

"I'll speak with Merissa." Katrin stepped closer, touching Matthias's beard. "You go see him. I'll be right there."

He nodded, glancing at the others.

Travel worn, they all looked horribly out of place within the decorated sitting room.

Failing to find his voice, he just nodded again and entered his father's bedroom.

A woman stood beside the king, pressing a damp cloth to his sweat-beaded brow. Her long raven hair hung down over her thin shoulders, almost as tall as his. Her bright green eyes darted up to meet his before they returned to the king as he wheezed. The auer, a new healer assigned by Merissa just before they left, bowed her head to the prince as she set the cloth aside. With her gaze still lowered, she stepped around the king's bed to the door.

Seiler stood from the chair in the corner of the room, silent until the auer closed the door behind her. "You'd think an auer could figure out what's wrong with him. But..." He held out his empty palms towards Matthias. "Nothing. They can't find anything."

Matthias strode into the room, the instinct to protect his younger brother from the pain of losing a parent resurfacing in his mind. He embraced his brother, grateful to feel Seiler's arms around him, too. "I should have been here. I'm sorry."

"You were doing important things. And you're here, now." Seiler moved back, squeezing his older brother's shoulder. "I worried you wouldn't make it in time." His voice held steady, as if too tired to show the emotion anymore. "I'm glad you did. He's been asking about you."

Matthias took a deep breath, patting Seiler's shoulder before approaching his father's bed.

The king lay amid piles of dark wool blankets, a black fur draped across his lap, arms over it. His brown hair, streaked with silver, stuck to his temples. Red flushed his cheeks even beneath his beard.

The crown prince dragged the stool next to the bed, sitting. "Dad? I'm here."

Geroth's eyelids fluttered before opening, and his mouth twitched in a smile as he saw his eldest son. "You made it home safe." He sucked in a tight breath, but didn't cough. "I'm glad. What of the others with you? Your bride?"

Matthias tried not to cringe, forcing a smile. "We're all safe. All here." His throat clenched, but he battled to keep the tears at bay. "Katrin's pregnant, Dad."

Geroth smiled wider, age lines creasing near his eyes. "That's wonderful."

Seiler turned his back, lifting a hand to wipe tears without their father seeing while he pretended to look out the window at the rest of the city.

Bowing his head, Matthias took his father's hand. "I'm so sorry I left you. If I'd known..."

The blue of his father's veins shone through his thinned skin, stretched across the bone and fading muscles like a man forty years older.

"Nonsense. It was just a cough. Until it wasn't. And what you were doing was important. *Is* important. For our country. You will make a fine king, and a fine father." Geroth's words came as little more than a whisper, his voice rough.

Matthias squeezed his eyes shut, his voice lowering as tears fell. "I'm not ready. I don't want to lose you. It's too soon."

Geroth wheezed another breath as Seiler took the stool across from Matthias. "Find joy, my sons. I get to see your mother soon. Rehtaeh is waiting for me beside Nymaera. I'll tell her all her sons have become."

Leaning over the bed, Matthias pressed his forehead to his father's hand.

"Tell her we love her," Seiler whispered. "And we love you, Dad."

Matthias nodded, his throat too tight for him to speak.

"I know." Geroth coughed, the sound like boulders in a landslide. "My boys. I'll always be with you, no matter what. Stay with me, won't you?"

Kissing his father's hand, Matthias straightened, briefly meeting Seiler's gaze. "We're not going anywhere."

Geroth grimaced, his next rattling breath shaking his entire body as he slipped his hand away from Matthias. He touched the gold signet ring on his left hand, slipping it from his too-thin finger. Cringing, as if the weight of the ring was too much, he pressed it into Matthias's palm. "This is yours, now. Take care of it?"

"I'll do my very best." Matthias closed his fist around the royal signet, swallowing as he met the king's eyes. "I love you."

Geroth squeezed his hand, closing his eyes. "One day, I will see you both again. And you will tell me all you have done in the years apart. The many, many years."

Matthias and Seiler fell silent, each holding one of Geroth's hands.

"Talk to me while I rest."

Matthias steeled the emotion from his throat as he nodded. The princes took turns telling their father stories from the past decade. What happened when Seiler first met Kelsara, how they'd butted heads in the beginning.

How Katrin had healed Matthias in the temple fire then accompanied him to the border.

The princes talked until Geroth fell asleep, his breathing uneven and raspy.

Matthias didn't look up from his father as he whispered to his brother. "Is Kelsara in Ziona already?"

"Yes. Her mother requested her presence."

"You'll join her, then?" Matthias couldn't say the word.

Seiler nodded, his eyes bloodshot, and spoke what Matthias couldn't. "After."

Geroth exhaled a shallow breath, and his chest didn't rise again.

Matthias breathed harder, tears wetting his cheeks. "May you find peace with Nymaera," he murmured, kissing Geroth's forehead. He laid his father's hand over his middle, his brother doing the same.

They remained beside him for some time, unaware of when the sun set, before a soft knock came at the door.

It swung open, and Katrin quietly entered the room, the skirt of a clean dress wisping along the floor. She paused as she met Matthias's eyes, tears already glimmering at the bottom of hers. "Is he...?"

Matthias bowed his head, shaking it. "He's gone."

Her shoulders drooped as she looked at the king's still body, approaching the bed. Running a hand over Seiler's shoulder, she continued to Matthias. She kissed the top of his head as she wrapped her arms around him, somehow keeping her voice steady. "I'm so sorry."

Seiler stood. "I'll go speak with Loryena."

"I've sent most of the advisors away," Katrin whispered, but didn't take her eyes from Matthias as she stroked his hair.

"Thank you." The younger prince nodded, his voice hollow.

Crossing the room, he exited, closing the door behind him.

As soon as it clicked shut, Matthias leaned into Katrin, shutting his eyes against her stomach. A sob escaped his throat, and he wrapped his arms around her.

She stood silently as she held him, offering what comfort her presence could provide. Holding him tightly, she ran her hands over him.

Sniffing, he straightened, wiping his hands over his face. "At least I got to see him. He deserved better."

Katrin ran her hands over his damp cheeks as he stood. "I wish there was more that could have been done."

"Me, too." Matthias nodded, taking a deeper breath. "I—"

A muffled shout reverberated from the front sitting room before the bedroom door jolted open.

Merissa walked inside, Liam and Dani on her heels.

"Have some respect. What's gotten into you?" Liam gaped as he paused in the doorway. His eyes darted inside to Matthias and Katrin before going to the king's body. Anger colored his face as if they'd already been arguing.

Matthias frowned at the healer. "This isn't the time. Leave."

"No, this is precisely the time." Merissa squared her shoulders as she stepped into the center of the open floor between Geroth's bed and the fireplace on the far side. The glowing flames sent her shadow over the four-poster bed, stretching across the room.

"You will leave." Dani reached for Merissa, but the healer spun and lashed a hand out. The flickering shadows cast by the fire twitched. The physical strike didn't touch the Dtrüa, but she flew into the far wall with a crash.

Liam gaped, turning towards Dani for only an instant before he drew his sword and faced the healer.

"I am *done* pretending to take orders from you," Merissa snarled at Matthias, her eyes dappled with black and gold. "The king is dead. The time has come."

Dread pooled in Matthias's gut. "What are you talking about?"

"Merissa." Katrin stepped beside Matthias, drawing the healer's obsidian gaze.

"*Merissa*," the priestess mocked, her tone sickly. "Always looking to Merissa. She knows best, doesn't she?" A wicked smile crept across the healer's face as her eyes darted back to the crown prince. "You've always trusted her. That's why she made the perfect vessel, even if her Art lacked *true* substance."

Memories flashed in his mind of all the times his healer hadn't seemed like herself. Ever since they'd left her at the temple. But the temple had been destroyed.

With only one survivor.

The prince gritted his teeth. "Who are you?"

"Such a smart little prince." Merissa smirked, her eyes drifting to the body on the bed. "Oops... king."

She was taking care of my...

Matthias stepped towards her, rage igniting in his chest. "Did you kill him?"

Gold flashed in her eyes, the black within them filling the rest of her iris and sclera. "Not personally, though I will happily claim the credit." Merissa rolled her shoulders, and the shadows at her feet rippled like a stone dropped in a pond. "I needed you to suffer."

Sidestepping, the prince put himself between Merissa and Katrin. His heart ached. "Why?"

Merissa hummed as she watched Katrin side-step towards the window. "So this would hurt more."

Shadow tendrils moved before anyone could react, lashing out at Liam, who'd crept forward with Merissa's distraction. Darkness circled the crown elite, burrowing into his flesh like a thousand leeches.

The prince lunged, but shadow rooted his feet to the floor. "Stop this!"

Dani staggered from where she'd risen and ran towards Liam's scream, only to have the shadow engulf her with him. They struggled to escape as color drained from their faces.

Wildly, Liam swung his sword at a rising tendril of shadow arcing to Dani, but the metal passed through it without connecting.

Merissa's hand twitched, and the tainted Art coursed through the air as Liam collapsed to his knees.

Matthias breathed faster, watching helplessly as Dani dropped, too. The Dtrüa choked, raking at her throat, and her eyes rolled back. Black ooze spurted from her mouth.

Liam cried out in rage as her body fell, but it faded beneath the sputter of inky black from his own mouth.

"No!" Katrin sobbed from behind him.

Micah and Stefan burst into the room, panting, only to be flung off their feet by another reach of shadow.

She wants me to jump.

"Hurry, Matthias. You're running out of *time*." Merissa sneered at the prince. Stepping towards him, she held out her open palm, a wriggling cloud of black swirling along her fingers.

It leapt at him, and pain sparked from the slice left on his forearm.

Matthias growled and shouted, "What do you want?"

"One." Merissa's smile held a sinister edge he'd never believed the healer's face capable of. "This will be further encouragement." Shadows writhed up the walls, and a pair shot out from the window frame behind Katrin, seizing her around the middle.

"No!" Matthias tried to move again, but his legs sat anchored in onyx stone, blood trickling down his arm.

The acolyte shouted in surprise as the darkness yanked her back, and glass shattered. Her body fell, disappearing beyond the window frame, and her scream faded as she plummeted towards the stone courtyard below.

"Fuck." Matthias flooded his veins with his power.

Merissa rolled her shoulders. "I needed you to suffer." Her eyes flickered over him, pausing at the blood welling through his tunic sleeve. "Ah, perhaps you already have."

Matthias panted, glancing at everyone still alive in that room. His eyes landed on Katrin, and his heart twisted. "Stand down." The command rang clear through the room, and everyone stilled as he met Merissa's gaze. "What do you want?"

The shadows at her feet gathered thicker, and the air hummed with power. With a snap of her fingers, a dart of obsidian lunged at Matthias's arm, directly beside the first mark, and tore through his flesh.

"Two."

The prince yelled, clutching his arm. "Tell me what you want!" He glanced at Liam, motioning with his gaze to the sword in the elite's hand. Matthias still had his, too, and kept a hand near the hilt.

Micah and Stefan entered the room, their faces grim, but halted when Matthias lifted a hand.

"I want you," Merissa purred. She looked down at her hands, aged and gnarled beyond her years. The fingers twisted by arthritis and blotched with sun damage. New wrinkles had formed on her face, and her hair looked thinner. "This body... won't last much longer. And she's... uncooperative, though she still told me plenty."

Fear spiked in the back of Matthias's mind. "You want... my body?" He shook his head. "What does that even mean?"

Merissa pursed her lips, the gold in her eyes flashing. "There are... rules." Annoyance tainted her tone. "Stipulations that must be met. But you will accept me, and you will grant me your power. Or everyone you care about will die."

Matthias looked at his hands before swallowing. "Who are you?"

How can I give this monster the kingdom when I just swore to protect it?

"I believe that requires a demonstration." Merissa turned, but then hesitated with a coy smile. "You'll have plenty of time to jump, my king. Let me properly show you."

Liam narrowed his eyes, and Matthias gave a minute gesture with his chin. It was all the soldier needed. He lunged into the center of the room and his sword connected with shadow, causing Matthias to question what he'd seen before jumping back.

A tendril lashed, pushing Liam's sword back, but the crown elite countered, swinging wide. His blade connected with Merissa's stomach, and she cried out as she stumbled back.

The shadows at her feet vanished, falling to the usual shapes the fire cast as Merissa clutched at the sword protruding from her gut.

"Run!" Matthias pulled Katrin sideways, shoving her towards the door.

Before his betrothed reached the doorway, it clouded over with darkness, and Micah grabbed her before she could fall into it.

Merissa's cries of pain morphed into laughter, and she pulled the sword out of herself. The flesh webbed together with tar, pulling it closed as if nothing had happened. "You know, your healer can feel that, even if I can't. Her cries are a great inspiration in my acting."

The black in the doorway surged, forcing all to step away from it before the entire wall became encompassed in writhing shadows, like a pit of snakes.

"More demonstration, Matthias?" Merissa mused as she peeked over her shoulder at him. Before he could say otherwise, a section of the wall collapsed onto Stefan, who'd skulked around the edge of the room towards the fireplace.

As the shadow fell over him like a sheer cloth, it tightened against his skin. The veins in his neck and face blackened. He collapsed to his knees. His body shriveled, the skin turning ashen as the skeleton beneath his muscles became more defined. A husk hit the floor, rivers of black oozing from it.

She breathed in a contented sigh. "Tastes lovely."

Matthias looked away, gulping back his fear as Katrin wept in Micah's arms. "Don't do this."

"You can stop it all if you accept me." Merissa waved her hand vaguely at Stefan. "Take that all back and make him alive again. No one will remember."

"I can't give you Isalica." Matthias cringed, thinking of all the innocent people who would be under the command of a vile monster.

"Think it... the lesser evil." Merissa stepped towards him. "Shall we go back so I can show you more? Or is this enough?" She stood beside him as she twisted her hand behind her, and the shadow wall fell on top of the rest of his friends like a thin sheet of snow.

Matthias watched in horror as the others slumped, weakened by the shadows the same way Stefan had been. Their bodies shriveled, and he stared at Katrin.

The acolyte balked as Micah collapsed, her eyes finding the prince in a panic. "Matthias, what's happening?" She gasped as her hands aged, skin peeling off her knuckles.

Matthias closed his eyes, his heart breaking.

I can't watch her die again.

"I needed you to suffer."

Matthias bowed his head, grabbing Katrin's shoulder and hauling her behind him. "Stand down. No one move."

Another slice of pain flashed over his arm.

"Three. Then it's time for the grand finale." Merissa's shadows pulsed outward.

"I don't need a finale. Please, what else can I offer you? What else will make you stop? I can't hand my country to a faceless creature." Matthias shook his head, his hope dwindling.

"Matthias?" Katrin's grip tightened around his wrist.

"She keeps killing you all," Matthias whispered, not letting go of her arm. "Stay behind me."

Merissa pouted, walking towards them. "Spoiling the surprise."

Matthias pulled Katrin to the side as Merissa continued past with an amused smile, crossing to the window.

"You worry about your kingdom in the hands of a monster?" Merissa's tendrils of shadow snaked up the walls around the window.

They passed through the glass, slithering out of sight. "What kingdom?"

The prince followed her gaze, and his breath caught in his chest.

Darkness crept over the streets, screams echoing from outside.

Matthias approached the window, taking Katrin with him.

The garden below withered to dust, trees lining the streets disintegrating before his eyes.

"Stop." The prince shook his head. "They did nothing to you."

The cries from Nema's Throne vibrated through his bones, seizing his muscles. Black masses emerged from within the streets, rising like giants to pull apart the stonework. The two dragon statues guarding the bridge to the city crumbled beneath shadow fists.

Behind him, Katrin sobbed, staring at the destruction as it wafted through the capital like a plague.

"Let's talk terms, shall we?" Merissa circled in the room as the fall of Nema's Throne continued outside. "I'm feeling generous. How about... I don't hurt your beloved acolyte?"

Reality of the situation crept into Matthias's mind like a predator stalking in the night.

I don't have a choice.

"You won't hurt anyone in this room. In this palace. Hells, you won't hurt any Isalicans." Matthias cringed, squeezing tighter to Katrin's arm.

Merissa frowned. "That's pushing it a little far. This room is plenty."

"And my brother." Matthias met Merissa's gaze. "You won't hurt or kill... or *have* anyone else hurt or kill those in this room and my brother."

Merissa gave a heavy sigh, waving her hand in the air beside her head. "Fine. But I will not be blamed for natural causes, or the actions of others outside my control."

"You will keep Katrin safe, though, in addition to the rest." Matthias swallowed, his insides quaking. "Keep her safe. You can take me."

"Matthias, don't." Katrin's voice shook.

"I have no choice," he whispered, his knees shaking. "If you can agree to these terms, you can have me."

The towers of the temple within Nema's Throne disintegrated behind Merissa as she smiled. "Done."

Another red-hot slash went down his arm, crossing the three marks from before.

The rumble of the city faded, and screams continued to echo into the clouds of dust and debris floating into the Isalican air.

Merissa held out her hand, a sly smile on her lips. "Shall we undo it together?"

Matthias huffed. "I think I'll ensure this doesn't happen for myself." He gripped harder to Katrin, and the Art scorched through them both.

"I needed you to suffer."

Matthias glanced at Katrin, finding the recognition he wanted in her eyes. "I've suffered enough." He wished he could tell her all the things he felt. "Everyone out. Leave us. Now."

Merissa smiled, eyeing the marks on his arm. "I can be quite persuasive, it seems."

He tilted his head at Katrin. "Forgive me."

Katrin's eyes brimmed with tears, and she hesitated as she stroked his cheek. "I'm sorry." She backed out of the room. "I love you."

The prince mouthed the words back to her, his hands shaking.

"What's happening?" Dani whispered to Liam as she rose, but they obeyed Katrin as she ushered them out of the room.

She turned back, her eyes meeting Matthias's for a long moment as she closed the door and it clicked shut.

I can't believe I'm doing this.

He glanced at his father's body.

I'm sorry, Dad.

"You'll have to repeat the terms, my poor, broken king." Merissa strode towards him, dragging her feet on the carpet. "Seeing as you've denied me the pleasure of remembering them myself."

Matthias's breath shook. "You can have me, but you can't hurt or kill Katrin, Liam, Dani, Micah, Stefan and Seiler yourself or by proxy. You will also keep Katrin alive and safe." He ran a hand over his beard, denial seeping through his veins at what he was agreeing to. "Don't destroy my country."

And I hope you never learn of my child.

His heart wrenched at the realization he'd miss the birth of their baby and everything that followed.

"Now, now, don't be dramatic. Destroying the country I rule would be counterproductive, wouldn't it?"

"If you break any of these rules... This ends."

"Of course." Merissa held out her hand. "Tell me. Did you see your city fall?"

Meeting Merissa's eyes, he swallowed. "Don't make me see it again."

"I won't."

Matthias took her hand, closing his eyes. "Take me."

Scorching darkness ripped into his veins, tearing into the corners of his soul like a starving beast.

The prince gasped, shouting as he opened his eyes, only to see swirls of onyx. He tried to retract his hand, but his muscles wouldn't respond. Agony boiled his insides until he blinked through a haze of inky mist.

A content sigh rippled through his mind, ending with a heave of his own chest, the sound reverberating through the room.

So many twists and turns. I will have great fun breaking you further. The voice echoed with a masculine tenor, sinister and inhuman.

Why can I still see what's happening?

The thought provoked a chuckle from his own mouth. *Who said you wouldn't?*

Dread eked through him, but he hovered in his mind, powerless against the being controlling him.

Matthias's body stepped forward, looking down to the rug where Merissa lay crumpled. Her body had thinned even further, her skin nearly translucent as she shook.

A sob ruptured from her like a crashing wave as she tried to rise, but fell back to the floor. "No, no, no," she whispered, each growing slightly more powerful. "Matthias, no!"

She's alive?

Regret sank like a stone in his stomach.

Don't kill her!

His hand flexed, cold rushing down his arm as shadows pulsed from his skin into his palm. The flicker bid those at his feet to follow, curling up Merissa's skirts as she trembled, forcing her body to straighten despite not having the strength herself.

Her irises had dimmed with the deterioration of her body, but a spark of defiance remained as the creature inside him wrenched her chin up.

Look in her eyes. She already knows what's coming. The creature purred, the sound echoing through every part of his being.

Matthias screamed, banging on invisible walls with what once were his hands. *You fucking asshole! Leave her alone!*

"My *name* is Uriel." The prince's voice held a lilt of humor. "And I will not."

Uriel reached out, his fist closing on air as the shadows obeyed, tightening around her body.

Merissa grimaced, holding in any cries as she glared up at his face. "You'll never be half the man you've embodied. I know your fears, your weakness. You will fail."

A hint of annoyance passed through him, and his grip tightened.

Merissa's body convulsed within the shadow, held by the necrotic power as it ate into the exposed skin of her neck and arms.

"If I do, you will not see it," Uriel whispered.

The tendrils of power unfurled, hurling Merissa sideways directly into the open fireplace.

Her broken body crashed into the flames, her skirts catching ablaze. She screamed as the fire consumed her, Uriel's tendrils preventing her escape.

Matthias tried to close his eyes, but couldn't. He withdrew, seeking refuge in the corners of his mind. He imagined Katrin's face, but it only brought pain.

What have I done? Gods, Kat. Please forgive me.

Chapter 42

"Kat, where are we going?" Liam's tight voice echoed his frustration.

"What's happening to Matthias? He screamed." Dani halted, forcing Liam to stop beside her since he held her arm. Her ribs ached from Merissa's attack, but leaving their prince alone with the corrupted healer made her nauseous. "I've felt that power before. We can't abandon him!"

"Not here," Katrin hissed, her hand closing over Dani's wrist to tug her forward again. "Please."

The Dtrüa snatched her hand back. "I'm not leaving him." She turned to go back the way they'd come, only to catch Seiler's scent approaching from the north wing.

Katrin had dragged them out of the royal chambers and down to the second floor without an explanation. She'd used the most commanding voice Dani had heard from her to order Micah and Stefan to follow.

"What's going on?" Seiler stopped in front of them, his tone masking his grief.

"Seiler," Katrin almost sounded relieved. "We need somewhere to talk no one knows about. Somewhere completely private."

"Where's my brother?"

"Gooseberries," Katrin blurted, her voice strained. "Please."

Huh?

"This way." Seiler's voice hardened.

"Wait." Command had returned to Katrin's voice. "Micah,

Stefan. I need you both to go to the southern barracks. Order them to prepare the drakes."

"But you just got back." Micah paused. "How many riders?"

Katrin hesitated, sucking in a breath. "Two."

Everyone stilled.

"Who is leaving?" Dani voiced the question no one else seemed willing to.

"No one. Not until we know what's going on." Liam's voice turned terse. "Katrin, you have to explain. We just left Matthias in a room with—"

"I know!" Katrin growled, her voice breaking, but she sucked in a deep breath. "Look, it's not him anymore. Please trust me and ready the drakes."

"Yes, ma'am," Micah whispered, and his footsteps departed with Stefan's.

Seiler exhaled slowly. "Come. Then you can explain." He strode down the hallway, and Dani reluctantly followed.

"I don't like this," she whispered to Liam. "Something is really, *really* wrong. Merissa was a *Shade*."

"No." Katrin's sharp tone dropped a stone in Dani's gut. "Merissa was something else. And now it's taking Matthias."

Anger rippled through the Dtrüa. "And we're letting it."

Seiler stopped halfway down the hallway, and a thunk emanated to the side.

A gust of stale wind rushed over Dani's face, pushing her hair back and meeting her nose with the scent of mildew.

Darkness overtook her blurry vision as they entered the space, footsteps echoing louder on the hard stone floor. A spot of light burst to life, adding contrast to the hazy shapes around her.

"Are there any tunnels Matthias doesn't know?" Katrin's voice came from near the lantern, the prince's name echoing through the tunnel as the door behind them slid back into place.

"This way." Seiler weaved through them, his scent still tinged with the salt of tears and grief.

They walked in silence, but the tension in the air between them grew thick enough a blade could cut it. The sounds changed, growing more cacophonous as they passed through another grinding doorway.

"All right, this is it. I'm not going any further until you explain." Liam's temper coated his words as he stopped, slipping from Dani to step towards the glow of Katrin's lantern.

Dani cringed and leaned against the wall, holding her side.

"What were those cuts on Matthias's arm? They just appeared." Liam's voice.

Katrin paced. "The thing in Merissa was counting his jumps. He took me with him for the last one. And I don't think it knew he could, otherwise it never would have let me leave." The acolyte's voice shook as she went on, explaining the threats and how she'd seen the capital city fall. "He didn't have a choice. He said it killed all of us the first few jumps, but then... the city..."

"What's happened to the real Matthias, then?" Dani clenched her jaw, her shoulders drooping. "There's nothing we can do?"

"I don't know." Katrin cleared her throat, her voice hardening again. "But whatever was in Merissa was making a deal, as if it needed his permission. I have to believe that Matthias is still in there somewhere. Right now, our focus has to be the kingdom."

"Matthias will be king, now. And you're saying he's not Matthias at all?" Liam sounded hollow. "How do we do anything? Are we supposed to pretend we don't know?"

"We have to. It killed Geroth. It could kill us, too." Dani ran a hand through her hair, listening to Seiler pace.

"What?" Seiler froze. "Merissa killed my father?"

"Not Merissa. Whatever is inside her. Whatever's in Matthias now."

"How long has Merissa not been Merissa?" The younger prince breathed faster. "She brought in Alana to help. There was always something off with that auer..."

"I have no idea." Katrin's voice broke again. "I didn't know this was possible. That things like this existed beyond children's tales."

"I need to find Lasseth," Dani murmured.

"Lasseth? That man who just appeared in our tent at the border?" Liam faced her. "That's right. You told me he was a Shade, too..."

"Yes. He said he took orders from someone, but I always assumed he meant Nysir. Who went missing..." Dani paused, remembering how the Dtrüa had tracked Nysir to the temple. "Nymaera's breath. Nysir. Merissa. It all makes sense."

"Nysir? Who is Nysir?"

"Nysir was our commander. Master Dtrüa. He went missing, but my old allies said he went to the temple with Tallos. Which means he was there when we left *Merissa* and continued on to Omensea. Lasseth took orders from Nysir. Lasseth... had that power. It smells like decay. The same, but weaker, than the Art Merissa used to attack me. *That's* when the creature... thing must have taken Merissa. At the temple. That's why she survived the fire."

"Decay." Katrin repeated slowly. "And the temple... Oh, gods."

"You two need to stop having revelations and not filling us in immediately," Liam grumbled.

Katrin huffed. "The body they found in that cave near the temple, the one that vanished. The soldiers who found it described it as extensively decayed, beyond natural decomposition. And all the lichen and ferns around the area were also dead, as if something had simply drained them of all life."

"Which means Merissa killed that priest?" Dani shook her head. "But why?"

"And to what end?"

"Information?" Liam's new leather vest creaked as he shrugged. "Why else would anyone torture anyone, but what would this creature want from the priest?"

"You said Matthias is still in there, somewhere." Seiler walked closer. "If Merissa was still in there, maybe torturing a priest would make her talk. Which would mean that by taking someone over, this thing doesn't get their memories."

"It also means the person's consciousness lives." Dani wasn't sure whether that was a relief or a horrible fate for her friend. "And if this thing is more powerful than Lasseth, maybe it isn't a Shade. But when Lasseth used the Art against me, everything around us died, too."

"This sounds an awful lot like stories I read in Ziona about Shades." Matthias's brother groaned. "Killing senselessly, without prejudice. Swathes of desiccated forest and gardens."

"Lasseth *is* a Shade." Dani nodded. "But he can't change bodies."

"So then Merissa must have been taken by the one giving Lasseth orders. Their master." Katrin breathed. "And it's in Matthias, now."

"My brother is the master of the Shades." Seiler gulped. "And he's also the king of Isalica."

"While it's possible it doesn't know all Matthias does, we have to assume it will try to learn everything." Katrin's voice grew quieter. "It clearly desires power, but the real question is if it's Matthias status or his Art."

"Or both," Dani whispered.

"We have to keep certain things secret. It can't know about the dragons, which means Matthias can't follow through with his promise to them."

"But we can." Liam wrapped an arm around Dani's waist, avoiding where her ribs ached.

"Good, it's better you all stay as far away as possible. You'll take the drakes. Then we hope the dragons come to you rather than Matthias."

"We can return to the mountain, but what about you?" The Dtrüa frowned, hating the idea of leaving Katrin in the palace.

Katrin reached for Dani's hand, squeezing it. "I have to stay here. It'll realize I know if I leave. But I'll be fine. I was part of the deal Matthias made with it. It has to keep me alive and safe. It also can't hurt any of us, but I don't trust it not to find a loophole."

Dani leaned on Liam, wincing. "What about Micah and Stefan? Seiler?"

"I can't leave my father's legacy in the hands of a monster." The prince huffed. "I can't leave you to handle all this alone."

"You must. We can't let it know. Go to Ziona as planned. I'll transfer Stefan and Micah to another outpost. I'll find a way to protect all of you and the country. I'll be able to as queen." A hollow determination colored Katrin's tone.

"You can't possibly think you'll go through with the wedding." Dani gaped at her friend.

"I have to. It's the only way." Katrin's dress rustled. "And I'll keep the pregnancy secret unless it becomes clear it knows. Matthias didn't mention the child, so I'll believe that means he won't."

Dani bowed her head. "I don't like this."

"Me either," Liam grunted. "I don't like leaving you here, Kat."

"I'll be fine. I just need to know you're both safe. And that the dragons are safe. We still need them to end this war." Katrin's voice hardened. "Go. There's no more time. Get out of Nema's Throne."

Chapter 43

All that could be done had been, and Katrin felt as if she'd been awake for a week rather than a day. Her body ached, and she longed to feel Matthias's touch. She'd seen him... it... several times, but his gaze never lingered on her. Instead, the creature within him put on a show of grief as he arranged the funeral and burial of Isalica's late king.

Katrin slipped through the door of their chambers, relieved when she didn't see the prince. A small tea setting she'd requested sat by the window, offering possible comfort for her twisting stomach.

Her eyes flitted to the bed, already turned down by the staff.

I'll have to sleep beside it.

The knot inside her tightened, a wave of nausea encouraging her to the tea. She twitched when the door behind her opened, and tea splashed over the rim of her cup onto her fingertips. Hissing, she refused to drop it. To give any indication of nervousness to the thing entering behind her.

Matthias's movements sounded exactly the same as he closed the door, but the lock sliding into place made Katrin's body numb.

She swallowed, burying the feelings. "Would you like some tea?" She didn't turn to face him, questioning her ability to keep her face straight.

"No." Matthias's deep voice held none of the usual softness. "And let's not pretend, shall we?"

Katrin's ceramic cup clinked as she set it back down, her heart thundering in her ears.

Were we wrong? Does he know everything Matthias knows?

She turned slowly, pursing her lips to harden her face. "Pretend?"

"Things are going to change." Matthias unbuttoned his formal coat, scowling. "We won't be getting married. You'll have a new chamber soon. All to yourself."

Katrin straightened, forcing herself not to back away as the creature stalked closer to her. He looked perfectly like Matthias, but as he approached, she saw a swirl of blackness gather in his eyes. Gold flecked around the rims of his stormy blue eyes, revealing the creature had no intention of hiding from her.

"Who are you?" Katrin's voice lowered to a whisper as she backed into the small table, making the tea set clatter.

"Someone you should fear." Matthias smiled, but it held no joy. "You should know... your beloved prince..." He touched a finger to his temple. "While he shall never return, is still here. He *feels* everything. *Sees* everything. And I have no qualms abusing that, should you cause trouble."

He promised not to hurt me, but Matthias never included himself in that deal.

Katrin had already considered one way to free Matthias of whatever malevolent creature had taken him. She spun to the tea set, plucking up a plate and snapping it against the edge of the table.

Before she could pull the sharp ceramic to her own throat, Matthias seized her wrist. He tutted his tongue. "See, now, that's the kind of trouble I mean. I can't have you plotting ways to rid me of my new favorite host." Twisting his grip, he forced her to face him, his face inches from hers. He pulled her hand, and the broken plate, closer to himself.

The ceramic touched the skin beside his collar.

Katrin's arm shook as she struggled to pull it away, but Matthias sliced through his own flesh, spilling blood over his sleeveless white tunic.

"He's screaming, child." Matthias chuckled. "Oh, how it hurts him."

Katrin let go with a sob, yanking her hands away as he released her. "Don't. Please."

"Your manners mean nothing to me," he snarled, smashing the plate on the rug. He circled her, flipping the rest of the tea set to the floor and forcing her back towards the center of the room. "I thought about giving you time to say goodbye, but you've forced my hand." He lunged at her, grabbing her forearm, and her vision flooded with darkness.

She screamed, but no sound came out as her surroundings whirled. A breath later, they halted. But they were no longer in the prince's chambers.

Blinking, she urged her eyes to adjust to the dimness of the space and stepped away from Matthias. It glowed with a strange pale green light, and she looked up at the ceiling to the roots swirling around it. The walls were rough and dark, like crumbling dirt.

Are we underground?

"I suspected your oh-so-valiant lover would want to keep you alive, but he said nothing about keeping you conscious." Matthias smirked, running his hand over a rectangle stone altar in the center of the room. "Have you been to Eralas, child?"

Katrin swallowed the horrid sickness rising in her. "Eralas?"

The darkness behind Matthias moved, and a woman emerged Katrin hadn't even seen there. Her emerald eyes pierced through Katrin, and the acolyte recognized the woman Merissa had brought to the palace to help the king.

The auer had likely caused the king's death.

In a rush, Katrin hurried to harden the aura of her power, hoping the creature wouldn't sense her delving into it.

Please don't be too far away.

Dani's consciousness snapped into her own with a worried timbre. *What's wrong?*

"What are you going to do to me?" Katrin looked at Matthias and the auer beside him, ignoring Dani's question when the creature didn't react to the change.

"I've brought a piece of Eralas to you." Matthias tucked a lock of the auer's hair behind her ear. "You'll be asleep. Therefore alive. Safe. Indefinitely. You won't even age." He smiled at Katrin. "Giving me eternity."

We're coming back for you. Right now. I'll find you. Dani's voice echoed in her head.

"No!" Katrin blurted to Dani, weakening her voice to repeat it for the creature. "No, why are you doing this?" She backed to the chamber wall, touching the dirt. "I won't try to kill myself again, I promise."

Dani gasped. *You what?*

The auer ran a finger down Matthias's jaw. "That didn't take long." Amusement laced her tone as she tilted her head to study the prince's face. "I approve of this new host."

Bile rose into Katrin's throat at the way the woman touched him.

Matthias's chest rumbled. "I do, too. It's good to be more like myself again. Male, at least." He smiled and turned his attention back to Katrin. "Don't make this harder than it has to be, child." He gestured to the stone table. "Just as I promised your lover, it won't hurt at all."

Katrin pushed herself harder against the curved wall.

Dani's tone grew determined. *Kat, where are you?*

Katrin cringed, wishing she could return her thoughts. Taking a breath, she forced herself to relax away from the wall with tentative steps. "You intend to keep me here, alive and unharmed, so I won't interfere with your plans. Without anyone knowing who you are." They weren't questions, and they weren't meant for him. "This is better, then. I won't need to live every day watching you destroy the memory of the man I love."

"Oddly agreeable." Matthias glanced at the auer.

"What will you tell everyone?" Katrin eyed the table as the auer stepped to the head of the altar.

"That you're dead, of course. Killed by the same illness that took my father. Tragic."

Katrin paused a few feet from the table at the center, glancing at the auer whose black hair blended in with the darkness.

A wicked smile spread over her ruby lips. "Lay your head here." Her black painted fingernails grazed over the divot in a stone headrest, carved with strange, swirling runes.

Dani's voice trembled. *How am I supposed to live my life knowing you can't live yours?*

"I'll only be asleep," Katrin whispered, hoping the creature would believe she was reassuring herself. "I'll wake up someday, when this is all over. Then maybe I'll have my Matthias back." She touched the cold stone, and it sent a shudder up her spine. "There's nothing you can do right now, Kat." She spoke to herself aloud, but prayed Dani understood. "But you'll find a way later." Her voice darkened. "Someone will."

He rolled his eyes. "I'm losing patience. I may be eternal, but I'd much rather return to *my* palace. I have work to do."

Katrin stilled her stomach from quavering at the idea of the creature ruling her homeland. Looking once more at the auer, she hoisted herself onto the stone altar, positioning her skirt around her legs as she lay back.

I promise, Dani whispered. *One day we will find you, and we will fix all this.*

Pausing before her head touched the rest, Katrin met Matthias's eyes. She focused on the blue that remained, holding back the tears that threatened. "I love you, Matthias," she whispered, hoping the creature spoke true and that he'd hear.

The auer gripped her shoulders, encouraging her down the rest of the way.

The world vanished in a flash of pale green light.

Chapter 44

"Dani!" Liam grabbed his wife's shoulders, shaking them harder after she'd ignored all previous attempts. "What's going on?"

The Dtrüa stood frozen near the gate of the drake pen, her hand resting on the latch she'd undone. Her eyes were more distant than usual, staring blankly while her mouth tightened in a frown. The usual cloudiness in her eyes had dissipated, revealing the grey shades of her iris Liam had never truly seen.

Ousa lowered his head, nostrils flaring as he brushed Dani's leg with the tip of his snout.

Something's wrong with Katrin.

He didn't know if it was the look on Dani's face, or some other familial instinct that roared through him. But without a doubt, Liam knew his sister was in grave danger.

"Shit." Liam pushed Ousa away from Dani, the drake letting out a perturbed groan as Liam tightened the buckles on his saddle.

Brek huffed, a rush of air rippling through Liam's hair, and he waved at the drake. "Back up, give her some air, boys."

Both drakes seemed overly curious about Dani's trance-like state, but a growl from Brek encouraged Ousa farther away. Still holding onto the straps of the beast's saddle, Liam slid along the dirt, his weight doing nothing to stop the drake.

A sudden gasp from Dani made everything in Liam leap, and he released Ousa so abruptly, his balance wavered.

Dani's eyes clouded over, and tears gathered on her lower lids. "He's hidden her. He's taken and trapped her, and she knows not where she is, and I cannot tell, her senses are duller than mine, and there were no doors—"

"Whoa, whoa." Liam gripped her shoulder again, brushing her hair back behind her ear. "Slow down. We'll find her."

The Dtrüa's bottom lip trembled. "Katrin wants us to stay the course and not look for her."

"She's stupider than Matthias if she thinks we'll listen." Liam turned towards their packs, now debating their purpose and the heavy winter cloaks rolled within.

"Liam," she whispered, reaching for him and finding his bicep. "Matthias put her into some kind of sleep. She won't age, and she... she seemed to want it that way."

He froze, staring at her. They were words that sounded like Katrin, but he didn't want to believe them.

"Even if we tried to find her, it's impossible. No doors. No stairs. The room was underground. It could be anywhere. We'd never find her." She cringed, swiping a fallen tear with the back of her hand. "We have no way to find her, and she told me to go. To be safe and find her later. When we have a plan. Answers."

Everything in him felt like it shook, yet he didn't move. "A plan." The idea sounded impossibly far away and tasted thick on his tongue.

Dani nodded, but a choked sob shook her shoulders, and she walked away, hands on her face. "This is too much. First Barim and Riez, then Matthias... Now Katrin. Gods, I..."

Liam jogged to her and wrapped his arms around Dani's waist from behind, pulling her tightly to his chest. Her hair smelled like berries as he brushed his cheek against the side of her head. His heart ached as he spoke. "We need to stay the course, then. If that's what Katrin said. We have to trust her."

Twisting in his embrace, Dani flung her arms around his shoulders and buried her face in the side of his neck. "This is all we have, now." Her fingers tangled into his hair, gripping at the roots.

"And it's enough." He kissed the top of her head. "We'll find a way to fix all this, but there are other... much bigger and scalier problems for us to deal with first."

Dani moved back and pulled his forehead to hers. "But we'll never give up. We'll do as she says and go deal with the dragons, but we will *never* give up trying to free her and Matthias. Promise me."

"Never." He closed his eyes, focusing on the gentle pulse of her breath on his lips. "I promise we'll never give up." His chest ached as he considered the next required step. "But we can't stay here. If Matthias has imprisoned Katrin, we might not be safe, either."

"I know." Dani loosened her grip, touching his cheeks. "Take Ousa. I'll take Brek. We need to get to the mountains. Maybe the dragons will send us a message."

"Or be royally pissed off when we show back up at their door when they told us not to."

"Zaelinstra said we couldn't return to Draxix. She said nothing about waiting by the portal in Thrallenax."

Liam smirked, kissing Dani's brow. He held it there, his mind whirling to the events of the day.

A single day since we returned from the mountains.

His gut twisted. "We can't let them know. The dragons. About Matthias. It will... destroy whatever chance we have at ending this war with their help."

Dani hesitated with a deep breath before nodding. "You're right. They cannot know. We'll tell them Matthias is unavailable with his father's passing. And he sent us, instead."

"Think Zaelinstra will believe us? Or that the Primeval will help?"

Drawing back, Dani centered her blurry gaze on his face. "They must. And we'll not leave Thrallenax until they do."

Twenty years later...
Summer, 2618 R.T.

Liam heaved the bale of hay into the pile with the rest beside the paddock, and Varin squeaked in surprise.

"Watch it, Dad. I was standing right there!" She brushed hay from her riding breeches, which she'd had no time to change out of after returning home from the mountains with her younger brother.

Dani had absconded with Ryen to have him help with a new clutch of drake hatchlings. Despite being adopted, the young man proved to have a touch with the animals like his Dtrüa mother.

"How was the air this time? Getting the hang of flying?" Liam heaved the next bale as his daughter jumped out of the way.

She picked a piece of hay from her strawberry blond hair, a telltale sign of her adoption. "Zeller tried to throw me off. Said it was funny to hear me squeal."

How many kids have dragon friends?

The old military fort turned homestead had seemed empty for the week the children had been away in Draxix, invited by the dragons for the extended stay never offered before.

Gaining a new level of their trust.

Liam brushed his hands together, the callouses catching on his palms. "I'm sorry I couldn't be there to see it."

"Oh, don't worry. Jaxx got plenty of a chuckle out of it for you. He wouldn't stop teasing me for the next couple days." Varin smirked at her father as he heaved another bale.

Dani had become pregnant with Jaxx shortly after they'd adopted five-year-old Ryen and his seven-year-old sister Varin, and they'd proven remarkable siblings from the start.

The early years of parenthood were busy, and Liam marveled at watching Dani embrace her role as a mother after they'd assumed they'd never have children. She gave them the childhood she never had, rolling around in the snow and starting snowball fights.

The Dtrüa's hunting ability sustained them through the long winters, and as the children grew, the burden eased off her and Liam's shoulders.

Everyone in their little family knew the dragons, caring for their eggs and protecting the mountains from Feyor. The attacks on the border had ceased shortly after they'd all returned to Nema's Throne decades earlier, the drakes and wyverns abandoning their masters.

The dragons had carried out their end of the deal and had grown slowly more trusting with the Talansiet family.

In all the years that had passed, they'd never seen the king again. And they maintained the secret from the dragons, despite the precarious line they walked.

Micah and Stefan visited occasionally, bringing treats and surprises for the children during their breaks from the border camps. The former crown elites had worked with Liam to station new camps around the base of the mountains, protecting the dragons without anyone realizing the purpose.

Life had moved on.

The books they'd gathered to research the being infesting Matthias collected dust on a shelf. Every avenue they'd explored hit a dead end, and they'd concluded that neither Katrin nor Matthias would wish they dwell on what they couldn't control.

Liam had attempted to play the part his younger sister often did, thoroughly researching during their visits to Draxix, but found the dragon's way of organizing legends and tales far too convoluted to follow. Speaking out loud about the creature that controlled Matthias seemed unwise, even when alone with Dani.

So they'd stopped.

The kingdom is still standing. Isalica is still prosperous. And the dragons are safe.

"How'd Jaxx do this trip?" Liam looked up as Varin unbuckled the harnesses she wore to secure her to the drakes as they climbed the mountains.

She met his gaze, her green eyes smiling. "He's getting better about the heights. But he still needs more time to bond with Zaniken before she'll take him flying. He's acting about how you'd expect a twelve-year-old to be when trying to make friends with a dragon."

Liam smiled, remembering when the dragon Varin mentioned had hatched. The first and only time they'd been allowed to witness the final processes observed near the lava pools deep within

Thrallenax. The dragons had insisted Liam and Dani bring their blood-child so that he might properly imprint with a new hatchling when he was only four. They'd put their faith in Zaelinstra, who'd continued to act as the ambassador between them and the Primeval within the dragon hierarchy.

"Good." Liam rubbed his hands on his breeches, cleaning off the dirt. "But it's good to have you all home, even if your mother and I enjoyed the peace for a few days."

Varin gave him a wide grin as she stepped out of the leathers. "Missed you, too, Dad." Her smile faded as she straightened, looking behind Liam towards the front gates of the homestead. Her smile returned as she lifted her hand in greeting. "Uncle Micah!"

"Hey kiddo!" Micah's voice carried over the snowy ground as he rode in.

Two more riders followed, their hoods obscuring their features. A man and a woman.

It can't be.

Liam's heart leapt into his throat, but defeat settled into his chest as the woman pushed her hood back from braided brown hair. And the man looked nothing like Matthias, other than the finely trimmed beard.

The stranger gave a respectful nod to Liam, but both kept their distance as Micah approached.

Who would he trust enough to bring here?

"Hey, Micah." Liam took the reins of the former crown elite's horse. "Wasn't expecting a visit. Did you send a messenger?" He wondered if Matthias would look anything like Micah now, with the age beginning to show in his friend's face. Lines at the corners of his eyes, and the salting of silver hair through his beard.

"I didn't want to trust anyone else." Micah dismounted, patting his horse's neck.

Varin jogged forward, wrapping her arms around Micah without giving him a choice.

"Varin, will you go get your mother, please?" Liam looked over

Micah's shoulder to the two strangers again and caught a glimpse of a navy tattoo on the edge of the man's neck.

Micah released Varin, watching her go before meeting Liam's gaze. "Is your family well?"

"They are. Have you been to the capital recently?" Liam hadn't visited Nema's Throne since they'd fled, unable to bear the thought of his sister trapped somewhere, asleep, and him not being able to help her.

And Matthias.

If there was a fate worse than eternal sleep, it was having a monster live your life in your place.

"Actually, I have. I accompanied a troop home a few months back. Caught a glimpse of our king." Micah shook his head when Liam opened his mouth. "It's still not him, but he looks exactly the same. Hasn't aged a day."

Liam winced, looking again to the strangers who were close enough to hear. And question what Micah suggested.

Micah followed his gaze. "Don't worry." His eyes drifted in the direction Varin had gone. "Well, that should spark more questions."

Dani loped through the frost, her big white paws crackling on the ground.

The ice from the night normally would have melted by then, but the overcast sky kept it chill enough.

Liam sucked a breath in through his nose as he considered the strangers again. He lowered his voice as he faced Dani so they wouldn't see his lips moving as he spoke to Micah. "You trust them?"

"If I didn't, they wouldn't be here."

Grunting in response, Liam greeted his wife with his customary stroke of her chin, lifting her panther head up to look at him.

Dani sniffed, her whiskers tickling his wrist. Her attention altered to the strangers, and she shifted. Her white fur receded from her face, and she smiled to greet Micah. "It's good of you to visit."

The strangers hardly reacted, even their horses steady with the approach of the panther turned human.

"We'll meet in the barn. I'd rather not introduce the kids until I can judge myself. And I have a drake nearby that can act accordingly if necessary."

"Perfectly understandable." Micah turned and walked to the strangers, speaking too low for Liam to hear clearly.

"Why are they here?" Dani whispered. "They don't smell familiar."

Liam narrowed his eyes as he watched the woman dismount first, the man shortly after.

The tattooed man turned his back to the homestead as he ran his hands up the horse's noses. Both seemed remarkably calm for how close they were to the drake pens behind the house. Micah's horse was accustomed, but the strangers'... He was surprised they'd made it past the gate without needing to dismount.

Dani tilted her head in their direction, focused on the man. "I'll tell Varin to keep Jaxx inside. Until we understand our guests." She turned, kissing Liam's cheek before heading for the house.

The strangers walked behind Micah as Liam took his friend's horse to tie it to the fencepost near the hay he'd just stacked, hoping the optional snack would keep him calm. He glanced back as the other horses grew closer, joining Micah's without any dramatics.

"Thank you for being willing to speak with us." The man held out his hand to Liam.

The ex-soldier examined the man's hand for a moment, noting the callouses that suggested he knew how to hold a sword even if he didn't carry one. A thin gold wedding band graced his middle finger, and a quick glance to the woman confirmed their apparent partnership with a matching band on her left.

The woman, slightly taller than Dani, smiled at him. Her eyes made him take a second look. One green, one yellow. "We've been looking forward to meeting you and your wife. I'm Rae, and this is my husband Damien."

Liam took the man's hand before offering his to the woman. "Liam, but I'm sure Micah already told you." He glanced at Micah, still debating his frustration for the visit with no warning.

But he said he didn't want to trust anyone else...

"Come. It's cold out here." Micah motioned with his head. "At least the drakes have a warm roost."

"Drakes?" Rae looked at Damien.

Liam couldn't help the smile as he turned to lead the way. "They're really quite docile once they know you. There might be a bit of a ruckus when we first walk in, but my wife will calm them quickly."

The primary barn for the drakes had taken Liam years to finish, the exposed wood already showing places where it'd need to be patched soon. The two story structure with massive side paddocks allowed the drakes a warm place to sleep among piles of hay.

Ousa howled in delight when he spotted Liam approaching, beginning his usual pacing of the tall fence line he could likely break through if he wanted to. Dani had moved his mate and her clutch of eggs to the other side of the property because Ousa had gotten overly protective.

Several of Ousa's hatchlings from the year before galloped beside their sire to look curiously at them.

"He's very excited to see you, it seems." Damien glanced at Liam, something in the man's hazel eyes suggesting he knew more, but wouldn't say it.

"We have quite the history together." Liam heaved against the reinforced barn door, pulling it open just enough for them to slip through.

Dani stood at the center, her hand on a small draconi's snout. She scratched it under the chin before sending it to join Ousa outside, not needing to speak a word aloud.

The little interior gate snapped shut behind the last drake to exit, leaving them alone.

Liam made the introductions, but Damien hardly seemed to pay attention to him, his eyes on Dani.

"You speak to them." Damien approached her, holding out his

hand. "I've never met a Dtrüa before, but I don't recall that being something they were capable of."

Dani straightened, facing him. She clicked her tongue and took his hand. "In a different way, I suspect, from how you communicate with your horses. It is not a Dtrüa ability." She tilted her head. "You know what I am, but what are you?"

Liam lifted an eyebrow.

Damien smiled. "That's a bit more complicated, I'm afraid."

"I doubt it." Dani turned his hand over, placing her other on the back of his. "Loosen your aura."

Liam exchanged a look with Micah, but his friend only shrugged.

Rae had wandered to the gate, watching the drakes outside.

Dani sucked in a deeper breath. "You're a Rahn'ka?" She focused near his face with wide eyes.

Damien's shoulders tensed, evoking the same in Liam as the barn hung silent.

Rae turned from her spot to stare at the two.

"How do you know about the Rahn'ka?" Damien's voice had dropped to a whisper, forcing Liam to strain to hear.

A smile tugged at Dani's lips. "I knew one, once. She helped me more than I can say."

Damien's eyes widened. "You knew Ailiena?"

The Dtrüa nodded. "She was living in Feyor at the time and helped me escape them during the Yandarin War."

"I'd very much like to talk about Ailiena with you further, though she has nothing to do with our journey here." Damien patted Dani's hand, facing Liam. "I'm afraid I come with other hard questions."

"About what?"

"About your king."

Dani stepped closer to Liam. "You want to know about Matthias?"

"We all know it is no longer Matthias." Rae approached from the gate. "I saw his face in Hoult. He is the beast who attacked Eralas."

"Hoult?" Liam strained to remember the relevance of the familiar name, and the mention of Eralas helped. The tale of the shadow beast attacking the auer homeland and razing the fishing village on Helgath's coast had even reached Liam and Dani in their mountain home. New fears had risen throughout Pantracia after it, yet the world had remained eerily quiet since.

"That was the thing in Matthias?" Liam studied the woman, gaze flickering between her different colored eyes. "You're certain?"

Rae nodded, a somber expression on her face. "I am. I was there. But I didn't know who he was until I saw him again and learned his name as Matthias Rayeht." She looked between him and Dani before letting out a steady breath. "That's why we're here. We want to free your friend."

To be continued...

The story continues with...

AXIOM OF THE QUEEN'S ARROW

www.Pantracia.com

Pierce her heart, but she may live.

Trapped for two decades and forced to witness his life pass before his eyes with cruel clarity, Matthias suffers. His sanity wanes, confusion clouding his mind to help him cope with the torment. The king's only chance for regaining control lies beneath the ground, but no one knows how to find her.

Micah surprises Liam and Dani by bringing unexpected guests to their mountainside home. They struggle to trust Damien and Rae with the secrets they guard, but the Helgathians may be their last hope to find Katrin and free Matthias. They know more about Uriel than anyone else, but all gifts—even those of knowledge—come at a cost.

Ending Uriel's twenty-year reign over Isalica could set a cascade of events into motion, causing destruction beyond what any of them have witnessed before. But Damien needs the final piece of his puzzle.

An abandoned host.

But only if the king survives.

Axiom of the Queen's Arrow is Part 3 of *Shadowed Kings*, and Book 10 in the *Pantracia Chronicles*.